He aimed his Walther at the terrorist's face. "No sudden moves or you're dead!" Then instinct made Katz glance down, and he realized the slide of the P-88 was locked back. He had burned up all the rounds from the magazine. The pistol was empty.

The wounded terrorist stared up at Katz and managed a twisted grin. He grabbed for the MAT chopper that lay on the floor nearby and seized the pistol grip in his good hand. He knew he could blast his captor by the time the spent magazine could be ejected, a fresh one drawn from an ammo pouch and the pistol reloaded.

Katz dropped his pistol, but his left hand streaked to the small of his back and grasped the metal handle of a small, black knife. He drew the weapon and pointed the five-inch blade at the terrorist.

The gunman's smile widened. What good would the knife do at more than three yards? Confidently he brought his weapon to bear and prepared to squeeze the trigger.

PHOENIX FORCE
COLD DEAD

GAR WILSON

A GOLD EAGLE BOOK FROM
WORLDWIDE®

TORONTO · NEW YORK · LONDON · PARIS
AMSTERDAM · STOCKHOLM · HAMBURG
ATHENS · MILAN · TOKYO · SYDNEY

First edition April 1990

ISBN 0-373-62203-1

Special thanks and acknowledgment to
William Fieldhouse for his contribution to this work.

1

Antarctica reminded Professor Linnson of an enormous white cathedral. A carpet of dense snow covered the surface of the frozen continent. The Transantarctic Mountains towered in the distance like ivory steeples. Pure and unspoiled by the corruption of man's technology, it was unlike any other place on earth. Linnson considered it God's last sanctuary on earth, the only place of peace on a troubled planet.

Those were largely romantic notions, of course, and Linnson realized they fell far from the truth. Man and the technology of the latter part of the twentieth century had obviously extended to the southern polar region. Linnson himself would not be there otherwise. He also admitted that such fanciful observations about Antarctica were hardly scientific, but Linnson was a climatologist and an environmentalist. He figured he could still cling to romantic views of nature, since he was one of the few scientists devoted to preserving the environment instead of engaged in destroying it.

Linnson wiped his goggles with a mitten-clad hand. Snow assaulted his face as the sledge traveled across the frozen terrain. The scientist was annoyed by the snow, which inhibited his view of the majestic white peaks, their destination. Linnson illogically blamed this inconvenience on Tad

Collier's driving. The younger man must be driving the sledge too fast, Linnson assumed. This worried him because the sledge was potentially dangerous. Sharp steel teeth on the runner treads at the underside of the carriage bit into the ice for traction, but the terrain was unpredictable. They had been warned to take care with the snow sledge because it could turn over, and besides the risk of breaking one's neck, a person could fall on the razor-sharp treads and be torn apart by the runners.

"Not so fast!" Linnson shouted, his voice muffled by the insulated face mask. "We're in no hurry, and we want to get to Beardmore alive."

"I'm not going that fast, Professor!" Collier answered as he sat in the driver's seat, mitten-sheathed hands on the controls. "Thirty-five miles per hour."

"Slow down!" Linnson insisted.

Collier reduced speed to twenty-five. Linnson grunted with satisfaction. He figured it was good to teach a young scientist like Collier some discipline. Linnson believed the fellows of Collier's generation had little dedication and too much ambition. Yuppie mentality, he thought with contempt. Collier was an ionospheric physicist. A specialized field, Linnson mused. Collier probably got into it so that he could get a high-priced job with one of the television networks or the federal government. No doubt he intended to help them develop improved methods of broadcasting so that they could contaminate the public with more video bubble gum for the mind, or more sneaky ways for the military or the CIA to transmit secret coded messages.

Linnson was proud of his record of commitment to environmental causes. He had been a regional organizer in New Jersey for the first Earth Day rallies. He'd participated in protest rallies at Boston Bay and Three Mile Island. He'd been arrested for handcuffing himself to a steel handrail at an Air Force base to protest nuclear testing. Pollution, acid rain, threats to the ozone layer, and other hazards to the environment had all been among his campaigns.

Young people were only concerned with making money, Linnson thought sadly. He hadn't been financially successful as a scientist. Linnson had moved from university to university, teaching climatology and lecturing about the environment. He'd acquired a reputation for being difficult and apt to criticize administrations of colleges where he worked. Tenure had been denied him more than once, but he always managed to find work somewhere.

Linnson's present assignment in Antarctica was due to his current staff position with the Foundation for the Protection of World Environment. His reputation wasn't entirely negative in some circles. A few people still cared about the environment. A few concerned and dedicated people were still willing to fight against the poisoning and destruction of the planet.

Tad Collier glanced over his shoulder at Professor Linnson as he drove the ice sledge. The older man was huddled next to the green tarp-covered bundles tied down to the carriage. Linnson looked like an Eskimo from another galaxy, Collier thought. Dressed in a heavy cold-weather parka with a fur-lined hood drawn over his head, gray mask and goggles, Linnson would have been unrecognizable without the name tag on his parka and the American flag on his left shoulder.

Of course, Collier was dressed in an identical manner. Parka, padded trousers, insulated boots, arctic mittens and face masks were necessary attire for protection from the weather. The temperature was sixty degrees below zero at the moment, not exceptionally cold for Antarctica during the austral winter.

Such extreme cold could be deadly. Without proper clothing the two scientists would be dead in no time at all. The danger had been one of the greatest attractions for Collier when he'd volunteered for the Antarctica assignment. Survival against nature's most deadly environment appealed to the young physicist's sense of adventure. He had chosen a field that largely consisted of evaluating satellite weather information, estimating smog content and its effects on the ionosphere, and checking the condition of the ozone layer. The work was interesting but seldom exciting. The trip to Antarctica was supposed to change that.

He was also pleased to be able to work with Professor Linnson. Collier had attended several of Linnson's lectures while in college and greatly admired the older man's dedication and years of hard effort on behalf of environmental reforms. Linnson had been an inspiration to Collier, and he had gone into ionospheric physics to combat the ravages of pollution and nuclear testing. Collier was convinced that if mankind didn't stop wrecking the atmosphere, the planet would be destroyed before the human race could get around to killing itself off by a thermonuclear war.

Yet Collier had been disappointed with his relationship with Professor Linnson so far. The older man seemed to resent him and paid little attention to anything he said. Collier was afraid that might be because Linnson's passion for environmentalist commitment had faded over the years. Perhaps he thought Collier was just a young, idealistic zealot. Maybe he didn't care about what Collier had to say. Sadly, Collier suspected, Professor Linnson may have given up the cause of environmentalism and was simply in Antarctica because the Foundation for the Protection of World Environment paid him.

A pity, Collier thought. So many people seemed to lose their drive and passion when they got older. They got too

tired to fight and were willing to take the easier path because there were fewer obstacles and disappointments.

The men continued across the miles of white territory in
silence. Neither realized how he had misjudged the other,
and they clung to opinions based on prejudices about age,
assumptions of a generation gap and fleeting first impres-
sions.

The sledge hurtled over the Ross Ice Shelf, largely following ill-fated British explorer Robert Scott's route to the
South Pole. Linnson had been maintaining radio contact
with the McMurdo Base. If they encountered any trouble,
a rescue unit would come to their aid. If they failed to
transmit every half hour, the base would assume they needed
help and would send a rescue team.

As the sledge drew closer to the brooding mountains in
the distance, Linnson opened a flap in the canvas baggage
and exposed the field radio to the elements long enough to
raise the antenna and transmit a radio message to Mc-
Murdo. He reported their position and assured the support
team that all was going well. The professor glanced up at the
black velvet sky, which was obscured by falling snow. The
night hadn't ended since Linnson had arrived in Antarctica.

The headlights of the sledge illuminated the path ahead
as Collier steered the vehicle over the bumpy terrain. Even
without artificial lights, Antarctica seemed to shine like
polished diamonds.

"Mount Erebus is the largest active volcano in Antarctica, isn't it?" Collier inquired.

"Erebus is the *highest* volcano," Linnson answered. "We
may yet discover other volcanoes that are *larger*. Two new,
smaller ones were discovered as recently as 1982."

"How far are we from Beardmore?"

"We're almost off the ice shelf. Not long, I'd say."

"Isn't there a temporary New Zealand station not far from here? We could stop there and make sure we have enough fuel in this rig," Collier suggested. "We could also get some hot food and coffee."

"I like the idea," Linnson admitted. "But our base might not approve. There's some political tension about certain claims New Zealand has made concerning territory here."

"To hell with politics," Collier snorted. "My stomach's rumbling, and a coffee would hit the spot just now."

"All right. Let's do it and contact—" The professor stopped in mid-sentence when he noticed floodlights in the distance. At least one vehicle was positioned near a hill about two miles away, just off the ice shelf. The number of lights suggested that someone was carrying out some sort of extensive research or exploration. "Odd," Linnson commented. "I wonder who they are."

"We can find out," Collier suggested. "They might be from a station closer than the New Zealand one. It'll save us time if they'll grant us hospitality instead."

"I doubt anyone would refuse to help us here in Antarctica. After all, we're all scientists seeking the same goals. That's one of the beautiful things about Antarctica. Everyone has to get along for mutual survival."

Collier didn't bother to give his opinion. The more he saw of Antarctica, the less he considered it to be beautiful or exotic. The younger scientist was now disillusioned with his adventure and simply wanted to get on with his job and leave Antarctica alive.

As their sledge drew closer, they saw two vehicles. A big snow tractor with a trailer bin attached was positioned at the base of the large hill, the trailer set near the face of the snow-draped slope. Another tractor with a huge metal drill set on a frame at the front of the vehicle stood next to the first rig. Floodlights shone from the tractors to cast bright white light on a hole twenty feet in diameter. Several figures were clustered around the cavity. They had seen the headlights of the approaching sledge and were waiting for Linnson and Collier to reach the site.

"A drilling operation?" Collier wondered out loud. "I didn't know anyone was drilling out here."

"Neither did I." Linnson frowned under his mask. Drilling into the earth seemed a violation of the environment, although he realized it was sometimes done for the sake of scientific research. He visualized the enormous metal shaft burrowing into the ground, powered by machinery in the hands of humans. It seemed a microcosm of man's rape of the planet.

Collier brought the sledge to a halt. The men at the drilling site waited for the scientists to climb out of the vehicle. They wore dark gray parkas with matching trousers and insulated boots. Even their protective cold-weather masks and arctic mittens were gray. Linnson looked for name tags and shoulder patches to see what nationality they were, but the men didn't wear any identification emblems. This seemed particularly odd since their clothing appeared to be uniform.

"Hello," Linnson said as he walked toward the group. "I'm Professor Linnson from the United States, McMurdo Base. Do any of you speak English?"

"I speak English," a tall man with broad shoulders and a massive chest announced as he stomped forward, folding his thick arms across his chest.

"Good, good," Linnson said, bobbing his head. The professor tried to guess what accent flavored the stranger's English. German or Scandinavian, he thought. Probably Norwegian. "Well, as I said before, I'm Professor Linnson, and this is Dr. Collier."

"You're Americans," the big man said. "I understand. What do you want?"

"We hoped you'd be able to help us," Linnson began. "Is your station located near by? Closer than that temporary weather post New Zealand set up recently?"

"No," the man answered. "Are you two alone?"

"Yes, we are," the professor stated. "You didn't mention your name, sir."

"Naakon," the big Norwegian replied. "Two men shouldn't go out on the ice alone. It can be dangerous. You have kept up radio contact with your base?"

"Of course," Linnson assured him. "I have to make the next call in about half an hour."

"Did you tell them about us?" another member of Naakon's group demanded as he stepped forward. His accent suggested he was probably Australian.

"Why are you concerned?" Linnson replied, wondering what these men were doing at the drilling site.

He glanced up at the hill and noticed that the top was flat and had little snow at the peak. A volcano, Linnson thought. Possibly an active volcano, because the heat at the summit seemed great enough to reduce the accumulation of snow. The professor recalled his own interest in volcanoes and the reason he'd come to Antarctica for research.

"We'd better be going, Professor," Collier advised. The younger man was getting nervous. They had come upon a group of odd characters who were involved in something they didn't want others to know about. Collier figured he and Linnson ought to leave while they still had a chance.

"Did you tell your base about us or not?" the Australian insisted. He held a two-foot-long steel pipe in one hand and tapped it against the other mitten-clad palm.

"Not yet," Linnson replied without paying much attention to the man. He was too intrigued by the volcano to notice the menacing gesture by the Australian. "Tell me, is this volcano recorded on your charts? I don't recall it on our maps."

"Professor," Collier hissed urgently. He glanced at the mysterious group of men in gray. They seemed hostile, even dangerous. Collier's nervousness transformed to fear and began to reach the level of sheer terror.

Two other members of Naakon's party approached the two scientists. One carried a length of steel pipe and the other held a large wrench. Collier grabbed Linnson's arm and pulled him toward the ice sledge.

The professor jerked away from the younger man's grasp. "What's the matter with you? These men are scientists, the same as we are."

"They're not like us," Collier replied tensely. "Look at them, damn it! They're carrying weapons!"

Linnson stared at the pipes and tools in the strangers' fists. He realized Collier was right, but he couldn't understand why they were being threatened by the group. This was Antarctica. People weren't supposed to fight down here. They were supposed to cooperate for mutual survival. This was supposed to be the last pure place on earth.

"Stay where you are," Naakon warned as he pried open a canvas pouch on his belt. He pushed back the flap and drew a blue-black pistol from the case.

"Good God!" Linnson exclaimed. He stared at the gun in the big Norwegian's fist. "What's the meaning of this?"

"I don't see any point in trying to explain it, Professor," Naakon stated. He gripped the slide of the pistol in his other hand and pumped it to jack a round into the chamber. "You won't tell anyone about us, anyway."

"Why are you doing this?" Linnson asked, stunned and confused by the man's behavior.

"It's just business, Professor," Naakon replied with a shrug.

The Australian suddenly stepped forward and swung his length of pipe. The steel tube crashed into Linnson's head before the professor could raise his arms to defend himself or attempt to avoid the blow. Linnson groaned and fell to his knees. The Australian grabbed the hood to Linnson's parka and pulled it back to expose the American's head. Crimson already stained the professor's hair. His assailant raised the pipe once more.

Collier saw the man hammer the improvised club across the back of Professor Linnson's skull. The scientist slumped onto his belly. Blood and gray matter spilled from his shattered head. The Australian swung the pipe again to make certain the professor was dead.

"Jesus Christ!" Collier exclaimed and ran for the sledge.

Naakon watched the American through the sights of his pistol. Collier nearly reached the sledge, his legs pumping with great effort to run through the ankle-deep snow. Naakon squeezed the trigger, and the pistol bellowed in the stillness of the Antarctic night. Orange flame spewed from the muzzle of Naakon's weapon and seemed to streak out at Collier like artificial lightning.

The projectile struck Tad Collier between the shoulder blades. The scientist fell forward and landed on the nose of the ice sledge. The bullet had propelled him off balance. He gasped in pain as his spine seemed to burst into sharp, hot needles that pierced his nerve endings to send messages of agony throughout his body. Collier slid to the ground, helpless and half-paralyzed.

Men closed in on the fallen figure. A wrench in a mitten-fist swung a vicious blow into Collier's masked face. His nose crunched and the frontal bone to his skull caved in.

Collier was already dead when other attackers smashed his shattered form with steel pipes.

Naakon slipped his pistol into the pouch and watched the men club and kick the American's lifeless body. Stupid waste of energy, he thought. It was obvious the man was dead. Naakon turned to stare at the drill and tunnel. They would have to take care of the tunnel and the bodies.

"That's enough!" he shouted in English, because it was a language all of his crew understood to some degree. "We've got work to do and little time to get it done. They'll send others looking for those two, and we can't afford to be here when they arrive."

"We can kill them, too," the Australian said with a cocky laugh.

"We didn't come here to kill anyone, Donaldson," Naakon told the Australian, clearly annoyed by the man's attitude. "Littering the snow with corpses won't make our job here any easier. As for killing, there'll be plenty of that soon enough."

$$\equiv 2 \equiv$$

Calvin James held the steel-blue pistol in a two-handed Weaver grip, right fist around the pebbled handle and left hand braced under the butt, fingers reinforcing the shooting fist. The feel of the thirty-two-ounce firearm finally seemed familiar to James as he peered through the sights at the gray silhouette target. His index finger squeezed the double-action trigger.

The pistol snarled and recoiled in his hands. James fired three more rounds and saw bits of paper burst from the center of the target. He raised the sights and fired four more shots at the "head." More paper fragments spit from the target. James extended his right arm and held the pistol in his fist, left hand at the small of his back in a classic dueler's stance. He fired the weapon one-handed and blasted three more rounds into the silhouette.

"Hot diddly damn!" James remarked, seeing bullet holes appear in the target's head as he squeezed off the last shot.

He switched the gun to his left hand, aimed and fired the remaining rounds from the magazine. Copper shell casings hopped over his shoulder as he fired. James pressed the button to the magazine catch on the left side of the pistol to expel the spent mag. The weapon was ambidextrous and featured a magazine catch on both the left and right side. James placed the pistol on the table and reached for the controls to the target wire. He pushed the forward button, and the silhouette target slid toward him on the trolley clip of the overhead wire.

Other weapons continued to bark along the firing line. James's partners were indulging in target practice at the other stalls. The Apache earmuff protectors on his head spared him the ringing pain of the report of loud firearms in an enclosed area. James's target arrived and he pulled it from the wire. He was pleased with the results of his shooting.

The new Walther P-88 had taken him a while to get used to after years of using the Beretta 92-F and various designs of the Colt 1911. Yet James had never scored hits with any pistol at the firing range to compare with the accuracy of the P-88.

Accuracy and dependability were vital to Calvin James and the other four members of Phoenix Force. They were the best special operations commando unit in the world. Trained in combat and survival skills, antiterrorism and counterespionage, Phoenix Force was a unique elite fighting team unlike any other. It consisted of the very best and most experienced experts assembled from the nations of the free world.

James was proud to be a member of Phoenix Force. The tall, lean black man was still in his early thirties, yet he'd had a lifetime of experience in combat survival, which had started as a youth on the south side of Chicago. Growing up in a ghetto had forced him to fight at an early age. By the time he'd joined the Navy when he was seventeen, Calvin James was already a seasoned knife fighter, a Golden Gloves contender and a student of karate.

However, James was intelligent as well as tough. The Navy allowed him to pursue interests in medicine and chemistry. This combination of brains and physical ability led to a Military Occupation Specialty as a hospital corpsman with the elite SEAL team, and the badass from Chicago needed all of his skills when he was sent to Vietnam.

When he returned to the World, James continued his education in medicine and chemistry in California on the GI bill. However, his plans for the future changed when his sister died from a drug overdose and his mother was murdered by muggers the same year. The double tragedy, which virtually destroyed what remained of James's immediate family, steered him in the direction of law enforcement. He joined the San Francisco police and became a member of the Special Weapons and Tactics squad.

James was with the SWAT team when Phoenix Force enlisted him for a mission against the Black Alchemist terrorist outfit. They needed his ability as a chemist as well as his highly developed skills as a warrior. James was originally intended to participate in only that one special assignment, but he'd been with Phoenix Force ever since.

"Looks like you've got that Walther zeroed in," Yakov Katzenelenbogen, Phoenix Force's leader, remarked as he appeared next to James and examined the target in the black man's hands.

The Apache ear protectors were designed to muffle loud noise yet allow one to hear relatively clearly. James turned to face Katz. Yakov Katzenelenbogen didn't look like a supercommando. Middle-aged and slightly overweight, he seemed to be a pleasant, well-educated intellectual.

In fact, that impression was accurate. Katz *was* a scholar, a linguist fluent in six languages and semifluent in at least a dozen others, and the author of numerous articles and two books on Middle Eastern history and archaeology. Yet he was also a veteran fighting man and espionage agent. His extraordinary career had begun as a teenager in Europe when he joined the French Resistance against the Nazis after his family was rounded up and sent to a concentration camp.

Later, Katz worked with the American OSS and British Intelligence before the end of World War II. He moved to Palestine and joined the battle for Israeli independence, eventually becoming a top agent in Mossad and occasionally working with most of the major espionage organizations of the United States and Western Europe. Promoted to full colonel in the Israeli military, Katz soon commanded an antiterrorist strike team for Mossad, which hunted down Nazi war criminals and terrorist groups that conspired against Israel.

"I've got to admit this P-88 is one hell of a gun," James told Katz now. "I've fired double-action 9 mm pistols, but I don't recall handling one that'll do everything this sucker does."

"Yes," the Israeli agreed. "I think we've finally come across the ideal side arm for Phoenix Force."

Katz carried another Walther P-88 in shoulder leather under his right armpit. The Israeli appreciated the fifteen-round capacity, deadly accuracy and reliability of the German-made pistol, but he especially liked the ambidextrous features of the new Walther. In addition to the right and left magazine catch, the P-88 also had a decocking lever on either side of the pistol frame. This same lever also served as the slide stop. Katz liked this multiple function, especially the fact that he could easily handle the weapon with just his left hand.

Yakov Katzenelenbogen didn't have a right hand.

His right forearm had been amputated after it had been mangled beyond repair by an explosion during a battle in the Six Day War. Katz had fully adjusted to the disability, but it certainly helped to have weapons designed to be fired left-handed or, like the P-88, ambidextrously.

"Yeah," James said with a nod. "All of us are convinced but one, and I don't think he's going to change his mind, Yakov."

"I know," Katz said with a sigh. "Few things in this world are as stubborn as the mind of David McCarter."

"Or as twisted," Gary Manning added as he joined the pair.

The big Canadian looked at James's target and whistled with admiration. The shot groups were very close. Most were bunched where the heart would be or dead center in the head. Manning slapped James on the back. It was meant as a friendly gesture, but the light pat jarred James.

"Shit, Gary," he complained. "Don't you know your own strength yet?"

"Sorry," Manning replied.

"Sorry isn't going to help if I start to spit up blood, man," James told him.

Manning was a powerful man who was built like a lumberjack with uncanny stamina. His physical and mental resources seemed limitless. Manning was the Force's demolitions expert and its best rifle marksman. His unique skills were developed during his teenage years and perfected with the 5th Special Forces in Vietnam. These abilities and other combat skills were honed to an even greater degree when the Royal Canadian Mounted Police enlisted Manning for an antiterrorist unit and sent him to West Germany to get on-the-job training with the elite GSG-9.

He served with the German antiterrorist squad in the early seventies and returned to Canada to discover that the RCMP had gotten into political hot water for illegal wiretaps and other embarrassing behavior, which led to the dismantling of the operation Manning had originally been intended for. The new Canadian Security Intelligence Service offered Manning a desk job, but he turned it down. When the opportunity to join Phoenix Force arrived, Manning encountered an offer he couldn't refuse.

"I've scored my best pistol shots with the P-88, too," Manning stated. "Of course, I've been using the Walther P-5 for some time now, but I think the P-88's even better."

Repeated three-round bursts erupted from another stall. The trio watched chunks of paper fly into the air. The silhouette's chest all but vanished as it was transformed into a ragged hole. They approached the nearby stall and saw Rafael Encizo remove a long magazine from the butt well of a compact machine pistol.

The weapon design was world-famous, with a charging handle at the top of the frame, a post front sight and open rear sight, and a stubby barrel. It looked exactly like what it was—a much smaller version of the Uzi submachine gun. However, the micro-Uzi had been altered to fire in three modes: semi, full-auto or three-round bursts.

Encizo glanced at his teammates and smiled. The handsome Cuban presented a good-natured, agreeable personality. It was genuine, but it also concealed the other side of Encizo, which could be incredibly deadly and even ruthless if necessary.

Muscular and physically fit, Encizo seemed at least ten years younger than his true age. Few would have guessed he was old enough to have participated in the Bay of Pigs invasion. Yet Encizo had been among the Cuban freedom fighters to hit the beach in that ill-fated effort to dethrone Fidel Castro. He had also suffered at the hands of the Cuban secret police in the political prison of El Principe. Encizo had endured torture and terror to escape and return to the United States.

Over the years Rafael had taken up a number of odd professions. He'd been a scuba instructor, a professional bodyguard, a treasure hunter and had occasionally worked with the DEA and the Justice Department in the United States and Central America. Encizo had been employed as an insurance investigator specializing in maritime claims when he was contacted to join Phoenix Force. The Cuban had eagerly accepted.

"Well, I'm getting the hang of this cut-down Uzi," Encizo stated as he placed the empty weapon on a table next to a thirty-two-round magazine. "I still say my Heckler & Koch MP-5 is better for range and accuracy."

"I know," Katz agreed. "The H&K is a full-size submachine gun, and naturally you'll have greater accuracy and a longer range. But we've needed more uniform weapons in Phoenix Force for some time. If the need arises to swap magazines or ammo with other members of the team, we'd better have the same caliber, and preferably magazines that'll feed into the other guy's weapon."

"We've been talking about it for a long time and I agree," Encizo said. "But the hardest thing for me to get used to on the new Walther is the lack of a manual safety catch. I'm not sure I want to carry a gun like that."

"Yeah," James agreed. "I've been worrying about that, too. I've had nightmares about dropping the son of a bitch and shooting myself in the nuts."

"The P-88's perfectly safe to carry," Manning said. "It has a passive trigger safety. It won't fire unless the trigger's pulled. The trigger's linked to the firing pin. The hammer can hit concrete from a fifty-foot drop and it won't fire, because the firing pin won't be in position."

"Thank you," Encizo said dryly. "I read the manual, too."

"Well, I agree the Walther P-88 and the micro-Uzi are first-rate weapons," James stated. "I don't have any complaints about either one except that it's a lot of gear for us to haul into combat if we're going to carry assault rifles as well."

"That's the reason for the micro-Uzi," Katz said. He scratched the side of his nose with the steel hooks of the prosthesis attached to the stump of his right arm. "It's around ten inches long, about the same size as the Ingram MAC-10, but it's certainly more accurate, and the rate of fire's more controllable. I'll agree, though, that it isn't as accurate as the MP-5, the standard-size Uzi subgun or the KG-99 McCarter's been using."

The Israeli stopped and glanced around the indoor pistol range. McCarter was missing. Encizo guessed who Katz was looking for and told him McCarter had left the range to use the bathroom in the corridor. As if on cue, the Briton returned from the hall.

Tall and lean with foxlike features, McCarter always seemed to wear wrinkled, ill-treated clothes. His hair was seldom combed, and ashes often covered his shirtfront, thanks to the Player's cigarettes he incessantly puffed. Smoking was one of his many nervous habits. The Briton tended to be restless and high-strung between missions.

McCarter was a tough cockney from the East End of London. He was a veteran of the British SAS and had seen action in Oman, Northern Ireland and Vietnam. McCarter had participated in the spectacular SAS raid on the Iranian embassy in London in 1980. The Briton thrived on adventure, and he had jumped at the opportunity to become a member of Phoenix Force.

A pair of Apache ear protectors hung around Mc-Carter's neck, and the butt of a pistol jutted from the shoulder holster under his left arm. He held a lighter to the cigarette in his mouth and fired the tip as he approached the other four men. "The answer's no," he declared in a firm voice.

"None of us asked a question," Katz said, eyebrows raised in mock surprise.

"You don't have to," the Briton declared. He patted the holstered pistol. "I'm not giving up the Browning, and that's bloody final."

"Oh, God," Manning muttered, shaking his head slightly. "I knew you'd never be willing to part with that pistol. You do realize the Browning Hi-Power's based on a design made back in 1925, don't you?"

"So it's passed the test of time for sixty-five years," McCarter said with a shrug. "I don't care if you blokes think it's outdated. I don't give a damn if this fancy Walther P-88 holds two more rounds in the magazine and has doo-dads and gizmos other guns don't have. I've used the Browning Hi-Power for nearly twenty years, and it's never let me down."

"I know you don't trust double-action autoloaders, David," Encizo said patiently, "but don't you realize the importance of having uniform weapons? In case one of us needs ammo or a magazine from the other guy, or if one of us loses a piece, somebody else can toss him a gun, if we're all using the same weapon."

"I've shot the Walther P-88," McCarter replied. "I'm familiar with it. I can use it for practical purposes in an emergency, but I'm not going to bet my life on a pistol with a load of extra gadgets that can foul up the mechanism. The single-action auto isn't complex, so you don't have a lot of junk that can break down in it. None of this double-action, ambidextrous and God knows what else added to it. The more complicated a firearm is—"

"The more things can go wrong with it," Manning said, completing the Briton's sentence. He was familiar with McCarter's philosophy about weapons. "The rest of us are using the Walther, David."

"That's your choice," the Briton replied with a shrug. "Hell, I'll even carry a spare magazine for the P-88, but I won't carry the damn gun. The Browning's the same caliber as the Walther—9 mm parabellum. I'll quit using the KG-99 and carry the micro-Uzi instead, and I'll agree with just about everything else we've been talking about for the past—"

"But you'll keep the Browning," Katz said with a sigh.

"Can't I finish a bloody sentence without one of you beating me to it?" McCarter growled.

"Okay," James said wearily, "we know where you stand on this issue. I think you're making a mistake. All of us have scored more accurate hits with the P-88 than we did with our other pistols. You're our all-time pistol champ and—"

"I was among the finalists for the Olympic pistol team," McCarter stated with pride, also happy that he had interrupted somebody else for a change. "I might have gone on to win a medal, but I was in the SAS at the time and they sent me to Oman before I could complete the final round of competition."

"Fate robbed you of greatness," Manning commented dryly.

"Sod off," the Briton told him.

"My point is," James continued, "that you can probably score better with the P-88 than any of us, David."

The British ace raised the Apache ear protectors from his neck and fitted the muffs around his ears. He walked to a stall, fitted a target to the wire clip and pressed a control button to send the silhouette sliding down the range. The other members of Phoenix Force slipped their ear protectors onto their heads as they watched the target travel toward its destination.

McCarter's right hand seized the Browning Hi-Power and pulled it from shoulder leather. His left hand grasped his right fist in a Weaver grip, and the pistol boomed. McCarter squeezed off three rapid-fire shots, then triggered three more and pressed the forward button of the control panel.

The silhouette target traveled toward McCarter from seventy-five feet away. The Briton opened fire once more as the target drew closer. The other Phoenix pros saw the holes in the center of the silhouette's body and in its head. McCarter fired the remaining rounds from the Browning magazine as the target approached. Bullet holes appeared above the hole in the silhouette's chest. A line of fresh holes extended from the center to the gap in the target's head. The silhouette resembled a connect-the-dots figure.

"God, what a show-off," Manning muttered.

The Briton returned the Browning to leather and yanked the target from the wire. He handed it to James and displayed a wolfish grin. The black warrior stared at the silhouette. The line of bullet holes between the head and chest wasn't quite straight, but otherwise the pattern was perfect. McCarter had fired all thirteen rounds, and every one of them would have been lethal for a human opponent.

"You were saying about accuracy?" McCarter asked smugly.

"Maybe David should keep his Browning," James remarked, and handed the target to Katz.

"Sure," Katz agreed, impressed by the Briton's marksmanship. "I'd say this is a good argument in defense of his position."

"I just hope you don't run out of pistol mags in a firefight," Encizo commented.

"There haven't been any firefights for a while," McCarter commented. "I can't recall the last time we went this long between missions."

"You afraid peace has broken out all over the world?" James remarked with a snort. "Don't worry, man. It won't last."

"Well," Encizo said, "it gives us a chance to get some training between missions. If we're going to make any mistakes, this is the time to make them, not in the field where someone can get killed."

"Hell of a way to spend our time off," Manning said with a massive shrug.

"We have to stay in peak condition to be prepared when we're called back into the field," Katz stated as he reached into a shirt pocket and removed his watch. "Our lives are on the line when we take on a mission. A lot of other people's lives depend on us, too. It's now 11:00. What do you say to another hour of training and then we'll call it a day?"

"Why not?" McCarter replied. "There doesn't seem to be much else for us to do right now."

3

The underground complex wasn't included in most blueprints of the White House. It had been built during a previous administration to protect the President from a terrorist-style attack on the White House itself. The chamber wasn't a bomb shelter in the sense that it had been constructed to survive a nuclear attack, but it would withstand an explosion capable of destroying the building above. That was the theory, anyway.

Hal Brognola was one of the few people outside the elite members of the White House security staff who knew about the complex. The big Justice Department agent stepped from the elevator and found himself in the entryway. Wooden panels and tiles on the walls, floor and ceiling concealed the steel-and-lead shell that surrounded the underground installation, which seemed agreeable, even pleasant. A battery-powered generator supplied electricity. Ceiling lights cast a soft glow across the sitting room. A filter system allowed fresh air through the vents, and the complex had an emergency oxygen supply if the vents had to be cut off.

An oak desk, a maple table, leather-backed armchairs and a sofa provided a comfortable living area. A well-stocked bookcase, a stereo, a color television and a VCR were available for entertainment. The kitchen contained bottled water, a two-month supply of food and other necessities. The complex also had bedrooms, a bathroom and its own plumbing system. One could stay in the subterranean fortress for weeks in relative comfort, safe from everything except cabin fever.

"Hello, Hal," the man next to the maple table greeted with a solemn nod. "I'm glad you could make it."

"Part of my job, Mr. President," Brognola replied.

The President of the United States gestured at an armchair, inviting his visitor to take a seat. Hal Brognola didn't fit the typical image of someone who would meet with the man from the Oval Office in a clandestine arrangement at a subterranean rendezvous. Middle-aged with a weary, haggard face, jaw carpeted by whisker stubble because he hadn't shaved in the past twenty-four hours, Brognola looked like a regular guy who had just left his white-collar job after putting in a lot of overtime.

The impression was misleading because Brognola never got off work. His suit was rumpled and his narrow tie askew. His black dress shoes had been hastily brushed off, and dust was still visible between the laces.

The Commander in Chief of the United States of America was no longer surprised by Brognola's appearance. His visitor was a man who didn't give a damn about polish and outward appearances. The President himself didn't seem very dapper today. He looked tired. The President's tie was loose and his shirt was open at the throat. Lines of tension at the corners of his mouth and on his forehead hinted of considerable mental and physical strain.

Brognola understood the strain of responsibility better than most men. His security clearance was higher than most government officials, although there was no record of his current position as chief of operations for Stony Man Farm. Unlike the CIA or the NSA, Stony Man was basically an enforcement organization, not an Intelligence network. In fact, it often got information by tapping into the computers and records of Intel outfits. Stony Man had managed to maintain airtight security because it consisted of a small number of extremely dedicated professionals.

The only man who gave Brognola orders was the President himself. The Fed had been accustomed to meeting with the former President and was still getting used to the new man in the Oval Office. The new President was no doubt adjusting to Brognola, as well. At least he appreciated the need for security. A former director of the CIA, he made certain their meetings were conducted in absolute secrecy.

"We have a serious problem, Hal," the President said, as he pulled a glass stopper from a bottle of water. "Of course, that's why you're here. Water?"

"Please," Brognola replied. "What kind of problem, sir?"

The President poured two glasses of water and handed one to Brognola. The big Fed noticed a file folder on the table next to the bottle.

"I'm sure you're aware the United States and several other nations have been conducting operations in Antarctica for decades," the President began. "Scientists mostly. Various types of studies are carried out there. The climate makes it difficult and dangerous, but some are willing to face the hardships and risks in the name of science."

Brognola sipped his water and waited for the President to get to the point.

"Two American scientists stationed at McMurdo Base went out on the ice and failed to make regular radio contact," the President continued. "Rescue teams carried out a search in the general area where the scientists supposedly vanished. They were on their way to Beardmore Glacier in the Transantarctic Mountains. The British, French, New Zealanders, Norwegians, Australians, even the Russians, sent search parties. Everyone tries to cooperate down there. Well, they found the scientists' snow sledge and eventually found them, as well.''

"Dead?" Brognola guessed.

"Murdered," the President said. "The corpses had been dropped into a tunnel of some sort. They were taken back to McMurdo. This is all a bit baffling and tragic for the families, but two men murdered in Antarctica wouldn't be a cause for international concern by itself. That all changed when the men who got the bodies out of the tunnel showed signs of significant exposure to radiation."

"Radiation?" Brognola said, raising his eyebrows.

"That's right," the President said with a nod. "They were lucky, though. The exposure might have been worse if they hadn't been wearing so much protective clothing due to the weather. Nonetheless, their clothes and the two dead men both registered worrisome levels of radiation, the sort that suggests someone may be doing nuclear testing in Antarctica. Of course, that's a violation of international law."

"Does anyone know what the Soviets have been up to in Antarctica lately?" the Fed inquired.

"No one seems to suspect them of anything like this," the President replied. "But, to be honest, we're putting the Soviets at the head of the list of suspects until we know more about the incident."

"I don't suppose there's any way to keep a lid on this?" Brognola asked, already aware of the answer.

"The story will be on the evening news tonight," the President answered. "Even if we could get our own media to keep this quiet for a while, other nations are involved. French and New Zealand rescue people helped get the bodies out of the tunnel and, as I said, their people were exposed to radiation. There's going to be a scandal about this. Accusations will start to fly, if they haven't already."

"If the Soviets are responsible, it'll sure put a crimp in *glasnost*," the Fed commented.

"It's not going to help our relations with anyone," the President added. "Seven countries claim ownership of territories in Antarctica. Neither the Soviets nor the U.S. recognize those claims. France and New Zealand are among the nations that feel they have a rightful claim to parts of Antarctica. So are Great Britain, Norway and Australia. Since they all had teams helping to search for the two missing scientists and know the men were found dead in a tunnel, they'll want to know what's going on down there. The French and New Zealanders already know the situation is more serious than two individuals who accidentally fell into a big hole and died."

"There will certainly be accusations that the cold war has surfaced in Antarctica," Brognola commented. "Considering the climate, that might be an appropriate place for it."

"Even if the Soviets are responsible," the President continued as he handed the file folder to Brognola, "America will catch hell, too. Some of the countries that claim part-ownership of Antarctica may press their claims and demand that both the U.S. and USSR get out and stay out. If all seven get together, it's hard to say how much support they could muster from other nations. Three European countries, two South American nations and Australia and New Zealand can put together a fair amount of influence if they can convince other countries that the superpowers have been carrying out illegal nuclear testing in Antarctica."

"Those countries are all allies of the United States, aren't they?"

"Yes," the President confirmed. "That's exactly why we'll get the bulk of the blame. They have more diplomatic and trade relations with America than with the Soviets. There are simply more ways they can strike back at us than at the Russians. The most serious concern for the United States is actually the same as it is for the other nations involved."

"Someone appears to be doing nuclear testing of some sort down there," Brognola said grimly.

"Exactly," the President said with a nod. "All I know for sure is that the United States isn't responsible for this. We've never conducted any nuclear tests of any kind in Antarctica. I've talked to top personnel from the Pentagon, the Nuclear Regulatory Commission, the Defense Department, the NSA, the CIA and Naval Intelligence. They all agreed this sort of thing would not only be a violation of the Antarctica Treaty of 1959, but potentially disastrous. Any serious damage to one of the polar caps could cause global destruction on an extraordinary scale—tidal waves, earthquakes, drastic changes in weather and possibly even an alteration in the earth's axis."

"The Soviets must realize all that as well," Brognola said with a frown. "Why would they pull a stunt like this?"

"My advisors tell me there's never been any evidence that the Soviets have ever conducted nuclear tests in Antarctica, either," the President answered. "We don't know the Russians are responsible for what happened in Antarctica yesterday, but we do know two men have been murdered and that others were significantly contaminated by radiation when they entered that tunnel. What few details we have are in that folder. I want your people on this and I want them on it immediately."

"Right away," the Fed assured him.

"Good. This situation can hurt us a dozen different ways, everything from trade and diplomatic relations to tearing down what progress we've made to reduce nuclear arms.

There's even the possibility the entire world could be at risk. I hope I don't sound too melodramatic, but I want you to fully appreciate how important this mission is."

"They're all important, sir," the Fed replied.

"So they are," the President agreed. "So they are."

4

Erik Heller exhaled as he thrust his arms high and stared at the barbell in his fists. He inhaled deeply and lowered the bar to his chest. Heller didn't think about anything except the weight and breathing. Concentration was vital to power lifting. He was bench-pressing four hundred pounds, nearly twice his own body weight, but Heller didn't dwell on how heavy the barbell was. He thought only of lifting and breathing.

Heller raised and lowered the barbell again and lifted it once more to place the bar across the iron brackets above the bench. Jason House stood by in case Heller had trouble with the weights, but his help wasn't needed. Heller sat up and flexed his broad shoulders in a great shrug. Muscles rippled in his powerful back. He gazed in the full-length mirror at the end of the gym.

His reflection stared back at him. A heavily muscled figure clad in white shorts and a red undershirt, his bare limbs bulged with power. Biceps and triceps resembled coils of thick rope under his tanned skin. Thigh muscles formed huge humps with a teardrop shape at the knees. His chest was like a keg of nails above a muscle-lined abdomen.

The head atop the bodybuilder's physique seemed older than the body. A lantern jaw with a small mouth, sleek nose and cool blue eyes formed a handsome yet cruel face. The years had left lines in his face, and gray had won over the dark brown hair at his temples. Heller combed his hair back to conceal the balding spot at the top of his head.

Heller hated growing older. He had spent his entire life as an athlete and physical fitness fanatic. Heller never smoked or drank alcohol. He consumed vitamin capsules, drank protein mixtures and watched his diet with greater care than a diabetic. Yet age, that ultimate destroyer and ravager of youth, slowly took its toll.

Erik Heller was only forty-four. Physically powerful and more fit than most men half his age, Heller still fretted about hair loss the way most might worry about cancer. He considered hair transplants, but that would be time-consuming, and he had businesses to run. Maybe later.

"My God, that's impressive," Jason House commented as he stared at the heavy plates attached to the barbell. "You should have tried out for Mr. Universe. Look what it did for Arnold Schwarzenegger."

"Schwarzenegger's a movie star," Heller remarked with a snort of contempt. "So what? My ambitions are considerably greater than that, Jason."

Heller still spoke with a Georgia drawl. There was arrogance in his voice. It had been bred into his family by 150 years of wealth and high social status. His ancestors had been plantation owners who'd sold cotton and bought slaves before the Civil War.

The Heller family had correctly predicted the South would lose, and had sold their property before the fighting had started. After the war they'd returned to Georgia and made deals with the carpetbaggers and Northern bankers to buy new land and start a new empire with lumber and paper mills. Clarence Heller had purposely hired former slaves to work in the mills because they'd accepted bottom-of-the-barrel wages and never dared complain about working con-

ditions or mistreatment. He was supposedly fond of saying, "It's just like the ol' days again with the Hellers on top
and the darkies in their place."

His family always found a way to stay on top. If they had
to hurt other people in the process, that was the other folks'
bad luck. Hellers had only one loyalty and that was to
themselves.

The Great Depression was little more than an inconvenience for them. They'd sold most of their stocks and in-
vested in commodities before the market crashed. They'd
sold scrap metal to the Germans and the Japanese until
Pearl Harbor. They'd sold munitions to the Soviet Union
until the American public had realized Stalin wasn't a nice
guy, even if he had fought against Hitler during World War
II.

Erik Heller had been born to a family of wheeler-dealers
and cutthroat businessmen. His father had been disappointed in young Erik because the boy's interest had been
in sports and exercise instead of finance and international
power. If his old man were alive and knew what his son was
involved with, Heller wondered what dear old Dad would
think. Would he be horrified and repulsed by Erik's behavior? Or proud to see his youngest son had become the most
ambitious, ruthless and unprincipled Heller of them all.

"Your guests will be arriving in about half an hour,"
House stated as he consulted his Rolex wristwatch. "You
might want to check security arrangements."

"That's your job, Jason," Heller replied. He rose from
the bench, eyes still fixed on his own reflection in the mirror. "I trust you to do it."

Heller raised his jaw and searched for any sign of a
dreaded double chin. He glimpsed House's reflection in the
mirror, as well. House was three years younger than Heller,
yet he lacked the American's bodybuilder physique.

Although tall with a lean face and long limbs, House had a slight potbelly, visible despite the baggy gray sweat suit he wore.

"You need to work on that gut, Jason," Heller commented as he turned away from the mirror. "Fifty sit-ups a day on the slant board ought to take care of it."

"The only muscles I need to worry about are in my trigger finger, sir," House declared, and patted the holster on his hip. The ivory handle of a .38-caliber Smith & Wesson jutted from leather.

House sounded confident and perfectly content with himself and the fact that he was growing older. Heller suspected this was because House was British. All that stiff-upper-lip, fatalistic crap. House had prematurely silver hair, clipped short as if he were still in the British army. His double chin and potbelly seemed out of place on the rest of his body. The Briton appeared to be both scrawny and flabby at the same time. Yet it didn't seem to bother House.

Nonetheless, House was one of the few men Heller trusted. A veteran mercenary with underworld connections, House had been a valuable ally and the closest thing Heller had to a friend. The Briton would certainly profit by his relationship with Heller. Indeed, he already had. That didn't bother Heller. Long ago his family had taught him that loyalty was something with a price tag on it.

"Suit yourself," Heller said with a shrug. "I'm going to work out on the heavy bag a bit and take a shower. You take care of whatever arrangements need to be made for security, but make sure you're in the den before our visitors get here. I want you with me."

"Absolutely," House agreed. "Some of those chaps are a bit unstable if you ask me. I especially don't trust those bloody wogs."

"You mean the Arabs?" Heller asked with a smile. "They're probably the most stable of the lot. They have a great tradition as traders and merchants, you know. The others worry me more than the Arabs, but keep an eye on all of them."

"I will," House assured him.

Heller nodded and walked across the hardwood gym floor to the heavy bag that hung from a short chain bolted to the ceiling. The bag was part of an assortment of combat training gear. A *makiwara* karate striking post and buckets of sand allowed him to toughen and temper hands and fingers. Heller slammed his fist into the bag. It swayed from the blow, and he hit it again with a left hook, followed by an elbow smash and the back of his fist.

Jason House watched the American hammer the heavy bag with a flurry of punishing blows. The British mercenary had noticed that Heller attacked projects with the same fierce determination. House was glad he was on Heller's side, because he suspected it would soon be very hazardous not to be.

THE LIMOUSINES approached the gate. Uniformed guards clad in khaki shirts, matching shorts and bush hats stood by the shack as the steel-wire gate rolled open. Each man carried an Australian-made F-1 submachine gun, a weapon similar to the British Patchett, with an unusual top-loading magazine located in front of the trigger mechanism. One man waited for the vehicles at the gate while the other moved to the shack to cover his partner if anything went wrong.

The cars came to a halt. The driver of the first limo rolled down his window and spoke with the closest guard. The sentry recognized the driver, but they exchanged passwords as a matter of standard security. The guards were then certain the passengers in the limos were the guests "Mr. Hellson" expected and not police, government agents or some other unwanted visitors. The driver was also assured that the ranch hadn't been raided by law-enforcement forces while he was at the airstrip to pick up the VIP visitors.

The guard waved the limos through the gate. The big black autos drove along the dirt road to the ranch house. Hundreds of acres of rich green New Zealand countryside surrounded them. The "Hellson" spread was fairly small, but well located with fine grazing land and underground streams that allowed for good irrigation and hydroelectric power. Four small windmills on tall aluminum stalks powered water pumps. The propellers whirled in the breeze as the cars rolled past a pair of wooden billets. Two men dressed in the same casual uniform as the sentries sat on the porch steps to one building. One guy oiled and cleaned an assault rifle while his companion guzzled beer and watched the limos with only passing interest.

Other men rode horses among the cattle in the grassland. The steers calmly chewed their cuds and swatted flies with their tails. Their keepers seemed bored with the task of tending the cattle. They sat in saddles atop their mounts while the horses simply walked around the lazy herd in a slow circle. The scene could have taken place in Wyoming or Montana, but these cowboys wore bush hats instead of Stetsons.

Some of the men at the "Hellson" spread were native-born New Zealanders. The majority were Europeans, mostly British and French with a few Scandinavians and Germans. The rest were Australians and, like "Hellson" himself, Americans. All were misfits of one sort or another. They were hard men—mercenaries, hoodlums and renegades who had found a gravy train with a private army that paid extremely well and required relatively little work. Many suspected they would soon be required to earn their keep. Something big was in the works. Something that would shake up the whole damn world.

The limousines pulled up to the house. A large split-level structure with whitewashed walls and picture windows, it was attractive and practical. Solar cell units on the roof fed an additional source of electricity to the house during the day. Two more armed figures stood at the doorway. A rectangular framework object of metal and plastic was mounted in front of the entrance.

The drivers of both limos got out and opened the back doors for their passengers. Abdullah al-Kalim and his aide Jaber emerged from the first vehicle. A small, slender man with proud features that many claimed resembled those of a desert falcon, al-Kalim stroked his neatly trimmed black beard and adjusted his gold-rimmed sunglasses. Sunlight flashed on the gold rings on several fingers.

"What's this?" al-Kalim inquired as he gestured at the object in the doorway. "A metal detector?"

"Oui," a French merc at the door confirmed. "It is a precaution, monsieur. You understand?"

"Of course," al-Kalim assured him. "A man in Mr. Hellson's profession must always take precautions."

He extended a hand toward Jaber and snapped his fingers. The aide reached inside his suit jacket and drew a 7.65 mm pistol from shoulder leather. Jaber placed the gun in al-Kalim's open palm. The French merc nodded as al-Kalim handed him the pistol.

"Just make certain you don't misplace it," Jaber warned.

"Of course, monsieur," the sentry replied with a nod.

Alberto Mancini and Dom Rigotti climbed out of the second limousine. The Italians were younger and less polished than the two Arabs. Mancini wore a rather shabby-looking suit, two sizes too big for his scrawny frame, and a black shirt without a tie. Rigotti was dressed in even more casual attire. The heavyset, tough guy from Rome wore a field jacket, denim trousers and a T-shirt. Both men had long hair and beards. Their appearance was part of their self-image as urban guerrillas.

"Why do we have to surrender our weapons?" Rigotti asked with a frown, wrinkles forming across his low brow.

"The American is nervous," Mancini replied with a shrug.

Al-Kalim had to go through the metal detector twice. Some of his jewelry set off the buzzer when he first stepped into the detector. He finally passed through the machine without triggering any alarms. Jaber followed. Mancini surrendered a .380 Beretta pistol to the sentries. Rigotti handed a flight bag to the French merc at the door. The sentry opened it and looked inside.

"Merde!" the Frenchman exclaimed when he saw a Czech-made Skorpion machine pistol and three Soviet F-1 hand grenades inside the bag. "How did you manage to get all this into the country?"

"We have ways," Rigotti snorted.

The French merc shrugged as he placed the flight bag on the porch. The Italians also gave up their wristwatches and keys before they stepped into the metal detector. Another figure emerged from the first limo and watched the pair enter the ranch house. A stocky Asian with a shaved head and thick gray eyebrows, he seemed amused by the precautions. General Ton Chi Dai was a dignified figure, clad in a black business suit and narrow black tie. The New Zealand climate was mild compared to his homeland of Vietnam. During the Southern Hemisphere winter, the weather seemed almost chilly to General Ton.

He unbuttoned his jacket with his left hand and pulled open his garment to reveal that he didn't carry a weapon.

Ton raised his right arm. The sentries stared at the large steel hook that jutted from the end of the sleeve. Ton smiled.

"I don't think I can pass through your metal detector without setting off the alarm," Ton declared in excellent English with a slight nasal accent. "If you must frisk me, I understand."

"That's not necessary, General," the Frenchman assured him. "Mr. Hellson wouldn't want you subjected to such an inconvenience."

"Merci beaucoup, monsieur," Ton replied as he watched the merc switch off the metal detector.

The Vietnamese officer walked through the contraption and entered the house. Ton joined the other four guests in the hall. Black and white squares formed a chessboard pattern on the floor. Two marble statues stood at opposite corners of the hall. One appeared to be a Roman warrior, naked except for a helmet and a loincloth of white stone. The nose guard of the helmet bisected the statue's fierce features. Blank stone eyes revealed no emotion, but the determination in the hard set of the lips suggested the warrior would never surrender unless the short sword in its cold white fist failed in combat.

The other figure was a female. Marble folds of a flowing robe hung from the graceful white shoulders. The statue sat on a short pedestal. The classical carving displayed spare breasts and slender limbs. Delicate features smiled with confidence, even arrogance. Marble replicas of bracelets, an ornately carved necklace and several rings adorned the statue. In one hand the lady figure held a small stone bag; in the other palm were three discs the size of silver dollars.

General Ton had been to the ranch house before and had noticed these statues, curious about what the figures were supposed to represent. The statues didn't fit the rest of the decor, but they did seem consistent with the character of

Erik Heller—even with his assumed identity of Edward Hellson. Yet Ton felt certain the statues were more than expensive decorations, garish displays of wealth, or tasteless efforts to impress others with the host's knowledge of classical art or his international globe-trotting. These Greco-Roman figures had to symbolize something of value to Heller.

"Welcome, gentlemen," a voice with a familiar Southern drawl announced from the end of the hall. "I'm glad to see that all of you are here."

Heller approached the group, his powerful physique clad in a short-sleeved white shirt and white duck trousers with gray slippers. He displayed a parody of a smile as he introduced himself as Edward Hellson for the sake of those present who hadn't met him before. Ton wondered if the others knew the man's real name or background. The Arabs probably did, the general reckoned, because they had Intelligence sources of one sort or another. Ton guessed the Italians knew only what Hellson-Heller had told them. Red Brigade zealots, Ton thought with contempt. He didn't feel such unstable amateurs belonged at this conference.

"Please follow me, gentlemen," Heller said, waving the group forward. "Everything's ready, so we can get on to business without delay."

"Of course," Ton said with a slight smile. "You Americans believe in coming straight to the point."

"We have our share of horse traders, too, General," Heller assured him.

"I was admiring your statues," al-Kalim said. The Arab was obviously as curious about them as Ton and had decided to ask Heller about their significance. "Do they symbolize strength and courage as opposed to the temptations of the flesh?"

"I don't know that those things are opposites," Heller answered. "The idea that strength is the ability to resist women and wealth, or that courage is the opponent of financial success, hardly suits me or my business. I may be many things, but even my worst enemies wouldn't accuse me of being a hypocrite."

The American gestured at the male statue. "This is Mars, the Roman god of war," he explained. "The lady is Fortuna, goddess of fortune. War and wealth are what my trade consists of. My good fortune is to be found in war."

"Perhaps you should include Thanatos in your collection," Mancini commented dryly. "The Greek personification of death."

"Death is a by-product of my business," Heller replied without a trace of remorse. "I'm not very concerned about it one way or the other. All of you, however, want a great number of people to die. That's why you're here."

Heller escorted his guests to the den. A large, comfortable room with armchairs and sofas, a well-stocked bar, a library and billiard tables, the den had been prepared for the visit. French wine, Turkish coffee and Chinese tea were offered to the five guests. A projector was set up on the leather-topped counter of the bar, lens aimed at a movie screen on the opposite wall. The shutters on the windows were closed for privacy.

Jason House waited for them in the den. The British merc wore a pressed uniform, well-shined low-quarter boots and a gun belt with the Smith & Wesson revolver on his hip. Two other men were present. A heavyset fellow with a brown-and-gray beard sat on a sofa, a short-stemmed pipe jammed into his mouth. He puffed billows of gray smoke across the room as he watched Heller lead the VIP guests into the den. A short, thin figure restlessly paced the hardwood floor. His long brown fingers tapped together in a nervous gesture, and his weary, heart-shaped face wore a brooding expression. A white turban was bound around his head. The Indian appeared to be well on the way to a nervous breakdown.

"Some of you have already met Jason House," Heller began as he steered the visitors toward the chairs. "I also want you to meet Gustav Kubler and Professor Morarji."

"A pleasure," Kubler replied, not bothering to rise from the sofa.

Morarji faced the group and bowed politely. Heller made certain his visitors were seated and then had House serve beverages. As Heller suspected, the two Arabs chose coffee, and General Ton accepted a cup of tea. The Italians seemed almost offended by the offer of wine. Mancini settled for coffee, while Rigotti reluctantly accepted a beer from the bar.

"Why does this one get to carry a gun and the rest of us must be unarmed?" Rigotti asked sourly as House handed him a mug of cold beer.

"Because he's my chief of security," Heller answered. "It's his job to be ready to protect me and my property. The gun is just part of the uniform."

"A man needs to feel secure in his own home," al-Kalim added with a shrug.

"None of us can truly feel secure these days," Heller declared as he stood by the bar and switched on the projector. "This is why."

House turned the dial of a control unit wired to the lamps, and the light dimmed as Heller's film cast images on the screen. A great mushroom cloud appeared on the screen. A brilliant light at the base and center seemed to push the sinister toadstool pattern of smoke wider and higher into the gray sky on the screen. There was no sound, but the black-and-white film didn't need an explanation.

"This footage is from the Nevada Proving Ground in the late 1950s," Heller said. "The weapon being tested here was far superior to the atomic bombs dropped on Hiroshima and Nagasaki in 1945. The nuclear destruction of those unlucky Japanese cities at the end of World War II changed the nature of warfare and international affairs forever. A new age began with the invention of the most fearsome weapon ever developed by man."

Another terrible mushroom cloud appeared on the screen. Smoke whirled and churned within the angry shape of awesome destruction. The scene changed to show a lifeless, grim collection of mangled buildings, scattered debris and charred earth.

"Here we see some results of a nuclear explosion," Heller explained. "This footage was taken at Hiroshima near ground zero. You'll notice most of the wooden structures were all but obliterated. Bamboo burned like paper in the blast. The fireball consumed dozens of houses and smaller buildings. Even concrete walls caved in from the blast. Cobblestones and cement melted in this nuclear inferno."

Japanese survivors of the bomb appeared on the screen. Nuked from the waist up, they displayed hideous scar tissue and clumps of tumors.

"This footage is also from Hiroshima," Heller continued. "Of course this is just the dawn of nuclear weaponry, the atomic Stone Age compared to what's been developed since 1945."

The images on the screen changed to a huge missile strapped to a platform and hauled by a tractor rig. Russian troops grimly marched alongside the monstrous weapon. Another missile appeared on the screen moments before it hurtled from the mouth of an underground silo to jet into the sky. A great submarine appeared briefly on the screen, slowly submerging into choppy waves. A white Polaris missile broke the surface of the water and shot up to the clouds above.

"Thanks to the efforts of scientists and military forces of the United States and the Soviet Union," Heller said, "nuclear weapons have become more powerful, more accurate and more lethal. The Little Boy fission bomb carried by the *Enola Gay* B-29 over Hiroshima was an oversize firecracker compared to the so-called H-bombs developed in the fifties and the ICBMs of the sixties and seventies. The warheads of these superaccurate weapons can deliver nuclear explosions greater than 180 kilotons of TNT. The Hiroshima bomb was only 12.5 kilotons. Correct me if I'm wrong on this, Professor."

"No, no," Morarji assured him. The Indian tried to avoid looking at the screen. "You have your facts straight, except nuclear weapons can be far more devastating than 180 kilotons. The largest ever detonated was by the Soviet Union in 1961. That was a fifty-megaton bomb."

"Thank you, Professor," Heller said, and returned to his role as lecturer. "Now these nuclear weapons are mostly in the hands of the superpowers. The United States and the Soviet Union lead the arms race, of course, but Great Britain, France, China and Professor Morarji's homeland of India also possess nuclear arsenals. Israel and South Africa almost certainly have nuclear weapons, as well. Dozens of other nations are trying to get into the nuclear weapons business. Pakistan may have already accomplished this, and it's probably just a matter of time before Saudi Arabia and some of the nations of South America do likewise."

Scenes of desert combat between Israel and Egypt during the Six Day War appeared on the screen. American soldiers in a rain forest followed. Some carried wounded troops on stretchers to a Huey in a clearing while others watched the surrounding jungle, M-16 rifles held ready. More combat footage followed. The Iran-Iraq War, Afghan freedom fighters battling Russian troops, civil wars in Nicaragua and Angola as well as more scenes of Vietnam and the Middle East flashed before the eyes of the group.

"There have been many wars and conflicts since World War II," Heller stated, "but nuclear weapons haven't been used in combat since 1945. Neither the Americans nor the Russians have used them. They've also tried to keep nuclear weapons from other nations, even those they support. Despite American support of Israel, the United States refused to give nuclear weapons to their Middle Eastern friends. It's believed Israelis actually hijacked a Greek ship to get their hands on approximately twenty tons of uranium in 1958 in order to build their own nuclear weapons."

"We've taken an interest in the activities of the Jewish State of Israel for some time, Mr. Hellson," al-Kalim said dryly. "Is this lecture on the history of nuclear weapons leading to something, or is this simply entertainment for your guests?"

"*Si,*" Mancini added gruffly. "I thought you Americans came to the point in matters of business. What is the purpose of showing these movies? You wish to make documentary films? Do that on your own time, but don't waste ours with this nonsense."

"My point is that governments with nuclear weapons don't intend to give them to others who don't," Heller explained, apparently unruffled by the criticism. "They don't want to give away such weapons or sell them to either foreign governments or allies. They certainly don't want them in the hands of private organizations, especially revolutionary groups such as the Italian Red Brigade, Mr. Mancini."

He switched off the projector. House turned up the lights, and Heller took a bottle of mineral water from the bar as he turned to face his visitors.

"The only nuclear weapons any of you can hope to get are those you purchase from me," Heller declared. "Before any of you decide to reject my offer, bear in mind I'm the only dealer with the merchandise willing to sell it to you. My prices are the best because no one else will sell these weapons to you at any price—period."

"What exactly are you selling?" General Ton asked with a sigh. "Everyone in this room knows you claim to have some sort of nuclear weapons for sale, but you've been very mysterious about details. I find it very hard to imagine that you've constructed long-range nuclear missiles that can rival those used by the United States and the USSR."

"Of course not," Heller confirmed as he took a sip of mineral water. "You've met Mr. Kubler and Professor Morarji. Now I think you should also know why they're here. As you may have guessed, the professor is a nuclear physicist, formerly employed by his government in India. For personal reasons he's now working for himself. Actually, he's working for me. Mr. Kubler was a munitions expert for the Austrian government, but now he's also a member of my staff."

"Do you want me to show them the merchandise?" Kubler inquired as he struggled to get his bulky frame off the sofa.

"Please," Heller confirmed.

The Austrian huffed and puffed as he succeeded in hoisting himself out of his seat and waddling to a bookcase. Kubler pulled the center shelf, and the case swung open like a door. A metal bin the size of a coffin slid forward with an electrical hum and locked into position at the end of twin girders.

Ton placed his teacup on the coffee table and walked to the bin. The Arabs and Italians followed his example. Inside the container was a large gray metal shell with a red warhead. It resembled a tank shell, Ton thought, roughly the same size as the 115 mm shells fired by a Soviet T-62.

"Professor Morarji and I made this at the Hellson Metallurgy Company," Kubler stated as he held a match to the bowl of his pipe. "It's a cannon shell with a nuclear warhead, a variation of an old idea. The Americans came up with a 280 mm atomic cannon in 1953, and nuclear warhead shells are found in NATO's arsenal. Most likely the Soviets have similar weapons among their Warsaw Pact forces."

"This is a lot smaller than 280 mm," Ton remarked.

"Naturally," Kubler said with a nod. "That would be too big and awkward for modern warfare. No, this shell is 115 mm. It can be fired by a tank gun or cannon. We've also built a nuclear cannon, based on my own design, for this purpose."

"Fascinating," al-Kalim said as he leaned over the bin for a closer look. "It doesn't seem to be any different from any other cannon shell. How powerful is it?"

"Approximately one to five kilotons," Morarji answered. "Small, even compared to Hiroshima, but the major tactical advantage is size and mobility. This shell can be fired from a cannon in the back of a truck."

"How much damage would that cause in the middle of a city?" Rigotti inquired. "Rome, for example?"

"The blast alone would destroy roughly one or two square blocks," Heller said. "The outer force would cause considerable destruction within several more blocks. Walls would come apart, buildings collapse. Broken glass, metal, wood splinters, other objects would become shrapnel. Bodies would be thrown hundreds of meters."

"How much do you expect to be paid for this nuclear cannon and shells?" Mancini asked, arms folded on his chest as he glared at Heller.

"The cannon alone will cost twenty million dollars, American currency or the equivalent," Heller answered. "The nuclear shells will cost considerably more."

"Twenty million dollars!" Mancini exclaimed. "That's absurd! The Red Brigade doesn't have that sort of money. We're not rich American capitalists. We're revolutionaries, fighting for the liberation of the people from imperialistic oppressors."

"You knew this would be very expensive," Heller sighed. "The merchandise will cost millions of dollars. Not lire. Dollars. You claimed the Red Brigade had a vast fortune, acquired by robbing banks and from kidnapping schemes and whatever else."

"A fortune, yes," Mancini insisted, "but not that much. We can't even pay for the cannon, let alone the shells."

"Then you're not able to participate in this business until you can afford it," Heller said with a shrug. "Perhaps you can convince some of your comrades in the Japanese Red Army or the German Red Army Faction to join forces with you to help finance the purchase in the near future."

"I don't see that we have much choice now," Mancini said, unfolding his arms.

He turned away from Heller to face Jason House. Mancini had pushed back his jacket to reach for something behind him. House recognized the motion, cursed under his breath and grabbed for the revolver on his hip. Mancini thrust his arm forward, a stubby yellow plastic object in his fist. It resembled a toy pistol, an exaggerated replica of a derringer with three barrels mounted one on top of another.

The plastic gun was pointed at House. The British merc's hand froze next to the grip of his holstered revolver. He knew Mancini's gun wasn't a toy.

The Italian's gun couldn't be the supposedly all-plastic Glock 17, which actually did have metal parts; he wouldn't have gotten it through the ranch house's metal detector. The Red Brigade terrorist had obviously come across the design for this nameless, unconventional firearm through Soviet connections. The KGB had developed such unorthodox, undetectable pistols for covert operations. All of the parts were plastic, even the bullets and shell casings.

"Drop the gun belt!" Mancini ordered, weapon trained on the Briton's chest.

"The rest of you stay where you are!" Rigotti snapped as he drew another plastic pistol from the small of his back and pointed it at the men at the bin.

Heller stared at the odd muzzles of the weapon aimed more or less at his torso. The American also knew the threat was serious. He raised his hands slowly, thick biceps bulging between elbows and shoulders. Heller glanced at the others and saw that they had also raised their hands. General Ton's steel hook was poised above his head as he looked from Rigotti's pistol to cast a disapproving glance at Heller. The Vietnamese officer shook his head slightly.

"What do you think you'll accomplish by this stunt, Mancini?" Heller demanded. "I've got forty men outside. How far do you think you'll get if you start shooting in here?"

"Shut up, you greedy Yankee pig!" Rigotti snarled as he stepped closer and pointed his weapon directly at Heller's barrel chest.

"We're leaving here with the cannon, at least one nuclear shell and you for a hostage, Hellson," Mancini announced, but he kept his attention and weapon fixed on House. "And tell this English stooge to do what I say, or I'll kill him."

"Take it easy," House urged as he slowly unbuckled his gun belt and let it drop to the floor.

The Briton wondered if the odd plastic gun would fire one shot at a time or all three simultaneously. He recalled reading that the KGB model could do both, but doubted the terrorists' weapons were that sophisticated. How effective were plastic bullets fired from a plastic barrel? Then he realized the guns might be loaded with wooden bullets, or even slugs made of carved bone, which could be just as deadly as steel shells.

House glanced at Heller and noticed his boss was slowly shuffling closer to Rigotti. Ton was aware of this, as well. The general slowly waved the hook at the end of his arm to keep Rigotti's attention from being fixed on Heller. But the distraction wasn't enough to allow Heller to rush his opponent.

The Briton returned his gaze to the stern face of Alberto Mancini. The terrorist's eyes seemed wild, desperate. Unstable bastard, House thought as he slowly lifted his hands to shoulder level, arms slightly extended. He judged the distance from himself to Mancini. House locked his gaze on the Italian's face and concentrated on the point between the eyebrows.

"You two had better think about what you're doing," Heller said in a loud voice.

"You should have thought about what you were doing when you decided to cheat us," Mancini replied, his eyes shifting toward Heller as he spoke.

Jason House thrust his left arm forward. A chrome-finished derringer with over-under barrels appeared from his sleeve and hopped into the palm of his hand. House instantly squeezed the trigger. The diminutive handgun roared in the confines of the den, and a .38-caliber slug smashed into the bridge of Mancini's nose. The bullet plowed through cartilage and bone to burn into the terrorist's brain.

The Italian collapsed to the floor, the unfired plastic pistol still in his fist.

Dom Rigotti's head swung toward the sound of the gunshot. Heller immediately charged the distracted terrorist and grabbed Rigotti's wrist above the plastic weapon. The American raised his arm and forced Rigotti's fist upward. The gun snarled with a loud, popping sound as if three firecrackers had exploded. All three rounds blasted into the ceiling.

Heller jabbed a fist into Rigotti's face while he held on to the Italian's wrist with his other hand. Rigotti was a strong man, but he was no match for the bodybuilder physique of the powerful American. Heller's punch rocked Rigotti's head and broke two front teeth. The muscular arms dealer retained his grip on Rigotti's wrist and clamped his other hand around the terrorist's elbow. Heller pumped a knee kick into his opponent's abdomen and pulled the captured arm forcibly.

Rigotti doubled up with a groan as Heller slammed the trapped arm across a knee as if breaking kindling for a fire. Bones cracked, and Rigotti screamed as his forearm seemed to explode with white-hot pain. Heller lashed a vicious back fist across his opponent's jaw. Blood spewed from the Italian's mouth. His knees buckled and he started to crumble to the floor.

Heller seized Rigotti by the throat with one hand and kept him from falling. With his other hand he reached between the terrorist's legs and grabbed the man's genitals. The American raised his opponent in the painful grip. Rigotti's feet kicked air above the floor as Heller lifted him overhead as if performing a military press with a barbell. Voices gasped as the others watched the remarkable display of strength.

Heller stepped forward and dropped to one knee. Rigotti cried out for help, but no one would heed his plea. Heller swung his arms forward and slammed Rigotti across a bent knee. The base of the Italian's spine smashed into Heller's knee with a crunch of breaking vertebrae. Rigotti's cries ended abruptly, and Heller dumped his limp body onto the floor. His back broken, Rigotti whimpered slightly before the pain and shock rendered him unconscious. Within seconds the Red brigade fanatic was dead.

"I'm sorry about the interruption, gentlemen," Heller declared as he got to his feet.

Al-Kalim and Jaber stared at him with amazement. The American seemed perfectly calm and composed, as if breaking a man in half was an everyday event. Kubler wiped his brow with a sweat-stained handkerchief. Morarji held one hand over his mouth and the other to his chest, uncertain if he might throw up or have a heart attack, or which to do first.

House had retrieved his gun belt and buckled it around his waist. The Briton then broke open his derringer and removed the spent cartridge casing. He replaced the shell with a fresh .38 Special cartridge in the top barrel. House snapped the derringer shut and fitted it to a metal clip at the end of his sleeve. He pushed to retract the derringer inside the sleeve until the spring-loaded tubes attached to the clip locked into place. The contraption strapped to his forearm would keep the derringer secure and hidden until House needed it again.

General Ton's expression remained inscrutable, but he was impressed with the deadly skill and cunning of both Heller and his British enforcer. The general knew these men were dangerous. He probably knew more about Heller than any other man in the room, and he was aware of how ruthless the American could be. A dangerous man to cross, Ton realized. Perhaps a dangerous man to do business with, as well.

The doors to the den burst open and four armed guards appeared at the threshold. Weapons ready, they stared into the den and saw the two dead Italians on the floor. Heller gestured for his men to lower their guns.

"Everything's under control," he assured the guards. "Two of my guests abused my hospitality. Please remove them so that we can continue our business without this unsightly clutter."

5

Phoenix Force sat at the conference table in the Stony Man Farm war room. Hal Brognola stood at the head of the table, an unlighted cigar jammed into the corner of his mouth and a computer printout in his hands. A stack of file folders, a combination television and videotape recorder remote control unit and a marble ashtray cluttered the table in front of Brognola. The five commandos knew the Fed had a mission for them, and the amount of paraphernalia in front of Brognola suggested it had already reached a critical level.

"I'm glad you guys were here training together," the Fed announced as he slumped into his chair. "Saves time not having to wait for you to come from all over the country or the world for a mission."

He noticed the Phoenix pros were still dressed in baggy sweat suits. Calvin James's navy blue sweatshirt had several white chalk marks across the sleeves and chest. Rafael Encizo's gray shirt was marked in a similar manner with streaks of red chalk. Brognola asked what had happened to them.

"Oh, we were just practicing knife fighting," James answered. "Rafael and I squared off with rubber knives and tried to slice each other up."

"Rubber knives?" the Fed asked with surprise.

"AF-AMK training knives," Encizo explained as he rubbed a damp cloth across the marks on his shirt. "The knives are designed so that you can practice knife fighting safely yet realistically. We put chalk along the edges of the rubber blades so that the marks would indicate where cuts were delivered."

"White chalk if your opponent wears dark clothing and red if his clothes are light colors," James added.

"Who won?" Brognola inquired.

"You called us up here before the match was over," Encizo replied. "I take it you've got a job for us, Hal."

"A great big messy one," Brognola confirmed. He told them about his meeting with the President and the mysterious murders in Antarctica.

The Phoenix Force veterans listened carefully, aware of the importance and serious ramifications if the radioactive corpses proved to be evidence of nuclear testing in Antarctica. Yakov Katzenelenbogen removed a pack of Camels from the breast pocket of his sweatshirt, shook a cigarette from it and stuck it into his mouth.

"Before we go any farther," Katz began, "what do you have on the two scientists killed down there? Were either of them CIA, NSA or connected to any Intel outfit?"

"Absolutely not," Brognola assured him. The Fed selected two file folders from the stack and passed them to Katz. "I had Bear run a check on Linnson and Collier."

"Bear" was Aaron Kurtzman's nickname. A huge, burly man with a shaggy beard and a deceptively gruff manner, Kurtzman was a brilliant computer technician and operator. Kurtzman had been seriously injured during an enemy assault on Stony Man. A bullet in his spine had left Bear semiparalyzed and confined to a wheelchair, but he was still a fighter and the best computer jockey in the business.

Brognola took the cigar from his mouth and placed it in an ashtray. "Linnson never worked for the government on any level. Check the file and you'll notice the guy was even investigated by the FBI in the late sixties. Linnson was an outspoken critic of the Vietnam War, and somebody in the Bureau got a notion he might be helping draft dodgers boogie up to Canada."

"Doesn't sound like the sort of guy the federal government would recruit for operations involving national security," Gary Manning remarked.

"He wasn't and neither was Collier," Brognola confirmed. "They were both environmentalists, politically liberal, generally antagonistic toward government and big business. Linnson was fairly well-known for protesting against nuclear power, strip mining, stuff like that. He rubbed the brass the wrong way all his life. Lost tenure at several universities because he refused to play ball with the administration. Collier was sort of a younger version of Linnson."

"So what were these two blokes doing in Antarctica?" David McCarter asked as he rose from his chair. The Briton could never stay put for long. He started to pace as he said, "Doing a bit of ice fishing?"

"It's in the reports," Brognola answered. "Linnson and Collier were down there doing tests on the effects of volcanic ash in the atmosphere."

"Volcanoes in Antarctica?" James said, eyebrows raised. "That's always seemed kind of weird to me. I always think of volcanoes in a tropical setting like Hawaii or Mexico."

"Yeah," the Fed agreed, "but there are still volcanoes down there. The scientists went to Antarctica to study the effects on the atmosphere of volcanic ash or fumes or whatever the hell comes out of volcanoes, because there's no man-made pollution in the air that far south."

"Sure sounds like the shit could hit the fan," James commented. "Barrels of it."

"The first few barrels have already landed," Brognola said as he reached for the remote control. "The incident isn't exactly a state secret. It's already a major news story all over the world."

The television set switched on and the VCR fed images and sound into the machine. A heavyset man in an expensive suit appeared on the screen. His face was solemn, almost mournful, with soft brown eyes and a long nose that seemed to be pulled down to accompany the frown on his wide mouth. Several microphones waved inches from his face as reporters tried to muscle in closer to the man. A name and title appeared on the screen below the fellow's shoulders. Roger LeTrec was a diplomat with the French embassy in Washington, D.C.

"All I know is what I've been told," LeTrec stated, hands raised in an exaggerated gesture of helplessness. "Frenchmen who helped remove the two Americans from the hole in the icy ground were apparently exposed to sizable doses of radiation. Someone's conducting nuclear experiments or perhaps dumping radioactive waste in Antarctica. Perhaps the United States or the Soviet Union. Either way the lives of people in Antarctica and possibly beyond are in jeopardy due to the cold war between the superpowers."

"Do you think American nuclear weapons are being tested in Antarctica?" a determined lady reporter demanded.

"I wasn't there," LeTrec answered. "Of course, we know the two dead men were American scientists. We don't know what they may have been involved with. As you know, France has claimed part of Antarctica, although the United States refuses to acknowledge this, and perhaps it's time to insist on recognition of this French dependency at a special meeting of the United Nations. Other nations have claims on other territories of Antarctica, and they may also demand recognition of these claims.''

"It's cold and miserable there," Encizo remarked. The Cuban despised cold weather. "Why would anybody want it?''

"Maybe they're low on ice cubes in France," McCarter suggested.

The scene on the television changed, and another man appeared in front of a column of microphones. A tall man with a strong jaw, brooding eyes and wavy gray hair stared into the TV cameras as his name and nationality appeared on the screen. He was Arthur Crowley, a representative of New Zealand's government.

"Well, we New Zealanders are naturally upset about this whole business," Crowley began, bobbing his head to emphasize his statement. "After all, New Zealand and Australia are a lot closer to Antarctica than the Americans, the Russians or the Europeans. We've told the United States for years we don't want any nuclear weapons of any kind in our country, and we most certainly don't want nuclear testing going on in Antarctica.''

"Does your government suspect the United States or the Soviet Union of violating the 1959 treaty?" a reporter inquired.

"At this point it doesn't matter who's responsible," the New Zealander replied. "Radioactive fallout is the same regardless of who sets it off. Right now we don't really want to see either the Americans or the Russians carrying out any sort of unsupervised activity in Antarctica until this business is resolved.''

"New Zealand claims territorial rights to parts of Antarctica, the same as France and several other countries," another reporter said rapidly as he tried to shove a microphone into Crowley's face. "Does your country intend to join in efforts to demand recognition of these claims at the United Nations?"

"I really can't say," Crowley answered, "but several New Zealanders who helped dig out a couple of dead Americans from a tunnel near the South Pole are now undergoing tests in a Wellington hospital to determine how serious their radiation exposure was. We don't want any more people victimized because someone is violating international law. We don't want another Chernobyl in Antarctica. We do want to know what happened. Why were those two Americans murdered, and why were the corpses radioactive?"

Brognola pressed the fast-forward button, and images became blurs of darting color on the screen. He stopped the videotape briefly and allowed it to play at normal speed. A different man was on the screen. He was stocky and dark and had a bushy mustache. The man spoke English with a thick Spanish accent as he addressed the reporters.

"Our country resents being denied our claim to Antarctic territory because the superpowers want to use it for a testing ground for nuclear weapons!" he exclaimed, jabbing the air to drive each word home.

"What country is he talking about?" James asked.

"Either Chile or Argentina," Brognola replied with a shrug as he switched the tape back to fast-forward mode.

"Argentina and Chile want to own chunks of Antarctica?" the black badass from Chicago said with surprise. "I never realized so many countries were interested in the giant freezer."

"Great Britain's on that list, too," McCarter informed the others. "Maybe I should remind you of something, Hal. I'm a British citizen, you know. I've been more than willing to fight for America because this country's interests usually agree with those of England. Besides, I feel sort of like a part-time U.S. citizen after so many missions with Phoenix Force over the years. Still, don't ask me to go up against my own country."

"This isn't about whether or not England or anyone else has a just claim to Antarctic territory," the Fed assured him. He watched the screen as he spoke. Distorted shapes flashed across the TV until he recognized the part of the tape he wanted Phoenix Force to see. "Here we go."

Yet another man appeared on the screen. A bullish figure dressed in a black suit frowned at a cluster of reporters. His hair was dyed black, gray roots visible at the hairline. The man's expression was grimly serious as his name and nationality appeared on the screen. Nikita Rykov was a representative of the Soviet embassy.

"The Union of Soviet Socialist Republics is alarmed and disappointed by the events in Antarctica," Rykov stated in slow, heavily accented English. "The threats of nuclear testing in that part of the world are very serious. People everywhere could be in danger due to this. Without more information we can't be certain what happened. Yet it seems most likely this action was taken by the United States, unmindful of treaties and arms agreements that the Soviet Union has respected and followed at all times."

"Mr. Rykov," a female reporter began, "I'm sure you're aware the dead men were civilian scientists and that they were murdered at the site."

"I know this, yes," the Russian stated. "I also know the American government is suggesting my country is responsible for this disaster. However, it seems more likely the two scientists weren't as innocent as you claim. They may have been working for the CIA. It's possible, even probable, the scientists were contaminated with radiation during whatever tests they were conducting at the site. The CIA may have killed them to keep them from seeking treatment and thus exposing their illegal activities in Antarctica. Then, of course, they try to accuse the Soviet Union of this terrible thing.''

"Do you think this will threaten the progress made in American-Soviet relations?'' another reporter asked.

"Relations between the United States and the Soviet Union will certainly suffer,'' Rykov confirmed. "If my country feels we can't trust America to keep its word about nuclear testing, the 1959 Antarctica Treaty and so much more, and blames its crimes on the Soviet Union, then *glasnost* will certainly come to an end between our nations.''

Brognola switched off the machine. "So you see,'' he said wearily, "things are already pretty hairy. The President wants you guys in Antarctica to find some answers as fast as possible before things go from worse to god-awful.''

"Maybe the President should consider somebody else for this job,'' Katz said as he drew on the cigarette held between the hooks of his prosthesis. "We've had cold-weather missions before, but those were in Alaska and Lapland. Conditions in Antarctica are considerably different. A team with extensive cold-weather experience would probably be better suited for what's needed there.''

"I've never been one to turn down a mission, but I'm sort of inclined to agree with Yakov,'' McCarter commented. He stopped pacing to reach for a pack of Player's. "Not that I see the climate as being that big an obstacle. I just don't see this as a Phoenix Force mission. It sounds like you need a bunch of nuclear scientist types to run experiments and such. We're not qualified for that sort of thing.''

"Gary has a degree in nuclear engineering,'' Brognola pointed out.

"Whoa, Hal,'' Manning began, one hand raised to urge the Fed to slow down. "I don't have a degree. I took some college courses on the subject at night school a few years ago. After that mission involving the Tigers of Justice ninja saboteurs who attacked nuclear power plants all over the country, I figured I ought to learn more about atomic energy, nuclear weapons and what have you. Phoenix Force has had me on a pretty heavy schedule for some time, so I never completed the course.''

"You still know more about the subject than most lay people," Brognola insisted. "Besides, Washington's sending plenty of scientists to investigate the situation. The Nuclear Regulatory Commission has experts in that field. The President wants you guys in Antarctica to take care of any murderous bastards who might be lurking around the snowbanks down there."

"The President figures the dudes who wasted those scientists are still hanging around?" James asked with a grunt. "Sounds pretty unlikely. The Soviets are the most obvious suspects, and I doubt they'd have kept the people responsible in the area after this radioactive tunnel was discovered."

"The NSA has an enormous and complex recon set up at McMurdo Base on the coast and Amundsen-Scott Station at the South Pole," Brognola explained. "They get reception from spy satellites, laser microphones with infinity amplifiers and all that other high tech sneak-and-peek stuff. They're keeping pretty close tabs on the whole damn continent, and they're reasonably sure none of the Russians have left Antarctica aside from a few high brass types who've headed back to the Soviet Union to make their reports to the Kremlin."

"We don't know enough yet to blame the Russians or anyone else," Encizo remarked. "Whoever's responsible for this mess may have already slipped away, undetected even by the NSA and its fancy surveillance gear. So we might head down to Antarctica and freeze our butts off for nothing.''

"Come on, Rafael," Brognola said with a massive shrug. "You know a mission has to start somewhere. This one has to start at the scene of the crime because it's all we've got to go on right now. You guys, the NRC or the NSA investigators and snoops might turn up a lead based on whatever evidence the killers left behind. I don't know what the hell that might be, but that's why you have to go there and find out."

"I hate cold weather," Encizo muttered. "Gary and I almost froze to death in Finland. Wolves damn near got us, too. Now we have to go to Antarctica and take our chances with even worse weather and try to fend off polar bears."

"Polar bears are found in the Arctic," the Fed corrected. "Antarctica is too cold for just about everything."

"Great," the Cuban moaned, already miserable with the prospect of traveling to such a godforsaken place.

"The climate's a definite problem," Brognola said, "so we're teaming you guys up with a man named Harold Swenson. He's got extensive experience in cold-weather assignments, both in the Arctic and Antarctica. He's a veteran Intelligence operative—former CIA and Naval Intelligence—and he's been recruited for a few missions by the NSA, as well. There's a file on him. He's kind of a weirdo, but I guess that's what it takes to keep going back to the biggest refrigerators in the world. Still, Bear ran a thorough check with his computers and reckons Swenson's the best man available to help you guys take on Antarctica."

"We'll need all the help we can get," Manning agreed. "Besides the other problems, we're also going to have trouble maintaining strict security since attention all over the world will be focused on Antarctica."

"I'll do what I can to help from this end," Brognola assured the commandos. "Even the President will pull some strings for us. He's particularly concerned about this mission because so much is at stake here. At the top of the list are foreign relations, especially with the Soviet Union."

"I'm not really convinced *glasnost* is any different than detente or the SALT talks," Encizo commented. "I've actually lived in a Communist country and spent time in a political prison. Castro's forces murdered my parents and turned my brother Raúl into a brainwashed goon. Don't expect me to be too quick to believe Moscow's claims of reform."

"Maybe *glasnost* will be another disappointment," Katz said, "but the situation in the Soviet Union is different. Economic problems, domestic unrest, trouble within the Russian military, all combine to make the Kremlin sit up and take notice. It's in their best interest to make some changes."

"It's also something of an embarrassment for the Soviets that even their satellite nations in Eastern Europe have a higher standard of living than the USSR," Manning added. "Creeping capitalism is hard for the Communists to condemn when it obviously works."

"That's why this might be an excellent chance for the U.S. to work with the Soviets to improve relations, ease tensions throughout the world, cut back Communist aggression in other parts of the globe and maybe even end some of the oppression in the world," Brognola said. "The President's a realist. He knows things might not work out, but it would sure be a pity to lose the opportunity to try because we started blaming each other before either side even knows what the hell has happened."

"The Soviets might know damn good and well what's happened," McCarter muttered. "If they're responsible for testing nuclear weapons in Antarctica, *glasnost* will be ancient history, anyway.''

"At least Uncle Sam won't take the rap for it," James said as he thoughtfully stroked his mustache. "If the Russians are testing nuclear weapons down there, they must have been hitting the vodka too hard. It's suicidal to start messing around with the polar caps."

"Maybe the Russians aren't responsible," Manning suggested. "That could be worse. Soviet scientists would appreciate the risks of such tests, but some fanatical terrorist outfit testing crudely made fission weapons might not."

"Well," Katz said with a sigh, "we won't find any answers here. Better pack our long johns and earmuffs before we leave."

"You'll need more than that," Brognola said, grinning. "Aaron ran an info sheet on Antarctica. This time of year it's winter down there. The temperature can drop to more than a hundred degrees below zero. That kind of cold can kill you as dead as a bullet."

"That's just wonderful," Encizo muttered, already shivering.

6

The Bell helicopter hovered over the green pastures of the quiet Vermont farmland. A few dairy cows grazed in the pasture, barely aware of the approaching aircraft. A clearing between the simple whitewashed house and red barn offered an ideal landing pad for the chopper. David McCarter worked the controls with the ease of an expert pilot and lowered the aircraft to the ground.

"We're still in one piece," Gary Manning remarked as he unbuckled his safety belt and rose from a seat in the cabin of the chopper. "We didn't crash for a change."

"I've never crash-landed any aircraft unless somebody was shooting at me or something was in my bloody way!" McCarter shouted from the cockpit.

"Don't get him started, Gary," Yakov Katzenelenbogen urged as he rose from his seat and pulled open a sliding door to the cabin.

The Israeli gladly emerged from the copter and placed his feet on the ground once more. Katz didn't have any reservations about McCarter's ability as a pilot. Despite Manning's snide remark, all of the members of Phoenix Force respected the Briton's flying skill and trusted him to handle almost any kind of aircraft under the most challenging conditions. Nonetheless, Katz still had a slight phobia about heights in general and flying in particular. It was nothing he couldn't handle, but he was always relieved to have the earth firmly underfoot again.

Manning stepped from the chopper and joined Katz. Both men headed for the farmhouse, ducking low to remain well below the still-whirling blades of the aircraft, which continued to hover above them. McCarter remained inside the copter and watched his partners approach the front porch.

The door to the house opened as Manning and Katz reached the steps. A tall man with broad shoulders and a potbelly filled the doorway. His long hair was dark blond and streaked with gray, but his shaggy beard had an odd salt-and-pepper texture that made him look like a dog with mangy fur. He examined the visitors, his baggy green eyes wary and unfriendly.

"That machine of yours sure makes enough noise," he growled. "If my cows don't produce any milk this month, I'll figure you scared it out of them."

"So give the Company the bill," Katz replied, supplying the prearranged response to the recognition code.

"I retired from the Company a few years ago," the bearded man commented. "Name's Swenson. What am I supposed to call you two?"

"I'm Ginsberg," Katz answered with his newest cover name. He tilted his head toward Manning and added, "This is Baxter. Are you ready to leave?"

"Almost," Swenson said as he moved back inside the house. "Come on in. You can help me carry my gear."

The front room was furnished with a Colonial sofa, a love seat and a walnut rocking chair. Photographs of snow-covered mountains, polar bears on ice floes and penguins clustered along frozen banks decorated the walls. Many photos included men dressed in heavy parkas with fur-lined hoods. Three large canvas-wrapped bundles sat in the center of the floor.

"I packed what I could manage on such short notice," Swenson explained as he walked to the closest bundle and reached down to grab a strap. "You people are sure in a hurry."

"The situation's critical," Katz replied. "You were certainly informed of that."

"Yeah," Swenson said with a wry grin. "I listen to the radio sometimes, too. The whole world's heard about what's happened in Antarctica recently. Doesn't take a genius IQ to figure out that's why I've been called back into the field to help you fellows handle a mission down there. Still, that's one of the things you'd better start appreciating about Antarctica before we head down there. You can't be too impatient on the ice. It's unforgiving. The ice makes the rules and you have to play by them. One mistake, rush into something without taking enough precautions and you're as good as dead. The Scott expedition back in 1911-12 was in too big a hurry, and you know what happened to them."

"They froze to death, didn't they?" Manning inquired as he scanned the photographs on the wall.

"Some died from the cold," Swenson confirmed. "The others starved to death. They buried Robert Scott down there. Somebody called it the 'grave kings would envy.' Funny thing, I don't recall any kings arranging to be buried in Antarctica. Damn sure none of them would want to go down there and die the way Scott did."

"Were these taken at the Pole?" the Canadian asked, indicating a trio of photos depicting a range of massive mountains.

"You mean the South Pole?" Swenson said as he hauled the first bundle onto his back. "No, those photos were taken in the Transantarctic Mountains, which from the description of where the dead scientists were found, is where we'll be heading. Mighty tough area. Hope you guys know what you're getting yourselves into."

"Not entirely," Katz admitted, and walked over to another bundle. "But we have some idea. We'll learn more after we get there."

Swenson stared at the Israeli's artificial arm and frowned. Katz seized a strap on the second bundle with his left hand and raised the burden over his shoulder.

"We were told you're an expert in polar exploration," Manning said, hoisting the last bundle. "They say you're the best."

"Amundsen was probably the best," Swenson replied. "He's long dead, of course. His plane went down somewhere near the North Pole when he tried to rescue Umberto Nobile's expedition in 1928. Guess he got another one of those graves for kings to envy. Shackleton, Stefansson and Byrd aren't around anymore, either, so I guess I might be the best polar explorer still alive. Not a hell of a lot of competition these days."

"What all do you have here, anyway?" Manning asked. He estimated his own bundle weighed at least a hundred pounds.

"Cold-weather clothes, a tent, a month of rations, a special heating unit, sleeping bags, blankets, lots of stuff," Swenson explained. "I understand you fellows will draw most of your equipment from the Navy before we leave."

"I hope we won't have to haul around as much gear as you've got here," Katz remarked.

"Nope," Swenson assured him, "but you'd better be sure what you have is what you'll need down there. Insulated boots, arctic mittens, face mask, goggles. I'll supervise when we get to the naval base."

"The mittens better have trigger fingers," Katz said.

"Like the Army TA-50 field gear," Manning added.

"That's standard military issue," Swenson commented as he moved toward the door. "You fellas figure you'll need firearms for this mission?"

"We think we might need them," Katz confirmed.

"I packed my trusty old .45 just in case," Swenson admitted. "After all, the news said those scientists were murdered. Do you guys know there are special problems with firearms in Antarctica?"

"How's that?" Manning inquired as he followed Swenson to the door. The powerful Canadian effortlessly carried the heavy burden across his brawny back.

"The cold," Swenson explained. "When the temperature drops to a hundred degrees below zero—or worse—you're talking about conditions that can freeze damn near anything with moisture. Gun oil can freeze and jam weapons. Metal parts stick together like glue. Rifle bolts freeze solid, cartridges stick together in magazines and refuse to feed into chambers, pistols get frozen in holsters."

"Standard carrying methods obviously won't work," Katz commented.

"You've got that right," Swenson said as he stepped onto the porch outside. "That's just one of the problems you've got in Antarctica."

"Problems are part of our business," Manning said.

Swenson waited for the other two men to haul their burdens across the threshold and paused to lock the door. They carried the gear to the helicopter and loaded it into the cabin. McCarter waited at the controls until the three passengers were inside and the sliding doors closed. The British ace made certain everyone was buckled in their seats before he raised the chopper into the sky.

"A friend of mine's going to take care of the place while I'm gone," Swenson remarked. "Just a small dairy farm, you know, but it still takes some work to keep it going. I make most of my profits from cheese."

"I wouldn't have expected a man with your background in Intelligence and polar expeditions to become a farmer," Manning confessed, raising his voice so he could be heard above the roar of the rotor blades.

"My father was a farmer," Swenson stated. "I was raised on a farm in Wisconsin. Figured I'd follow in Daddy's footsteps until the Korean War came along. I enlisted in the Navy and things just sort of changed after that."

"Eventually you got a farm again," Katz reminded him.

"Uncle Sam set me up with it," Swenson said. "Don't make much money with the spread, but I get a pension for twenty-five years in the navy—most of it in the reserves—and another pension from the CIA. Never expected to be in the field again, but they told me this mission was very important and that they needed me pronto. I've never told my country to go to hell, and I'm not gonna do it now."

"We appreciate that, Swenson," Katz assured him. "I'm sure you must be curious about exactly what this mission is, so we'll brief you as best we can on the way to Annapolis. The rest of our team will meet us there, and you can help us select cold-weather gear and everything else before we continue on to Antarctica."

"You guys must be able to cut through a lot of red tape to move this fast," Swenson said, genuinely impressed.

"We've got White House authorization," Manning explained. "Anybody gives us a hard time, they can take it up with the President."

"Well, hell," Swenson said, chuckling, "sort of wish I'd voted for him now. By the way, Ginsberg, are you going to Antarctica on this job?"

"That's right," Katz confirmed, and raised his prosthesis to display the trident hooks. "You worried about this?"

"To be honest, yeah," Swenson said with a nod. "Not to mention your age. Frankly, I figure I'm really over the hill for this sort of thing, but I still have two good hands and I'm in pretty good shape for a guy in his fifties. The ice is tough enough for men half your age, without any physical handicaps to deal with."

"I appreciate your candid observations," Katz assured him. "There are some things a man with two arms can do that an amputee can't, but you'd be surprised how few they really are. I understand my limitations, and I won't insist on doing anything to satisfy my ego if it might endanger the mission. Fair enough?"

"Okay," Swenson replied. "I just hope you're up to it. No place on earth tests a man quite the way Antarctica does."

"Is that why you've gone back so many times?" Manning asked.

"That's part of it," Swenson admitted. "Supposedly my ancestors were Vikings. Story is that one of them sailed with Erik the Red when he discovered Greenland. I don't know if it's true, but maybe some of that Viking blood never filtered out of the Swenson family. Maybe I'm just a little crazy."

"That may be a job requirement in this profession," Katz said with a shrug.

THE CHAIRMAN SAT at his desk and glanced up at the photographs on the wall. Mikhail Gorbachev, the current president of the Soviet Union, stared back at him from one picture frame. Former Soviet leaders also hung on the wall. Brezhnev, Andropov, even Chernenko still held an honored place in his office. Gorbachev had publicly condemned Stalin, so the face of the Soviet iron man no longer hung in the chairman's office.

Of course, there was still Lenin. A painting of the hero of the Revolution hung higher than any of the other pictures in the chairman's office. Lenin, the father of the Soviet Union, would always have pride of place.

The chairman felt that the pictures on his wall revealed the decline of the Soviet Union. They had fallen from revolutionary fire to whimpering cowardice. Gorbachev met with their enemies to discuss reduction of arms that would weaken the Soviet Union, pulled out all troops from Afghanistan instead of pushing for victory and even spoke of changes that would bring capitalism to the masses.

Perhaps things would have been different with Yuri Andropov, who had also once been chairman of the KGB. If he had lived long enough after he had risen to the leadership of the Soviet Union—and the politburo had supported his decisions—Andropov might have returned the USSR to its former glory.

The current head of the KGB was almost grateful for the recent incident in Antarctica. It seemed obvious that the Americans had violated international law and half a dozen treaties by conducting nuclear tests near the South Pole. The capitalist swine even had the nerve to try to blame the USSR when their crimes became public knowledge. The chairman believed the United States was a nation of gangsters, and one didn't negotiate with such trash. Gangsters belonged in prison or in front of a firing squad.

Gorbachev didn't have the backbone for such actions, the chairman thought, so it was up to the KGB to take immediate and direct action for the sake of the nation. Of course, the president would be furious if he learned the KGB chief had taken it upon himself to carry out an unauthorized operation of this sort, but that was unimportant. After the KGB exposed the Americans' heinous crimes against humanity in Antarctica, Gorbachev would be kicked out of office and probably internally exiled, just as Khrushchev had been. The president had many powerful enemies in the politburo, which was the real ruling force of the Soviet Union. These men already wanted Gorbachev out of office and replaced by a hard-line Communist spokesman. If the other members of the politburo could be convinced of the folly of *glasnost*, Gorbachev would be nothing but a painful and embarrassing memory by the end of the year.

A knock at the door drew his attention from the pictures on the wall. The chairman turned to face the door and barked, "Come in!"

The door opened and two men entered the office. Both wore Red Army uniforms with two silver bars and a silver star on each shoulder board. The insignia indicated they were majors. Neither man had met the chairman before that day, yet the head of the KGB had read the files on the two majors and recognized them from photographs.

Major Nicolai Semyonovich Morozov was a veteran field agent. Despite his army uniform, Morozov wasn't a member of the GRU—Soviet military Intelligence—but a high-ranking operative of the Second Chief Directorate of the KGB. Of average height, a bit stocky in build with a bland face, Morozov was the sort of man one would seldom take a second look at on the street, a desired quality in an espionage agent.

Yet those who observed Morozov's face with more than a glance noticed the hard lines around his mouth and the cool intelligence expressed in his deep-set eyes. His body language was subtle, each movement precise, eliminating all unnecessary gestures. Morozov was a man who gave nothing away concerning his thoughts or emotions.

Major Anatoli Konstaninovich Remizov was a little over six feet. His body was lean and hard. Remizov carried a handsome blue beret tucked under his arm. The badge on the beret displayed a white parachute capped by a red star, symbol of the Red Army paratroopers. The medals on his chest included the highly honored Gold Star of Valor, which he had received for his courage and dedication fighting in Afghanistan.

Remizov was the kind of soldier the Soviet Union could still be proud of, the chairman thought. The paratrooper's face was angular, with a strong jaw and eyes as clear as a winter morning above the Ural Mountains. Remizov was a living weapon, trained in karate and boxing as well as sambo wrestling. The paratrooper was also an expert in small arms, demolitions and survival techniques. Most important of all, Remizov had extensive experience in cold-weather operations.

"Good afternoon," the chairman greeted with a nod. "You've been introduced, so I won't waste time with social pleasantries. Since you've both been fully briefed before coming here, I also won't bother repeating the details of your mission, unless you have some questions concerning it."

Morozov repressed a smile. He had heard stories that the chairman was afraid to discuss assignments in his office because he feared the room might somehow be bugged. Spies were always spying on spies in the Soviet Union. Paranoia was an occupational hazard for anyone involved in espionage; it was also a necessary character trait for survival.

"Only one question, Comrade Chairman," Morozov said. "Who's in charge of this mission? Major Remizov or myself?"

"This is a KGB operation," the chairman replied. "You're in charge, but you're to bow to the expertise of

Major Remizov. He's far better trained and experienced in cold-weather conditions. If necessary, Major Remizov's ability as a combat commander may be drawn upon to conduct a military action. I trust I needn't explain that in any greater detail."

"I understand, Comrade Chairman," Morozov assured him.

"Major Remizov?" the chairman inquired.

"Any time the army works with the KGB the latter outranks the former," the paratrooper said evenly. Remizov was careful not to reveal any resentment toward the chain of command, but the two KGB veterans were aware it existed. "Naturally, I accept those conditions. I will, of course, obey orders and serve my country as I have throughout my military career."

"I have total faith in both of you," the chairman declared. He placed his hands on the desktop and stared at the pair to emphasize the importance of his words. "The security of our state is in jeopardy. The Americans have violated international treaties and are trying to convince the rest of the world that we're responsible for their crimes. You must prove they're lying. You must help us expose the Americans for the criminals they are."

The chairman's gaze turned toward the painting of Lenin as he continued. "This is a very dangerous mission. Major Remizov has selected ten of his best men to accompany you. I'm not encouraging you to use violence, but don't hesitate to do so if the situation demands it. The CIA has already killed two of their own people just to cover up their crimes and throw investigators off their track. They certainly won't hesitate to kill you if they get the chance."

"If we kill them first, one might call it self-defense," Morozov said.

"Do whatever you have to do," the chairman told the two majors. "If you can't find evidence, create it."

"That could backfire if we get caught doing it," Remizov warned. "It could trigger an international incident."

"An international incident already exists, Major," the chairman informed him. "Make certain your men understand their duties. Your plane will be ready to transport you to your destination by the time you have your gear packed. I want you there as soon as possible. I won't tolerate failure. Too much is at stake."

"Yes," Morozov said, "we'll do whatever the mission requires, Comrade Chairman. If anyone gets in our way..."

"As the Americans say, terminate with extreme prejudice," the chairman replied tersely.

7

General Ton Chi Dai and Abdullah al-Kalim peered through the thick Plexiglas porthole of the steel chamber. Within the metal shell a robotic arm lowered a transparent tube to the dome of a smaller steel vessel in the center of the chamber floor. The tube was the barrel of an industrial laser, attached to the mechanical limb.

"There is an opening in the vessel dome to allow the laser to be inserted," Professor Morarji explained, his singsong English rising and dropping in pitch due to the nervous tremor in his voice. "The laser beam is carefully regulated to feed exact degrees of energy to the uranium in the core of the vessel. This is a delicate procedure, but less expensive and requiring less equipment and technology to transform uranium ore to uranium-235."

"This uranium-235 is the sort used for nuclear weapons?" al-Kalim asked, staring at the vessel as he spoke.

"Correct," the Indian physicist confirmed. He nodded his head so hard that his turban nearly came apart. "The uranium must be enriched, yet remain at a subcritical mass."

General Ton turned from the chamber to face Erik Heller, Jason House and Gustav Kubler. Jaber, al-Kalim's aide, stood by silently and watched the trio like a suspicious hawk. Of course, the Arab bodyguard was aware they were on "Hellson's" turf. They had been taken to the Hellson Metallurgy Company in Wellington. The mill was well equipped for smelting metals, producing alloy metal products and numerous other functions.

However, Heller had taken his visitors to a restricted area of the plant, off-limits to the majority of his employees. The forbidden section was heavily guarded by armed security officers—mercenary soldiers in Heller's private army. Although General Ton and the two Arabs had come to New Zealand to do business with the American, they felt uneasy and vulnerable in Heller's lair.

Morarji seemed more nervous than any of the others present. Odd, Ton thought, the Indian helped design nuclear weapons, yet he seemed terrified by the possibility of any type of violence. Perhaps the man's nerves had been frayed by being forced to work on construction of such fearsome devices under less than ideal conditions. Enriching uranium with a laser beam was no doubt a highly stressful operation.

"Uranium-235 isn't as powerful as plutonium-239," Heller declared. "However, we can't produce the latter and we have a growing supply of the former. Besides, the uranium-core weapons may better suit your needs. Plutonium is considered the deadliest material in the world and produces extremely poisonous dust. The larger blast and wider pattern of fallout would threaten your own forces if you were fighting opponents near your borders. Israel is close to your borders, Mr. al-Kalim."

"Israel also has one of the most efficient air forces in the world," al-Kalim replied grimly. "They almost certainly have nuclear weapons—far superior to what you can offer us. We strike with tank shells and they retaliate with missiles. That doesn't seem to be a formula to ensure victory for my country, Mr. Hellson."

"I'd be willing to negotiate selling nuclear missiles to you if I had any," Heller said with a shrug. "Your country has done a great deal of trade with the Soviet Union, but the Russians have no intention of letting you have such weapons. The Americans certainly won't sell nuclear arms to your government. Nuclear shells and the cannon to fire them are more than what you have now. What you do with the weapons and how you plan to use them isn't my concern."

"What if we choose to use them against the United States?" Ton inquired with a faint smile.

"Go right ahead," Heller answered with a nod. "I don't live there anymore. I don't give a damn what happens to America now. In fact, I'd say they deserve what they get, regardless of how bad that might be."

"I see," Ton said, returning the nod.

Heller was slightly annoyed by Ton's question. The general knew enough details about Heller's past to be aware that Heller felt no loyalty toward the United States. Ton was aware Heller had deserted from the army during the Vietnam War. He knew Heller had been involved in mercenary operations, smuggling, gunrunning and narcotics before setting up his current front as Edward Hellson in New Zealand. Perhaps Ton still distrusted Americans because of the war and hadn't fully accepted the idea of doing business with one—even a renegade like Erik Heller.

"You've shown us how you enrich the uranium for the warheads," al-Kalim remarked as he walked from the chamber to move closer to Jaber. "I confess I know little about such things, but I've heard that it's possible to use lasers to transform uranium ore in this manner. In theory, at least."

"The shells will work," Heller assured him.

"We can't be certain of that, Mr. Hellson," Ton stated. "After all, you haven't detonated any of these weapons, have you?"

"I assure you the nuclear shells will work, gentlemen," Professor Morarji insisted, wringing his hands nervously. "The bullet of uranium-235 is inserted in uranium ore with more conventional explosives jacketed around the core. This method has been used numerous times and has never failed to cause the chain reaction necessary for an atomic explosion."

"Has it ever been done by uranium processed by this laser-enriching technique?" al-Kalim demanded. "Have any of these weapons been tested? What proof do you have that these nuclear shells will perform as you claim?"

Gustav Kubler sighed and shook his head. The Austrian munitions expert had helped construct the shells and designed the atomic cannon to fire them, but he realized there was no point in adding his claims that the weapons would work to what Morarji and Heller had already told the two clients. Kubler looked at Heller and shrugged. He handled the technical mechanics of weaponry; it was up to Heller to convince potential buyers to purchase the arms.

"So you want a demonstration of the product in action?" Heller inquired. He didn't seem surprised by the clients' cynicism. "I can arrange that, but it'll be expensive and risky. Are you prepared for that?"

"I'm prepared to pay for one of the shells," Ton assured him. "In advance."

"You'll have to purchase the cannon, as well," Heller told the general. "That will be twenty million dollars for the cannon and, let's say, forty million for the shell. It will, of course, be the least powerful explosive in our atomic arsenal. Forty million is also the least expensive."

"You may not regard yourself as an American, Mr. Hellson," General Ton said dryly, "but you're certainly a capitalist."

"And an opportunist," Heller admitted without a trace of guilt. "Can you afford it or not, General?"

"Yes," Ton answered. "Payment will be made in gold and precious gems. We can discuss details later in private."

"Of course, General," Heller replied. He turned to face al-Kalim and Jaber. "Well, gentlemen? Do you want to pay for a demonstration also, or perhaps assist General Ton in paying for this one?"

"That hardly seems necessary," al-Kalim said with a slight smile. "If your nuclear device really works, we'll surely know it after the demonstration. A nuclear explosion won't go unnoticed or unreported."

"I should have been less eager to take on the burden of financing the demonstration," Ton remarked. "I commend you on your patience and wisdom, al-Kalim."

The Vietnamese officer raised his right arm and cast a mocking salute with the steel hook. The gesture was silently threatening. The hook was a large, curved single piece of solid blue-black metal with a wicked point. It obviously served little use as a functional replacement for Ton's missing hand—except as a weapon.

"Your country and mine have similar goals and many of the same enemies," Ton told al-Kalim. "Both are committed to the struggle for international unity and peace through the success of the socialist revolution."

"The version of socialism in Islamic nations is different from that of Vietnam," the Arab stated. "However, we certainly have much in common. I'm not certain you're actually working on orders of your government, but we're not enemies and we will surely fight shoulder to shoulder against the infidels and imperialists in the future."

COLD DEAD   89

Ton nodded. The Asian was less than pleased with al-Kalim, yet each man appreciated the need of allowing the other to save face. Jason House glanced at the pair and eyed Jaber with extra suspicion. After the unexpected trouble with the two Italian terrorists at the ranch, House was less than confident that al-Kalim or his bodyguard didn't carry hidden weapons that had eluded the metal detectors.

"So you want to just sit back and see if our merchandise is all that we claim?" Heller said in a calm, slightly amused voice. "Under the circumstances, that's understandable. Still, I must remind you our supply of uranium has limits. How many weapons we can produce is questionable."

"I was under the impression that your people could produce more than a hundred nuclear shells and dozens of cannons," al-Kalim said with a frown.

"We can," Heller assured him, "but you must realize we can choose clients from all over the world. There are many, many nations and organizations who would be willing to pay any price for such weapons. We can't really be certain how many we can produce within a short period of time. Supply and demand. First come, first served."

"I see," al-Kalim said with a slow nod. "So we need to make a deposit to be certain there will be weapons available for us when the demand for your products begins to exhaust the supply. Correct?"

"Arabs are known to be shrewd businessmen," Heller said, smiling. "I'm glad to see you understand the principles of free enterprise and the natural order of supply and demand."

"American jackal!" Jaber hissed angrily. The bodyguard trembled with rage, but he didn't approach Heller. "We are fighting for our nation! The Zionists threaten to destroy us and steal our homeland, just as they did to the people of Palestine! This means nothing to you."

"That's right," Heller confirmed. "I just don't give a shit one way or the other. I may even sell my atomic cannons and nuclear shells to Israel if I think I can deal with them. It doesn't matter to me who uses these weapons, or who they use them against. I'll sell to the Afghan rebels or the contras just as willingly as to any Communist nation or left-wing guerrilla army. I don't care if they're Arabs, Jews, Christians or atheists. If the Martians invaded and had the money to buy these weapons, I'd sell to them just as eagerly."

"I don't suppose you're offended if a person considers you a most disgusting excuse for a human being," al-Kalim remarked. It wasn't a question. "Very well, Mr. Hellson, how much do you want for this down payment?"

"Twenty million dollars will assure you a cannon, and at least three shells will be reserved for you," Heller replied. "Payment can be in American dollars, West German marks, Swiss or French francs or British pound notes. Of course, gold, diamonds, silver or other precious metals and gems may be used instead. Please bear in mind that this is a metallurgy establishment. My people can easily detect impure metals and fake gem stones. I've been involved in a couple of counterfeit currency schemes and I can certainly spot fake money of almost any sort. I have forgers and counterfeiters on my staff. If anything gets past me, I assure you, my experienced experts in the field will indeed catch what I failed to detect."

"If you were a man of honor, I would be insulted by such a suggestion," al-Kalim said, his voice as hard as diamonds. "Yet cheating is no doubt a natural process with a person of your mentality, so I will assume your warning is due to your personal character flaws and not directed against myself or my country."

"Fine," Heller said with a shrug. "My merchandise is good and my security and confidence among clients is reliable, even if my other character flaws repulse you. Twenty million dollars is still the price. An oil-rich nation such as your country probably spends that much on ivory door-knobs at the presidential palace."

"I'm authorized to give you three million pounds British sterling," al-Kalim announced. "That's less than half of what you require, but I'll have to return to my country and discuss this with the proper government officials before the rest of the payment can be delivered."

"We'll talk again at that time," Heller assured him. "Mr. House will see you out. General Ton and I still have some business to iron out. A pleasure doing business with you, Mr. al-Kalim."

"I hesitate to say this has been a pleasure," al-Kalim replied grimly. "Yet the troubled times we live in sometimes force us to do business with individuals we might not otherwise associate with. The ways of Allah are indeed a mystery. We'll await news of your demonstration, Mr. Hellson, and we'll make our decision at that time."

"Don't wait very long," Heller advised with a smug smile. "The world is going to change forever. You'd better be prepared when it happens. Most of the people on the planet won't be ready, you know. They'll pay most dearly for that."

8

The plane descended to the icy surface. Sheets of snow whipped across the windscreen as if nature intended to sabotage the aircraft before it could land. The skis of the landing gear touched down and the plane skidded across the ice. The aircraft slid across the slippery surface as torrents of snow spewed from the landing gear.

"Oh, shit!" Calvin James rasped as he stared out a window at the blur of white outside the plane. "Are we headed toward that radio tower?"

"I can't tell," Gary Manning replied, his voice deceptively calm, although his heart hammered rapidly with apprehension and tension. "I can't see a damn thing in this blizzard."

"The pilot's made this trip many a time in the past," David McCarter assured the other Phoenix Force passengers. "He can probably land this crate blindfolded."

"I hope so," Rafael Encizo muttered. The Cuban was already beginning to shiver just from looking out the window at the snow. "As far as I can tell, he must be flying blind already."

Yakov Katzenelenbogen pressed his lips together firmly and resisted the urge to tell the others to shut up. The Israeli's fear of flying had been escalated by the terrible weather. He avoided looking at the windows and tried to ignore his partners' comments. Katz had learned long ago that sometimes a man can't do anything about his fears except recognize them, understand them as best he can and simply wait until the reason for the fears subsides.

Harold Swenson seemed perfectly relaxed as he sat strapped in his seat with a map sprawled across his lap. The veteran visitor to Antarctica obviously expected such conditions. The plane trembled and weaved in the violent wind, but Swenson wasn't unduly alarmed. Hell, it was winter in Antarctica. The worst time of year to come to the frozen continent.

"Getting here's the easy part, fellas," Swenson declared. "You'll find out just how tough this place is after we land. Assuming we survive the landing."

"That's an encouraging observation," James said dryly. "Got any other great news for us? Like freezing to death is just like going to sleep and never waking up?"

"I wouldn't know," Swenson said with a shrug. "Never froze to death, but this is sure the right place to be if that's how you want to go."

"I don't," Encizo said with a trace of misery in his voice. "When I die, I want to feel the sun on my face and a warm breeze on my skin. If it's the last thing I'll ever do, I'd like it to be as agreeable as possible. Not that I've seen many people die in an agreeable manner."

"Timing is usually off," McCarter commented. "Most folks die when it's bloody inconvenient."

"Especially for them," James added.

The five commandos and Swenson were uncomfortably warm in insulated field pants, heavy wool shirts and cold-weather boots that resembled those worn by Boris Karloff in *Frankenstein*. They also wore special arctic long johns and extra pairs of warm tube socks. Swenson had told Phoenix Force to pay particular attention to their feet. He'd said he'd seen dozens of serious frostbite victims and many lost toes or a part of a foot because people had failed to protect their feet from the cold.

The bulky clothes made them sweat inside the plane, but the men realized they would need all the protection possible from the killer cold of Antarctica. Each man also had heavy cold-weather parkas, face masks and arctic mittens as well as other gear packed and ready for the adventure ahead.

At the moment the passengers were wondering if they would even survive the landing on the ice. The plane seemed to spin across the slippery surface, completely out of control. The sensation was terrifying as the plane seemed to gain momentum. Clumps of snow rushed against the metal hull of the aircraft and seemed to roar like an angry monster trying to crush the plane. Even Swenson, despite his numerous visits to Antarctica in the past, began to worry that the craft wouldn't stop until it crashed into the radio tower or the weather station.

Finally the plane stopped whirling across the ice and gradually slowed to a halt. The passengers uttered a collective sigh of relief. The navy copilot called out to them and asked if everybody was still alive.

"Just barely," Manning replied as he unbuckled his safety belt and rose from his seat.

"Bundle up," Swenson instructed. He slipped into his parka as he spoke. "It's eighty degrees below zero out there."

"¡Madre de Dios!" Encizo rasped, shaking his head. "It's hard to believe anyplace can be that cold."

"It can get colder here," Swenson warned. "Don't forget the masks and goggles."

"I thought goggles were worn to protect you from snow blindness," James remarked. "If it's night virtually twenty-four hours, the sun won't produce glare on the snow, so I wouldn't imagine snow blindness would be a problem."

"It's cold enough to literally freeze the water in your eyes," Swenson explained. "Your eyes could be welded shut and sealed with a layer of ice."

"Well," Katz began as he adjusted a gray protective mask over his face, "this will certainly be a different experience."

Phoenix Force discovered Katz's remark was an understatement. They emerged from the plane to set foot on a land that could have been found on another planet. The white terrain extended for miles in every direction. Snow underfoot was hard-packed and frozen. The area was practically featureless beneath the black night sky. Only the collection of sturdy brick buildings and the sixty-foot-high radio tower broke the monotony of the barren white landscape.

McMurdo was the largest U.S. base in Antarctica. It was located on Ross Island, right next to the Ross Ice Shelf. The structures were ugly, functional single-story buildings. Walls, doors and windows were thick and built to withstand the harsh climate. The radio tower was also simple in appearance. Steel girders formed a crisscross pattern along the tower with the rod of the antenna and pipe in the center. It reminded James of a skeletal version of the Washington Monument.

Two figures trudged through the snow as Phoenix Force and Swenson hauled their gear from the plane. The commandos carried less equipment than Swenson, because the explorer had brought tents, stove, heaters and weather-gauging devices. Nonetheless, Phoenix Force was heavily burdened with packs filled with rations and survival gear as well as plastic-alloy rifle cases and side arms stored in thick canvas pouches attached to utility belts.

"Welcome to Antarctica," one of the men who approached the group greeted. "I'm Fennimore and this is Eisley. How do you like the place so far?"

"Might put a bit more rock salt on the runway," McCarter replied. The Briton shifted about his bundles of gear until he could better manage the burden.

Fennimore seemed to stare at the new arrivals. His protective mask and goggles concealed whatever expression he wore, and it was difficult to even tell what direction he was looking at. Eisley also wore the bulky cold-weather garments and face gear necessary in Antarctica. It seemed odd to converse with people wearing masks. They seemed to have no identity. Even their voices were distorted and muffled.

The pair helped Phoenix Force with their gear. The Navy pilot and copilot emerged from the plane and assisted Swenson, who had a far greater burden than the commandos. Fennimore and Eisley marched across the frozen ground to a building near the radio tower. Phoenix Force and the others followed. They were glad to get out of the cold. Even with the protective clothing, a few minutes in the subzero climate was a shivering experience.

Fennimore escorted them into the building. The interior was Spartan. A sofa that appeared to be made of plastic, metal folding chairs, a card table and a stove comprised the furniture in the front room. The two Navy flyers left as soon as they finished helping deliver the gear to the building. They knew the NSA shack was top-secret, and they didn't have high enough security clearance to be present during any meeting held in the place.

Swenson shoved the bolts of the door into place to make certain it was locked. Fennimore pulled back the hood of his parka and removed his goggles and mask. His face was longish with a narrow, almost fragile nose and small, thin lips. Fennimore's sandy hair was gray at the temples, and worry lines formed a crease across his forehead. Phoenix Force removed their parkas and masks, as well. Fennimore nodded in recognition when Swenson doffed his mask.

"They told me you'd be here, Harry," Fennimore said. "Thought you retired."

"I am retired," the explorer replied. "Just came back for one last job, Lee."

"Maybe you can help us figure out how the Russians managed to get away with nuclear testing for any length of time without us knowing about it," Fennimore remarked.

"I wasn't aware there was any firm evidence the Soviets are responsible for what's happened here," Katzenelenbogen said as he pulled the insulated sheath from his prosthetic arm.

"So what if there isn't?" Eisley inquired. "If the Russians aren't responsible, who is? The Australians? The French? Shit. Don't believe that *glasnost* crap. The USSR is still the 'other side,' and they're behind this thing as sure as a bear shits in the woods."

Eisley was slightly shorter than Fennimore, younger and more aggressive. His black hair was cut in a style reminiscent of Moe Howard from the Three Stooges, but his drooping mustache would have done justice to a Hollywood version of a *bandito*.

"We've had a few encounters with the KGB in the past," Katz said, taking out a pack of Camels from the pocket of his wool shirt. "Many words might describe the Soviet Intelligence network, but careless isn't one of them. Conducting nuclear experiments in Antarctica seems a bit foolhardy, since there are expeditions from all over the world here virtually year-round."

"Maybe the KGB isn't in charge," Fennimore suggested. "There's some evidence of friction between the KGB chair-

man and the president these days. Could be a military Intelligence operation. The GRU is pretty closely linked to the
KGB, but Gorbachev or some big shots in the politburo may
have decided to assign a mission directly to the GRU and
keep the KGB out of the picture.''

''Trying to keep a secret from the KGB in Moscow is
about as easy as me trying to convince people I'm from
Sweden,'' Calvin James commented.

''I don't understand why the Soviets would test nuclear
weapons here,'' Manning announced. ''If they wanted to
carry out underground testing, they could do it in their own
country. The USSR is the largest country in the world. Like
Ginsberg said, there are scientific teams in Antarctica all the
time, and the Soviets certainly know there are CIA listening posts here. They'd have a much better chance of getting
away with illegal testing in Siberia than here.''

''We have a hell of a lot more than a listening post here,
fella,'' Eisley declared. ''Maybe that's why they're doing
this shit in the first place.''

''You think the Soviets are trying to get you guys shut
down?'' Encizo asked, shaking his head. ''That seems pretty
farfetched to me. Especially since the Soviets are getting as
much flak as Uncle Sam.''

''They don't have as much to lose here,'' Fennimore
stated. ''Let me show you gents something.''

''The grand tour, huh?'' Swenson inquired.

''You never saw one like this,'' Fennimore assured him as
he led the visitors into another room.

They felt as if they had stepped onto the set of a science
fiction movie. Steel and plastic were everywhere. Technicians sat at computer terminals while data appeared on the
screens. Information was fed into memory banks. Translator reels whirled, and decoding machines printed out sheets
with words and numbers. Television monitors displayed

aerial footage of icy terrain, ocean waves, grassy plains and busy city streets. Yellow letters appeared on the screens. Each site was identified and analyzed. Important features were magnified for greater detail.

"This is SIGINT," Fennimore declared proudly as he escorted his guests between the desks and computer terminals. The technicians barely glanced up from their machines as the men filed past them. "Signals Intelligence. We're collecting information electronically and from communication sources of all types, including reconnaissance satellites, Soviet as well as European, Japanese and American."

"You're getting Intel from Russian spy satellites?" Swenson asked with astonishment.

"Incredible, isn't it?" Fennimore replied with obvious pleasure. "We're tapping into the radio wavelengths and laser radios of allies and enemies alike. See that third monitor?"

The others looked at the screen. The images were green and yellow, various shapes and shades. Information appeared on the screen. Most of the data was written in abbreviations and code numbers. It vanished to be replaced by new data in less than ten seconds.

"That's electro-optical reception from a Soviet spy satellite," Fennimore explained. "It's gathering photo-Intel over New Zealand and Australia. Our computers evaluate the images, translate data and extrapolate as to the value of the information to the Soviets."

"And the Russians don't know they're broadcasting the Late Show to the NSA?" James inquired.

"They might know," Eisley answered, "but there isn't much they can do about it. You see, the pull from the South Magnetic Pole makes it difficult to trace interference. Our equipment allows us to use the magnetic pull to our favor.

It's a new type of electromagnetic radio cannon that puts us ahead of the Soviets in the spy game at last."

"It gives you a technological advantage," Encizo commented.

"Espionage is technology these days," Fennimore declared. "HUMINT or Human Intelligence methods are outdated. Cloak and dagger have been replaced by computers and lasers. TECHINT is what matters now. Technical Intelligence acquired by our most advanced machines. And the SIGINT equipment here is the best in the world."

"It's pretty fancy," Manning agreed, "but I'm still not convinced the Soviets would risk their own operations in Antarctica just to put you guys out of business. After all, they've got equipment similar to this, even if it isn't as advanced as your SIGINT gear. They must also realize there are other NSA bases throughout the world with the same technology you have here."

"So the Commies plan to pull similar stunts elsewhere to try to put a dent in our operations," Eisley insisted.

"Oh, hell," McCarter snorted, "that doesn't explain how you blokes failed to know about the alleged nuclear testing at the base of that bleedin' volcano. I've seen this sort of mentality before. You spend so much time playing with your *Star Trek* gadgets, figuring they're so damn infallible, that as long as you don't blow a fuse everything is going fine. You tend to rely on them too bloody much. You also have a habit of associating everything in the world as being part of your job, as some sinister conspiracy against your precious machines."

Fennimore and Eisley glared at the Briton. Katz sighed and stepped between the two NSA operatives and McCarter. The Phoenix Force commander couldn't argue with anything McCarter had said, but it had been a very inopportune time for the British ace to exercise his sharp tongue.

"Gentlemen," Katz began in a calm, even voice, "we're all on the same side here. Everything thus far has been speculation. The first thing we need to do is examine the site where the two murdered scientists were found."

"That's near Beardmore Glacier," Fennimore stated. "We have a base there, too, but it's closed in the winter. You'll have a tough journey, but Harry is probably the best guide you could have. It looks like you guys came armed and ready for bear."

"We were told there aren't any bears in Antarctica," Encizo replied. "Bears don't carry guns, anyway. The sort of opponents we're prepared for shoot back."

"Some men arrived at the Soviets' Vostok Station, and believe me, they look like they know how to shoot back," Fennimore warned. "They arrived in a Soviet military transport plane less than two hours ahead of you guys. Some of their equipment resembled rifle cases, too. We figure they might be Russian commandos."

"You sure about this?" Manning asked.

"Picked 'em up on an optical scan of the area," Eisley assured him, "We've been monitoring Vostok Station around the clock since this goddamn thing happened. Got about a dozen new Ivans in the neighborhood. They brought along some extra sledges, too. That suggests they don't intend to just hang around the area. Maybe they're going to provide extra security for their comrades, or murder some more Americans."

"Well, I noticed the autopsy on Collier mentioned they'd removed a bullet from his spine," Manning commented. "Nine-millimeter parabellum. Maybe the shooter was a Soviet, but he wasn't using a Russian pistol."

"The Russkies don't carry Tokarevs anymore," Eisley snorted. "Nowadays they pack 9 mm Makarov pistols."

Manning smiled. The Canadian and the other members of Phoenix Force were familiar with Soviet weaponry. They had all fired Makarovs, and opponents had fired the double-action Russian pistols at the commandos on numerous occasions during previous missions. Eisley had probably never even seen a Makarov except for photographs in reference books.

"Both the Makarov and the Stechkin machine pistol are 9 mm weapons made in the USSR," Manning said, "but both fire the Russian 9 mm cartridge, not the 9 mm parabellum. Ballistics on the bullet removed from Collier were unable to pinpoint the exact type of firearm used, because the slug was deformed when it struck bone. Most likely choices for the murder weapon seem to be a German-made Walther P-38 or its Norwegian look-alike the M-38. Odd weapons for Soviet assassins to use. If they wanted to cast suspicion on the CIA or the NSA, American-made pistols would make more sense."

"Maybe they didn't intend to frame us for the murders when they killed those two poor bastards," Fennimore suggested. "You fellas were sent here to find answers. Maybe you can learn the answer to that little puzzle when you find out who's really responsible and why they did it. Still, I don't like the Soviets calling in reinforcements at Vostok. It makes me a bit uneasy after everything that's already happened here."

"It would be ironic if the cold war gets hot in Antarctica," Katz remarked. "We'd better start planning our expedition to Beardmore and get some rest before we have to leave. It's going to be a very long day out on the ice."

9

The caravan of ice sledges rode across the frozen desert. Snow spewed from the treads of the vehicles. White froth trailed the sledges like water in the wake of a speedboat. Harold Swenson piloted the lead vehicle, followed by McCarter and Katz in the second sledge. James operated the third rig, accompanied by an unhappy and shivering Rafael Encizo. Manning had the last sledge and followed the others, the craft burdened with extra gear secured to the carriage.

The vast terrain of unspoiled white plains extended beyond the view of Phoenix Force and their guide. The Transantarctic Mountains stood in the distance, ivory sculptures that seemed to beckon the team onward. The emptiness of Antarctica was both eerie and fascinating. The only sound was the rumble of the sledges' engines. The constant night of the austral winter sky displayed a remarkable array of stars set on black velvet.

Yakov Katzenelenbogen viewed the setting with something akin to awe. It seemed they had traveled back in time to the last ice age. Indeed, Antarctica had been in deep freeze for millions of years.

However, Katz couldn't allow himself the luxury of wandering thoughts for long. The terrain gradually became more rugged as they approached the mountains. Rock formations, covered with centuries of ice, dotted the landscape. Swenson signaled to the others that he was going to reduce speed; they had to watch out for crevasses. McCarter obeyed the instruction and passed on the command with another hand signal for James. The black commando also slowed his vehicle and gestured for Manning to do likewise.

The Canadian pressed the rudders and eased back the throttle as the caravan reached a cluster of icy monuments. Manning felt the sledge hit something as he started to reduce speed. The machine rose with the impact and canted sideways in midair. It nearly stood erect on one end, leaning toward the heaviest portion of the equipment in the rear of the rig. Manning tumbled from his seat and fell out of the open-top sledge.

He hit the hard, frozen earth and slammed against an ice-coated boulder, which dazed him. His vision cleared in time to see the sledge descend. The belly of the vehicle was headed straight for the Canadian's prone form. The razor-sharp steel teeth of the treads whirled like giant meat saws.

Manning couldn't move fast enough to get clear of the sledge. There was no time. He pressed his back against the base of the boulder and held his arms against his chest. The sledge crashed, and tread blades struck the rock formation. Manning gasped as he stared up at the knifelike runners. The machine was tilted against the boulder with Manning trapped beneath. Chunks of ice shot from the blades as the treads sawed into the frozen shroud around the rock.

Ice cracked, and pieces showered Manning's mask-covered face. His goggles became fogged by heavy breathing. The treads shifted on the ice and moved closer to the Canadian's pinned body. He tucked his arms and legs in to avoid amputation, but the treads ate through more ice and inched closer to him.

The Canadian closed his eyes and gritted his teeth. Manning had always realized the risks involved in the sort of work he did with Phoenix Force. He knew eventually his luck would run out, but he had expected it to end with an enemy bullet. It seemed almost absurd to get killed in a freak accident after surviving so many firefights in the past.

The treads suddenly stopped whirling and the engine ceased. Manning opened his eyes and saw that the blades were still above him. They were no longer moving. He heard voices and the crunch of boots on frozen ground.

"Baxter!" a familiar voice called. "Baxter, can you hear me?"

It took Manning a moment to remember that Baxter was his current cover name. "I hear you!" he called out hoarsely. "I think I'm okay, but I can't move."

"Just stay where you are," James's voice told him. "We're going to lift this sucker off you."

"That would be nice," Manning replied, trying to sound more relaxed than he felt.

The sledge slowly rose. Gloved hands pushed the carriage and lifted it high enough for Manning to crawl out from under the machine. He discovered that all four of his Phoenix colleagues and Harold Swenson had come to his rescue. The five men pulled the sledge away from the boulder and eased it to the ground once more. Manning got to his feet. His knees wobbled, and he was still breathing hard, but he had suffered no worse than a few bruises from the accident.

"Nasty spill," Swenson remarked, as if he saw such near-fatal accidents everyday. "I don't think the weight on the load is evenly distributed. We'd better rearrange the equipment before we go on."

"You feel up to making this trip, Baxter?" Katz inquired.

"I'm fine," Manning assured him. "Just rattled me a bit."

"Maybe I ought to drive the sledge the rest of the way," Encizo reluctantly volunteered. "It's similar to a hydrofoil. I think I can handle it."

"It's more like a cross between a hydrofoil and a snowmobile," Manning said. "I'm okay. The accident didn't happen because I don't know what I'm doing with the rig."

"Could have happened to any of us," Swenson confirmed. "The terrain gets trickier when we get closer to the mountains. We'll have to be careful and go nice and slow."

"Are you familiar with the region, Swenson?" James asked.

"I've been to the Transantarctic Mountains a few times," the explorer answered, "but I won't claim to be familiar with the entire range. Saying you know the Transantarctic Mountains is like saying you know the Alps or the Rockies. Not *all* of it, you don't."

"How about the part we're headed for?" James inquired.

"I know where it is," Swenson said, "but I don't recall ever coming across a volcano in that region. Doesn't really surprise me. There are lots of things in Antarctica no man has ever seen. We might think we've conquered the place, but it still has plenty of surprises."

"It's hard to conquer something when you're freezing your ass off," Encizo muttered.

The Phoenix Force expedition didn't have any more drastic incidents as it continued its journey to the Transantarctic Mountains. The great white giants were magnificent. Draped in snow, much of it dozens of feet deep, the mountains stood out like sculptures of marble. The peaks of smaller mountains were barely visible among the layers of snow. Some gorges between mountains were filled with snow, and one could only guess how deep the ravines might be.

They discovered the site of the double murder with less difficulty than they had expected. A row of aluminum poles formed a token fence around the tunnel at the base of the volcano. Each pole was labeled with three red triangles set against a yellow circle. The universal symbol for radiation warned that the site was still regarded as potentially dangerous.

"I thought the NRC was supposed to send us somebody to check out this goddamn hole," James remarked as he climbed from the driver's seat of his sledge.

"We didn't find any nuclear scientists waiting for us at McMurdo," Encizo replied. The Cuban unbuckled the straps securing their cargo as he spoke. "If we were smart, we would have waited for an NRC expert to join us. Of course, if we were smart, we probably wouldn't take on assignments like this in the first place."

"The way Washington drags its feet and binds everything up in red tape, the NRC might take a week to finally get somebody to Antarctica," James said. "God knows what kind of shit could happen between now and then."

"I don't like the idea of any of us going down there," Encizo said as he pulled back the protective tarp from the gear. "Nobody knows what's in that tunnel except that the last men to go in got exposed to radiation."

James searched through the bags of equipment and found one marked with a triple pyramid symbol. He opened the container and pulled out an oversize silvery garment. Boot covers and mitten-style gloves were built into the outfit. James pulled down the zipper to the garment and shoved a leg into it.

"None of those guys had radiation suits," he told Encizo as he stepped into the silver coveralls. "Besides, they only got a mild dose of radiation. Not that any radiation is a good thing. Still, from what I can gather from the medical reports available, the New Zealanders and French who pulled the corpses out of the tunnel didn't come down with anything worse than a little nausea. Even the bodies of Linnson and Collier had relatively low levels of radiation, considering how long they must have been stuck in that pit."

"I noticed that, too," Manning began. The Canadian was also dressed in radiation-proof coveralls. He zipped up the suit and inspected the metallic-weave fabric for tears. "What sort of nuclear testing leaves such low levels of radiation?"

"This whole business seems pretty weird to me," Encizo confessed as he helped James with his helmet.

The headgear resembled a clear plastic bucket. An air tank was attached to the back of the helmet and fitted between James's shoulder blades. Encizo helped James attach the helmet to the suit while McCarter assisted Manning with his protective garments. The Canadian had also taken a Geiger counter from the equipment supply bags on his sledge.

"If you get a dangerously high reading," Katz said as he approached Manning, "I want you to get out of there immediately. These radiation suits are designed to protect the wearer from a lethal exposure, but the term radiation-proof is like bulletproof."

"I know," Manning assured him. He realized that a bulletproof vest wouldn't stop armor-piercing projectiles and that a powerful dose of radiation would go through his protective suit like penny nails through cardboard.

James and Manning armed themselves with flashlights and ice axes. A sturdy nylon rope was secured around each man's waist. The remaining men would hold on to the other end to anchor the line while James and Manning made their descent. Another rope would allow the pair to signal if they needed to be hauled out of the tunnel in a hurry, or if they needed more line to go deeper.

"How did we wind up volunteering for this?" Manning muttered as he and James approached the mouth of the tunnel. "McCarter can usually be counted on to take on the really crazy stuff. Son of a bitch let us down this time."

"Little late to complain," James replied. "We got the job 'cause we're better qualified. Lucky us."

"Lucky," Manning said tensely as they drew closer to the ominous black gap at the base of the volcano.

They were clumsy and slow, limbs burdened by the bulky radiation suits as well as layers of clothing for protection from the cold. The two men stepped between the warning posts with the radiation symbols mounted on the poles. The others watched the pair slowly enter the mouth of the tunnel. McCarter and Encizo gripped the main line in their fists. They tossed out several feet of rope as James and Manning disappeared into the pit.

Katz, who was holding the signal line in his left fist, felt the cord yank forward. "One tug," he announced. "They're okay."

"Does that mean the Geiger reading isn't high enough to worry them?" Swenson inquired.

"I hope so," the Phoenix commander replied.

NICOLAI MOROZOV PEERED through his binoculars as he watched the American team at the base of the volcano. The KGB agent grunted with grim satisfaction. He turned to look at Major Anatoli Remizov. Morozov wouldn't have known which paratrooper was Remizov if the man's name tag hadn't been sewn on the chest of his white cold-weather parka. The Russians were all clad in heavy arctic clothing, faces concealed by masks and goggles.

"It seems we already have our proof, Major," Morozov remarked. "The Americans have returned to the scene of the crime, so to speak."

"But what are they doing?" Remizov wondered aloud.

"Two of their people are in the tunnel," the KGB man replied. "No doubt to remove some evidence that would prove the CIA has been conducting nuclear testing."

"One moment, Comrade," Remizov said as he placed a mitten-clad hand on Morozov's arm. "If the Americans have been testing some sort of nuclear weapon in that tunnel, the radiation level would still be dangerously high. Too high to venture inside, even with radiation suits. Besides, that big hill is an inactive volcano. Why would anyone be willing to carry out any sort of nuclear tests at the base of a volcano, even an inactive one? It's suicide."

"Americans are insane," Morozov offered as an explanation. "In California a nuclear power plant is supposedly located along an earthquake fault line."

"Chernobyl was still using technology and equipment that were thirty years out of date," Remizov replied. "It's no wonder a disaster occurred there. All nations make such careless mistakes, but I can't imagine the CIA doing something as foolhardy as nuclear testing next to a volcano."

"Yes, Comrade!" Morozov declared, as if a revelation had suddenly struck like lightning from the sky. "You're right! They aren't carrying out nuclear testing in the conventional sense. It's obvious now. The CIA has been experimenting with a way to cause dormant volcanoes to activate. If they can perfect this, they could make volcanoes erupt in other countries and make it appear to be natural disasters instead of enemy sabotage."

"That's a rather farfetched theory with little to support it, Comrade," Remizov said, shaking his head slightly. The paratrooper thought the KGB thrived on paranoia, and Morozov seemed living proof of such an opinion.

"We're going to get evidence, Major," Morozov assured him.

He glanced at the other paratroopers under Remizov's command. Ten highly trained, well-armed commandos, the flowers of Soviet manhood. Dressed in white camouflage parkas with protective masks and goggles, the soldiers could have been a product of advanced cloning. Morozov found comfort in this. He didn't want to see their faces. It was easier to deal with men who had no identity, especially if one's decision might cost some of them their lives.

"I want the men to surround the enemy," Morozov announced. "Don't use the ice sledges. They make too much noise, and the headlights could give us away to the enemy."

"They're more than a kilometer away," Remizov commented. "It'll take a while to get into position. The volcano will block them unless they're foolish enough to run into the tunnel. We'll position men at every other avenue of escape."

The major turned to face his men. "Unload one of the sledges. It'll be light enough for three men to tow it manually. If the Americans manage to reach their vehicles and try to run, we'll be able to catch them with little difficulty. A sledge without the extra burden of equipment will easily outrace one weighed down with gear."

"Good thinking," Morozov said with approval as he opened a pouch on his belt and drew his Makarov. "We'll wait for the two badgers to come out of their burrow. Then we take them."

"No shooting unless it's necessary," Remizov said. The command was more a reminder for Morozov than instructions to his men.

"We certainly don't want to kill all of them," the KGB agent replied as he worked the slide on his Makarov to chamber the first round. "But it has been my experience if you shoot one man, the others will be more inclined to talk."

10

Gary Manning checked the Geiger counter as he and Calvin James descended into the tunnel. The radiation level increased slightly as they moved deeper. Rock walls surrounded the pair, and the faint light from the mouth of the cave gradually faded. The footing was better than either man had thought it would be. The rock underfoot was frozen, but it was less slippery than they'd expected, due to the lack of moisture in the tunnel.

The tunnel wasn't as steep as they'd expected, either. They could have scaled the rocky interior without the assistance of the rope. The passage was narrow and extended into the ground at an inclined angle. Their flashlight beams stroked the black walls of the tunnel. The stone seemed almost polished, and it shone with a stunning luster.

"Radiation level is higher here," Manning announced as he moved the Geiger counter toward the black substance. "Still nothing the suits won't protect us from."

"I hope that Geiger counter's reliable," James said as he drove the blade of his ice ax into a rock wall. "This shiny shit must be a layer of pumice from the volcano, but the black rock doesn't look like coal."

"Hey, Calvin!" Manning exclaimed. He had felt something harder than rock at the outer edge of his foot. "I found something."

James trained his light on the object. The men had trouble looking down through the plastic helmets, goggles and masks. They had to crane their necks and turn their heads at unnatural angles, but finally they saw the shape of two iron rails along the rock surface.

"Son of a bitch," James whispered. "Is someone planning to run a streetcar through here?"

"No," Manning said. "An ore car. This isn't a tunnel drilled out to test explosives or radioactive gases. It's a mining shaft. The rails would have linked together to extend outside. Whoever built it must have taken the closer rails out when they left, but they must have been in a hurry and failed to measure the length. These were left behind."

"Oh, man," James said as he examined a chunk of black rock in his double-gloved hand. "I think I know what this stuff is. Pitchblende."

"Pitchblende?" Manning asked with surprise. He studied the sample and nodded as best he could with the bulky headgear. "My God, Cal. I think you're right."

"Yeah," James said as he began to unscrew the back plate from his flashlight. "Wish we'd brought a mineral sample box. I'll have to improvise."

He dumped the batteries from his flashlight and tried to shove the pitchblende chunk into the hollow tube of the flashlight shaft, but it didn't fit. Manning took the sample, braced it against a rock wall and tapped it with the blade of his ice ax. The pitchblende broke in half. Manning handed a portion to James. It fitted into the black commando's flashlight now, and James screwed the rear plate back in place.

"Thanks," James told the Canadian. "Let's get out of here."

Manning tugged the signal line once to let the others know they were still all right. Then he pulled twice more to signal they were coming out. They climbed back up to the mouth of the tunnel, assisted by the strong, steady pull of the main line attached to their waists.

The pair emerged from the tunnel. The other three Phoenix Force commandos were relieved to see their partners again. James placed his flashlight on the ground before he stripped out of his radiation suit. Manning did likewise. Then both men stepped away from the discarded garments. Encizo approached them with a Geiger counter in one hand and a metal cylinder that resembled a fire extinguisher in the other.

The Cuban extended the Geiger counter and ran it near James and Manning. The machine ticked softly. Encizo noticed the reading was less than the usual radiation reading from a color television set. He nodded at the pair. "It's okay. You guys are safe."

"Glad I won't be glowing in the dark tonight," James said. "Let me have the spray shit before the canister explodes in this cold."

"I'd rather it explode while you've got it than me," the Cuban declared as he tossed the canister to James.

"You guys are all heart," James said as he headed for the discarded radiation suits. He switched on the nozzle and sprayed the suits with a special chemical compound. Then he sprayed the flashlight and Manning's Geiger counter, as well.

"What did you find down there?" Katz asked as he approached Manning and James.

"Enough to be pretty sure everybody's been barking up the wrong tree," the Canadian replied. "The hole in the ground is a goddamn mining shaft. We brought a mineral sample out. Somebody better qualified will have to confirm what it is, but we've got a strong suspicion it's pitchblende."

"Are we supposed to know what that is?" McCarter inquired gruffly. "Sounds like some sort of mixed drink for baseball players."

"Pitchblende is a mineral that contains large amounts of uranium," Manning explained.

"Pitchblende and carnotite are two of the main sources of both radium and uranium," James added as he turned from the radiation suits to join the conversation. "I don't figure anybody was conducting secret mining operations to get their hands on radium."

"Jesus Christ," Harold Swenson rasped as he joined the others. "Somebody found uranium ore under this volcano?"

"You bet," James replied. "Looks like those scientists and the guys who pulled them out of that hole got exposed to radiation thanks to natural uranium, not nuclear testing."

"Two men were murdered because of that mine, and we've still got an international hornets' nest—" McCarter began. He stopped in midsentence when he heard a faint scraping sound on the wind.

"I don't think that was some mice building an igloo," James whispered tensely.

McCarter opened the pouch on his belt and extracted his Browning Hi-Power. The Briton folded his arms on his chest and tucked the pistol barrel under an armpit. James pulled back the flap on his pistol pouch, as well, but didn't draw his weapon. Encizo placed a hand on the sheath to his side arm, and Manning slowly moved toward an ice sledge where his rifle was stored.

Katz inched closer to the sledge, but remained in the open. Experience had taught him that if someone was close enough to be heard, they were probably close enough to start shooting. If someone was getting in position to attack them, they were holding their fire for the moment. That meant there was probably still time to spare before the unseen enemy struck . . . if indeed there was an enemy in the area. Katz chose to risk those moments in the open to prevent startling the opponents into taking action. If a couple of members of their team stood by the sledges, anyone watching wouldn't be unduly suspicious. If they all seemed ready to head for cover and grab their rifles, the other side might be inclined to open fire.

Swenson helped James load the radiation suits, flashlights and ice axes into a heavy rubber bag. Despite the decontamination spray, those items were still radioactive. A Geiger counter reading of the gear was unreliable because the chemical cleanser might have masked the true level of radiation. The men used aluminum tongs to stuff the materials into the bag and then closed it with an airtight seal.

"I think I saw somebody move by the foot of that hill to the west," Swenson remarked. He had already opened his Colt .45 belt pouch.

"Yeah," James said. He looked down at the rubber bag as he spoke. "I saw somebody by those rocks to the east. They're wearing white and they move damn good. Not easy to spot 'em. Whoever they are, they've had some decent training, and they're not going to make too many mistakes."

"That's not the most comforting thing you could have said at a moment like this," Swenson growled through clenched teeth.

Three figures appeared from the base of a hill to the west. They walked boldly forward. Two men carried AK-74 assault rifles. The third held a Makarov pistol in a white-gloved fist. They wore white parkas with the letters CCCP printed in red over the right breast. The Soviets had landed.

"Stay where you are and do not move!" Morozov ordered as he trained his pistol on Katz. The KGB agent's English was rusty, and he barked out each word as if eager to get it out of his mouth. "My men surround you. They can shoot you all immediately if you resist!"

"I understand," Katz replied. "What do you want? Why threaten us when we haven't done any harm?"

"CIA assassin!" Morozov snapped. "We know what you've done here in the past and what you are doing here now! Testing your illegal nuclear weapons to use against the people of the workers' socialist movement throughout the world."

"Whoa!" Swenson declared. "Hold on, fella! Let's not kill each other over a misunderstanding."

"Shut up!" Morozov bellowed. "All I want you to do is confess."

Major Remizov and other members of the Soviet team covered Phoenix Force from the east side. Rifle barrels jutted from behind rocks, and a couple of white parka hoods were barely visible from the Russians' cover. The Phoenix Force team realized that for every opponent they could see there was probably at least one they had yet to detect.

"We're not going to confess to something we didn't do," Katz said. "But before you do anything else, look at what we found in the mine."

"So you're the leader of this group?" Morozov declared, a chuckle in his voice. "Without you these other dogs will start yapping."

The KGB agent pointed his Makarov at Katz's chest. It was more difficult to aim than he expected due to the mask and goggles, but Morozov figured if the first bullet didn't kill the man, he could finish the job with the second or third. "Shoot one," he said. "The others are more eager to talk."

The pistol shot erupted like a clap of thunder in the Antarctic silence. The muzzle-flash streaked from the weapon, and a high-velocity projectile pierced the mask above and between the goggles. Morozov's head recoiled from the impact. The KGB agent literally died on his feet, his brain torn asunder by the parabellum slug. He toppled to the ground, his unfired Makarov still clenched in his fist.

McCarter had removed the Browning Hi-Power from its hiding place under his arm as he'd unfolded his arms from his chest. The British pistol champ hadn't hesitated to shoot when he'd seen that the Russian commander was about to kill Katz. McCarter had relied on years of marksmanship training and combat experience to nail the KGB man with a fatal one-shot round to take him out instantly.

The shot was the signal for all hell to break loose. Katz and Swenson immediately dived for cover next to the sledges as Soviet rifles opened fire. The two paratroopers with Morozov were taken off guard by the KGB man's sudden death and wasted a vital split second trying to determine where the shot had come from. McCarter dropped to one knee and gripped his pistol in both hands. The Briton concentrated on the two soldiers in the open. He heard automatic fire and the whine of ricochets near his position. McCarter kept his attention focused on the opponents he could see and trusted his teammates to cover his ass as he aimed the Browning and squeezed the trigger.

McCarter drilled a 9 mm round into the chest of one paratrooper. The bullet struck the Russian in the breastbone, shattered the sternum and knocked him off balance. The other Soviet trooper swung his AK-74 toward McCarter, but the Briton fired first. He squeezed off two shots that hit the Russian in the chest. His heart stopped midbeat, and he collapsed next to his wounded comrade.

The paratrooper with the smashed breastbone lay on his back, unconscious and in a state of shock from the massive damage caused by the bullet. Three opponents were out of the fight, but Major Remizov and eight of his soldiers remained. A burst of 5.45 mm rounds snarled from the rock formations to the east. Snow and bits of ice kicked up from the ground near McCarter as the high-velocity hailstorm missed the Briton by less than a foot.

The British ace rolled away from the geysers of snow and ice fragments. He landed on his belly and sprawled flat. McCarter was pinned down and could do little except wait for his fellow Phoenix fighters to bail him out of the tight spot so that he could move into a better position and resume an active role in the firefight.

James and Manning spotted the Soviet rifleman among the rocks. The Russian leaned around the edge of an ice-coated shoulder of rock to take better aim with his assault rifle. The masks and goggles inhibited the combatants' marksmanship, but both Phoenix Force and the Soviet troops had experience using weapons while wearing gas masks and other headgear that restricted vision.

James drew his Walther P-88 and fired at the paratrooper while Gary Manning yanked a Heckler & Koch PSG1 rifle from an insulated canvas scabbard among the gear on the sledge. The Russian gunman convulsed as James blasted two 9 mm rounds into the man's upper torso. Manning swung his H&K at the opponent as the Russian staggered away from cover, and squeezed the trigger.

The 7.62 mm NATO projectile punched through the hollow of the Russian's throat. It split his Adam's apple and knifed through vertebrae at the back of his neck. The man's head wobbled loosely as if his neck had been turned into rubber. His knees folded and he slumped to the ground in a lifeless lump.

"Take it!" Manning shouted as he handed the rifle to James and began to reach inside another equipment bag on the sledge.

The Soviets returned fire with a vengeance. AK-74 rounds smashed into the frame of the ice sledge and ripped into the tarp over the gear. James ducked low as several slugs narrowly missed his head. One bullet tugged at the fur liner at the top of his parka hood. Manning barely seemed to notice as he continued to search through the equipment, even as bullets plowed into the sledge.

"Whatever you're after, it better be good," James advised. "They're going to be feeding us grenades any second now."

"Let's feed them first," Manning announced. The Canadian held up an orange metal sphere with a red stripe painted across the middle. "I've got some fraggers and concussion grenades in this bag, as well. Grab some."

"Shit, man," James rasped, "I hope the bastards don't hit this stuff. We'll all go up like fireworks on the Fourth of July."

"We wouldn't know if it happened," Manning replied dryly. He pulled the pin from the orange-and-red grenade in his fist. "Don't look at this thing when it goes off."

"I don't even want to look at it now," James assured him as he reached inside the bag for more grenades.

Manning swung his arm and hurled the orange ball at the rock formation. The grenade sailed high and descended in an arc toward the enemy position. It exploded in midair. The magnesium charge burst in a brilliant white glare like a miniature supernova.

James handed the H&K rifle to Manning, drew his Walther and bolted from the cover of the ice sledge. Manning shouldered the rifle and covered James. The Canadian saw a white parka hood pop up from behind a rock ledge. The face under the hood was covered by a gloved hand as well as a cold-weather mask. The paratrooper had slapped a hand over his goggles after the glare of the magnesium blast had temporarily blinded him.

Manning immediately seized the opportunity. He fixed the H&K on the target and stared through the scope. The cross hairs found the hooded head of the paratrooper. With the center marked at the back of the hand across the man's face, Manning squeezed the trigger. The Canadian warrior felt the recoil of the rifle and saw a bullet hole appear in the Russian's glove. The man's hand flew away from his face to reveal another bullet hole in his mask at the bridge of the nose. The paratrooper fell from view behind the rocks.

"Damn it," Manning grumbled bitterly as he dashed from the cover of the sledge to follow Calvin James.

The Canadian was upset because he had been forced to kill the Soviet soldier. The battle was unnecessary. If the leader of the Soviet team had been willing to talk and simply look at what they had found in the mine shaft, there would have been no need for killing. When the bastard insisted on trying to murder Katz, Phoenix Force had been forced to defend themselves. The Russian soldiers were just doing their job and had no more choice than the Phoenix team when the shooting had begun.

James and Manning ran for the rock formations. The black American fired three P-88 rounds at the rocks to discourage the remaining paratroopers from raising their heads to take aim with their weapons. Manning held his fire. The H&K was semiauto only and less maneuverable than a pistol. They ran as fast as possible, burdened by their bulky clothing and the ankle-deep snow. They felt clumsy and slow, as if trapped in a dream, a nightmare that might end in death for both men.

An object was hurled from behind the rock formations. They glimpsed the metal egg as it sailed overhead. A stubby steel stem poked from one end of the Soviet grenade. The

Phoenix fighters knew what it was—an F-1 fragmentation grenade. The Russian blaster had a five-second fuse, but it was likely that the paratrooper who had thrown it had pulled the pin and held the F-1 for a second or two before lobbing it at the Phoenix pair.

Manning and James dived forward. They rolled onto their bellies and covered their heads as best they could. The grenade exploded some distance behind the pair. Clumps of snow and shards of ice showered down on them as the earth trembled beneath the pair.

RAFAEL ENCIZO HAD ALSO REMOVED extra weaponry from an equipment bag on a sledge. The Cuban selected two concussion grenades and an Uzi machine pistol in addition to his Walther pistol. Yakov Katzenelenbogen was also armed with a micro-Uzi, held in his left fist and braced across his prosthetic right arm. Harold Swenson crouched by the sledge next to Katz. The explorer held his Colt .45 in his fist. The big revolver was a popgun compared to the automatic rifles and explosives wielded by the Soviet ambushers.

McCarter darted to the cover of the sledges as another burst of enemy fire raked the ground near his feet. The Briton leaped forward, tucked his head and hit the frozen ground in a fast shoulder roll. He reached shelter and ducked behind an ice sledge, Browning Hi-Power in his fist. He wiped snow from a goggle lens with a gloved thumb and gripped the pistol with both hands.

"What the hell are we going to do now?" Swenson asked tensely. He glanced around and saw that Manning and James were busy fighting the opponents on the east side, but Soviet gunmen to the west still had the rest of the team pinned down.

"Try to get their attention," Encizo replied as he pulled the pin from a concussion grenade. "With a little luck we can turn the tables on them."

"We'll need more than a little luck," Swenson muttered, but he aimed his Colt at the muzzle-flash of the enemies' weapons and squeezed the trigger.

The .45 boomed, followed by the crack of a 9 mm round as McCarter fired his Browning. Katz added to the firepower with his micro-Uzi. The weapon sprayed a salvo of high-velocity slugs across the ice-caked face of the hill. Bits of ice hopped from the surface and sparks struck off rock as bullets ricocheted with angry whines and hisses.

Encizo hoped the barrage of bullets would distract the enemy as he stood and lobbed the grenade at the hill. The grenade exploded with a violent shock wave when it hit a rocky ridge. Snow whirled from the rock wall like water from the hide of an enormous beast attempting to shake itself dry.

Katz took a deep breath—as deep as possible with the mask over his nose and mouth—and bolted for the base of the hill. The distance was less than a hundred yards, but it seemed like twenty miles as he ran through the deep snow, fully aware he was vulnerable to the Russian troops stationed among the rocks.

The notion that he might be getting too old for combat duty flickered through his mind, but his reflexes responded to more than four decades of experience and training. Katz triggered two three-round bursts with the micro-Uzi and ran in a fast zigzag pattern, back arched and head low. His bullets slashed the rock wall to further discourage retaliation by the enemy. He reached the base of the hill, still alive.

Encizo followed the Israeli. He carried his Uzi machine pistol in one fist and the second concussion grenade in the other. McCarter and Swenson continued to fire at the rocks while the Cuban galloped through the snow. He fired the micro-Uzi one-handed at the mountain and saw the spark of bullets on rock. It seemed a waste of ammunition, yet the shooting helped keep the enemy pinned down long enough for Encizo to reach a large boulder next to Katz.

"Try not to kill any of them unless you have to," the Israeli urged.

"I just wish they felt the same way," Encizo replied. The Cuban pulled the pin from his grenade and moved around the base of the hill. Katz followed, Uzi held ready. As McCarter and Swenson continued to exchange fire with the Soviet paratroopers, Encizo and Katz could only hope the enemy would remain distracted and preoccupied long enough for them to carry out their plan.

The Cuban tossed the grenade. It sailed over the shoulder of an icy boulder and descended on the other side. Encizo placed his back flat against a rock wall. Katz followed his example and braced himself for the explosion, which occurred a split second later.

The hill trembled as if an earthquake had shaken its base. Katz and Encizo were nearly thrown off balance by the violent tremor, but they were unharmed by the blast. Encizo drew his Walther from its belt pouch. Micro-Uzi in one fist, the Walther in the other, the Cuban hurried to the other side of the hill. Katz was right behind him, machine pistol held ready. Either McCarter or Swenson had taken an automatic weapon from the gear on the sledges and blasted additional full-auto fire at the hill to keep the enemy pinned down. However, the Soviet forces had ceased fire. Maybe the concussion grenades had taken the Russians out of action. Maybe...

Encizo swung around the edge of the hill, both weapons in his fists. Two dazed Russians were at the base. One man lay sprawled on his back. He had fallen from a rock ledge when the grenade had exploded. Stunned or unconscious, the paratrooper didn't present an immediate threat, but his comrade was still on his feet. The Russian held a gloved hand to his hooded head and used his AK-74 as a crutch to stand erect, fist around the barrel and metal stock braced on the ground. A third Soviet gunman was still positioned on the rock wall. He was on all fours, obviously rattled by the concussion, but he had managed to stay perched on the ledge. The paratrooper had dropped his assault rifle and was shaking his head to clear it.

"Nyet!" Katz shouted as he appeared behind Encizo and saw the man on the ledge reach for a Makarov side arm.

The Russian ignored the warning and yanked the pistol from its belt pouch. Katz raised his micro-Uzi and triggered a three-round burst. Parabellum slugs smashed into the soldier's face and upper chest. The Soviet jerked from the impact of the bullets and tumbled over the lip of the ledge. His lifeless body plunged to the frozen earth below.

The soldier who had been using his rifle as a crutch saw his comrade fall and reacted by raising the AK-74 and grabbing the pistol grip. His trigger finger slid into position as he dropped to one knee and tried to aim his weapon at the Phoenix pair.

"Damn idiot!" Encizo exclaimed, and triggered both the Uzi machine pistol and the Walther P-88.

The Russian had left him no choice, and Encizo had responded with swift and deadly action. Three Uzi slugs slammed into the Russian's chest as the machine pistol spit a long tongue of orange flame. The Walther in Encizo's other fist barked twice and drilled a 9 mm death into the paratrooper's stomach and solar plexus. Torso riddled with ragged bullet holes, the Russian staggered two steps backward and dropped his unfired AK-74. He tried to speak but could only gurgle. Crimson appeared at the mouth of his cold-weather mask, then the man collapsed, twitched slightly and lay still.

JAMES AND MANNING ROSE from the snow-laced ground. Neither man had been injured by the F-1 grenade blast. They scrambled to the base of the rock formation where the remaining members of the Soviet hit team were located. James pulled the pin from an M-27 fragmentation grenade and lobbed it over the edge of the natural fortress. The Phoenix warriors ducked low, and the grenade exploded on the opposite side of the rocks.

The Canadian commando dashed around the outcropping first. He nearly stepped in the splattered gore and dismembered remains of a Russian soldier. The man had been torn to pieces by the grenade. Manning barely glanced at the grisly display. The Phoenix demolitions pro had seen such carnage many times before.

He found another Russian ten yards from the mutilated corpse of the first man. The second paratrooper had been stunned and shaken by the blast, but his slain comrade had absorbed the bulk of the explosion. Manning pointed his H&K rifle at the soldier. Although dazed, the Russian was still armed with an AK-74.

"Drop it!" Manning shouted, hoping the paratrooper understood the tone if not the words in English.

The Russian raised his assault rifle. Manning peered through the telescopic sights of his H&K and centered the cross hairs on the soldier's upper right arm. He triggered the weapon, and a 7.62 mm slug punched through the Russian's biceps to shatter the underlying bone. The Soviet gunman screamed as the assault rifle hurtled from his grasp. Manning altered the aim of his H&K and fired another round. The second bullet smashed through the Russian's left kneecap. The man collapsed in a thrashing heap, howling in agony as he rolled onto his back and clutched at his wounded leg with his left hand.

"That all of 'em?" James asked. He stood behind Manning and glanced about at the nearby rock formations. "Figured there were more than two of 'em left."

"Yeah," Manning agreed, a trace of apprehension in his voice.

The growl of engines drew their attention to a passage between a cluster of boulders and the base of another large hill. Headlights knifed through the gloom, and a bright red ice sledge suddenly burst from cover. Two figures were aboard the sledge, which had a gold star painted on its side. The driver steered the rig directly for Manning and James while the passenger crouched in the rear, both hands gripping a light machine gun mounted on the sledge.

James leaped around the edge of the rocks and ducked low as a barrage of rounds exploded from the Soviet sledge. Manning dived for cover behind a trio of cone-shaped boulders near the splattered remnants of the dead Russian. Bullets chipped ice and bounced off rock. Ricochets wailed, and tracer rounds streaked through the shadows like jet-propelled fireflies. The Soviet sledge charged forward, headed for the Phoenix vehicles in the clearing next to the base of the volcano.

"Fuck!" James exclaimed as he poked his P-88 around the edge of the rocks and opened fire.

The Walther pistol snarled in a vain attempt to take out either of the Russians. James fired blindly, unable to expose himself long enough to aim. The superior firepower of the light machine gun made such an effort virtual suicide. Manning faced a similar problem. He could put his rifle barrel between the conical rocks, but he couldn't aim it at the Russian sledge without presenting a target. With more than a thousand rounds for the chain-fed weapon, the Soviets could afford to waste ammo blanketing the rocks with firepower to keep the Phoenix defenders pinned down.

Manning set the H&K rifle aside and reached into a parka pocket to remove an aluminum packet. The size of a pack of cigarettes, it contained five ounces of C-4 plastic explosive, a detonator and a timing mechanism. He pressed a red button on the pack as the sledge drew closer, then hurled it into the path of the Soviet vehicle.

The Russian rig bolted forward and ran straight into the merciless blast of C-4. The explosion lifted the sledge from the ground and threw it backward onto the ice. The machine gunner flew from the rig and plunged into a snowbank. The driver fell out of the sledge and landed on the ground as the vehicle tipped over in a manner similar to the sledge accident Manning had experienced earlier that day. However, the Russian paratrooper wasn't as lucky as the Canadian had been. No barrier of ice and rock protected the fallen soldier from the treads of the ice rig.

The sledge slammed down on the helpless Russian. Steel blades rolled across the man's chest and abdomen. The weight of the vehicle pushed the metal teeth deep into clothing and flesh, and the treads slashed the paratrooper as if he were pinned under a giant chain saw. A terrible shriek of agony and fear erupted as blood jetted from beneath the sledge. Scraps of clothing and bits of bone flew from the treads, and then the man's screams ceased.

Major Remizov slowly crawled from the snowdrift. The deep pocket of white flakes had effectively broken his fall and saved the Soviet officer from bone-breaking injury. He shook snow from his hood and face mask as he dragged himself from the soft drift on all fours. Remizov glanced up and discovered a figure standing in front of him with a pistol pointed at his head.

"Hold it, pal," Calvin James declared, covering the Russian with his P-88. "I hope you understand a little English, 'cause I want you to move real slow."

Remizov suddenly swung the back of a fist against James's wrist to deflect the aim of the commando's Walther. James held his fire, reluctant to shoot the Russian. Enough killing had occurred due to a misunderstanding and the Soviet commander's arrogance. James wanted to take this guy alive. Remizov's other hand delivered a deft karate chop to James's ulna and knocked the P-88 out of his hand.

The American commando then swung a left hook at the Russian's face. It struck the rim of Remizov's padded hood, which cushioned the blow. Remizov powered himself forward and rammed the top of his skull into James's stomach. The black man's parka also reduced the impact of the head butt. Yet the blow knocked him back two steps, and he felt his foot slip on the icy ground.

Remizov grabbed an ankle and yanked James's leg forcibly. The black man's feet left the ground and he fell on his back. Again the heavy cold-weather clothing cushioned the blow. Remizov started to get up, still holding James's ankle in both hands. James braced himself on his back and thrust his other leg forward. His booted foot slammed into Remizov's ribs and knocked the paratrooper to the ground. James yanked his ankle free and tried to throw another kick at the Russian's head, but Remizov had already rolled clear of the attack.

Both men got to their feet. Fighting in heavy cold-weather garments with slippery footing was awkward, but Remizov was more accustomed to combat under such conditions due to training in Siberia. James raised a hand in a feint and attempted a karate snap kick, aiming for his opponent's groin. The insulated trousers and heavy boots slowed his leg and telegraphed the kick. Remizov countered by chopping a hand across James's ankle to stop the kick. The Russian's other hand grabbed James's right arm. The American lashed out with a left hook, but Remizov stepped forward and directed his right arm under James's triceps to parry the attack.

Remizov turned sharply and hauled James onto his hip. He tossed the black warrior in a sambo wrestling move similar to a judo hip throw. However, James held on to his opponent. The Phoenix pro hit the ground and pulled Remizov forward. The Russian folded at the middle, startled by James's tactic. The Red Army major's head bent low, and James raised his knee sharply and cracked Remizov's skull soundly.

The Russian tumbled to the ground. James rolled onto his knees and got to his feet. Remizov also rose and adopted a sambo fighting stance, knees bent, weight evenly distributed on his feet, hands held at chest level for grappling. James lifted one arm high to block, and moved his other hand to hip level for counter attack.

Remizov made the first move. He raised a boot as if to throw a kick, but only stamped it in a feint and lunged forward. He raised his arm and chopped at James's face and neck. The Phoenix fighter raised his arms swiftly, crossing his forearms to block the Russian's attack. Then James whipped a knee into Remizov's abdomen.

The paratrooper groaned, and James shoved the man's arm downward. The black commando slammed another knee kick into his opponent's belly and hooked a fist under the Russian's rib cage. Remizov doubled up from the assault but attempted a wild back fist at James. But the Chicago badass blocked the attack with an elbow to Remizov's forearm and slapped a palm over the paratrooper's shoulder. He shoved down hard and swung a knee at the nerve cluster in the Russian's armpit.

Remizov quivered from the pain, and James grabbed the rim of his opponent's hood and yanked the soldier's head back. The American thrust a *seiken* karate punch at Remizov's chin. The big knuckles of forefinger and middle finger struck hard. Remizov's knees buckled and he started to sag. James felt the man's body go limp. He let go of Remizov and tagged him on the jaw with a left hook to be certain the Russian went down. The paratrooper crashed to the ground, arms sprawled apart and legs splayed.

"Is he alive?" Manning asked as he approached James, H&K rifle canted over a shoulder.

"Just taking a nap," James assured him, breathing heavily from the battle. "Tough dude. He'll be able to talk when he comes to. Sure hope he can give us some answers."

11

"How did the Russians find you people?" Lee Fennimore wondered aloud as he marched into his office, followed by Katz and Swenson.

"Same way you knew the Soviet commando team had arrived at Vostok Station," the Phoenix Force commander answered. "The Russians have obviously been spying on this base with their satellite surveillance systems and have probably been watching the area around the volcano where the mine's located. We may as well be carrying out this mission in front of TV cameras."

Fennimore had been stunned when Phoenix Force had radioed the NSA base and informed him they were bringing in four Soviet prisoners, three of whom would need medical attention. "This whole business is incredible," Fennimore said with a sigh. He moved behind his desk and reached for a telephone.

"Who do you intend to call?" Katz demanded, his tone as sharp as a razor, with an implied warning that Fennimore had better not touch the phone without the Israeli's permission.

"I'm going to call the Navy Intelligence chief of operations and tell him what's happened," the NSA agent answered. "We'll turn the Russians over to Navy Intelligence and contact the director in Washington, D.C., or perhaps the President himself...."

"We're not contacting anyone yet," Katz insisted. He pulled a pack of cigarettes from the pocket of his wool shirt, then hesitated, remembering his labored breath during the firefight. Maybe he should quit. Reluctantly he put the Camels back in his pocket. "We have three injured Soviets in your dispensary. One of them probably won't survive. He was shot through the breastbone, and that's not a minor wound under the best of circumstances, let alone being exposed to extreme subzero temperatures. I'm not sure how bad the other two are, but we've only got one man fit enough to question right now. We've also got eight dead Soviets lying out there in the foothills of the Transantarctic Mountains. We need to be able to give a proper explanation for why those men are dead."

"Your team acted in self-defense," Fennimore said, taking his hand away from the phone. "The Russians are responsible for the illegal mining operation and they attacked you because you were about to learn the truth...."

"The man who seemed to be in charge accused the CIA of nuclear testing at the site," Katz stated. "He intended to kill me to convince the others to confess. The Soviets think we're responsible for violating treaties here and testing nuclear weapons. Someone else has been mining uranium from that hole in the ground. Whoever they are, they murdered Linnson and Collier and stirred up this political whirlpool that has the U.S. and the Soviet Union barking accusations and veiled threats at each other."

"How do we find out who the mysterious 'they' are?" the NSA man inquired.

"First, Jackson and I are going to interrogate our healthy prisoner with scopolamine," Katz began. "Hopefully we'll be able to learn some details about what the Russians are up to. If we can find out what they think about this incident, we'll be better able to mend fences with Moscow and try to repair damage done to our foreign relations with the USSR and other nations that have been threatening to muscle us out of Antarctica."

"Scopolamine's kind of tricky," Fennimore remarked. "I've heard of people dying under the influence of that drug. Besides, isn't it possible to lie under the influence of truth serums?"

"Jackson has administered scopolamine to subjects many times in the past," Katz assured the NSA agent. "None of them have ever died from the drug. It's possible to resist the effects of scopolamine, but not without giving away telltale evidence that a person has been conditioned by posthypnotic suggestion or some other method. We'll catch it if that's the case."

"You'll need a Russian translator," Fennimore said. "I have a number of men who speak the language fluently."

"So do I," Katz replied. "As for who's responsible for the mining operation and the murders, your computer complex here may be able to help us figure out who they might be. You have information on personnel stationed in Antarctica. We're looking for someone who's either still here or was here at the time of the murders. Someone involved in mining in Antarctica or with a background and expertise in mining."

"Probably mining in arctic regions," Swenson added. "That takes special equipment and unique expertise. Mining for cryolite in Greenland is a hell of a lot different from coal mining in West Virginia."

"The equipment is another possible lead," Katz said. "The type of drills used, radiation detection equipment, rails and ore cars, whatever else they'd need. Just about anyone knows more about mining than I do. Get your experts and the computers on ferreting out who might be the people we're looking for.''

"Okay," Fennimore said with a sigh. "I've never heard of anyone mining for uranium in Antarctica before. In fact, mining operations of any sort are so difficult in this climate that it's practically unknown. Mostly digs done by geologists and mineralogists to learn more about the continent.''

"People have been coming to Antarctica since 1820, and there's still a lot we don't know about it," Swenson said. "Obviously somebody found out about that uranium deposit. Maybe one of those geologists detected radioactivity in lava samples from the volcano. Doesn't matter now. What does matter is that whoever the bastards are they've already killed two people and they're probably planning to use that uranium to construct nuclear weapons. It sure doesn't sound as if these are nice people who intend to use that stuff to benefit mankind, Lee.''

"Nobody's going to argue with that, Harry," Fennimore assured him. "If the Soviets aren't responsible, the situation might be even worse than we originally thought it was. Whatever else can be said about the Russians, they haven't been irresponsible with nuclear weapons. They've had atomic bombs almost as long as we have, and they haven't used them in actual combat.''

"They've also refused to give nuclear weapons to countries that might be inclined to use them," Katz remarked. "Libya, Syria, Iraq, Vietnam, to name a few. Even the missiles in Cuba were under strict control by Moscow and not left in the hands of Castro's regime.''

"There are certainly a lot of countries that want nuclear weapons but either lack the raw materials or the technology necessary to build them," Swenson added. "One thing's for sure, nobody would be mining for uranium in Antarctica if they could get it somewhere else.''

"Washington has been having nightmares about the high probability that Khaddafi has been producing chemical weapons," Fennimore said. "It's believed Libya has the largest plant for producing chemical weapons outside of the Soviet Union. It was scary enough to think a guy like Khaddafi might be building an arsenal of nerve gas. If he or somebody like him has finally gotten access to nuclear weapons, the whole goddamn world could be in deep shit."

"Yes," Katz agreed, "and radioactive excrement at that."

DAVID MCCARTER, Gary Manning and Rafael Encizo were dangerously close to being bored. There was little they could do at the NSA base at McMurdo. Katz and James interrogated the Soviet prisoners. Fennimore and his NSA technicians ran personnel checks with their computers. The remaining three members of Phoenix Force weren't qualified to participate in either activity, so they simply had to wait.

"I wonder how many people go crazy down here," Manning remarked as he sat on a plastic-backed chair at a table in the lunchroom. "Imagine being cooped up in these little buildings for months. Go outside and there's nothing to look at but snow and ice. Not a single tree on the whole damn continent. Not even a blade of grass."

"I couldn't take it," McCarter admitted. The Briton had found one small comfort at the base. One of the vending machines in the lunchroom had Coca-Cola. He had a Coke bottle in his hand as he paced the floor. "Boring bloody place. Like going to the office and never leaving."

Encizo sat at the table and stroked the blade of a Cold Steel Tanto across a whetstone. The knife was a favorite weapon of the Cuban warrior. The heavy six-inch blade with a slanted point was designed in the manner of a samurai fighting knife. Encizo had learned to use a blade in battle long before he'd picked up a gun.

"Antarctica is my idea of hell," he said now. "Cold, bleak, always dark. Never hear children laugh. I haven't heard anyone laugh or sing since we got here. Can't even step outside and take a deep breath without a mask over your face because the air's so cold it'll freeze your lungs. God, I hate this place."

"You know," the Canadian said as he raised a cup of vending machine coffee to his lips, "the people stationed here must have a special kind of courage—scientists, Navy personnel, NSA operatives like Fennimore, explorers like Swenson and all the others who come here and stay in this environment for long months and don't leave until their tour is over."

"They've got to believe in what they're doing to make that kind of sacrifice," McCarter said. "Living in isolation like this is damn sure a sacrifice. Maybe it takes as much courage as facing the enemy on a battlefield. That little firefight we had with the Russians was almost a relief."

"This coffee isn't," Manning muttered as he put down his plastic cup and grimaced. "Why is it everywhere in the world coffee from a vending machine tastes as if it's been brewed with a sweatsock?"

"They have to do something with old sweatsocks," Encizo suggested with a grin.

Katz entered the lunchroom. He looked tired, and an unlighted cigarette hung from his lips. The Israeli still hadn't smoked since he'd returned to McMurdo, but the temptation was growing stronger. The other three men looked at him with expectation, eager to learn what Katz and James had discovered after interrogating the Soviets.

"The fellows we brought back here are Russian paratroopers," Katz explained. "Major Remizov is the man we questioned with scopolamine. He said a KGB agent named Morozov was in charge of the group. Remizov and his men had strong doubts about the claims that the CIA was conducting nuclear experiments or testing or whatever at the base of a volcano. He tried to convince Morozov to wait before charging in and accusing us of crimes against humanity. Needless to say, the KGB didn't listen to the soldiers."

"They never do," Manning replied. "So Moscow believes the U.S. is the villain."

"Moscow may have some doubts about whether America is really guilty of violating treaties here," Katz answered. "Morozov and Remizov received their orders directly from the chairman of the KGB himself. Remizov is almost positive the chairman was acting on his own without authorization from the president. So we weren't ambushed by order of the Soviet government. This was strictly a KGB action, and probably one Gorbachev would never have approved had the KGB chief gone through proper channels."

"I've read that the KGB isn't exactly thrilled with *glasnost*," Encizo remarked. "I've also read that Gorbachev is planning to replace the old head of the KGB with a new man."

"When he finds out about this stunt, I think he'll follow through with that plan immediately," Katz declared. "I also think we'll find Remizov quite willing to testify against the KGB chairman. He's very unhappy about this entire mission, and particularly upset that several of his men were killed because of the KGB. By the way, the major doesn't blame us. He realizes we acted in self-defense, and he stated, under the influence of truth serum, that he would have responded to the situation the same way if things had been reversed."

"Sounds like a decent bloke forced into an indecent assignment," McCarter commented as he took out a pack of Player's. The Briton stuck a cigarette into his mouth and flipped open his lighter. "Where's Cal?"

"You mean Jackson?" Katz replied, subtly reminding McCarter that they had to address one another by cover names during the mission.

"Hell, you know who I mean," McCarter said as he leaned forward and offered the flame of his lighter to Katz.

The Israeli had forgotten he had an unlighted cigarette in his mouth. He almost accepted McCarter's invitation, but reluctantly shook his head. The Briton shrugged and fired up his cigarette. Katz jealously watched gray smoke jet from McCarter's nostrils.

"Jackson is at the dispensary helping the medical team with the wounded Soviet paratroopers," Katz explained. "Has Fennimore turned up anything with his computer search?"

"He hasn't mentioned anything to us," Manning said with a shrug. "Maybe he doesn't know we're in here."

Swenson appeared at the doorway. The explorer grunted as he entered. He held a bottle of beer in his hand as he gestured at the vending machines. "Figured I'd find you guys in here. Is the coffee still as shitty as it used to be when I was stationed here?"

"I don't know how bad it was then," Manning answered, "but it's pretty lousy now."

"Get your goodies from the kitchen personnel," Swenson advised. "Mess hall is open twenty-four hours a day here. The people work around the clock at this base, so they have to be able to eat something when they get hungry. Usually pretty good food, too. They do that to help keep the morale up. Most people start to feel isolated and depressed in Antarctica sooner or later."

"I can't imagine why," Encizo cracked.

"Well, this might lift your spirits," Swenson announced as he pulled a chair away from a table and took a seat. "Fennimore and Eisley came up with a list of possible suspects. About two hundred names so far. I took a look at the list and recognized a few of the names. There aren't that many of us crazy suckers who specialize in extreme cold-weather operations in the Arctic and Antarctic regions. After a while you get to know some of the other guys in the same line of work. One name especially rang a bell. Olav Naakon."

"What's special about him?" McCarter inquired.

The Briton blew some smoke toward Katz. The Israeli's nostrils twitched, and he started to suck on the unlighted Camel in his mouth.

"Naakon's a Norwegian mining engineer," Swenson explained. He took a swallow of beer before he continued. "I met him on Ellesmere Island a few years ago. I was working as an adviser at one of the Canadian military bases up there. Naakon had been hired by a Canadian outfit that thought they could find gold or silver or something. He had quite a reputation in certain circles. Supposedly Naakon had been pretty successful with mining operations in Iceland."

"So why do you remember him?" Encizo asked. The Cuban slid the Tanto into a leather sheath on his belt. "Was he a sparkling conversationalist?"

"As a matter of fact, Naakon's a surly, unpleasant, antisocial son of a bitch," Swenson replied. "That's one reason I remember him. The main reason is he got into a fight with one of his workers and killed the guy with a pickax. Supposedly it was self-defense, but they shipped Naakon back to Norway because the rest of the miners didn't want to work with the bastard. Most of them figured Naakon had gotten away with murder—literally."

"Sounds like a charming character," Manning remarked. "Still, it's possible Naakon did kill the man in self-defense and that the local miners believed it was murder because they resented the fact that a foreigner had killed one of their own. He was probably a rotten boss, from what you say. That wouldn't help sway their opinion about how the killing had occurred."

"Yeah," Swenson agreed, "but after Naakon left, the mining operation discovered that the payroll for the men had been stolen. The company manager said Naakon could have taken it, but they couldn't prove he was guilty. The guy was already in Europe, and he couldn't get Interpol to track him down without any serious evidence. Anyway, the mining operation shut down and that was that."

"Interesting set of coincidences," Katz said. "Is Naakon with a Norwegian team here in Antarctica?"

"No," Swenson replied. "That's the most interesting part. Naakon is with a New Zealand outfit. Hellson Metallurgy is sponsoring an expedition to investigate Antarctica for geological purposes and to search for mineral deposits that could be used for metal alloy developments in the future. It's odd that they'd have a guy like Naakon in charge of a scientific expedition on the ice, isn't it?"

"Curious to say the least," Manning agreed. "Any idea what sort of equipment they brought?"

"Fennimore's trying to find out, but I don't think the NSA will have that kind of information," Swenson said. He finished his beer and placed the empty bottle on the table. "After all, New Zealand's an ally. We spy on the Russians most of the time here. Sometimes we try to catch some Intel by eavesdropping on the British and the French. We might even keep tabs on the Chileans and the Argentines. South American politics being what it is, we tend to be a bit suspicious of those guys. The Australians might even get surveyed from time to time, but New Zealand? The NSA doesn't figure their expeditions are anything to worry about, and they don't think the New Zealanders have any covert Intelligence worth looking into."

"The metallurgy company isn't part of the New Zealand government," McCarter pointed out. "We should try to find out some details about it—who runs it, who it does business with, that sort of thing."

"Good idea," Katz said. He took the unlighted cigarette from his mouth and tossed it into a trash can. "All right, we've got a possible lead. Let's see what else these NSA snoops can come up with before we concentrate on Naakon or anyone else."

Calvin James walked into the lunchroom. He wore a green smock stained with blood. A surgical mask hung from his neck. The black commando looked grim as he approached the other men of Phoenix Force.

"One of the Soviet soldiers died," he announced. "Chest wound, heart and lungs were damaged by bone fragments as well as the bullet. We didn't think he'd make it, and we were right. They had to amputate another Russian's leg at the knee, and he'll probably only have partial use of his right arm. They were lucky they could save it. The third guy has a broken hip and some dislodged vertebrae in his lower back. He's young, so he might make a full recovery."

"You did all you could," Encizo said gently.

"Yeah," James replied, "but it pisses me off, because none of those guys should have gotten hurt to begin with. We shouldn't have been forced to shoot it out with them. Somebody ought to pay for this shit, man."

"Somebody's going to," Katz assured him. "We'll make sure of that."

12

The Land Rover bounced over the dirt road. For miles in every direction the land seemed barren, with only a few trees and rugged tufts of grass to break the monotony of dry sand and distant hills. General Ton stared at the setting with amazement. Vietnam was a densely populated country with an abundance of rain forest. The Gibson Desert in Western Australia was unlike anything he'd seen before.

Erik Heller sat in the back of the vehicle next to Ton. The renegade American was unimpressed by the desert and eager to reach their destination. Jason House sat in the front seat with the driver, an Australian named Abe Samels was at the wheel. Another member of Heller's private syndicate, Samels was familiar with the desert. It was a very bad place to get lost in.

The blue-and-white sky was clear and almost painfully bright. The afternoon sun seemed determined to subject the men to ovenlike temperatures. The desert appeared to be too formidable to sustain life, yet insects harassed the Land Rover, and an occasional lizard or snake appeared along the road. Heller eyed the latter reptiles with fear and loathing. He despised snakes of any kind and knew that more than seventy species of poisonous serpents were native to Australia. Heller realized the snakes wouldn't attack a moving vehicle, but he was still relieved when the Land Rover passed the legless reptiles and the serpents were no longer in view. One reason he lived in New Zealand was because there were no snakes there.

"We're almost there, gents," Samels announced as he tugged on the brim of his Australian bush hat. "Enjoyin' the view, are ya?"

"It's interesting," Ton replied sincerely. The Asian raised his right arm and gestured at the desert with the big steel hook at the end of his sleeve. "Is much of Australia like this?"

"Quite a bit," Heller answered. "Australia's almost as large as the United States, but it has less than ten percent of the population. The majority of the people live along the coastal regions. Australia's an ideal place for privacy."

At last they saw a pair of small shacks in the distance. The run-down, weather-beaten structures appeared deserted at first glance, but a battered old truck was parked between the shacks, and a few chickens and some pigs wandered about the property. Two men emerged from the larger dwelling as the Land Rover approached. A bearded figure dressed only in khaki shorts and sheepskin boots carried a double-barreled shotgun canted on a shoulder. His wiry companion was clad in baggy trousers, boots and a stained undershirt. The pair waited for the Land Rover to roll to a stop.

"G'day, mates," the scrawny man greeted with a display of tobacco-stained teeth meant to pass as a smile. "Beginnin' to wonder if ya was gonna make it."

Samels put on the brakes and switched off the engine. He pushed his bush hat back high on his head and fixed his cool blue eyes on the pair with a hard stare. "Lucky for you two you didn't run off somewheres," he declared as he climbed out of the Land Rover.

"Oh, we wouldn't let Mr. Hellson down," the skinny man assured Samels. "Pleased to meet ya, sir. I'm Bart Tibbs and me mate here is Rob Ethan."

"We need to see the merchandise," Heller said in a flat, hard voice. He stepped from the Land Rover and flexed his powerful shoulders in a massive shrug. The fabric of his bush shirt stretched taut across the weight lifter's muscular chest.

Tibbs had heard that Hellson was a muscle boy, but he was still surprised by the American's physique. He didn't figure a wealthy and influential man like Edward Hellson would be such a big, strong son of a bitch. Of course rich people could afford fancy equipment and training coaches and all that. Tibbs also noticed the Smith & Wesson revolver holstered on House's hip, but the real surprise was the stocky Oriental with a steel hook for a hand.

"Who's the zipperhead?" Ethan asked in a whispery voice that was only meant for Tibbs to hear.

"Hush up, Rob," Tibbs snapped through his teeth. "He's probably the bleedin' client."

Samels gestured for the pair to move to the second shack. Tibbs and Ethan hurried to the crumbling structure. Samels turned to face Heller. The American folded his muscular arms on his chest and glared at Samels. "Couldn't you have found somebody better than those two?" the American arms dealer inquired.

"They're not bright, but they follow orders," Samels told him. "Their assignment wasn't very complicated. They just had to stay at these rat shacks a few days and baby-sit your merchandise. It doesn't take much to give the impression that this is a desert hermit's little dirt farm."

"I wouldn't be surprised if those two mental dwarfs could fail at even the most simple tasks," House muttered sourly. "I can't say I trust them to keep their mouths shut, either."

"I'm not worried," General Ton declared. The Vietnamese looked at the shack that Tibbs and Ethan had entered. "What are they doing in there?"

"Come take a look," Samels invited as he led the others to the shack.

They found Tibbs and Ethan inside the shabby structure. The interior was filthy, the wooden floor littered with pig and chicken excrement. Sunlight streamed down from holes in the tar-thatched roof. Some chickens and a pair of pigs poked about the shack, searching for food. Ethan stood in a wire-frame chicken coop, back arched as he pried the floorboards with a crowbar. Tibbs was busy cutting the suspension links to the chicken wire. The clippers snapped, and wire fencing fell to the floor.

"Bloody pests!" Ethan snapped as he kicked a curious pig and sent the animal skidding across the floor.

"Hurry up, ya lazy sods!" Samels ordered, embarrassed by the amateurish behavior of the two men he had assigned to the dirt farm.

"Just need another minute or so," Tibbs replied as he gathered up another crowbar.

The two flunkies pried up the half-rotted floorboards with little difficulty. Chunks of wood and splintered planks gave way under the assault of iron tools. Tibbs and Ethan soon dug up enough of the floor to reveal a large metal crate in a trench. They finished the excavation and pried open the lid of the metal casket.

"Here it is, gents," Tibbs announced with a grin. "All safe and sound."

Heller and Ton stepped to the edge of the trench and gazed down at the open crate. A huge steel log was packed in the container. The enormous barrel extended from a thick steel sleeve attached to the box-shaped base.

"This is your atomic cannon, General," Heller declared.

"Perhaps it looks more impressive out of the box," Ton replied dryly.

"Hook up the chains to that thing," Samels told Tibbs and Ethan. "I'll get the truck and we'll tow the cannon out."

The chore required nearly two hours. Samels's truck was a three-ton military surplus rig, which pulled the chains attached to the cannon. The barrel, recoil sleigh and breech-lock assembly weighed close to a ton. They towed the cannon from the shack and opened the canvas flap at the rear of the truck. Samels climbed out of the cab and moved to the back of the rig. He entered the trailer and turned on a crane unit installed at the opening. The crane hauled the carriage for the cannon out of the truck and lowered it to the ground. The oversize wheels on the carriage touched down, and Samels's hired hands attached the chains to the barrel so that the crane could raise the cannon and fit it into place on the carriage.

"You'll notice this weapon is designed in a manner similar to a howitzer," Heller told Ton. "It's bolted to the carriage at the cradle and elevation arc. The trail and spade allow it to be attached to the rear of a vehicle and pulled for short distances. Of course it weighs approximately two tons fully assembled, so the vehicle used to transport it must be capable of handling the load."

"Is the breech lock the same as with a howitzer?" Ton asked.

"Yes," Heller confirmed, "but the breech-lock ring has been replaced with a time-set firing mechanism. You can press the buttons for three minutes to ninety minutes. There's also a remote control unit with a range of one and a half kilometers."

"You told me the explosion wouldn't be life-threatening to those using the weapon," Ton said with a frown. "The nuclear blast isn't supposed to reach the cannon."

"If you have adequate range," Heller confirmed. "However, we suspect there may be circumstances when our clients may be forced to use the cannon on a close target and be forced to abandon the gun while firing it by a set timer or remote unit. Kubler came up with that idea and I readily agreed. This way the cannon can be concealed in a garage or in the back of a truck and detonated in the heart of a major city like an enormous time bomb."

"I see," Ton remarked as he stepped closer to examine the weapon. "You tried to think of everything. When do we test it?"

"We need to go farther into the desert," Heller answered. "A site has already been chosen. It's important that we maintain security and reduce the likelihood of the explosion being detected and investigated before we can clear the area."

"A nuclear explosion will surely be detected," Ton remarked.

"Of course," Heller agreed. "But nuclear testing has never been carried out in Australia. Not until now."

"So we'll all be part of a historic event," Ton said dryly. "One of the darker chapters of history."

"Having second thoughts, General?" Heller inquired. The renegade didn't like the idea that his client might have an attack of conscience and decide to back out of the deal.

"I'm having the same thoughts I've had since this business began," Ton replied. "The thoughts that war is a terrible thing, yet necessary if certain goals are to be achieved. The leaders of my country are too concerned with the opinions of Moscow, and the Soviets have been acting like cowards instead of revolutionaries. The task of doing what is necessary has fallen to me. I won't turn from my duty. We go on with the test, Hellson.''

OLAV NAAKON SAT at his field desk and examined the charts made by geologists based on the mineralogical readings of another volcano in the Transantarctic Mountains near Nimrod Glacier. The big Norwegian grunted with gruff satisfaction. Evidence suggested there was a strong possibility of another deposit of pitchblende among the mineral deposits at the site.

He stuck a black briar pipe in his mouth and struck a wooden match on the iron rim of the desk. Naakon held the flame to the bowl of his pipe and puffed gently as he considered the risks involved in carrying out another mining operation. So far there was no reason to believe anyone suspected the Hellson Metallurgy expedition was involved in the incident that had the entire world up in arms. Naakon had heard enough on the radio to know the Americans were blaming the Soviets and vice versa for killing the two scientists and conducting alleged nuclear testing in Antarctica.

Nuclear testing! Naakon had been astonished when he'd heard that that was the conclusion everyone was jumping to. Australia, New Zealand, Chile and Argentina were threatening to drive the U.S. and the USSR out of Antarctica. Britain, Norway and France were also upset.

It wouldn't be long before they realized the so-called underground testing was a mine shaft and that someone had been digging for pitchblende at the base of that volcano. Naturally they'd realize that the reason for covert pitchblende mining was to get uranium for nuclear weapons. The superpowers would certainly blame each other, and the rest of the world would join in, East and West taking their appropriate corners and accusing either the U.S. or the Soviet

Union, depending on which side their politics placed them. Still, the confusion wouldn't last forever, and eventually they'd start looking at other possibilities.

The sheer magnitude of the escalated attention on Antarctica presented a serious risk to Naakon's mining operations. However, Heller's supply of uranium was running low, and the renegade paid very well for the radioactive mineral. If Naakon could hit one more deposit of uranium and deliver one last shipment to Heller, he would be a millionaire. A multimillionaire with enough money to go anywhere and do anything he wanted. He could live like a king for the rest of his life and never have to stick his neck out in another dangerous or illegal project again.

Naakon figured he deserved to be rich. He'd spent most of his life handling dirty, backbreaking jobs for wealthy corporations that made the bulk of the profit from his labors. Naakon had worked on ice-covered oil derricks in the North Sea, frozen mine shafts in the Arctic and weather stations in Queen Maud Land, the Norwegian territory in Antarctica. They had been cold and bitter jobs that had paid well, but never well enough. Not until Heller had hired him.

"You know, the last time I was in this frozen dung heap I was working at Mawson Station in the Australian territory," Donaldson commented as he moved a folding chair closer to the space heater. "Miserable bloody job. At least we've had a spot of excitement on this trip."

"We don't need any more excitement," Naakon told the Australian. "This operation is supposed to be a secret. Leaving corpses stuffed in mining shafts isn't the best way to keep people from being curious about activities in Antarctica."

Donaldson stretched out his long legs and held his bare feet near the heater. The Australian's lanky frame was clad in thermal long johns. He took advantage of the opportunity to relax without being forced to wear the bulky clothing necessary to survive in the Antarctic cold. The Australian looked at Naakon and shrugged. "You told me to get rid of the bodies. I couldn't dig a hole in the bloody ice. You'd have to dynamite to get through that stuff. What was I supposed to do? Dump the corpses in a snowdrift?"

"It would have been better than putting them in the mine," Naakon replied. "Still, I should have seen to the bodies myself instead of leaving it in your hands, Donaldson. What's done is done. We would have had to abandon mining at that site, anyway, after those two Americans showed up. Dead or alive they were a problem. At least they couldn't describe our parkas, vehicles and drills."

"Nobody even knows we're responsible for that business," Donaldson snorted. "You heard the news reports. We're still safe."

"But we don't have enough uranium, yet," Naakon reminded him. "Maybe we would have if we'd been able to finish mining at the original site. There was still a fair bit of pitchblende there."

"You've been going over that volcano information," Donaldson remarked. "Thought it was agreed we'd dig there and get what we need. Hell, the lads are getting the drill ready. Equipment's all packed. You said we'd start out today."

"I'm a bit worried about this one," Naakon admitted. "So are the geologists on our team. This other volcano, near Nimrod Glacier, is active. Lava is bubbling in the crater at the peak. Besides, Nimrod isn't far from Beardmore, our other dig, and I don't like an operation that close to a murder scene. It's also pretty close to our base, which will make it easier to trace it back to us."

"Who's going to trace us, Naakon?" the Australian asked. "Nobody suspects us."

"Let me remind you that we're on the Ross Ice Shelf," Naakon said in a weary voice. "Now that's New Zealand territory, but it's not very far from McMurdo, which must be crawling with the CIA or Navy Intelligence or whatever the Americans have as part of their spy outfits. They must be spying in every direction."

"The Yankees are spying on the damn Russians," Donaldson said with a barklike laugh. "That's all they ever do. Looking for Commies under their beds. Who the hell's going to suspect a bunch of blokes from a private firm in New Zealand? Nobody frets about New Zealand. Not even Aussies. Hellson's a respected businessman in his country. Come to think of it, he's an American by birth."

"Yes," Naakon muttered. "And I know more about his background than you do. Hellson isn't even his real name. The Americans would have him drawn and quartered if they knew who he really was and what he's been up to since Vietnam."

"Really?" Donaldson raised his bushy eyebrows. "I didn't even know he'd been in Vietnam. I heard he had connections with some high-muckety-mucks in Southeast Asia, but I always reckoned those would be Thai gangsters. You know, drug lords in the jungle and all that."

"I've told you more than I should have already," Naakon declared. "If we're going to make another dig, we'd better do it now while the Americans and the Russians are still accusing each other and things are still confused enough that nobody's paying much attention to what we're doing. Of course, we can leave now with the uranium we've got, pick up our pay and be on our way. That means we'll only make about half of what we hoped to earn on this venture."

"To hell with that," Donaldson said. "After freezing our arses off down here, working our fingers to the bone and killing two men? I say we do the dig and get our full pay so we can all retire as rich as lords. This is our chance at the gold ring, Naakon. There won't be another opportunity like this."

"I know," Naakon assured him. He glanced around the plastic-wrapped walls of the hut. Fiberglass insulation was visible under the clear wrappings. "I've spent so many years living in cold-weather sheds like this. I swore this would be the last time I'd live like a damn rat and work like a pack-horse when I wasn't hibernating in an artificial burrow."

"So we do the dig?" Donaldson asked anxiously.

"We do it," Naakon confirmed. "Tell the men to get ready. We're going out on schedule. I want everything ready to hit the ice within the next two hours. Sooner if they can manage it. That includes weapons. If there are any more wandering morons like those two Americans we came across before, they may be armed this time. Might even be escorted by military personnel. Let's be ready for anything those bastards might throw at us."

"We'll be ready," Donaldson said with a wolfish grin. "I didn't mind killing two blokes, and I don't care if we have to deal with twenty more before we leave. Anybody who gets between me and two and a half million dollars is clearly suicidal."

13

The green and yellow shapes moved across the television monitor to a panel in the data center at the NSA base at McMurdo. Eisley operated the controls of the satellite receiver unit, while Katz and Fennimore watched the caravan of boxlike figures move across a field of pale yellow.

"These transmissions are from a spy satellite TV cam with a special optic-fiber night sight lens," Fennimore explained. "That's why everything's a funny color. It magnifies reflected light instead of producing its own the way infrared does."

"I see," Katz replied. Actually, he was familiar with the system. It was essentially the same as that used for the Starlite night scopes Phoenix Force had used on numerous assignments. "You're sure we're looking at vehicles from the Hellson Metallurgy camp?"

"Absolutely," Eisley declared with a nod. "I've been keeping them under surveillance ever since the computers came up with Naakon's name and Swenson told us about the Norwegian son of a bitch. I synchronized three dishes to pick up transmissions from five different satellites, including a couple of foreign models as well as our own spy birds."

"I'm impressed, Eisley," Katz said sincerely. "That's quite a trick to come up with on such short notice."

"Not as hard as it would be under ordinary circumstances," Eisley assured him. "We were already monitoring the Russians. I just rerouted some of our transmissions. When I knew the camp was on the Ross Ice Shelf not far from us, I just called Scott Base, the New Zealand station next to us, and requested the exact coordinates of the Hellson camp."

"Did they ask why you wanted the information?" Katz asked as he once again reached for the pack of Camels in his shirt pocket.

"Please don't smoke in here," Fennimore urged. "These machines are very sensitive, and smoke isn't good for them."

"Not good for anybody," Katz muttered, and left the cigarettes in his pocket.

"The New Zealanders asked, and I told them we suspected the Hellson group was getting in the way of one of our geological teams and that we just wanted to keep tabs on them in case they were up to something questionable," Eisley said with a shrug. "They knew it was bullshit, but they also know who we are, and they didn't want to piss off Uncle Sam. Luckily we get very good reception off satellite transmissions in Antarctica. No pollution in the atmosphere, no forests to block the view, and the magnetic pull from the Pole tends to hold satellites in the general area above the continent before continuing in their orbits. We've got Antarctica covered like the TV security system in a department store."

Katz was genuinely surprised by Eisley's efficiency. The NSA agent hadn't made a very good first impression with Phoenix Force. He was abrasive and unpleasant, but he knew how to handle the fancy hardware of the NSA's high tech SIGINT.

"Now here's a heat reading," Eisley continued as he punched some keys on a terminal. Another set of shapes appeared on the screen with a variety of colors—red, orange, white and blue, as well as yellow and green.

Katz examined them and noticed that some of the colors formed human outlines. "Looks like they sent a pretty large team."

"Fifteen warm bodies down there," Eisley confirmed. "Heat readings are even better than optics in Antarctica. There isn't much heat from surrounding objects to distort the readings. Anyway, they seem to be headed for Nimrod Glacier."

"That's in the Transantarctic Mountains, too," Fennimore remarked. "Do we have a heat scan of the area?"

"Yeah," Eisley said as he worked the keys to show his boss another heat reading of the glacier region. "There's nobody there. Not a soul within fifty miles in any direction aside from Naakon's crew."

The glacier reading was almost pure white, surrounded by mountains that registered no more heat than the giant sheet of ice. However, a cone of red-and-orange light burned among the lighter mountains.

"What's that?" Katz asked. He pointed the hooks of his prosthesis at the orange shape on the screen. "It seems to be inside that mountain or hill."

"Probably volcanic heat," Fennimore replied as he leaned closer to examine the screen in more detail. "Eisley, what do you think?"

"I'm eighty-five percent sure of it," the other NSA agent confirmed. "It's an active volcano in the area Naakon's group is headed for."

"The mine shaft we found was at the base of a volcano," Katz stated. "Print up a detailed map of the glacier region and bring it to Swenson. If Naakon's team is responsible for

the crimes that have already occurred, they might be involved in another mining operation at the site of this new
volcano.''

"We could get reinforcements from the Navy," Fennimore suggested. "There are only six men in your team, including Harry. Naakon's group outnumbers your team more
than two to one."

"They've also got a head start and they're closer to the
volcano, so we'll have to move quickly to catch up with
them," the Phoenix commander replied. "That means there
isn't time to get reinforcements. In fact, we'll want to leave
most of our supplies here to lighten the sledges. Besides, the
element of surprise is more important than extra man-
power. We can't catch them off guard if they see us coming
miles away. A small group has a better chance of achieving
this than a large one."

"They'll certainly reach the volcano before you do,"
Eisley said. "Of course, maybe it would be better if you can
catch them out there digging for uranium."

"That's rather what we hope will happen," Katz assured
him. "We also want to bring them back here for interrogation. That means our first concern is to get evidence that
Naakon and his people are the scum we're after, or enough
evidence to scratch them from the list of suspects and continue looking elsewhere. Our second concern is to learn who
they're working for. But there isn't enough time to discuss
this now. See to those maps and meet us in the bay area."

"You got it, Ginsberg," Eisley said with a nod. He shifted
his swivel chair to another control panel and started a computer scan of the data on the screen.

The memory banks would give all available topographi-
cal information about the area on the screen. A printout
would produce a detailed map with the approximate size of
landmarks and additional information about the terrain.

Katz left the NSA data center. Computers and other high tech equipment weren't his field of expertise, and he was glad to get away from the SIGINT hardware.

Phoenix Force had been created to serve largely as an enforcement unit. Katz and his teammates were better suited for battlefields than computer centers. They specialized in direct action, and it seemed the time had come for them to go into the field and stalk a group of men who might very well be the enemy. Katz felt the familiar rush of anticipation as he hurried to inform the other members of Phoenix Force.

TWO SLEDGES RACED across the ice. Phoenix Force and Harold Swenson had once again ventured into the frozen, hostile environment of Antarctica. They'd left the base at McMurdo as quickly as they could pack the necessary gear and bundle up to protect themselves from the killer cold. Swenson had been reluctant to set out on the ice with a minimum of equipment, but Katz had insisted they didn't have time to pack the tent, rations, extra clothing and other gear Swenson had brought in case the team was stranded on the ice due to unforeseen circumstances. They would remain in radio contact with the NSA base, and Katz assured Swenson they would call for help if needed. Fennimore had told him a rescue team would be on alert and ready to hit the ice if the Phoenix unit sent out an SOS.

The Ross Ice Shelf terrain was mostly smooth and easily traveled by the ice sledges. With three men in each vehicle and a minimum of gear, the sledges raced across the glossy white surface, leaving behind the glowering peaks of Erebus and Terrar. Ahead, in the distance, the ivory sentinels of the Transantarctic Mountains stood like an army of great white colossi crowned by halos of colored light.

"Holy shit!" James exclaimed as he pointed at the shimmering spectacle in the sky. "Look at that!"

The sight startled the other members of Phoenix Force, as well, except for Gary Manning, who told James it was nothing to worry about. Swenson calmly brought the lead sledge to a halt, and Manning followed his example. The men gazed up at the mysterious luminosity, which seemed to vibrate in the dark sky.

"It's the aurora australis," Swenson announced. "Quite a light show, isn't it?"

"I've seen the aurora borealis in Canada," Manning said. "You usually don't see it unless you're fairly far north."

"You wouldn't believe what I thought when I first looked up at those lights," Rafael Encizo commented sheepishly.

"Yeah," Swenson said with a trace of amusement. "I think this might be how all those silly stories about a secret UFO base at the South Pole got started. You ever hear any of those idiotic theories?"

"I never pay any attention to that kind of crap," James said. "I just thought it looked like ball lightning at first."

"Well, I've seen the northern lights in Scotland," McCarter confessed, "but it never looked like this. It looked like peaks and swirls of light in the sky. This is more like the descriptions of Saint Elmo's fire."

"Probably a similar phenomenon," Swenson said. "The southern lights are particularly impressive here because we're right next door to the South Magnetic Pole and there's no pollution in the sky or city lights to interfere with the view. Something more important is associated with the lights. Ginsberg, try to radio Fennimore."

"All right," Katz replied as he reached for the radio unit. He switched on the transmit button and held the microphone to his mask. "Apple Pie, this is Ice Rover. Come in, Apple Pie. Over."

The radio crackled with static. There was no reply from the NSA base. Katz repeated the transmission, but received no answer. The static just got louder.

Swenson grunted. "I was afraid of that."

"You mean the lights affect radio transmissions?" Katz asked as he tried the radio one last time.

"Aurora phenomena—north or south—follow the cycle of sunspots," Manning explained. "You've heard how sunspots can affect transmissions of radios, telegraphs and telephones? The aurora creates even greater interference due to the concentrated disturbance in terrestrial magnetism during the time of the light display."

"In other words, we've been cut off from contact with McMurdo," Encizo said grimly.

"You got it," Swenson confirmed with a nod. "Those pretty lights in the sky have sabotaged our lifeline by radio to the NSA base. We get in any kind of trouble, have any sort of emergency, we're on our own. No rescue team will be sent and we can't send out an SOS for one. Since we don't have the tent, extra supplies and all the rest of the stuff you guys forced me to leave back at the base . . . well, I'd say we could be up a frozen shit creek close to a hundred degrees below zero without a decent icicle for a paddle."

"Oh, shit," James muttered. "That means we take the additional risk and go on, or wait for the aurora to subside. Right?"

"Those are the choices," Swenson said, nodding. "I've been with you guys long enough to know which one you'll pick. You crazy bastards want to go on despite the additional risk, don't you?"

"We have to," Katz confirmed. "The mission comes before personal safety. You ought to know that, Harry. You spent enough time in the military and Intelligence."

"Yeah," Swenson answered with a sigh, "but I'm retired. Well, I just hope nothing happens to these sledges before we can reestablish radio contact with McMurdo. It'll be one hell of a long walk back in some mighty cold weather."

"Nobody said this job would be easy," McCarter commented.

"Nobody mentioned the possibility of losing all our fingers and toes due to frostbite," Encizo said with a miserable groan.

"Hell, that won't matter much if we're dead," Manning told him. "That's a risk we ought to be used to by now."

"I just don't want to die of bloody boredom," McCarter declared. "Are we going on or just sitting around here talking about it?"

"Let's go," Katz announced. "This mission won't be any easier if we waste time that needs to be spent catching up with Naakon."

14

Olav Naakon watched the drill rig attached to the lead tractor. The giant bit tore into the layers of ice at the base of the volcano. Ice spit from the drill like chips of white rock. Naakon marched through ankle-deep snow to approach a pair of men by the drill. The uniform worn by the group consisted of gray parkas with matching trousers, boots, masks and gloves. They didn't wear name tags or emblems to identify nationality. Naakon couldn't tell which man was which unless he recognized an individual's voice.

"Dubou?" he asked, addressing the man examining a geologist's chart of the volcano. "How far can we drill without hitting lava?"

"This is a central-vent volcano, *Monsiour*," Dubou replied as he folded the chart. "Drilling at the base should be safe until we go deep enough to hit a dike or the chimney in the center of the volcano. The magma chamber itself is probably hundreds of meters under the volcano. Eventually there may be a risk of drilling into a laccolith. That could be quite dangerous."

"As if the uranium wasn't enough to worry about," Naakon muttered. He glanced around, searching for Donaldson. The Australian managed to swagger even when dressed in bulky cold-weather gear, which made him recognizable even from a distance.

"Looking for me, mate?" Donaldson's familiar voice asked from the rear of the drill tractor.

Naakon turned to stare at the mask and goggles of the cocky Australian. Donaldson stood at the tractor near the drill bit. He held a large stainless-steel wrench in a gloved fist.

"I don't want this drill to dig more than two meters," the Norwegian declared. "Dubou will examine rock samples and estimate how close we are to lava."

"It's your show," Donaldson assured him. "This volcano doesn't seem like much to me, but we'll do it your way."

Naakon glanced up at the volcano. The cone of rock was roughly two hundred feet high. It wasn't very impressive in size, but the columns of ash and smoke from the mouth of the crater worried Naakon. The damn thing was an active volcano. Regardless of its size, the lava within was bubbling at temperatures that exceeded a thousand degrees. The geologists had assured him that the volcano showed no signs of an impending eruption, but Naakon was still leery of it and didn't intend to take any more chances than necessary.

The other men in the team were positioned at different points in the area. A pair of mineralogists had climbed the rock wall to take samples and Geiger counter readings near the crater. Four other men were on sentry duty during the dig. The others were busy helping with the drill rig or checking equipment at the ice sledges and a second tractor rig with a trailer bin attached. Most of them frequently gazed up at the stunning display of southern lights that continued to shimmer in the night sky above them.

"Pay attention to your work, damn it!" Naakon shouted at one of the sentries gaping at the light show instead of watching for unwanted visitors.

He repeated the order in German and signaled for Dubou to translate the warning in French, as well. Naakon wasn't sure what nationality the sentry was, but he was certain the man wasn't Norwegian. There was only one other Norwegian in the unit, and Naakon knew the man wasn't on guard duty. He had too much respect for the national intelligence average of his countrymen to waste a Norwegian on a task a lesser being could handle just as easily.

The sentries seemed unhappy with their assignment. Naakon didn't blame them. Each man was perched on a slippery rock ledge along the face of one of the surrounding mountains. They were all experienced ice climbers and wore crampons strapped to their boots and safety harnesses with ropes secured to the rock wall by pitons. Nonetheless, it was hardly a desirable station to stand on an icy surface, hundreds of feet from the frozen ground with a terribly cold and merciless wind to contend with.

Unpleasant job, but Naakon had insisted that sentries be posted during the dig. The guards had assault rifles in protective scabbards and Steiner binoculars. Naakon carried his pistol in a pouch on his belt, and other weapons were stored among the gear in the ice sledges. Yet Naakon was less worried about human opponents than the possible hazards of drilling for radioactive materials in an active volcano.

One of the mineralogists on the rock wall of the volcano waved at Naakon with a walkie-talkie in his gloved fist. The Norwegian reached for the radio unit on his belt, but realized the beeper must have failed on his walkie-talkie thanks to the aurora australis. Naakon groaned with misery as he approached the foot of the volcano and grabbed the line.

He attached the line to a carabiner on his climbing harness and wound the rope around his waist. Then he strapped a set of crampons to his boots. The steel spikes on the soles of his feet allowed him surer footing as he climbed up the ice-coated surface of the rock wall. The Norwegian swung an ice ax occasionally to secure a temporary handhold with the pick end of the blade as he scaled the volcano. He was an accomplished mountaineer and no stranger to ice climbing, but scrambling up the side of an active volcano made the familiar chore unnerving.

A wave of hot air rushed into Naakon's masked face as he reached the ledge where the two mineralogists stood waiting for him. The heat came from the crater. It was a shocking contrast to the bitter subzero cold. The men on the ledge pulled the rope to help haul Naakon up the rock wall.

"I hope this is important," the Norwegian declared as he dug the spikes on his boots into the icy ledge.

"I believe it is, *Mein Herr*," a German mineralogist named Gerber said. He held a Geiger counter in one hand. "The readings here are very low. Much lower than those reported by the scientists who previously investigated this volcano. With the greater activity in the volcano vent, the radioactive level should be higher."

"How do you explain that, Herr Gerber?" Naakon inquired, not certain he wanted to hear the answer.

"The pitchblende in the lava may have been churned around and forced deeper into the lava," the German explained. "Or it's possible the previous evaluations were incorrect, probably based on faulty readings of the mineralogist's Geiger counter. The gauge on the machine may have been damaged, or the man's parka may have been slightly radioactive from other pitchblende sites."

"We're not going to drill inside the heart of the volcano, so this doesn't change much," Naakon said.

"Except the deposit of uranium in the pitchblende will probably be much smaller than we had anticipated," Peters, the other mineralogist, informed him. "That's not exactly good news, Mr. Naakon."

"Then we'll dig for what we can get," the Norwegian replied gruffly. "We've come this far and—"

"Naakon!" a voice shouted from the foot of the volcano. The howling wind almost blotted out the voice, but a trace of an Australian accent still identified the speaker. "Naakon! A sentry spotted somebody headed this way!"

The Norwegian stared down at Donaldson. The Australian looked like a cartoon insect from that angle. Head covered by the parka hood, face concealed by a protective mask with bug-eyed goggles, Donaldson seemed tiny and less than human from a hundred and fifty feet.

"How many are there and which direction?" Naakon shouted back.

"He saw a bloody ice sledge, and he didn't tell me how many bastards are on the goddamn thing!" Donaldson bellowed. "The radio still isn't working! He just shouted down to me!"

Naakon glanced around at the sentry posts. Two guards were once again admiring the southern lights in the sky. Another seemed bored with his station, but at least he was paying attention to the surrounding area. The fourth sentry had opened his rifle scabbard and extracted an Australian version of a Belgian FAL. He slapped a palm on the magazine and raised the walnut stock to his shoulder. The guard's arctic glove held the pistol grip, trigger finger ready to fire as the man took aim at a target approaching from the south.

A rifle shot erupted with a loud roar as a high-velocity round broke the stillness. The guard dropped his rifle. He staggered slightly and turned to reveal a scarlet bullet hole in the left breast of his parka. The sentry didn't cry out or clutch at the wound. He fell silently from the rock ledge. His body plunged eight feet before the safety line attached to his climbing harness was pulled taut and stopped the descent.

The corpse dangled limply at the end of the line, causing it to resemble a puppet immobilized by tangled strings.

GARY MANNING SAW the man drop from the mountain. He watched through the telescopic sights of his H&K PSG1. The Canadian sharpshooter had drilled the sentry through the heart. Manning, McCarter and Encizo had approached the enemy position from the south on foot. They were using the rock outcroppings for camouflage while the other members of the Phoenix Force team approached openly in an ice sledge to distract any sentries posted by Naakon's drilling team. The assumption that their quarry would have lookouts posted had proved correct.

The guard had aimed his rifle at the sledge, threatening Katz, James and Swenson. Manning hadn't hesitated to take the guard out with a rifle shot. Now he swung his H&K toward another sentry who had seized a weapon scabbard. The cross hairs of Manning's scope marked the guard's chest. Manning altered the aim slightly and found the padded canvas sheath that contained the man's assault rifle. He triggered two shots.

Both bullets tore into the sentry's scabbard and sent the man's sheath and rifle hurtling from his grasp. The guy cried out in surprise and fear as he saw his weapon spin into the air and fall to the ground more than two hundred feet from his position. He tried to sprawl on his belly along the ledge, but the rock shelf was too narrow and slippery. The man screamed as he slid off the edge. He thrashed his arms and kicked wildly. His safety line stopped his fall abruptly, and he hung helplessly suspended by the rope attached to his climbing harness. The man swung slowly at the end of the line like an oversize pendulum.

The men in Naakon's drilling outfit exploded into frenzied activity. Most ran for cover behind ice sledges and tractor rigs. Some grabbed rifles and handguns from padded cases and belt pouches. Others simply made do with wrenches or lengths of steel pipe, since they were unable to reach the firearms cache. The sentry on the mountain perch to the south was closest to Manning's position and swung his assault rifle toward the rock formation where the Canadian crouched for cover.

The enemy rifleman triggered a burst of full-auto fire. Ice and rock shattered as 7.62 mm slugs hammered Manning's shelter. The Canadian Phoenix fighter ducked low and listened to the whine of ricochets, feeling the rock formation vibrate from the impact of multiple high-velocity bullets.

Encizo moved from the cover of another boulder while the sentry was preoccupied in an effort to blow away Manning. The Cuban raised an M-16 assault rifle, black plastic stock braced against his shoulder. He quickly lined up the front and rear sights and centered on the sentry's upper torso. Encizo triggered a three-round burst and nailed the gunman in the chest. The sentry dropped his weapon and toppled backward to sprawl across the rock ledge.

"Throw down your weapons and step forward with your hands raised!" David McCarter shouted as he moved to a pile of boulders near the volcano. "No tricks! We know there are fifteen of you bastards, so don't think you can hide and try to catch us by surprise!"

The Phoenix Force commandos crept closer to the enemy position. They were burdened with weaponry. All three men carried rifles, Uzi machine pistols, side arms, grenades and spare magazines for their weapons. They checked on the remaining sentry to discover the guy had decided he was a sitting duck and had chosen to abandon his post rather than risk being picked off like his comrades.

Katz, James and Swenson approached from the southeast in their ice sledge. They parked the vehicle next to a cluster of boulders. James climbed from the rig with an M-16 in his fists. A micro-Uzi hung from a shoulder strap, a Walther P-88 was in a pouch on his belt and a case on his left hip contained four 40 mm grenade shells for the M-203 launcher attached to the underside of the M-16 barrel. Katz didn't carry a rifle because the padded cover over his prosthesis prevented him from using the steel hooks at the end of his right arm. With only one hand to rely on, Katz was armed with an Uzi machine pistol and his P-88, with some grenades and spare ammo.

The Israeli stepped from the sledge and gestured for Swenson to stay with the vehicle. The explorer shook his head. Swenson was only armed with his .45, but he didn't intend to stay out of the fight. He joined Katz and James as they headed for the volcano. The gunshots announced that either Naakon's forces or the other three Phoenix commandos had started shooting. Probably both sides were exchanging fire. They could only hope any casualties had been among the enemy.

A few of Naakon's people opened fire when they glimpsed movement in the rocky terrain. Bullets sparked off rock and tore out fragments of ice, but none found human flesh. Other men in the Norwegian's team realized they were just wasting ammunition. They held their fire and waited for the mysterious opponents to present a clearer target.

Naakon himself was still positioned near the summit of the volcano. Gerber and Peters shared the ledge with the ringleader. They looked at him as if he ought to know what they should do. Naakon was tempted to throw the two mineralogists off the volcano just to have more room on the ledge. They couldn't descend the rock wall without exposing themselves to enemy fire. If they climbed higher, they would be at the rim of the crater, with molten lava waiting for them to fall in. The only option seemed to be to stay put and hope a better choice of action would be possible.

At the foot of the volcano, a gunman poked his Australian assault rifle around the nose of a tractor and leaned forward to try to get a better view of the approaching invaders. Manning spotted the gunman and got his hooded head in the cross hairs of his H&K scope. The Canadian triggered his rifle and pumped two 7.62 mm rounds through the guy's skull.

The gunman fell from view, and more enemy rifles swung toward Manning's position and opened fire. The Canadian ducked as a wave of high-velocity slugs raked his shelter. McCarter and Encizo took advantage of the distraction to lob two concussion grenades at the enemy vehicles. The twin blasts erupted near the tractor and a sledge. Explosions knocked opponents to the ground. Some screamed when their eardrums burst. Others were simply bowled over, but otherwise unharmed, ears protected by the padded hoods of their parkas.

One member of the drilling unit panicked and jumped into an ice sledge. Donaldson screamed at the man to stop, and threatened to shoot him if he tried to run out on them. The terrified man ignored the order, aware that Donaldson didn't have a gun and that it was unlikely any of the others would be willing to satisfy the Australian.

The sledge bolted forward and headed east in a blindly desperate effort to flee. Another member of the team was hiding behind the vehicle. Stunned by the blast and suffering a ruptured eardrum, the man didn't even notice his cover rolling away. Encizo and Manning both spotted the exposed figure, but held their fire. The guy didn't present any danger and appeared to be disabled by the grenade explosions.

Snow spit from the treads of the sledge as the panicked driver raced for a narrow pass in the mountains. The guy must have thought he could make it, although what he would do once he got into the mountains would be a problem. He was heading straight for the interior of the continent—certain suicide. Then, suddenly, an object streaked from a nearby pile of rocks. The driver barely glimpsed the blur of movement before the projectile crashed to earth directly in front of the sledge.

The M-203 grenade shell exploded with a blast of orange light and a mighty roar. The sledge was thrown sideways and tumbled end over end. The driver shrieked as he was crushed under the machine.

Calvin James lowered his M-16 and opened the breech to eject the shell casing. Smoke rose from the grenade launcher as James fished another 40 mm shell from the case on his hip. He reloaded the grenade launcher and pointed the assault rifle at the enemy position. The Chicago commando fired a short burst of 5.56 mm rounds at the remaining vehicles in Naakon's unit. It was more a warning than an attack. He wanted to let the enemy know they were surrounded and that any attempts to flee would meet with the same fate as the man in the sledge.

Manning, Encizo and McCarter lobbed more concussion grenades at the enemy position while James and Katz got closer to Naakon's group. Several members of the Norwegian's team were already dead, unconscious or otherwise removed from the battle. Within less than two minutes Naakon's team had virtually been cut to half strength. Most of the men who remained on their feet were dazed and disoriented by the grenade blasts.

Manning and James pelted the enemy vehicles with rifle rounds to keep Naakon's people pinned down while the other members of Phoenix Force charged forward. Encizo and McCarter attacked from the south. Katz and Swenson closed in from the east. They hit the enemy shelter at both ends to catch their opponents in a cross fire.

McCarter reached the position first and thrust the stubby barrel of an Uzi machine pistol around the rear of the second ice sledge. The Briton and Encizo had left their rifles behind. The micro-Uzis and their pistols were better suited for close combat. McCarter spotted two opponents still on their feet. One held an assault rifle and tried to aim the weapon at Manning. The British ace didn't hesitate. He triggered the micro-Uzi and blasted a trio of 9 mm rounds into the gunman's rib cage.

The man screamed and spun around from the impact of the bullets. He still clutched his assault rifle, so McCarter nailed him point-blank in the chest with another burst of deadly hornets. The Aussie assault weapon flew from the triggerman's hands as he thrust his arms wide apart and fell backward onto the snowy carpet. The other man stared at the machine pistol in McCarter's fists and glanced down at his slain comrade. He raised his hands in surrender.

"Good decision, mate," the Briton informed him.

Encizo swung around the end of the trailer bin to find only one opponent. The guy was fumbling with the magazine on his assault rifle in a clumsy attempt to reload. Encizo whistled sharply to get the man's attention, then pointed his machine pistol at the gunman's mask and goggles.

"Merde!" Dubou exclaimed when he saw the Cuban ready to blast him into oblivion.

He dropped the rifle and raised his hands. Encizo stepped closer and gestured for Dubou to face the vehicle. The French geologist understood and placed his mitten-clad hands on the trailer. He adopted a spread-eagle posture.

"Do not shoot, *Monsieur*," the Frenchman urged. "I surrender."

A burst of M-16 shots snarled as James noticed that one of the figures on the rock ledge near the volcano summit had drawn a handgun. Peters, the British mineralogist, had unsheathed a .38 Special and tried to fire at Encizo, but James had been faster and more accurate with his assault rifle. Peters jerked from the impact of three 5.56 mm projectiles in the center of his chest. His arms rose to shoulder level and pulled the revolver trigger. The Smith & Wesson roared and fired a harmless bullet at the shimmering southern lights. Peters's corpse fell from the ledge as far as the safety line permitted.

Encizo hadn't flinched when he'd heard the pop of James's M-16, aware that the enemy was armed with larger-caliber assault rifles. However, the unexpected boom of the .38 from the volcano did catch his attention. He swung the micro-Uzi around to confront the possible threat, and saw Peters dangling from the rope attached to his climbing harness. The Cuban was distracted for only a second, long enough for Dubou to take action.

The Frenchman pushed away from the trailer and lashed a savate kick at Encizo. The edge of Dubou's boot struck the micro-Uzi and sent it flying from Encizo's grasp. Dubou lashed out with his other foot and slammed his toe into Encizo's abdomen. The Cuban's heavy parka protected him from the full force of Dubou's kick, but he groaned and started to double up from the unexpected blow.

Dubou threw a left hook at Encizo's face. The Phoenix warrior ducked under the other man's fist and lunged forward to drive a shoulder into Dubou's breadbasket. Using his arms, Encizo encircled Dubou's legs above the knees to prevent him from throwing another savate kick. He pulled hard to yank Dubou off his feet, then pivoted to throw the Frenchman into the trailer.

Encizo heard Dubou gasp when he slammed into the steel frame of the vehicle. The Cuban drove a fist into his opponent's torso in the general area of the solar plexus. It was impossible to judge exact targets with an opponent dressed in a bulky cold-weather parka. With his other hand, Encizo grabbed the rim of Dubou's hood, gripping it like a handle and smashing the back of Dubou's head into the trailer. Then he grabbed the parka hood with both hands and whipped a knee between Dubou's legs. The Frenchman moaned in agony from the blow to his genitals.

The Phoenix pro slammed his opponent's skull into the trailer once more, harder than before. Encizo nearly repeated the action a third time, but refrained for fear of killing Dubou. He held on to the geologist's hood with one hand and yanked the man's head forward as he raised his other fist in a short uppercut. The punch caught Dubou squarely on the chin, and he collapsed against the trailer, unconscious.

Katz and Swenson charged the drilling rig and remaining tractor. A figure appeared near the drill frame, and Katz fired his micro-Uzi. Bullets sparked off metal, and the figure retreated behind the machinery. The Phoenix commander noticed another figure on all fours near the drill bit at the base of the volcano. The man was obviously stunned and armed only with a large steel wrench. Katz concentrated on the opponents behind the drill rig because one or more might be fully alert and carrying firearms.

Swenson galloped to the opposite end of the tractor as fast as he could manage in the deep snow. With years of experience in the formidable weather and quite accustomed to the bulky cold-weather garments, Swenson moved rapidly under conditions that would have severely hampered most men. He gripped his .45 in both hands as he jogged around the corner.

A burly figure in gray suddenly appeared in front of Swenson. The veteran explorer pointed his Colt. 45 and squeezed the trigger as a reflex reaction to the unexpected danger. He didn't even realize he'd shot the gunman until he saw him collapse to the ground with a bullet hole in his chest.

Two other figures, lifeless or unconscious, already lay on the crimson-streaked snow behind the tractor. Another opponent was positioned hear the drill frame. Startled by Swenson and the fact that his comrade lay dead at the explorer's feet, the man swung the barrel of his assault rifle toward Swenson. The explorer cursed under his breath as he ducked for cover and fired a hasty, unaimed shot at the enemy gunman.

Swenson missed his opponent by more than a foot, but the pistol shot forced the rifleman to drop into a crouch and trigger his rifle off-target. Bullets hammered the steel body of the tractor near Swenson's position. The explorer gasped as a ricochet round sizzled scant inches from his nose. Swenson had had no idea what he was getting into when he'd been recruited to assist the five mysterious commandos on the mission. He sure as hell didn't expect to find himself in the middle of one gun battle after another in Antarctica.

The enemy rifleman had turned his attention from Katz to Swenson and had momentarily forgotten the Israeli. That was a fatal mistake. Katz moved to the drill frame and trained his machine pistol on the gunman. He blasted a trio of 9 mm slugs between the thug's shoulder blades. The man dropped his rifle and staggered forward three steps before he fell facedown into the snow. Backbone shattered, spinal cord severed, the man was instantly thrown into shock and died within a few seconds.

Katz's hood, mask and goggles all but blocked out his peripheral vision, yet he glimpsed movement to the left. Donaldson had been stunned by the grenade explosions, but he had managed to clear his head and get to his feet. The Australian was still armed only with a steel wrench, hardly a match for the Israeli's machine pistol under ordinary circumstances. However, Katz hadn't gunned down Donaldson when the Australian was still on his hands and knees, still dazed. That had given Donaldson an opportunity to get behind the Phoenix commander. If he could get close enough, the wrench could be as lethal as a firearm. Donaldson had used the improvised weapon on Linnson and Collier. It would work just as well on the one-handed commando.

When Katz turned, Donaldson swung the wrench. Steel clanged on steel, and the tool knocked the micro-Uzi out of Katz's left hand. The Australian snarled with rage and slashed a backhand sweep at the Phoenix fighter's head. Katz ducked and the steel club whistled above his head. It brushed fabric at the peak of his parka hood, but failed to connect with the Israeli's skull.

Katz thrust his prosthesis forward. The artificial limb was sheathed in a padded sock that rendered the hooks useless, but the steel cap at the end of his arm struck like the punch of a heavyweight prizefighter. Donaldson gasped from the blow and raised the wrench to retaliate, but Katz grabbed the Aussie's wrist with his left hand, preventing him from swinging the makeshift club.

The Israeli's prosthesis rammed an uppercut under his opponent's ribs. Donaldson groaned as the wind was driven from his lungs. Katz shoved the Australian's arm down and raised a knee to meet it. The hard blow dislodged the wrench from the Australian killer's fingers.

With his free hand Donaldson swung a short hook at Katz's jaw. He broke free of Katz's grip on his wrist and slammed a fist into the Israeli's chest. Katz was propelled backward by the blows and staggered awkwardly in the deep snow. His feet slid on the icy surface as he struggled to keep his balance.

"You're dead, cripple!" Donaldson snarled as he charged forward and swung a boot at the Israeli's groin.

Katz jabbed his prosthesis low and punched the steel plate into Donaldson's shin to block the kick. The Aussie killer howled from the sharp pain that streaked up his leg. He lashed a left hook at Katz's head. The Phoenix commander countered with a karate block. His left forearm parried Donaldson's punch and increased the attacker's momentum. Donaldson stumbled past Katz, and the Israeli slammed his prosthesis into the small of the man's back.

The Australian plunged forward, off balance, heading directly for the overturned ice sledge, which was still running. He screamed when he saw what lay before him and raised his arms to protect his face as he fell into the whirling blades. The powerful treads raked steel teeth through the fabric, flesh and bone. Donaldson's arms were chopped off in an instant. Blades slashed the parka hood and mask. His shriek ended with a liquid gurgle, and blood spewed from the treads in a crimson fountain.

"It's over!" Encizo shouted as he pointed his micro-Uzi at the two figures remaining on the ledge near the top of the volcano. "You bastards are finished!"

"Get your asses down here!" Swenson added. He raised his Colt .45 and aimed it at Naakon and Gerber.

Naakon stared down at the devastation below. It was hard to believe that only five or six opponents had taken out his entire team. Naakon considered his options. Death, or life in a maximum-security prison. Neither fate was appealing, but at least the former offered him a chance to go down fighting. Gerber didn't share his boss's opinion. The German held up his hands to show he was unarmed, then grabbed the main line to descend to the ground.

"What's that other son of a bitch up to?" Swenson wondered out loud as he stared up at the Norwegian.

Naakon swung his ax and drove it into ice and rock. He climbed higher and inched his way around the cone of the volcano near the crater. Manning and James emerged from cover and approached their teammates. The Canadian raised his H&K rifle and followed Naakon's progress through the telescopic lens.

"Hey, man," James said as he watched Manning. "You're not going to shoot that sucker off the rocks, are you?"

"I just want to see what he does," Manning replied, rifle stock braced on his shoulder, barrel trained on Naakon.

"He's trying to get to the other side of the volcano," Katz observed as he watched Naakon creep along the cone. "Let him know it's a waste of time."

"Right," Manning replied, slightly altering the aim of his rifle before he squeezed the trigger.

A 7.62 mm slug smashed ice and chipped rock six inches from Naakon's right foot. Manning raised the sights and fired another round, blasting a bullet close to Naakon's hand. The Norwegian froze in his tracks, aware the shots were a warning that the sharpshooter below could pick him off if he continued to move around the volcano. Calmly Naakon drew his M-38 pistol and swung it toward the figures below.

Manning saw him pull the gun, trained the cross hairs on the next target and triggered the H&K. A bullet tore through

Naakon's biceps. The Norwegian's fist popped open, and the M-38 fell from his hand and dropped to the ground two hundred feet below. Naakon cried out and braced his wounded arm against his torso. Bone had been shattered and the pain was terrible. He clung to the shaft of the pickax desperately. The point was still lodged in ice and rock. Naakon's eyes watered and his head spun. He could barely think as the pain increased. He felt close to losing consciousness.

"Can't go around," he mumbled to himself through clenched teeth in his native language. "Never make it down. I'll have to go higher."

Only half aware of what he was doing, Naakon swung the ax and dug in with his spiked boots. He hauled himself up the rock surface and hooked the pickax onto a ridge of stone. A furnace seemed to open as he dragged himself onto the rim of the crater. The heat started to revive him as he swung his legs over the other side. Then, too late, he realized what he was doing.

Naakon's vision cleared and he stared into the bubbling pool of molten lava. He screamed and twisted his body in a wild effort to swing up from the crater. The violent movement only served to dislodge his ax. Naakon cried out in terror as he plunged into the smoking inferno. The lava sucked at his body, filled his open mouth and poured into his throat. It ate through flesh and bone and consumed him in the blink of an eye.

"Oh, my God!" Swenson exclaimed as he stared up at the smoldering cone of rock. "Why did he jump?"

"I'm not sure," Manning confessed as he lowered his rifle. "But I'm sure as hell not going up there to try to pull him out of the lava and ask him about it."

15

Aaron Kurtzman rolled his wheelchair to the radio receiver in the communications center of Stony Man Farm. He growled an unintelligible complaint as he steered around a swivel chair in his path. The wheelchair had a battery pack and he didn't have to push the wheels, but Kurtzman had learned he could maneuver the chair better manually when unexpected objects were in his way.

His deft fingers hit the keyboard on the receiver as a blue light continued to flash in time to an annoying buzzer. Kurtzman punched out the numbers for the scrambler code. The radio transmission was an ultrasecurity, laser-intensity frequency. The sender transmitted to a radio satellite that scrambled the transmission and transferred a jumbled message on the special frequency of the Stony Man receiver. Kurtzman had to insert the proper code to descramble the reception and program the transmitter to use the same laser-intensity frequency in order to communicate.

"Alpha One, this is Cold Duck," a deep voice with an electronic quiver to each word announced. "Do you read me? Over."

"Read you, Cold Duck," Kurtzman said into the microphone. "Hold a minute. I'll get the boss. Over."

Bear started to roll the chair away from the radio to try to find Brognola. He turned the chair toward the entrance and spied the Fed in the doorway. As usual, an unlighted cigar jutted from Brognola's mouth as he marched into the commo center and eagerly approached the radio unit. "Is that Phoenix?" he asked.

"Yeah," Kurtzman confirmed. "Code name Cold Duck. I bet Antarctica can freeze anybody's feathers."

"Well, the President would like to know how things are going down there," Brognola said as he reached for the radio mike. "Who's on the line? Katz?"

"Can't tell," Kurtzman answered. "The voice is electronically distorted, which means that everybody who uses this frequency sounds like a robot with a frog in its throat. By the way, I'd appreciate it if you'd push the swivel chair back after you're done."

"Sorry, Aaron," Brognola replied. "I'll try to remember in the future. Hang around. We might need you to run some computer checks and conjure up some information with your magical keyboards."

Kurtzman grunted in gruff agreement. Brognola keyed the transmit button on the microphone and called for Cold Duck to come in.

"We've had some progress, Alpha One," the voice declared. "Original objectives of the mission have been completed. We learned who's responsible for the problems. We have ample proof, and we learned why they're doing it. Over."

"You don't sound as if you intend to come home just yet, Cold Duck," Brognola observed. "What's up? Over."

"Discovered the tip of an iceberg here," the voice explained. "We're still interrogating prisoners and getting information. Can't give many details even on a secure line. We plan to contact Soviet and New Zealand bases here."

"The Soviets and New Zealanders?" Brognola exclaimed. "Why those two? Are the Russians involved or the New Zealanders? Last I heard they weren't exactly allies."

"Neither government's involved," the Phoenix spokesman said. "The KGB caused us some trouble, and we want to make sure they don't repeat it during the mission. A meeting's a good way to ease international tensions, especially if we share some information and evidence with the Soviets. They've been blaming our side and we've suspected them, but a third party was responsible. We have to go to New Zealand to take care of them before a serious matter becomes an international tragedy."

"Sounds like you uncovered something pretty nasty," Brognola remarked.

"If anything, the truth is more alarming than what we thought was going on down here," the voice said. "Suggest you contact the President and tell him of our progress and ask that he contact Gorbachev. Tell him both Washington and Moscow will receive details and evidence of a private conspiracy that threatens both East and West. We have to concentrate on finding the conspirators and put them out of business. Our companion will return home and pass on all information gathered so far."

The Fed realized the "companion" was probably Swenson, or possibly one of the NSA agents at McMurdo.

"We'll need cooperation from authorities in New Zealand," the Phoenix Force representative continued. "Direct action is necessary. We'll need the best people they've got."

"Understood," Brognola assured the caller. "Anything else?"

"Run a check on Edward Hellson," the voice said. "He's a New Zealand businessman. Metallurgy, cattle, shipping, other businesses that are less public. He was originally an

American, and Hellson is probably an assumed name. We don't know much else about him except that he ranks high in the conspiracy. May even be the leader.''

"We'll get on it right away," Brognola promised. "You've given me a pretty sketchy report. Anything definite I can tell the President when I meet with him?"

"Our companion will fill in the details when he comes home," the Phoenix voice replied. "We can tell you there has been no nuclear testing in Antarctica. However, the threat to innocent lives is actually greater than anticipated. There's even a risk that the conspiracy we uncovered here may trigger World War III.''

"Oh, I'm really looking forward to telling the President that," Brognola muttered. "Understood, Cold Duck. Sounds like you've done a good job so far. Keep it up. Good luck. Over.''

"We'll do our best," the voice confirmed. "Over and out.''

The Fed placed the microphone on the radio and turned to face Kurtzman.

"I'll see what I can dig up on this Hellson character," Bear said as he started to wheel away from the radio set. "I'll also find out who to contact in New Zealand to arrange security clearance and government cooperation for Phoenix Force when they arrive. What about transportation from Antarctica?"

"They would have mentioned it if they needed it," Brognola said. "They must be confident they can handle it at their end. I'd better arrange a meeting with the President and tell him our relations with the Soviet Union and the rest of the world should improve unless the apocalypse occurs before we can sort this mess out.''

COLONEL MIKHAIL IVANOVICH MERKULOV removed his white parka and handed it to his aide. A stocky man with a strong, square-shaped face, his gray eyes peered from shaggy thick brows with equal degrees of curiosity and suspicion. "This is a very unusual situation, gentlemen," he remarked in heavily accented English. "I do not recall ever hearing of a Soviet officer being invited to McMurdo Base before."

"It's a first for us, too, Colonel," Rear Admiral Arnold Clayton said as he gestured at a chair at the head of the conference table.

Clayton was the second-in-command of the U.S. naval forces in Antarctica and temporary commander of the Navy research and weather operations at McMurdo. A tall, well-built man with an oval face and compact features, he seemed as uncomfortable with the Russian's presence as Merkulov seemed about being at the U.S. base.

Merkulov nodded and took his seat. He glanced at the other men present in the conference room. A middle-aged man with a prosthesis sat to the right of Rear Admiral Clayton. Seated beside him were two men clad in blue denim shirts. They wore handcuffs on their wrists and their expressions suggested abject misery. A lean, fox-faced fellow sat on the other side of the prisoners, his attention fixed on the pair, a pistol clearly displayed in a shoulder holster under his left arm. A man with clipped sandy brown hair and a trimmed mustache sat to the left of Clayton. He wore a khaki uniform, and Merkulov guessed the man wasn't an American. Possibly British or Australian, he thought.

The biggest surprise, however, was the tall figure dressed in the uniform of a Soviet paratrooper. Merkulov had spoken with Major Remizov on the radio before arriving, and they had exchanged salutes when the colonel had entered the room. Yet Merkulov was still stunned by the major's presence. Remizov seemed calm and relaxed, almost pleased by the circumstances that still baffled his superior.

"This is Colonel Hodden from Scott Base, our New Zealander neighbors on Ross Island," Clayton said. The rear admiral turned to Katz. "And this is Mr. Ginsberg, and one of his men who is kindly guarding the two prisoners whose names I don't recall."

"Gerber and Dubou," Katz supplied. "They're still a bit hung over from the scopolamine we used to interrogate them earlier, but they've both decided to cooperate with us in the hope that it'll weigh in their favor when they stand trial. You've already met Major Remizov."

"Yes," Merkulov said with a nod. "I am also aware the major was part of a unit of twelve Soviet military personnel who were engaged with American forces in a gun battle in the Transantarctic Mountains. I have been promised an explanation concerning this matter, which cost the lives of several of my countrymen."

"You can blame that bloody mess on the KGB," David McCarter remarked sourly. "Don't take our word for it. Ask Remizov."

"I will," Merkulov assured him. "What do you intend to do with the major? Is he a prisoner?"

"Not at all," Katz replied. "We hope you'll take Major Remizov and the other surviving paratroopers from his unit back to Vostok Station and from there to Moscow. They have a very important message for your president, concerning the current chairman of the KGB. You won't be too upset if he loses his job, will you?"

"I choose not to comment," Merkulov said with a slight shrug. "I was told you will share information about the nuclear testing being done down here. Is this a confession or another accusation?"

"A confession," Clayton declared, "but not from the United States government. Those two men in chains can do the talking."

"You heard the man," McCarter told Dubou and Gerber.

Gerber and Dubou reluctantly confessed to their participation in the covert uranium mining operations for Hellson Metallurgy. They admitted they had witnessed the murders of Linnson and Collier, but insisted they hadn't taken part in either killing. The pair also stated that the secret mining operations in Antarctica had been going on for more than a year and that they had supplied Edward Hellson with several hundred kilos of pitchblende. They could only guess how much uranium Hellson had extracted from the mineral delivered to his metallurgy company in New Zealand.

"This man Hellson has been building nuclear weapons in New Zealand?" Merkulov asked in astonishment. His gaze shifted from the prisoners to Colonel Hodden.

"Don't look at me that way," the New Zealand officer told him. "We didn't know anything about this uranium mining business. Hellson Metallurgy is regarded as a respectable outfit, and Nuukon's research unit was supposed to be looking for ore deposits for new metal alloy products. Neither my base nor my government had any idea what that bastard was really up to."

"No one's accusing you or your country of anything," Katz said quickly, eager to keep tempers cool. "To answer Colonel Merkulov's question, Hellson has munitions experts and at least one nuclear physicist working for him. He also has an industrial laser, and he can manufacture lead and steel vessels or whatever else he'd need to create rather primitive but very dangerous nuclear warheads."

"And what does he intend to do with them?" Merkulov demanded. "Is he a lunatic?"

"I don't know if he's insane or not," Katz replied. "From what we can gather about the man from interrogating his people, Hellson's apolitical and amoral. He may be power hungry and might be insane, but he isn't stupid enough to try to use the weapons himself. Hellson supposedly has a background in illegal arms dealing, narcotics, smuggling and God knows what else. Most likely he intends to sell the nuclear devices to buyers who want such weapons but can't build their own or get them from countries with nuclear arsenals. Hellson's probably dealing with Third World countries or terrorist outfits that can come up with enough money."

"You see, Colonel," Clayton began with a sigh, "that's why you're here. This could be as big a threat to the Soviet Union and its allies as it is to the United States and our allies."

"This madman must be stopped immediately!" Merkulov declared. He waved a hand across the room to include everyone present. "Have you ordered this man's arrest?"

"Goddamn right we will," Hodden stated. "I'll radio Wellington and we'll have the bastard in irons within an hour."

"Wait a minute," Katz urged. "Think, gentlemen. Hellson has a private army with men stationed at both his metallurgy company and his ranch. He may have nuclear weapons at either or both sites. If the police and the military swoop down on him, he may use those weapons. Besides, we need to know if he's sold any bombs and, if so, who the buyers are."

"That means we've got to handle this with tight security and a minimum of personnel," McCarter added. "If we nail Hellson without learning where all the weapons are, whoever has them might decide to use the bloody things as soon as they hear Hellson got the chop. They'll probably figure we'll find out about them, and they'll have to use their nuclear toys before we come after them, as well. Some of the fanatics we've crossed swords with over the years wouldn't hesitate to blow themselves to bits if they could take enough of their enemies with them."

"So what do you suggest?" Hodden asked, hands outstretched in a frustrated gesture. "Hellson's got to be stopped."

"Your government's probably being informed of a crisis situation with limited details by the President of the United States even as we speak," Katz explained. "Your prime minister will know we're coming and will arrange clearance for our security, permits for special weapons and equipment and cooperation with your intelligence and military people. We need you to get us to New Zealand as quickly as possible and to report this situation to the necessary authorities and confirm that it's true."

"I'll do that and anything else you need," Hodden said firmly.

"Thank you, Colonel," Katz said. He turned to Merkulov. "We ask a similar favor of you and Major Remizov. The President's also going to talk to Mr. Gorbachev and give him a general idea of what's happened, with the promise that he'll be given more details soon. If you two will return to the Soviet Union and deliver this information, it'll help to patch up the problems that have occurred between our countries."

"Do you think you can trust us?" Merkulov asked with a smile. "We are Communists, after all."

"I doubt I'll ever trust communism as a form of government, and I'll always be suspicious of those in power in a Communist nation," Katz answered in a direct, matter-of-fact tone. "But I also feel that nations have to accept the right of others to have a different ideology. That means we have to trust individuals even if we don't trust their system of government."

"What you ask us to do is in the best interest of my country as well as yours," Merkulov said. "I think that is why you trust us. That is enough, Mr. Ginsberg. We will do our best to impress our president with the need to maintain secrecy about this matter until you have taken care of Hellson. I just hope you succeed. If you do not, we may all find ourselves in a far worse situation than we are now."

"Oh, yeah," Katz said with a nod. "We're aware of that, too."

PHOENIX FORCE PACKED their gear for one last journey by ice sledge across the frozen terrain of Antarctica. Encizo whistled cheerfully as he secured the canvas bag that contained his micro-Uzi and several hundred rounds of ammunition. The Cuban was delighted to be leaving Antarctica. Phoenix Force would leave McMurdo with Colonel Hodden and travel to nearby Scott Base. From there they would fly to Campbell Island to refuel and then on to New Zealand. Encizo was anxious to feel sunlight once again.

"Well, my plane leaves before yours does," Swenson announced as he slipped into his parka. "But I've got a lot farther to go before I reach America."

"Yeah," James said with a grin. "You're going to meet the President. That ought to be exciting."

"I've had enough excitement for a while," Swenson assured him. "That little dairy farm of mine in Vermont seems awfully good to me now. It's time to go back to retirement for this old war-horse."

"You've certainly earned it," Manning said. "We couldn't have managed down here without you, Harry."

"I know the neighborhood," Swenson said with a shrug. "Frankly, I never saw this much action when I was stationed in Antarctica in the past. Maybe it's best that my last assignment be the most memorable. I'm sort of sorry I can't see this mission through to the end."

"You'll find out how it turns out," Katzenelenbogen assured him. "It's been a pleasure working with you, Harry."

"Same here," Swenson said with a smile. "Although I think I'd have a heart attack if I went out with you guys on the ice again and somebody started shooting at us. Things might get pretty tough in New Zealand, too."

"Even if it's tough, it'll still be warmer," Encizo declared. The Cuban figured any place would be better than Antarctica.

"Well, good luck, anyway," Swenson told the commandos. "I have a feeling you're going to need it."

16

Streaks of gold and pink formed halos along the rims of a scattering of clouds on the horizon. The terrain was silent except for the lonesome call of a desert bird. Gray boulders clustered together like a huddle of sleeping giants. A cold wind swept across the desert and stirred drifting sand among the rocks.

Erik Heller shivered and turned up the collar of his bush jacket. He had forgotten how cold the Gibson Desert could get before sunup. At least the cold would keep the snakes away, he thought with relief.

General Ton held a pair of binoculars in his left hand and raised them to his eyes. The Vietnamese examined the cluster of boulders and estimated the distance to be at least twenty kilometers. Ton lowered the glasses and turned to stare at the nuclear cannon.

Jason House stood next to the cannon and opened the lid to the casket-style crate that contained three 115 mm shells. The British merc glanced at the rock formation in the distance. His hands were sweaty and his knees quivered. House hadn't expected to be so frightened of actually loading and firing the cannon, but the full meaning of setting off a nuclear explosion had suddenly hit him with mind-jarring force.

"What are we waitin' for?" Rob Ethan asked as he leaned against the rear of the truck and popped the tab from a quart can of beer.

"Mr. Hellson hasn't given the order yet," Abe Samels told Ethan, his tongue as sharp as a razor. "So just shut up and wait for our employers to tell us what to do."

"I'd just as soon not touch that cannon after they load it," Tibbs said nervously.

"Are you ready, General?" Heller asked Ton in a soft, calm voice. The renegade American sounded more relaxed than he felt, but he had no intentions of letting the others see the fear he felt at the moment. They had enough trouble dealing with their own negative emotions without wondering if Heller shared their doubts.

Ton raised his binoculars again and tried to estimate the distance a second time. It seemed more like fifteen kilometers than twenty. "Are you certain we're far enough from the target?" he inquired with a frown.

"We're safe here," Heller assured him. "Jason, load the cannon. That is, if it's okay with the general."

Ton continued to gaze through his binoculars, then reluctantly nodded. House opened the cannon's breech and reached for one of the shells. His fingers shook as he touched the torpedo-shaped explosive. The Briton took a deep breath, gripped the shell in both hands and hauled it from the case. It was heavier than he'd expected. House grunted as he shoved the shell into the breech.

"We've never fired one of these cannons with a nuclear round before," the Briton remarked. "I hope Kubler knew what he was doing when he made this thing."

"Kubler's an expert in designing munitions," Heller declared. "He's one of the best in the field, Jason. You know that."

"Sorry if I disappoint you, sir," House replied in a hard voice, "but I'm about to crap in my trousers."

"It's loaded," Heller said with a shrug as he approached the cannon. "I'll fire it myself."

"The sights are locked on the boulders," House said. "They're about twelve miles away."

"If it'll make you feel better, I'll set the timer for five minutes and we can drive off in the truck to get a bit farther away," Heller told the merc. He was actually glad to have an excuse to put some more miles between himself and the weapon.

House didn't argue. He gestured for the Australians to help him load the metal casket with the other two shells into the truck. Heller punched out the number code on the timing mechanism for the cannon. General Ton started to lower his binoculars when he noticed movement among the rocks.

"There's someone out there, Hellson," the Asian announced.

Heller looked up with surprise and peered at the boulders. He could barely see the rocks at that distance without benefit of binoculars, let alone see any figures moving near the boulders.

Samels grabbed his binoculars and examined the rocks. He saw three small, slender shapes walking near the rocks. The men were naked except for loincloths made of tanned kangaroo hide. They carried spears as long as the men were tall. "Christ," he muttered. "Aborigines."

"What?" House asked.

"Aborigines," Heller said with a sigh. "That's a polite term for savages. A few less won't be much of a loss."

"I didn't know you were going to kill somebody when you tested this cannon," Tibbs said nervously.

"We didn't plan it," Heller said as he stepped away from the cannon. "It's just going to turn out that way."

Ton lowered his binoculars and silently walked to the truck. The Vietnamese wasn't pleased that three innocent people were about to die because of the test, but he realized many innocent people would be killed if the nuclear shells and cannons were used for their intended purpose. Ton had seen hundreds of innocent lives snuffed out during the war and since. He had killed many himself and ordered the slaughter of many more. Ton had learned to accept these sacrifices as necessary to achieve greater goals. It was a justification, of course, but it made him sleep easier to think of genocide in this manner.

"Bad luck for them," House commented as he climbed into the back of the truck. The British mercenary was too worried about his own hide to be concerned about the three aborigines. "Let's make some tracks, gentlemen."

"Right," Heller agreed. The American joined House and Ton in the back of the vehicle.

Ethan drove the truck with Tibbs in the passenger seat of the cab. Samels was alone in the Land Rover. He started the engine and prepared to shift gears. The Australian felt the hairs at the nape of his neck rise. Samels was tempted to turn and examine the aborigines with his binoculars once more. He felt them watching him. Felt their eyes on the back of his neck in a silent accusation of his part in their destruction. Samels told himself it was nonsense. His imagination had gotten the better of him. Hell, the aborigines couldn't see them well enough to suspect what was about to happen.

Samels shivered, stomped on the gas pedal and sped away from the cannon. Dust spewed from the tires of the Land Rover as he raced from the scene, more eager to be clear of the aborigines than the nuclear explosion that was scant minutes away. The truck had a slight head start, but Samels soon passed it. His vehicle was smaller and faster than the three-ton rig, and the flat, arid land let him cover distance rapidly. Then, suddenly, he realized he was going close to eighty miles an hour, and slowed before he lost control of the four-wheel-drive vehicle.

The truck and Land Rover were still racing across the desert when they heard a monstrous roar. The glare erupted behind them, yet even from a distance of more than twenty miles the flash was considerable. A terrible, angry growl continued to fill the predawn morning as the vehicles came to a halt.

"Christ!" Samels exclaimed when he turned to stare at the great mushroom cloud in the distance. A brilliant orange-and-yellow light burned in the desert. Smoke seemed to turn and tumble with atomic rage, extending at least a mile into the sky and nearly as wide across. Samels had never witnessed a sight more terrifying than the nuclear devil unleashed by Hellson's terrible cannon.

Heller and General Ton drove the Land Rover back to the cannon. The others were afraid to return to the site until they knew for certain that the radiation level was low enough to be safe. Heller had followed a standard rule of successful leadership for commanders of men in a dangerous profession. He didn't order them to do anything he wouldn't do himself.

Ton was no more anxious to return to the area than the other men, but he felt it necessary to impress the others with his courage. It was a matter of saving face that he appear as brave as Heller, for he, too, was a leader of men in his homeland. Ton also needed to get a better look at the results of the nuclear blast. But the Asian didn't want to get any closer than necessary. The mushroom cloud had subsided into a whirling mass of dust in the distance, and the earth still trembled from the aftershock of the explosion.

Heller stopped the Land Rover near the cannon and reached for a Geiger counter. His pulse hammered as he switched on the machine. Heller had studied the hazards of radiation when he first began his scheme to get into the private nuclear arms dealing trade. He knew any radiation could be biologically dangerous over time. More than a hundred rems would mean a high probability of leukemia or other types of cancer. Poisonous radioactive substances such as strontium-90 and iodine-131 attacked the bones and glands. If the Geiger counter reading was above four hundred rems, Heller and Ton might as well make out their wills.

The American's stomach constricted with fear as the Geiger counter crackled and he watched the needle jump. Heller loved his body and prided himself on his health and extraordinary physical strength. Radiation poisoning, cancer, bleeding gums and greater hair loss frightened him much more than armed opponents on the battlefield. His vanity was his greatest weakness, although his arrogance and supreme self-confidence had always been his greatest strengths. Heller felt Ton's gaze as he waited to hear the verdict. The American peered down at the meter gauge.

"Ten rems," he said with a sigh of relief. "It's okay, General."

Ton nodded and raised his binoculars. He had to brace the field glasses with the curved steel of his hook to hold it steady. Ton's single hand was still shaking. He stared at the swirling fog of dust where the nuclear shell had exploded. The boulders were gone. They hadn't been pulverized or reduced to piles of pebbles; the big rocks had vanished from the face of the earth as if they had never existed. The aborigines had also been vaporized by the blast. Only a steaming crater marked the spot where the boulders had been.

"Incredible," Ton said as he lowered the binoculars.

"I trust you're pleased with the merchandise," Heller remarked. He raised an arm and waved for the others to come forward.

"Perhaps *satisfied* would be a better term than *pleased*," Ton replied. He glanced at the atomic cannon. "Such destruction, and the nuclear shell is one of the least powerful of weapons of this sort. Fascinating and terrible."

"And expensive," Heller added. "But worth every penny to make your country a member of that elite international community armed with nuclear weapons."

"The cannon isn't going to my country, Heller," Ton declared, using the renegade's real name while the others were absent. "You know that. The delivery is part of our deal."

"I know," Heller said with a nod as he watched the truck approach. "That may be the most difficult part. We'll have to move quickly."

"Yes," Ton agreed. "I doubt a nuclear explosion will go unnoticed even in a place like this."

"*Especially* in a place like this," Heller amended. "Let's get a move on. It's a long way to Darwin."

"And you're certain our cargo ship will be ready?"

"Don't worry, General. Before you know it, we'll be out of this godforsaken desert and sailing the high seas."

17

From a thousand feet in the air, New Zealand seemed peaceful and pleasant. The capital city of Wellington was a less hectic version of a European port. The green harbor waters appeared as calm as a pond, and little traffic competed in the streets, but less than an hour had passed since dawn. The plane circled the city as the pilot searched for the landing field.

Finally the pilot located the airstrip at the edge of the city and descended. It was a small independent field with three hangars and a fuel station. However, a pair of government limousines and a pair of deuce-and-a-half trucks were present. When the plane touched down on the runway, a pair of men dressed in suits and two others in army uniforms stood by the entrance to a hangar and waited for the craft to taxi to a halt.

The five men of Phoenix Force emerged from the plane. They had changed clothes since leaving Antarctica and now wore brown-and-green camouflage fatigue uniforms, paratrooper boots and light headgear suited for a warmer climate. Katz and McCarter both sported berets. Manning favored a boonie hat with a wide, shapeless brim, and Encizo chose not to wear any headgear at all. Each man carried aluminum rifle cases and had pistols in shoulder holster rigs.

Colonel Hodden also climbed from the plane. The four men at the hangar approached. Phoenix Force had dealt with government personnel in dozens of countries, and they could almost identify a civil servant a hundred feet away. The guy dressed in a dark blue single-breasted suit with a houndstooth tie was their choice as the most likely representative of the New Zealand government. Federal agents tended to wear the same style of suits in either black, blue or gray anywhere in the world. The houndstooth tie was something of a special badge for Intel personnel associated with the British Commonwealth.

"Hello, gentlemen," the man in the blue suit announced with the modified British accent associated with New Zealand. "I'm Gavin Ford, Security Intelligence Service."

The Phoenix Force commandos nodded as if they were surprised.

"This is Inspector John Briggs, CID," Ford said as he tilted his head toward the man beside him.

Calvin James had already guessed Briggs was a cop. The heavyset, fortyish man with a haggard face wore a baggy sport coat and pants. His necktie was flowery and wide, loose at the collar, but his shoes were neatly polished. A plainclothes dick, James had thought the moment he'd seen the guy. He might as well have had his gold shield pinned to his breast pocket.

"And Colonel Gerrard and Captain Todd are, of course, with our armed forces," Ford added. "Army Intelligence and New Zealand Special Air Service. Are you familiar with the British SAS?"

"I've heard of them," McCarter said dryly.

"Good," Ford said. "Todd and his mates are trained in the same manner. Commandos. Sort of like you fellows, I imagine. Shall we continue this conversation in the hangar?"

No one agreed or argued, so Ford turned and led the group back to the hangar. A table and a dozen chairs were set up as an improvised conference room. Sweet rolls, coffee and tea were also on hand. Ford took a seat and pulled out a pack of cigarettes from a pocket.

"So, why don't we get down to it right away?" the SIS man suggested. "Just what *is* going on?"

"There's a very dangerous conspiracy based here in Wellington and at a cattle ranch on South Island," Katz answered. "Both are owned by Edward Hellson."

"Yes," Briggs said as he reached inside his jacket and removed two folded computer printouts. "We got some information on Hellson from some blokes in Washington, D.C. Some real surprises popped up."

"I've heard of Hellson," Ford remarked. "He's a respectable businessman. Captain of industry and all that. Probably one of the richest men in New Zealand. Unlike you Americans, we don't have many people who are really wealthy here, but we don't have many living in total poverty, either."

"The CID and the local police have had some doubts about how 'respectable' Hellson has been in the past," Briggs said, obviously pleased he could hit Ford with something the SIS man wasn't expecting. "Hellson's hired quite a lot of blokes with questionable background. Some are native New Zealanders with criminal backgrounds. Others are Aussies with a history of trouble with the law. Quite a few are Europeans and Americans. Sketchy information on those blokes, but we know some of them have hoodlum pasts and others were employed as mercenary soldiers in dirty little wars and would-be revolutions in parts of the world most people don't pay much attention to. Still, there was never any evidence Hellson was doing anything illegal, and he has friends in high places. Rich people usually do.''

"Didn't it seem odd that he was hiring so many foreigners with bad backgrounds instead of locals?'' Colonel Gerrard inquired with a frown.

"Odd but not illegal,'' Briggs answered. "For one thing, we know Hellson has never hired any Maoris or anybody else who isn't one hundred percent white.''

"So Hellson's probably a bigot who only wants white guys in his neighborhood?'' Calvin James asked.

"White guys with criminal backgrounds,'' Briggs corrected.

"What have you got on Hellson?'' Katz asked.

"Correct me if I'm mistaken,'' Ford said with a sigh. "Aren't *you* supposed to be telling *us* about Hellson?''

"I'm sure there's one thing about him they don't know,'' Briggs said as he unfolded a printout. "Hellson isn't his real name. He appears to be Erik Heller, who was supposedly killed in Vietnam in 1971.''

"That's a surprise,'' Gary Manning commented as he helped himself to a cup of coffee. "Are you sure?''

"Not a hundred percent, but Heller seems pretty likely to be Hellson's true identity,'' the CID man answered. "Take a look. Age, background, physical description, they all fit. Great bloody weight lifter type with lots of muscles. Heller was—or should I say *is*—a nasty bastard. According to the U.S. Army, Lieutenant Heller was due to be court-martialed for killing three of his own men when they refused to obey his orders to butcher an entire village in the Mekong Delta.''

"Son of a bitch,'' James rasped through clenched teeth.

"Right you are,'' Briggs said with a nod. "Apparently Heller thought the Vietcong were hiding in the village, so he wanted his troops to kill every man, woman and child until somebody confessed. When his men refused to carry out the order, he accused them of treason and promptly shot five of them. Three died. The rest of his platoon jumped him and knocked him unconscious. At the inquest they stated it took four of them to bring him down—and they'd jumped him from behind. They had to hit him on the head with a steel helmet to finally knock him out. The blow probably would have killed an average man, but whatever one might say about Heller, average he isn't."

"How'd they figure he was dead until now?" James asked.

"He broke out of a stockade in Saigon and fled into the jungle," Briggs explained. "They thought he set off a claymore mine and got blown to bits. Apparently those bits belonged to somebody else, probably some idiot who helped him escape. Anyway, I imagine the Army was glad to be able to close the case without the embarrassment of a trial and all the bad publicity that would have gone with it. God knows they got quite a bit back in those days."

"Yeah," James said bitterly. "Every guy who served in Vietnam had to pay for the 'publicity' that a handful of assholes like Heller gave us."

"Don't worry," Katz assured him. "Heller won't get away with anything much longer."

Phoenix Force and Colonel Hodden explained what they learned about Heller's secret mining operations in Antarctica and the strong probability that he had nuclear weapons at either the metallurgy company, his ranch or both. Ford, Briggs and the New Zealand officers were naturally stunned by this news.

"We've got to take care of these bastards, fast and hard," Captain Todd declared. The New Zealand SAS commander fixed his gaze on Katz and asked, "How do you suggest we handle this?"

"We split into two units," the Israeli replied. "Your men and mine. We can't use large forces, or they'll realize we're coming before we reach them. For that matter, it's even possible Hellson, excuse me, Heller, has informers within the military and the police. We can't risk tipping him off, not when he has nuclear weapons."

"You don't think he'd actually use them here in Wellington or at the South Island ranch?" Ford asked in amazement.

"We can't be sure one way or the other, so we'd better assume he would use them if he's cornered," Katz insisted. "That's also why we'll form two strike force units. One will hit the metallurgy center and the other will hit the ranch. That way there won't be time for any of Heller's goons to radio either base and warn them in advance. Both attacks will be carried out simultaneously."

"I agree," Todd said. "It's the best way to handle it. I have twenty crack SAS troops under my command. Will that be enough?"

"Hopefully," Katz replied. "Your second-in-command, Mr. Baxter and myself will take the detachment to hit the metallurgy base, Captain. You and my three other friends will take the second unit to the ranch. Make certain your men understand how important this mission is. We can't take any chances with the enemy. This is virtually a state of war with Heller's forces."

"Don't worry about my men," Todd urged. "They've been well trained. We New Zealanders have fighting in our blood, you know. New Zealand had the largest percentage of population in the armed forces of any Allied nation in World War II other than Great Britain. Our lads were in Korea, Vietnam and the Falklands."

"We all appreciate the contributions of our fighting men in the past," Ford assured him. "But the threat of nuclear weapons is something our country has gone to considerable effort to avoid. Our prime minister vowed to keep American vessels with nuclear weapons out of New Zealand waters and ban NATO missile sites here. Remember that fuss in 1985 when U.S. warships weren't allowed to make port calls here? The American secretary of state accused us of undermining the so-called nuclear deterrent against the Soviets.''

"If Heller already has nuclear weapons here, they won't go away because we pretend they don't exist," Colonel Gerrard said with a sigh. The army Intelligence officer obviously felt neglected in the conversation and eagerly participated when he saw the opportunity to add his opinion. "I'm afraid nuclear weapons will endanger everyone, including New Zealand, whether we try to keep them off our soil or not. Look at what Heller managed to do right under our collective nose.''

"We couldn't have predicted he'd find uranium in Antarctica," Ford stated. "Some small uranium deposits have been found in boulders and such here in New Zealand, but never enough for mining operations.''

"Well, you've got a problem with nuclear weapons now, Ford," Encizo announced in a flat, hard voice. "It came from a source no one expected, but it's here and we've got to take care of it here and now.''

"No doubt about that," Briggs said. "What bothers me is that everybody on Heller's payroll isn't part of this conspiracy. Maybe everybody working at his ranch is a villain, but not all of the blokes employed at the metallurgy center. I don't want innocent people to get killed if you commando fellows start shooting it out with these bandits.''

"We'll take as much care as possible to protect the innocent," Katz assured him. "But there's no realistic way we can promise you no innocent people will be hurt. It's obvious more innocent lives will be in jeopardy if we *don't* take action."

"If we can get blueprints and other information on Hellson Metallurgy, it might help reduce the risks," Manning suggested. "The more we know about how the place is set up, the better. That might give us some idea where Heller's weapons might be stored. He'd obviously want someplace private and off-limits to the bulk of his employees."

"When this business about Hellson came up, I looked into that," Briggs announced with a smile. "We've got the blueprints and I had the police pick up a couple of blokes who recently worked at the metallurgy outfit. They should be able to fill in a few details not included on the prints."

"We'll question them over the phone," Katz said. "There isn't any time to waste. We don't know how long it'll take before Heller gets suspicious. His commander in Antarctica, Olav Naakon, had been making radio reports to Heller on their progress with the mining operations. Naakon's dead and the two flunkies willing to cooperate at McMurdo can only make a few reports back before Heller will wonder what happened to Naakon."

"He wound up bobbing for lava in an active volcano," McCarter said in case the New Zealanders were curious. "We know what has to be done. Let's bloody well get on with it."

"I hate to agree with him," Manning commented, "but he does have a point."

"Try to be patient long enough for us to organize this operation and plan it out as best we can," Katz urged. "Don't worry. You won't have to wait long."

18

The impression that Wellington was a peaceful and pleasant city seemed to hold true as Yakov Katzenelenbogen rode in the back of a green sedan with Inspector Briggs. There was more traffic in the streets than they had observed earlier that morning from the air, yet the traffic was still pleasantly light. Of course, there were fewer than a hundred and fifty thousand people in the city.

Shops, markets and a variety of stores were open for business. Men dressed in business suits hurried along the sidewalks on their way to work. They carried briefcases and anxiously glanced at their wristwatches, concerned about the possibility of being a minute or two late for work. Wellington was the headquarters of commercial trade and banking in New Zealand. The stockbrokers and junior executives were off to the corporate jungle with the same nervous and unsure expressions common to men who flirted with high finance, board meetings and ulcers. Katz wondered if it was better to face human opponents on the battlefield than the stock exchange and commodities trade.

"We're almost there, sir," the CID man at the steering wheel announced. "I hope this idea works."

"We all feel that way, Sergeant," Briggs assured him as he reached inside his jacket to draw out a snub-nosed .38. He opened the chambers to make certain it was loaded.

Briggs's gesture didn't reassure Katz. Any man who had to inspect his weapon minutes before reaching a destination where he might need it was probably unfamiliar with the gun. Katz guessed the inspector only fired the weapon once or twice a year for qualification at the police range. The Phoenix commander hadn't brought Briggs along because he expected him to be an expert marksman. He just hoped the inspector didn't get himself killed.

The car approached the metallurgy company. It was located near Port Nicholson Bay. A pair of large concrete buildings with towering smokestacks sprawled across more than a city block. A steel-wire fence surrounded the property. Piles of scrap metal and iron bins were located at the rear of the second building. A uniformed security guard was stationed by a truck gate to screen and record vehicles going in and out of the plant.

"Hellson has about four hundred employees in this place, and about one-third are working here on an average daytime shift," Briggs commented. "I wonder how many of them are hired killers."

"Not all hoodlums are willing to put their life on the line for their boss," Katz said. He held a Camel cigarette in the steel hooks of his prosthesis, but he still hadn't lighted it. "That's one thing in our favor. Terrorist fanatics might not object to giving their lives for a cause—whatever it might be—but mercenaries and gangsters seldom have that sort of dedication."

"It's not their willingness to give up *their* lives that worries me," Briggs replied.

The driver parked across the street from the plant. Katz picked up a two-way radio unit and pressed the transmit key. He pushed the button on a beeper twice and waited for a reply. Two beeps came through the receiver in response.

"The rest of the team's in position," Katz announced.

"Right," Briggs said, and took a deep breath. "Here we go."

The inspector and the driver emerged from the car and headed for the front entrance of the plant. Katz watched them as he opened a briefcase and removed his micro-Uzi. The Walther P-88 was already in shoulder leather under his right armpit. Katz also carried one SAS flash-bang grenade, two tear gas canisters and a gas mask. Spare magazines for the firearms and a ballistic knife in a scabbard at the small of his back completed the Israeli's arsenal.

For the moment he could only wait for others to help set the stage for the raid. Katz wondered if everyone was ready to carry out each individual role in the operation. There had been no time to rehearse the plan. They had been forced to call in others on short notice, dedicated personnel who understood the task was potentially very dangerous, although they hadn't been given any details of the hazards involved. Timing was important, and everyone would have to carry out his job precisely if the operation was to be successful.

Katz knew Manning and the ten SAS troops were in position. He had total faith in the Canadian professional's ability and would trust Manning or any of his fellow Phoenix warriors with his life. The New Zealand commandos had been trained in the traditional manner of the British SAS, and Katz appreciated the high quality of that elite fighting unit. His only qualms about the New Zealand soldiers with Manning was their relative inexperience and lack of actual combat time. No degree of training equalled the real experience of the battlefield.

"GOOD MORNING, GENTLEMEN," the young woman at the reception desk in the foyer to Hellson Metallurgy inquired as she looked up from her desk. "How may I help you?"

Briggs removed an identification card and showed it to the receptionist. "I'm with the Occupational Health and Safety Commission," he declared. "I need to talk to the man in charge. Is Mr. Hellson here?"

"No," the woman said, frowning. "Mr. Hellson hasn't come in today, but the plant manager is here. He's also senior vice president of Hellson Metallurgy. I'll ring him."

"Please do," Briggs replied. "This is a rather serious matter we've got concerning the safety of this plant."

The receptionist dialed an in-house phone number and spoke briefly. Two minutes later a sour-faced man with thinning hair appeared in the foyer. He wore a short-sleeved white shirt, a polka-dot tie and a pair of safety goggles suspended from his neck by an elastic cord.

"I'm Foley," he announced. "What's this about, gentlemen? The laser again? I've got certificates from the Safety Commission national office as well as here in Wellington that the laser has been inspected and declared perfectly safe and acceptable for industrial use. My God, you'd think by the latter part of the twentieth century people would realize the laser isn't some science fiction weapon out of a bad Hollywood film. It happens to be a perfectly sound and safe piece of equipment."

"I don't doubt that, sir," Briggs assured him. "I don't really know anything about lasers. That's not why I'm here. We've had some complaints about your furnaces."

"Furnaces?" Foley asked with a frown.

"Yes," Briggs said as he took a clipboard from the sergeant. "The furnaces used here for processing steel. You have both blast furnaces and an electrical air furnace. Correct?"

"A blast furnace is used for cast iron and isn't necessarily used for the production of steel," Foley replied. "But we do have blast furnaces. What about them?"

"Well, the cables and chains to the blast furnaces aren't completely secure," the CID inspector explained.

"Cables and chains?" The manager knitted his brow. "Now you're talking about the open-hearth furnaces. You don't know anything about making steel, do you? What's this business about our furnaces not being secure?"

"That's what we've been told by a number of current and former employees at Hellson Metallurgy," Briggs answered. "We've got signed statements, all claiming the same sort of violations. Worn cables, badly rusted chains with obviously weakened links, and exposed electrical wiring at the arc furnace and motors to the rollers. That's for sheet metal, right?"

"Molten steel," Foley said with a sigh. "Look, Inspector, or whatever your title is, these accusations are absurd. They've obviously been made by incompetents who have been fired and want to get even with the company."

"Some of the claims are supported by individuals who *still* work here," Briggs insisted. "I'm sorry for this inconvenience, but the Commission believes there's more than enough reason to justify an investigation."

Foley rolled his eyes toward the ceiling. The receptionist seemed worried. She twisted a long lock of honey-blond hair in an unconscious, nervous gesture. Briggs and the sergeant kept an eye on her. The young woman was attractive and appeared harmless, but every veteran cop had seen big, strong men who had been killed by innocent-looking females.

"Mr. Hellson isn't here today, and I don't think he'll be in for a day or two," Foley began, clearly frustrated. "It would make more sense if you'd come back when he's here, and bring someone better qualified to make the inspections than you are, sir. No offense, but you don't even know the difference between a blast furnace and an open hearth, or sheet metal and molten metal."

"I admit I know very little about steel or how it's made," the CID officer admitted. "That's why the fire department has been called in to help."

"The fire department?" Foley was stunned by this remark. "What the hell for? What do you people think you're doing?"

"The fire department has experts on fire safety, wiring hazards and all the rest," Briggs explained. "They'll conduct the mechanics of the investigation. You can, of course, remain and help supervise the inspection. Your expertise will no doubt be appreciated and very valuable."

"You don't intend to do it now?" Foley demanded. "I've got men working here. The furnaces are in use now."

"You'll simply have to get them out of here until we've finished the inspections," Briggs insisted. "If all goes well, your company can sue those who made the accusations, but if we find violations..."

"I can't authorize this!" the manager said sharply. "We can't just shut down work here!"

"We'll be as quick as possible," Briggs assured him.

The wail of a siren issued from the street. Foley moved to the glass door and stared at the fire engine rolling up to the truck gate. Red lights flashed atop the large vehicle. The manager cursed and spread his hands in a helpless gesture.

"Are you people bloomin' nuts?" he demanded as he glared at Briggs. "That thing's taking up half the street! There's no need for a goddamn fire truck down here with its bleedin' siren going!"

"I can't quite hear you, sir," Briggs replied as he raised a hand to his ear. "That siren's making a lot of noise."

THE UNIFORMED SECURITY GUARD emerged from his shack by the truck gate and stared at the fire engine, bewildered and startled by the unexpected arrival of the big red truck. He didn't see the figures climb over the wire fence near the scrap metal bins and stacks of steel tubing. Gary Manning dropped from the fence and moved behind an iron bin. The Canadian carried a small backpack in addition to a micro-Uzi, Walther pistol, grenades and a gas mask.

Five New Zealand SAS troops also mounted the fence. The soldiers wore brown-and-green striped camouflage uniforms and sand-colored berets. They were armed with British-made 9 mm L2A3 submachine guns, American-made .38 Special revolvers and Australian versions of the famous Fairbairn-Sykes Commando dagger. One SAS soldier crept along the piles of scrap metal to conceal his movement from the guard or anyone who might be watching from the windows or bay doors at the rear of the building. He got as close to the truck gate as possible without exposing himself, then whistled.

The security guard turned and saw the trooper's Sterling subgun pointed at him. The commando gestured for the guard to come forward. The guy started to raise his hands in surrender, but the SAS soldier shook his head and snapped a hand down, open palm, to signal the guard to keep his arms down. The rent-a-cop got the idea and obeyed. The troop repeated the gesture to urge the guard forward. He reluctantly obeyed and approached the commando's position.

"Easy with the gun, fella," the guard muttered softly. His hand crept to the holstered pistol on his hip.

"Don't try it or I'll kill you," the soldier warned. "Get over by that bin and sit your arse on the ground. Hands on top of your head."

The guard saw the other SAS troops and realized resistance would be suicide. He followed instructions and got down behind the bin. The sergeant nodded his approval to the soldier who had nabbed the guard, then relieved the captive of his side arm. The NCO bound the guy's wrists together at the small of his back with a set of unbreakable plastic riot cuffs, then manacled his ankles the same way.

"Good work," Manning whispered to the soldiers. He peered around the corner of a bin and scanned the windows and bay doors.

It was difficult to say which was louder—the fire engine siren or the fiery roar and clash of metal within the metallurgy plant. Some workers at the bay section closest to the truck gate stood at the opening and watched the fire engine, confused and curious. No one seemed to notice at the other bay door. Manning didn't see anyone at the windows facing his direction, either. He motioned for the soldiers to stay put and tried to visually measure the distance to the bay doors.

The Canadian took a deep breath and bolted to the second bay entrance. He kept his back arched and head low as he ran. Manning reached it without hearing anyone yell out an alarm. The Phoenix pro entered the bay section and found workers busy at their stations. No one noticed Manning shuffle along a wall to a door labeled Loo.

He stepped into the bathroom and nearly bumped into a startled laborer clad in heavy coveralls. The Canadian shoved his micro-Uzi into the man's chest and pushed him into the room. A second man, his back to the door, stood at a urinal.

"Stand still and keep quiet," the big Canadian ordered, pointing his machine pistol at the pair.

"Jesus," the guy in the coveralls rasped, slowly raising his hands. The other man followed suit.

"All right," Manning said. "No sudden moves from either of you or you're both dead."

Keeping a wary eye on his two prisoners, Manning slipped the backpack off and opened the canvas flap. Inside there was an assortment of plastic explosive compounds, prima cord and a dozen plastic riots cuffs. He removed four unbreakable red plastic strips and ordered the man in the coveralls to bind the ankles and wrists of his fellow worker. That finished, Manning did the same to the guy in the coveralls, an easy task since the man was petrified with fear. His task completed, Manning placed adhesive strips over the mouths of both men, then consulted his watch. He was twenty-eight seconds behind schedule.

Cursing, he picked up his machine pistol and headed for the bathroom door. He opened it a crack and peered at the rolling mill and the workers positioned next to it. Time for a grenade, he whispered to himself. Careful not to be noticed, the Canadian stepped from the bathroom, pulled the pin on the grenade and tossed it into an iron bin loaded with scrap metal. Then he hurried back to the bathroom.

Columns of thick gray-green smoke spewed from the grenade. The smoke poured through the workplace. Several voices called out in surprise and alarm, then someone yelled the word Manning was counting on.

"Fire!" a voice cried. "Something's on fire!"

Manning could see little except the dense fog from the smoke grenade. Figures darted everywhere in the dark cloud. The Canadian remained hidden in the bathroom and allowed the confusion to build among the men in the plant.

"Shut the machines down and get some fire extinguishers!" a gruff voice ordered. "Not that way, damn! Keep away from the fire area!"

"Where the hell's it coming from?" another man exclaimed.

"Bloody hell!" someone added. "There's a fire engine outside!"

"The whole damn plant must be on fire for it to be here already!" another yelled. "Let's get out of here!"

Please do, Manning thought as he listened to the boot leather on concrete, hoping it meant the men were leaving the area.

THE TELEPHONE RANG at the receptionist's desk. The woman picked up the receiver as Foley opened the front door and leaned out to stare at the smoke streaming from the rear of the plant. Briggs and the CID sergeant exchanged glances. Both knew the others ought to be carrying out their role at that moment and hoped the plan was going smoothly.

"The foreman in Building Two has been trying to locate you, Mr. Foley," the receptionist announced, her hand tightly clenched around the receiver. "He says there's a fire. The men are evacuating the building."

A voice bellowed from the earpiece of the receiver, and the woman started nervously. Whatever the foreman was saying, it was obvious he was angry. Foley glared at Briggs as if convinced the inspector had somehow caused the fire by telepathy.

"I'd say this is pretty obvious proof the fire hazards we discussed are genuine," Briggs told him. "Good thing we happened to be here."

"You bastards expect me to believe this is just a coincidence?" Foley said, his fists clenched in rage as he marched toward the CID officer.

The sergeant grabbed Foley by the back of his neck and shoved him face first into a wall. He adroitly twisted the manager's arm in a hammerlock and pressed Foley against the wall as he pulled a pair of handcuffs from his jacket.

Briggs drew his .38 and pointed it at the receptionist's face. Forgotten, the receiver was still clutched in her hand as she stared, her eyes wide with fear.

"Hang up," Briggs said sharply. "Now!"

She obeyed and raised her hands. The sergeant hand-cuffed Foley as the manager demanded to know what the hell was going on. He was still protesting when Yakov Katzenelenbogen entered the foyer. The receptionist gasped as the new figure arrived, dressed in combat uniform, a set of steel hooks for a right hand and armed to the teeth.

"You," Katz said, pointing the metal claws of his prosthesis at the woman. "Outside. The police are out there. They'll want to talk to you."

"Yes, sir," she replied, unsure of what else to say and glad to have an excuse to get out of the building.

The receptionist hurried out the door as the CID sergeant swung Foley around to face Katz. The Israeli suddenly grabbed the manager by the shirtfront and tie. He dragged Foley to the desk and shoved him across the top. Foley cried out in terror, but fell silent as Katz thrust the hooks of his artificial arm in front of the manager's face.

"This plant has a public address system, correct?" Katz asked in a hard voice that suggested he wouldn't tolerate any lies or attempts to stall for time.

"Y-yes," Foley confirmed, afraid to nod his head because the steel talons seemed dangerously close to his eyes.

"Tell me the number to the PA system," Katz commanded. "I'll dial it and you make the announcement that everybody has to leave the plant immediately because the buildings are on fire. If you give me the wrong number or try any other type of trick, your face will have a great deal in common with three pounds of bloodied hamburger. Understand?"

"Yes," Foley croaked. "I understand."

A young SAS lieutenant named Jennings appeared at the foyer entrance. Other commandos followed while Foley made the announcement as Katz had instructed. When the manager was finished, the Phoenix commander released him.

"Inspector Briggs," Katz began as he braced his micro-Uzi across his prosthetic arm, "take this man outside and help supervise the police and firemen. They were called in on very short notice and may need your help."

"All right," Briggs replied. He stuck his revolver into a holster under his jacket and uttered a deep sigh. "I sure as hell hope you know what you're doing, or we're all in a hell of a lot of trouble."

"Someone is certainly in for trouble," Katz confirmed. He turned to Lieutenant Jennings and his troops. "Let's go."

19

Hellson Metallurgy was a scene of mass exodus as workers poured out of the plant. An SAS soldier slipped into the guard shack and operated the buttons to release the truck gate. It slid open with an electrical hum before the onslaught of the laborers who were anxiously swarming from every exit. Many were astonished to encounter armed and uniformed men going in the opposite direction at the front of the building and at the bay doors. The SAS troops instructed everybody to keep moving and waved their weapons to urge the workers to get out of the way.

Outside, they found three police cars and two paddy wagons waiting for them. More than a dozen Wellington policemen corralled the plant workers and frisked them for weapons. Fire department personnel assisted in crowd control to keep back innocent bystanders. The police and firemen knew there was a good possibility that firearms might be used so they did their best to keep people as far away as possible.

Gary Manning had joined two SAS soldiers who were shooing workers out the bay door. They scanned the workplace and saw several figures scurrying among the rolling stands and presses. The PA announcement of a fire, and the order for all employees to leave the building immediately, clearly hadn't convinced these individuals. Based on his knowledge of the plant's layout, Manning realized that the men who remained in the building were heading toward the location of the industrial laser.

The Phoenix commando ran along the rolling stands, keeping low in case he needed to use the machinery for cover. The two New Zealand soldiers separated and approached the men from different directions. As one SAS trooper lobbed a tear gas grenade at the group, Manning yanked open the canvas bag on his left hip and extracted a gas mask. He slipped it over his head and tightened the straps to the rubber face guard. The Canadian breathed through the plastic filters, satisfied the gas mask would protect him sufficiently.

But the laggards were unprepared, and they coughed and choked on the gas. They groped about, half blinded and rapidly becoming ill. Manning closed in on the group and counted three unarmed opponents and a fourth with a small pocket pistol.

"Drop the gun!" Manning ordered, his voice muffled by the mask.

The armed man either didn't hear or didn't choose to obey. He swung the pocket piece at Manning. The Canadian triggered his machine pistol and blasted a trio of 9 mm parabellums into the gunman's chest. The man spun around from the impact and collapsed to the floor, lifeless. Another opponent dived at Manning, his hands clawing for the micro-Uzi in a desperate effort to disarm the Canadian.

Manning sidestepped the attack and slapped the steel frame of the machine pistol against his opponent's skull, dropping him to the concrete. A third man jumped Manning while the fourth wiped his teary eyes and stooped to reach for the fallen pocket pistol.

The Canadian drove an elbow at his newest attacker's face and hit him flush in the mouth, snapping the guy's head back, then the Phoenix pro followed up and slammed the micro-Uzi across the side of the face. The unconscious man folded up as Manning turned to confront the character who had scooped up the pistol.

A figure appeared behind the gunman. The bug-eyed lenses and filter snout of a gas mask concealed his features, but the Sterling submachine gun clearly identified him as one of the SAS soldiers. He quickly smashed the metal stock of the weapon into the nape of the gunman's neck. Moaning, the man wilted to the floor.

One of the attackers made an attempt to get to his feet, but Manning swung a boot and kicked him hard in the face. The man flopped onto his back, no longer a threat to anyone. The other SAS trooper approached the scene and whistled softly as he glanced at the four figures sprawled on the concrete.

"You blokes have been busy," he remarked.

"There may be more of them around, so stay alert," Manning urged. He spotted a thick metal door on the east wall. "The laser should be in there."

He slipped off his pack, opened it and removed a packet of C-4 plastic explosive. The Phoenix fighter tore off a portion of the white puttylike substance. He judged the amount needed for the task and jammed the C-4 into the doorjamb. The Canadian demolitions expert then reached into his breast pocket and removed a pencil detonator. The two SAS soldiers stood away from the door as Manning inserted the detonator into the C-4 charge and set the timing mechanism for two seconds.

The Phoenix commando stepped to the side of the door away from the charge and covered his ears with his hands. One of the New Zealand troopers held a flash-bang grenade in his fist as he waited for the explosion. The blast wasn't as loud as the SAS commandos had expected. A brilliant glare erupted from the door as the C-4 blew the lock and threw the door open. The soldier immediately pulled the pin from the grenade and tossed it into the room.

The grenade sounded like a large firecracker as it burst in a blinding flash of white light inside the room. Manning ducked low and entered the room, micro-Uzi held ready. He dropped to one knee and trained the machine pistol on a pair of tough-looking characters positioned near a large steel-and-lead vessel. Both men were pawing at their eyes, temporarily deprived of vision by the glare of the grenade. But they still had their Bren submachine guns.

One of them swung his weapon toward Manning. The Canadian fired his micro-Uzi and nailed the gunman with a three-round burst. As the man toppled backward, he triggered his Bren SMG. The weapon spit a short burst of 9 mm rounds into the reinforced concrete ceiling. Bullets ricocheted and whined angrily within the confines of the chamber, and a voice cried out in terror. Manning noticed somebody curled up in a corner, arms wrapped around his turban-clad head.

The second gunman's vision had cleared, and he stared down at his slain companion. He raised his Bren and tried to aim the weapon at Manning, but an SAS warrior's Sterling poked through the doorway and fired a volley of full-auto rounds. The enemy gunman caught the blast in the upper torso and face, and his body was hurled backward into a wall.

Manning glanced around warily. The industrial laser was positioned near the bulky vessel, and he also noticed some coffin-shaped metal cases were also stacked in the room. But Manning didn't see any more humans in the chamber except the one cowering in the corner, apparently unarmed and overwhelmed with fear.

"Don't shoot me!" Morarji exclaimed, slowly raising his hands above his head. "Please, I don't have weapons. I'm a scientist, not a gunfighter."

"Get up slowly," Manning told him. "So you're a scientist?"

"Yes," the Indian said nervously. The two SAS commandos also entered the chamber, and Morarji's eyes opened wide with new terror. "Tell them not to shoot!"

"Don't worry about that," Manning assured him. "What sort of scientist are you? A nuclear physicist?"

"That's correct," Morarji said with surprise. "You already know who I am?"

"I have a pretty good idea what you've been doing here," Manning replied as he pointed the micro-Uzi at the vessel and the laser. "Enriching uranium for the use of nuclear weapons. Right?"

"I believe I have a right to a lawyer," the Indian declared. "Why should you be charging in here and shooting indiscriminately—"

"Shut up," an SAS trooper snarled. "You are in here making nuclear warheads to sell to bloody terrorists, and you have the nerve to question the way this raid is handled?"

"I only did what Hellson made me do," the physicist claimed. "I never wanted to be part of this madness. I'm willing to help testify if it'll help my... uh, situation."

"We can probably, uh, squeeze the information out of him," the other soldier remarked.

"It might work, but it wouldn't be practical," Manning told him. "We still have some work to do here."

The sounds of gunshots echoed within the plant. Three other SAS commandos were in the building and were obviously clashing with more of Hellson's hoodlums. Katz and five more soldiers were supposed to hit the first building from the entrance. Odds were high they had also encountered armed opposition. The battle was far from over.

"We need this jerk alive and able to talk," Manning told the two troopers. "We don't want any damage to happen to the equipment here, either. Especially this vessel. It might contain radioactive matter."

He looked at the metal caskets. "And what are these?" the Canadian asked. "Nuclear vampires?"

"Those contain shells with nuclear warheads—115 mm cannon shells," Morarji answered.

"That's the same caliber cannon used on many types of Russian tanks," an SAS soldier said grimly. "Sellin' to the Commies, eh?"

"I'll tell you more if you keep me alive and get me somewhere safe," the Indian said, aware he had some leverage due to his knowledge and expertise.

"Don't push your luck with us," Manning warned him. "In case you failed to notice, we're not following the usual rules much." Manning turned to the SAS soldiers. "You two guys had better stay here and guard this chamber and everything in it, including our mad scientist."

"What are you going to do?" one of the troopers asked.

"See if the others need a hand," Manning answered as he headed for the door.

He stepped into the bay area once more. Tear gas and smoke continued to drift within the building, and molten metal glowed along the rolling stands. The machinery had been shut down, but the hot liquid metal remained. Shots resounded father up along the conveyors, and he moved toward the sounds of battle.

Manning soon spotted two New Zealand SAS commandos who were positioned at a sheet metal press. They were using it for cover as they exchanged fire with a lone gunman stationed next to the motors and great iron rollers of a rolling stand. He was armed with a Beretta M-12 and a Bren. The guy's heavy firepower and solid cover had allowed him to pin down the SAS troops. The soldiers were returning fire with their Sterling blasters.

As Manning drew closer, he saw a third SAS warrior sprawled near the press. Bullet holes riddled the fallen soldier's back. Apparently the enemy gunman had managed to ambush the troops. The commandos lobbed a tear gas grenade at the triggerman's position. Noxious fumes poured across the ambusher's hiding place. He coughed and spit, but continued to fire his subguns at the SAS fighters.

Manning was in a better position to take out the gunman, and he hadn't been spotted yet. The Phoenix pro aimed his micro-Uzi and opened fire. A trio of 9 mm slugs hit the ambusher in the upper arm and rib cage. The force of the high-velocity bullets spun him around and sent the Beretta flying from his hand. Manning triggered another three-round burst and finished him off.

A man suddenly bolted from behind a metal pillar near Manning. The Canadian swung his machine pistol toward the new threat, but a long wooden pole crashed down on the micro-Uzi and knocked it out of his hands. His opponent was a large man armed with the shaft of a push broom. The improvised weapon was no match for a micro-Uzi or a Sterling subgun, so the guy had hidden and waited for someone to get close enough.

The hood raised the pole swiftly and chopped Manning across the chest, driving him backward. His boots slipped on a concrete lip, and he stumbled into a gutter along the rolling stand. The gutter was littered with debris, among them a few glowing blobs of molten metal. Heat from the slag seared Manning, making him feel as if he'd fallen into an oven. He was four feet from the stream of molten steel on the conveyor. Too damn close.

The guy with the pole leaned forward and swung the shaft at Manning's head. The Canadian danced away from the slashing stick, then quickly grabbed the shaft with one hand and seized his opponent's coveralls with the other. He pulled forcibly, rotating his hips to add power to the thrust. The man was suddenly hurtling forward and plunged into the molten steel. He screamed as the hot metal made short work of him, then was forever silenced by merciful death.

Manning climbed out of the gutter and retrieved his machine pistol, and the two SAS soldiers stepped from cover and waved an all-clear. One knelt by the fallen soldier to check if he were alive, but he wasn't.

"Thanks for bailing us out, mate," a trooper told Manning through the gas mask. "We planned to soften him up with tear gas and try to rush the bastard, but you saved us the trouble."

"Glad to help," Manning said, glancing at the dead SAS man. "Sorry I wasn't a minute or two sooner."

They still heard the sounds of battle, but the reports were distant. The action seemed restricted to the other building where Katz and his SAS unit conducted the second front of the raid on Hellson Metallurgy.

YAKOV KATZENELENBOGEN and a pair of New Zealand commandos had passed through the foyer and headed for the small office section while Lieutenant Jennings led two more SAS troops into the heart of the plant where the furnaces were set up. The Phoenix commander eyed the glass door to the office area with suspicion. The rows of small metal desks and swivel chairs looked innocent, but Katz figured it was better to assume danger than blindly walk into an ambush.

"Be ready to lob tear gas," the Israeli informed his companions as he pointed his micro-Uzi at the door.

One soldier took a gas grenade from his webgear while the other donned his gas mask. Katz fired a short burst and blasted the top pane of glass from the door. Broken fragments crashed to the floor inside the office section, then the commando threw his grenade through the shattered pane. A cloud of fumes immediately exploded within the room.

The head and shoulders of a young man dressed in a white shirt and tie popped up from behind a desk. He thrust an arm across the desktop, a blue-black pistol in his fist. Both Katz and the SAS trooper who had already donned his mask opened fire. Twin streams of full-auto 9 mm slugs raked the desktop and ripped into the pistolman's exposed head and blew off the top of his skull.

The other New Zealand trooper slipped on his gas mask and both men rushed to the door. Katz yanked open the canvas case at his right hip with the steel hooks of his prosthesis and extracted his own mask. The Israeli pulled it onto his head and adjusted the straps with his hooks, then headed for the door while the two SAS soldiers searched among the desks in the office section but found no other holdout.

Suddenly a door burst open and a heavyset figure appeared from a smaller, private office. He had improvised a mask to protect himself from the effects of the tear gas. Crouching, he thrust the barrel of a semiauto Browning shotgun around the edge of the doorway. One of the SAS commandos triggered a hasty salvo of Sterling subgun rounds at the gunman and ducked behind a desk. The thunderous clap of the shotgun responded.

Buckshot smashed into a computer terminal on the desk the soldier used for cover, and the monitor exploded in a spray of plastic and metal fragments. The soldier stayed down, but the other SAS trooper and Katz fired at the shotgunner's position. Parabellum slugs chewed away chunks from the doorway of the private office. The gunman tumbled backward into the room and fired a random burst of buckshot.

The soldier scrambled from behind the desk and slid across the floor sideways. He spotted the wounded enemy gunman at the doorway just as he was trying to swing the Browning blaster toward the threshold.

The SAS commando fired a long burst and slashed half a dozen 9 mm slugs into the enemy's torso. The gunman's body convulsed wildly from the force of the multiple high-velocity projectiles in a last show of life that lasted mere moments.

Katz had already turned his attention to the two doors at the opposite end of the main office section. One door opened a crack, and a fist with a revolver appeared. The Israeli triggered his micro-Uzi and blasted a trio of bullets directly above the hidden gunman's fist. The door swung open, and the owner of the hand tumbled across the threshold, his lifeless eyes staring up at the ceiling.

The SAS troopers quickly swept through the rooms for more opponents while Katz guarded the entrance to the office section. They found no more enemies and left the area. Katz led his New Zealand allies into the plant section where Lieutenant Jennings and his men searched among the steel furnaces. The insane metallic chatter of automatic weapons alerted Katz's three-man team that Jennings had encountered armed opposition.

The machinery in the plant was enormous. The open-hearth furnaces were eight feet high with heavy doors operated by thick cables and chains. Three hearths were open, and white-hot flames burned within them. Plates of cast iron formed huge stacks near the furnaces, and a set of tracks ran along the hearths to accommodate ore cars. A huge crane stood in the center of the plant, its great skeletal frame extending to the crisscross pattern of catwalks near the ceiling.

The huge electric arc furnace, however, was the largest and most impressive item of machinery. Its metal dome was more than twenty feet high and almost sixty feet in circumference. Its exceptional capacity made the arc furnace ideal for tonnage steel and processing alloy metals. Above the dome, a set of heavy beams formed a huge square around the furnace, with heavily protected cables and pipes extending to the monstrous machine.

A burst of automatic fire erupted from a pile of iron plates. Two figures clad in coveralls fired down at the plates from the catwalks above. A gunman was positioned near the crane, and yet another combatant had taken cover next to a large forklift. Two coverall-garbed corpses already lay sprawled on the concrete floor.

Katz raised his micro-Uzi and triggered a volley at the opponents on the catwalks as he lunged for cover behind a steel pillar near the open-hearth furnaces. One of the gunmen screamed and fell backward over a handrail. His shrieks continued as he plunged from the catwalk and until he smashed into the concrete below.

Katz's position was sprayed with a burst of Bren subgun slugs, and the SAS forces retaliated with a wave of Sterling rounds. The man on the catwalk dropped his Bren as bullets shredded his flesh, and found himself draped over the railing in a dead heap.

Katz ejected the spent magazine from his micro-Uzi and reached for an ammo pouch on his belt. Suddenly a muscular young man in baggy trousers and a T-shirt appeared from behind an ore car. He snarled at Katz as he swung a ten-foot length of steel chain. Heavy metal links clanked across the barrel and frame of the micro-Uzi, knocking the weapon from the Phoenix commander's left hand.

The attacker raised his arms and whirled the chain in a fast arc aimed at Katz's head. The Israeli ducked, and links slammed into the pillar inches above his bowed head. Katz jabbed his prosthesis forward and snared the chain. With his left hand he reached for the Walther P-88 in shoulder leather.

Enraged, the man with the chain tugged hard and nearly threw Katz off balance. He charged forward and whipped the opposite end of the chain across Katz's arm to prevent him from drawing the pistol. His face contorted in a mask of rage, the hired thug slapped his hands together with the chain bunched between his palms. He swung his arms as if delivering a blow with an ax.

Katz lashed out with his artificial arm, clamping the steel hooks under his opponent's left arm. Sharp metal bit into the nerve cluster in the underarm, and the man screamed from the terrible pain.

The wounded attacker swung a kick at Katz's groin, but the Israeli blocked the attack by stomping on his opponent's shin. The thug's damaged left arm refused to function, and he swung his right fist in a wild roundhouse. Katz stepped forward and raised his left forearm to block the punch as he drove the curved steel of the hooks into the other man's solar plexus. The big brute groaned as the blow drove the breath from his lungs.

Katz seized the man's arm above the elbow, jammed his right shoulder under it, then heaved and sent his opponent hurtling over his back in a judo shoulder throw.

The man sailed six feet through the air. Katz couldn't see the airborne figure because the glare of the open-hearth furnace blinded him. The shriek of pain told Katz which direction his opponent had been tossed. The Hellson flunky hit the floor directly in front of the open furnace, less than a foot from the raging fire, and the enormous heat ignited his hair and set his shirt ablaze.

The man stumbled around mindlessly, his body shrouded in fire. Katz drew his Walther P-88 when he saw the hardguy suffer the torments of a living hell and ended the man's agony the only way possible.

A burst of full-auto slugs sparked off concrete and the iron rail less than a yard from Katz's feet, forcing the Israeli to jump back for the cover of the iron pillar. He glanced around the edge and glimpsed a muzzle-flash among the beams above the electric arc furnace.

Katz fired his Walther, although he realized the chances of being on-target were slim. Automatic weapons fired streams of 9 mm rounds at the same target. Katz noticed that the muzzle-flashes of these subguns came from the iron plates, where Lieutenant Jennings or his SAS companions were obviously pinned down.

One of the New Zealand commandos with Katz's team darted toward the arc furnace and fired up at the gunman. Another salvo of automatic fire spewed from the crane in the center of the workplace. The SAS warrior stopped abruptly as bullet holes appeared across the front of his uniform shirt. The soldier dropped to his knees and tried to point his Sterling chattergun at the assassin, but the submachine gun slipped out of his lifeless fingers.

An engine growled to life and the forklift suddenly lurched forward. The enemy gunmen at the crane and at the top of the arc furnace fired at the vehicle. Bullets clanged against the frame of the forklift, but the SAS trooper at the steering wheel stayed down as he aimed the lift at the crane. Jennings broke cover from the iron stack and bolted toward the rig. He fired up at the opponent on top of the arc furnace as he ran to keep the gunman occupied. Katz also abandoned his shelter and jogged to the plates. The Israeli triggered two pistol shots at the crane as he darted to his next cover.

The soldier on the forklift suddenly jumped from the vehicle and hit the floor in a fast roll. He tumbled to the base of the crane, a .38 Special Colt Diamondback in his fist. He triggered the revolver at the enemy gunman stationed at the crane. A figure dressed in coveralls tumbled from behind the machine. The gunman still clutched a Bren submachine gun, although the bullet holes in his chest and forehead proved he would no longer be able to use the weapon.

The driverless forklift rolled into the crane and jammed its twin forks and lift carriage against the network of iron girders. The SAS trooper with the revolver fired two .38 rounds at the gunman on top of the electric arc furnace while Jennings dashed to the cover of the forklift. The vehicle continued to run, but the wheels spun vainly as the forklift remained lodged at the base of the crane. Jennings and the other soldier exchanged a few brief words. The officer nodded and raised his Sterling subgun to trigger another burst at the elusive gunman stationed on the beams above the furnace.

Katz guessed what strategy the SAS commandos had decided on. The trooper who'd driven the forklift clearly had hands-on experience with heavy machinery. If so, he might be at the controls of the crane. The crane engine came to life with a growl. Katz glanced up and saw its massive arm slowly move toward the electric arc furnace. A large steel hook swung at the end of the hoist ropes as the crane rose above the furnace to the beams where the gunman was located.

The crane arm shifted into position, its hook dangling above the gunman's cover. Pulleys turned, and the jib slid forward as the hook descended. The gunman tried to avoid it, but there was nowhere to move except into the line of fire over the side. He stepped clear of the hook as the curved steel swung lower. The man sighed with relief.

Suddenly the hook rose and turned, crashing into the chest of the gunman and knocking him backward off the edge of the beam. He cried out in terror as he fell into the glowing stems of the furnace's electrodes. White sparks burst from the poles of light. Electrical snakes crackled and streaked across the fallen body of the Hellson triggerman. Clothing burst into flame, and the twitching form slid down the electrodes to the roof of the furnace to be consumed by the heat.

Katz nodded his professional approval of how the New Zealand SAS troops had dealt with the situation. Then the report of an automatic weapon burst from a stack of pallets, and he saw an SAS soldier sprawled on the concrete. The Israeli glimpsed the muzzle-flash of the assassin's subgun behind the pallets.

The Phoenix commander crept toward the killer's position, then silently drew even closer as the assassin's hands and arms came into view. The Israeli aimed carefully and squeezed the trigger.

A well placed parabellum slug slammed into the enemy's left arm. The 124-grain Hydra-Shok Federal round struck the elbow joint. The hollowpoint slug mushroomed on impact with bone and shattered the target. The killer's MAT-49 few from his hands as he screamed and stumbled forward, weak and stunned by the terrible pain that burned up through nerve endings in his bullet-smashed limb.

"Freeze!" Katz commanded as he pointed his Walther at the guy's face. "Make a sudden move and you're dead."

Then, suddenly, Katz realized the slide of the P-88 was locked back. The Israeli had burned up all the rounds from the magazine. The pistol was empty.

The wounded opponent stared up at Katz and managed a twisted grin. He also saw that the Walther slide was back and recognized what that meant. He grabbed for the MAT subgun on the floor and seized the pistol grip in his good hand.

Katz dropped his useless pistol, but he only raised his abbreviated right arm and prosthesis in surrender. His left hand streaked to the small of his back and grabbed the black metal handle of the ballistic knife. The Israeli drew the weapon and pointed the five-inch blade at his opponent.

The gunman's smile widened. Confident, the man pointed his MAT-49 and prepared to squeeze the trigger.

Katz's thumb pressed down on the lever in the handle of his knife. The pressure on a powerful steel spring inside the hollow handle was released, and the spring shot the blade forward like a projectile from a cannon. The gunman was taken off guard and didn't fully understand what had happened until the point of the ballistic knife blade struck him in the chest and sunk deep into his flesh.

The Phoenix commander dived to the floor. A blink of an eye later, the MAT subgun blasted a poorly aimed volley, but the gunman's aim had been thrown off by the awful pain in his chest. He tried to correct his aim, but his punctured heart stopped. The man glared at Katz as if accusing him of cheating, then his eyes closed abruptly.

"Ginsberg!" Jennings's voice shouted. "Are you all right?"

Katz slowly rose from the floor. His knees buckled, but he managed to stand upright before the SAS troops rushed to his position. Katz pulled at his gas mask and pried it from his face and head. He'd noticed that Jennings and his companion weren't wearing their masks and assumed no tear gas had been used in the furnace area.

"I'm okay," Katz replied, breathing heavily. "Just a bit close that time. Better search the building and see if there are any more of the bastards in hiding."

"We will," Jennings assured him. "Still, I think we've already won. There's no more shooting in the next building, either. Looks like our mates there succeeded, as well."

"You may be right," Katz said as he reached for a pack of cigarettes that weren't in his pocket. "But let's make sure, Lieutenant."

"Yes, sir," the SAS officer said with a nod.

"Do you have a cigarette, Lieutenant?" Katz inquired.

"Of course," Jennings answered as he took a pack of Player's from a pocket and offered them to the Israeli. "I didn't think you smoked, sir."

"It's not a good time for me to try to quit," Katz remarked as he took a cigarette and happily accepted a light from the SAS officer. He sucked in the smoke with relish and felt his body relax. "Maybe I'll give it another try when I don't have so many people shooting at me."

20

New Zealand's South Island might have easily passed for paradise. Vast grasslands extended for miles in all directions, and the magnificent Southern Alps stretched across three-fourths of the length of the island that comprised the largest portion of New Zealand. The scenery that greeted the three-vehicle caravan was tranquil and beautiful.

The clear blue afternoon sky was bright and inviting. Rafael Encizo enjoyed the warmth of the sun after spending forty-eight hours in Antarctica. The climate was somewhat less than the tropical environment Encizo had anticipated, but the sixty-degree weather was still a pleasant relief after the deep freeze of Antarctica. The Cuban rode in the lead Land Rover, seated next to an SAS sergeant named Winslow. Another Land Rover and an army deuce-and-a-half followed Encizo's vehicle.

The caravan bounced along the rolling terrain, skirting a forest of beech trees. The snowcapped peaks of the Alps towered above the treetops in the distance. Skylarks and songbirds chirped pleasantly among the branches, and a small red deer stood by the tree line and watched the vehicles pass by.

"Heller's ranch should be just beyond the trees," Captain Todd announced. The SAS officer sat in the back of the Land Rover with a detailed map of the area across his lap.

"Best stop here and continue on foot. Less chance we might be spotted by any sentries that might be posted."

"Yes, sir," Winslow declared as he stepped on the brakes.

The other two vehicles came to a halt behind the first. David McCarter and another NCO were in the second Land Rover. Calvin James emerged from the passenger side of the truck cab. Seven New Zealand SAS soldiers climbed from the rear of the deuce-and-a-half, and the truck driver stepped from behind the wheel. Captain Todd assembled his men in formation next to the first Land Rover. The young warriors came to attention, stamped their feet together and saluted in the manner peculiar to the British-influenced military.

Encizo attached a foot-long silencer to the barrel of an M-16 assault rifle.

James, too, had an M-16, already fitted with a silencer. An M-203 grenade launcher was attached to the underside of the barrel. He opened the breech to the M-203 and inserted a 40 mm cartridge grenade. "Pretty little place here," he said. "Too bad it won't stay that way for long."

James also carried his micro-Uzi and Walther P-88 in a leather rig, with the pistol holstered under his left arm and a Blackmoor Dirk in a leather sheath under his right. Encizo's Cold Steel Tanto was in a belt sheath, and a Gerber Mark I fighting dagger was clipped to a boot, as well. The Cuban also carried a micro-Uzi and a Walther P-88. Encizo was inclined to carry more weapons into combat than any other member of Phoenix Force. Three *shaken* throwing stars were attached to the harness of his shoulder holster rig. He would have included a backup pistol and another blade or two, but the additional gear would have been too cumbersome in what might be a full-scale battle.

McCarter was armed with his pet Browning Hi-Power in shoulder leather and an Uzi machine pistol with silencer attached to the stubby barrel. He also carried a Barnett Commando crossbow, a favorite of his. A quiver of bolts was attached to his left hip. The feathers at the ends of the fiberglass shafts were different colors. Green feathers labeled the plain steel-tipped bolts, while red meant the shaft at the tip contained a lethal dose of cyanide. The poisoned bolts could deliver almost instantaneous death.

Captain Todd and four of his SAS troops were armed with Sterling submachine guns. The other soldiers carried FAL assault rifles. The best marksmen of the lot had silencers attached to their FAL barrels and telescope mounts. All eleven New Zealand commandos packed .38 Special revolvers on their hips, and all fourteen members of the assault unit carried grenades, spare ammo and gas masks.

"All right, men," Todd addressed his troops. "We all know why we're here, and I won't waste time with a pep talk or telling you blokes why this is so important. The Heller ranch is about two miles east of us. It covers quite a bit of territory, and we have to consider it all to be behind enemy lines. We can only estimate how many opponents may be there, but it's certain we'll be outnumbered. The odds might be as high as eight to one."

That didn't appear to worry any of the SAS soldiers. Of course, they were young and inexperienced in actual combat. That made it easier for them to regard themselves as indestructible. They had never been wounded in battle or seen their friends collapse with blood streaming from flesh torn by bullets or shrapnel. Unfortunately some of the troopers would soon learn the reality of war...if any survived the battle.

"All of you also understand that you're to take orders from these three men just as you would from me," Todd continued as he gestured toward the Phoenix Force commandos. "Perhaps I should say as you would from a *field-*

grade officer. I'll be taking orders from them, as well.'' Todd turned to the Phoenix Force commandos. "Any comments for the lads?''

"Just use good sense and remember your training,'' McCarter declared. "Remember the strengths and weaknesses of your weapons. Try to keep your head. It can get pretty crazy in the heat of battle. Hell, you blokes have been through lots of simulated battles in the past. Draw on that experience, because it's the best thing you've got until you've gone through the real McCoy.''

"We'll probably need to separate into smaller teams after we're inside,'' Encizo added. "Try to stay together in two-man teams. A rifleman for distance and a man with a submachine gun for close quarters.''

"Don't look at me,'' James said with a shrug. "I figure we've talked enough. Let's go get the bastards.''

The strike unit approached the trees carefully, alert to the possibility of surveillance cameras or electronic eyes installed in the forest. They scanned the tree branches, trunks, tall grass and dense growth of ferns, but found no signs of such devices. The Phoenix trio was more familiar with sophisticated surveillance contraptions than the SAS. They realized some devices were virtually undetectable. Microphones could be hidden inside tree trunks, and miniature cameras could be concealed in a small bird's nest among the highest branches.

A shape appeared from the ferns. It was the size of a large hen and walked on short, stubby legs. The creature's brown feathers resembled matted hair, and a long needlelike bill extended from its head. McCarter thought it looked like the product of an impossible union between a stork and a hedgehog. Actually, it was a kiwi, the best known of several species of flightless birds native to New Zealand.

The bird was an interesting zoological curiosity, but it also reminded Phoenix Force that a surveillance device could be hidden among the ferns. There was never any way to be one hundred percent certain of avoiding alarm systems, just as no security precautions were one hundred percent efficient. They could only take what measures of care that conditions and time allowed. Katz and Manning were still in Wellington with the rest of Captain Todd's SAS forces. They had probably hit the Hellson Metallurgy plant already. The enemy in the city base may have managed to radio a message to the ranch and warn them to expect trouble. The second Phoenix Force unit and their New Zealand allies had no idea what they might be walking into.

At the end of the tree line the strike team came to the perimeter of Heller's ranch. Barbed wire surrounded the grazing land. A Land Rover patrolled the grounds along the opposite side of the fence. Two men dressed in khaki uniforms and bush hats rode in the vehicle. One drove the rig and the other glanced around, a French FAMAS assault rifle canted on his shoulder.

The FAMAS was easily recognizable because it was one of the oddest-looking pieces of military hardware ever conceived. At first glance it appeared that someone had slapped the FAMAS together with spare parts from other firearms. The barrel and pistol grip resembled that of a German MP-40 Schmeisser, the butt stock looked like it had been borrowed from an M-60 machine gun and the carrying handle might have been an oversize version of the one found on an M-16. The most unusual feature was the box magazine between the pistol grip and butt. Although the FAMAS looked like a weapon designed by the late Salvador Dalí, it was a serious piece of equipment that fired a thousand rounds per minute.

The Phoenix trio and the New Zealanders stayed low as the Land Rover passed their position. They waited for the patrol to roll out of sight before they approached the fence. Encizo inspected the wires for an alarm. He signaled the others to stay back as he knelt by the post and examined the center strand of barbed wire. He found a thin rubber-coated wire woven in with the barbed wire.

"Found one," he announced. "Simple trick, but it usually works because people don't look for it. An electrical current runs through a wire concealed in the strand. Cut the wire and it triggers an alarm. Cute gimmick. Inexpensive, too. It's also the sort of alarm system that won't go off every time a steer wanders into the fence. Usually put it at the bottom wire or the middle because those are the strands usually cut for an intruder to slip through the fence."

"Can we cut it without setting off the alarm?" Captain Todd asked. He looked around nervously, half expecting the patrol to return any moment.

"Simpler just to leave it be," Encizo said as he checked the other strands to be certain. He also inspected the posts to make sure there wasn't a pressure-operated alarm concealed in the innocent-looking supports. "Everything else is clear. We can just cut the bottom strand and crawl under the fence."

"Be sure to nail down the wire at the posts before you cut," Sergeant Winslow advised. "Otherwise you could end up having yards of wire springing loose along the fence."

"You sound as if you've had some experience with this sort of thing," McCarter said.

"I was raised on a sheep ranch," Winslow explained with a shrug. "The land is better for sheep than cattle, you know."

"Sounds like you should handle this," Encizo said as he handed the sergeant a pair of wire cutters. "Tell us how to do it."

Winslow told them to nail down the wire at each post on either side of the section they wanted to enter through. Then he cut the bottom wire at both ends and removed it. One by one the men crawled under the fence. They kept a collective eye peeled for the patrol as they slipped into the ranch grounds. The team headed for the only available cover—a cluster of shrubs and a few small evergreens.

They discovered that the trees and shrubs were at the perimeter of a valley. At the ridge they peered through the branches and stems. Below them, a herd of steers roamed the grazing land, and several men on horseback kept the cattle from straying. Some carried lariats in one hand and held the reins of a mount in the other. A truck with a trailer attached was parked near the herd. An outdoor mess had been set up behind the trailer. A serving line, butane stove and metal trash cans for washing pots, pans and trays were supervised by a heavyset man in a stained leather apron.

"I'll be damned," Calvin James whispered. "Looks like a rerun of *Rawhide* down there."

"Well, let's head 'em up and take 'em out," McCarter replied.

"Those blokes may be innocent ranch hands," Winslow reminded his teammates.

"Possible," Encizo allowed. "But we'd better assume they're bad guys in the saddle, even if they're wearing tan bush hats instead of black Stetsons."

"What?" Captain Todd asked, confused by the Cuban's remark.

"Never mind," Encizo said. "We'll try to take these guys out without killing them, but we can't afford to take any chances. Those guys might not be hired killers, but they're still not complete innocents unless they're awfully stupid. They'd have to know something about Heller's operation if they've been working here for any length of time."

"So we don't just gun them down, but we don't use kid gloves on the bastards, either," McCarter muttered. "They won't go away just by wishing."

"We can't hide fourteen dudes on this knoll behind some skimpy bushes," James rasped. "If we don't boogie soon, somebody's going to spot us."

"Well, there's more cover along the side of this hill," McCarter observed as he adjusted the shoulder sling of his micro-Uzi to better handle the Barnett crossbow with both hands. "Let's make the most of it, mates."

THE STEERS BECAME restless and bellowed nervously. One of the wranglers noticed that the cattle seemed frightened by something in the bushes at the foot of the hill. His horse also snorted and tried to turn away from the brush. The rider forced the reins back to keep his animal under control. He scanned the trees and shrubbery, unsure if he saw something move among the foliage, or if it was just his imagination or shadows caused by clouds drifting across the path of the sun.

A loud rustle drew the wrangler's attention to a large bush surrounded by ferns and thistles. The bush seemed to be trembling. He placed a hand on the button-flap holster on his hip and cocked his bush hat high on his head with a thumb. He was originally from Australia and still found himself looking for snakes and dingoes on the range, but he reminded himself that neither animals were native to New Zealand. There were a few wild dogs and house cats that had run off and reverted to predomesticated ways. Still, he thought as he urged his mount toward the shrubbery, it would take one hell of a big kitty to shake a bush that size.

He drew closer as the bush shook harder and faster. The wrangler tried to get a better look at a dark figure behind the plant. His fingers opened the flap to the holster and touched the grip of his side arm.

Suddenly a figure jumped up from behind the bush. David McCarter's head and shoulders appeared at the top of the leaves. The British ace held up his hands, palms open to show he didn't hold a weapon. The wrangler jerked back in the saddle, startled by the stranger's abrupt appearance.

"Don't shoot," McCarter urged in a friendly voice. "I surrender, mate."

The wrangler was so surprised by this discovery and McCarter's actions that he didn't notice Calvin James emerge from the bushes next to his horse. The black commando dashed forward and reached up to grab the wrangler. James seized the man's jacket lapel in one fist and the collar with the other. He pulled hard and yanked the wrangler out of the saddle. The man cried out as he fell from the horse and crashed to the ground.

James dropped onto the wrangler's chest and swung a fist at the man's jaw. He followed with the back of his other fist and watched the wrangler's head bounce against the ground. James used his hand like an ax and chopped the hard edge across the side of his opponent's neck. The wrangler uttered a sound that resembled a sigh of relief as he lost consciousness. An SAS soldier appeared from the bushes and helped James drag the wrangler from view.

Another wrangler noticed the riderless horse gallop away from the brush. He frowned as he watched the animal trot some distance, then look around as if puzzled. It was Kingsley's horse, he noticed. The Aussie must have fallen from his mount. What the hell, he thought. Was the idiot drunk or what?

He steered his horse toward the bushes and trotted forward. The wrangler grunted sourly. He couldn't find the Australian. As the man drew closer he saw a figure move near a tree. A bush hat on the shape's head bobbed slightly. The wrangler snorted with contempt. Kingsley was apparently taking a leak or something.

"Hey, you thick-skulled Aussie!" he called out as he approached the brush. "You forgot to hobble your bloody nag."

McCarter stepped from his place of concealment while the wrangler's attention was focused on the SAS trooper impersonating Kingsley. The Briton silently moved behind the horseman. The wrangler noticed that his horse was nervous, and he patted its neck as he stared at the figure in the bushes. Something about the Australian seemed different. The wrangler strained his eyes and craned his neck in an effort to get a better look at the man in the bush hat. Suddenly he realized what was wrong. The guy he had thought was Kingsley was dressed in a camouflage fatigue uniform.

The horse swatted McCarter's elbow with its tail as the Briton crept along the right side of the animal and reached for the rider's ankle. He grabbed it with one hand and yanked the wrangler's foot out of the stirrup as he raised the micro-Uzi in his other fist. The wrangler gasped and reached for his side arm, but McCarter punched the barrel of his machine pistol under the guy's ribs and knocked the breath from his lungs. The British warrior pushed the wrangler's leg and sent him hurtling out of the saddle in an awkward cartwheel.

Bone crunched in the rider's left ankle as he failed to kick his other foot from the stirrup. He moaned and slammed into the ground on his neck and shoulders. James rushed forward, prepared to karate chop the guy into dreamland, but the fall had already rendered the wrangler unconscious.

The black badass pulled the man's left foot out of the stir-rup as the horse whinnied and rose on its hindlegs in fear. James jumped back to avoid a hoof. The animal spun around sharply and bolted into a full run, nearly trampling its rider in the process.

Another man on horseback saw the second mount gallop from the brush without a rider. He also saw James drag the unconscious wrangler into the bushes. The third wrangler cursed and reached for a carbine in a saddle scabbard. An SAS marksman spotted the new threat, aimed his rifle and triggered a three-round burst. The silencer rasped harshly, and the wrangler pitched backward across the rump of his mount, his chest ripped apart by a trio of 7.62 mm slugs. The guy's horse panicked and rose with a terrified whinny. It bucked the corpse from the saddle and galloped away.

The steers bellowed with fear and tried to get clear of the area. The frightened horses and the smell of blood had triggered panic among the cattle. The remaining wranglers cut off the herd and drove it back. They noticed the rider-less horses galloping around the range, but the chaos was confusing and too much was happening at once for them to fully comprehend what was wrong.

One wrangler realized that the situation entailed more than a few spooked steers and a couple of runaway mounts. One horse getting free of its rider was understandable, and two might be a coincidence, but three suggested something had happened to the riders. The worried wrangler left his comrades to deal with the cattle and headed for the trailer. He brought his horse to a halt, dismounted and ran for the door at the side of the rig.

When he reached for the handle on the door, a sharp pain suddenly erupted in his upper arm as pointed steel stabbed the triceps muscle. The wrangler staggered back and clutched at the source of the agony. His gloved fingers touched a five-pointed star. Two sharp tines were lodged in his flesh. He cried out and yanked the *shaken* from his arm.

"Shut up and raise your hands!" Rafael Encizo ordered as he approached from the front of the truck.

The Cuban had approached the trailer during the confusion and spotted the wrangler about to enter the rig. He'd thrown the *shaken*, nailing the guy with the Japanese *shurikenjutsu* star. Now he pointed his M-16 at the wrangler in case the man was gutsy enough to reach for his side arm. The wrangler stared at the black muzzle of the silencer attached to Encizo's rifle and slowly raised his hands.

The door to the trailer opened and a bearded man poked his head outside. The man saw the wounded wrangler and barked a startled curse. He was unaware of Encizo's presence until the Cuban rushed forward and stamped the butt stock of his rifle against the door. The blow slammed the door into the man's head and smashed his skull against the metal frame. He groaned and slid forward. Encizo quickly slapped the barrel of his M-16 behind the stunned man's left ear.

The guy collapsed in the doorway and fell from the trailer to the ground. He was unconscious when he hit the dirt, but the wrangler figured now was the time to jump Encizo. He lunged for the Cuban, hands like twin claws aimed for the Phoenix fighter's M-16. Encizo raised the rifle in his fists and used the frame as a bar to block the wrangler's desperate attack. The guy's forearms banged painfully into steel. Encizo swung a hard butt stroke at his opponent's jaw and dropped the wrangler beside the other figure who was taking a nap on the ground.

Then Encizo heard a voice hiss something that sounded like angry French. He turned and saw the blur of an object crash into his arms and chest. The M-16 was knocked out of Encizo's hands, and the unexpected blow knocked him three feet backward. The swivel chair that had hit the Cuban clattered near his feet.

The man who had thrown the furniture jumped from the doorway and charged toward Encizo. He was taller than the Cuban warrior, but slender and less muscular than the Phoenix commando. Encizo grabbed the micro-Uzi that hung by a strap near his right hip. His opponent was unarmed, and the Cuban didn't want to kill unless the guy forced him to blow him away. Encizo hoped pointing the machine pistol at the son of a bitch would be enough to make him stop.

"Cochon!" the lanky opponent hissed as he swung a roundhouse kick at the micro-Uzi before Encizo could aim the weapon.

The machine pistol flew out of the Phoenix pro's grasp. His opponent's foot touched the ground, and he pivoted on it to thrust a whirling side kick at Encizo's abdomen. The Cuban gasped and doubled up from the boot to his belly. Another French kick boxer, Encizo thought as he staggered away from the lanky enemy. He could learn to hate savate if he had to keep going up against practitioners of that martial art.

The Frenchman raised his fists and danced forward. He feinted a snap kick and swung a left hook at Encizo's head. The Cuban blocked with his forearm and threw a left jab at his opponent's chin. The flunky's head snapped back from the punch, but he retaliated with a high roundhouse kick aimed at the side of Encizo's skull.

Encizo ducked, and his opponent's foot whirled above his bowed head. He lunged before the Frenchman could regain his balance and hooked a fist into a kidney. His opponent fell against the side of the trailer. Encizo hammered a fist between the guy's shoulder blades and slipped an arm under the Frenchman's left armpit. With his hand he clasped the back of the goon's neck in a half nelson. Using his other hand, Encizo grabbed the Frenchman's right wrist and twisted the man's arm in a hammerlock. He rammed a knee into his opponent's tailbone and slammed him face first into the trailer.

The man's knees buckled and he started to sag in Encizo's grasp. The Phoenix fighter was about to slam the guy into the trailer again to make certain he was unconscious, when another figure appeared from the rear of the trailer. Encizo thrust the dazed Frenchman at the bulky shape. A terrible scream erupted, and the French opponent convulsed in a ghastly parody of a jitterbug. The other man shoved him aside. The Frenchman dropped to the ground, both hands clutching a crimson blot spreading on his stomach.

Encizo faced his new opponent. The big man with the leather apron glared at the Cuban and pointed the bloodied tip of a twelve-inch butcher knife at Encizo's face. The cook didn't seem very upset that he had stabbed the Frenchman when Encizo had shoved his comrade into the guy. Maybe the cook figured it was the Cuban's fault and he would concentrate on settling the score now and weep for his slain comrade later.

The cook growled at Encizo like an angry watchdog. He was a nasty-looking thug with a bullet-shaped head, a low brow and a jaw covered by a carpet of ten-day-old whiskers. The guy seemed more like a blacksmith or a professional wrestler than a cook.

Encizo instinctively reached for the Tanto on his belt instead of the Walther P-88 in shoulder leather. The Cuban's early years as a knife fighter triggered this response, but he realized it was the right move because he could draw the Cold Steel blade faster than the pistol, and close-quarters combat made a knife as lethal as a gun, anyway.

The cook slashed his big butcher blade at Encizo's arm in an attempt to disable and disarm the Phoenix warrior before he could draw the Tanto. Encizo danced away from the flashing steel. The butcher knife missed by less than an inch. The cook uttered a bestial snarl as he saw Encizo's Cold Steel Tanto slide from leather. He lunged and tried to thrust the butcher blade into the Cuban's chest.

Encizo dodged the enemy blade and slashed the Tanto at his opponent's wrist. Steel clanged on steel when the blades met. The cook's free hand suddenly snared Encizo's wrist above the Cold Steel weapon. The brute raised the butcher knife for a circular swing at the Cuban's neck, but Encizo's free hand streaked out and caught his opponent's wrist before the cook could carry out the attack.

The two men struggled, each trying to hold his opponent's knife at bay while trying to bring his own blade into play. The cook was bigger, heavier and at least five years younger than Encizo. The contest was definitely in the larger man's favor, but Encizo wasn't about to play by the rules. He stomped a boot heel into his opponent's kneecap and whipped his knee into the guy's thick gut. The gorilla groaned and Encizo turned suddenly. He shoved his wrist against the cook's thumb to concentrate on the weakest point of his opponent's grip. The Phoenix fighter's wrist broke free of the hold, but the cook managed to yank his knife hand from Encizo's grip, as well.

The cook raised his butcher knife for a diagonal cut, but Encizo raised his Tanto in a swift cross-body stroke that slashed his opponent's chest from right rib cage to breastbone. The leather apron protected the big man from the full fury of the ultrasharp Cold Steel edge, but blood still poured from the wound. The cook bellowed with pain and rage as he struck out with his butcher blade.

Encizo ducked low and leaned away from the slashing steel. He thrust his blade beneath the attacker's arm and drove the slanted tip of the Tanto into the cook's chest. The thick steel blade punctured flesh and muscle to stab upward through the solar plexus into the man's heart. The cook howled in agony as the mortal wound announced his death. His final act was an attempt to take Encizo with him. The goon tried to execute a backhand slash with his blade, but Encizo slammed a palm heel into his opponent's forearm to check the attack.

The Phoenix commando hooked the back of his heel and calf muscle across the cook's ankle and pushed his opponent. The judo throw sent the man crashing to the ground. Encizo stepped back and watched the dying cook twist around on the ground and finally twitch before the butcher knife slipped from lifeless fingers.

CALVIN JAMES AND SEVERAL SAS troopers took advantage of the stampede to close in on the remaining wranglers. They stayed low as they approached and used the running cattle for concealment. One wrangler rode around the herd and tried to corral it back into a smaller area. He didn't see the two SAS soldiers until he almost ran over them with his horse. The pair jumped apart to allow the rider to gallop between them. One soldier grabbed his FAL assault rifle by the barrel and swung it like a baseball bat. The butt stock hit the wrangler under the heart and knocked him out of the saddle.

However, another wrangler spotted an SAS trooper first and hurled his lariat before the lone soldier realized the danger. The loop fell around the trooper's head and shoulders. The noose tightened with a hard tug and constricted the soldier's arms and chest. His arms pinned by the rope, the soldier couldn't raise his weapon as the wrangler wound the main line of the lariat around the horn of his saddle. The rider dug his spurs into the horse's flanks and it broke into a run. The soldier was pulled off his feet and dragged at the end of the rope.

James saw the trooper hauled across the ground and heard his screams as flesh was torn on rocks and thistles. The wrangler dragged his victim deliberately into the path of several steers. Hooves trampled the fallen soldier. His screams ceased as his chest was smashed apart as if it were made of cheap plywood.

"Rotten bastard!" James snarled as he raised his M-16 and aimed at the wrangler's back.

He triggered a three-round burst and drilled the killer between the shoulder blades. The silencer-equipped rifle coughed angrily, and James watched with grim satisfaction as the wrangler toppled from the saddle and fell among the charging cattle. He landed on the head of a steer. A horn pierced the man's belly. Blood spurted across the animal as it thrashed wildly and threw the dying wrangler to the ground. The body was crushed by cattle hooves that trampled out whatever trace of life remained.

A loud crack, similar to the report of a small-caliber pistol, exploded and something struck James's M-16 with considerable force. A lash of twisted leather wrapped around the barrel, and a hard tug yanked the weapon from the Phoenix warrior's hands. He turned and saw the bullwhip whirl upward. A wrangler on horseback wielded the eight-foot whip and swung it overhead in a wide circle.

"Gotta problem, nigger?" the man sneered. His accent sounded more Mississippi than southern New Zealand.

James ducked low and grabbed the micro-Uzi on the shoulder strap. The redneck shot his arm forward, snapping his wrist to lash the whip. It struck James across the left shoulder and back. Skin split and the black commando felt blood ooze across his shirt. The blow nearly knocked him off balance as he triggered the machine pistol. James swore angrily when the micro-Uzi blasted a useless trio of 9 mm slugs into the ground.

The wrangler whirled and lashed out with his whip once more. James raised the micro-Uzi in one fist, and the lash struck the frame and curled around the machine pistol. James immediately reached out and grabbed the whip with his other hand before the wrangler could pull the lash and yank the weapon from his grasp.

"Now you've got a problem, asshole!" James growled as he held the whip in one fist and triggered the micro-Uzi with the other.

The nine-inch silencer sputtered at the end of the stubby barrel of the machine pistol. Bullets ripped into the chest of the whip expert. The guy's body convulsed in the saddle as he stared at James with an expression of astonishment. He slumped forward, the whip handle still in his fist. James pulled the leather cord and watched the dead man tumble from the back of his mount.

"What a dumb shit," James muttered as he unwound the whip from the frame of his micro-Uzi. He winced from the pain in his shoulder and back, but he was aware the wound wasn't serious. "Only a brain-damaged, illiterate, peckerwood moron would use a whip against a guy armed with a submachine gun."

James glanced around and found his M-16. Luckily the steers hadn't stomped it into the ground. The black commando was still growling under his breath about the idiot with the bullwhip. The bastard must have read *Uncle Tom's Cabin* too many times and adopted Simon Legree as his hero, James thought sourly as he retrieved his rifle.

A wrangler at the opposite side of the herd fired a pistol at an SAS soldier before the New Zealand Commando blasted him with a silenced Sterling SMG. Until that shot, not a single weapon without a silencer had fired, a noisy report that would no doubt be heard for miles. The cattle bellowed in greater terror and ran in a wild charge toward the heart of the ranch. The assault team gave the beasts plenty of room and allowed the steers to flee.

THE PATROL IN THE LAND ROVER heard the shot and the commotion in the valley. The vehicle rolled to the ridge and came to a halt. The driver reached for a two-way radio transceiver while his companion with the FAMAS rifle stood up in the Land Rover to examine the valley with a pair of binoculars.

"The bleedin' cattle are panicked," he announced. "I can't see any wranglers ridin' herd on the beasties, either."

"All hell has broken loose," the driver said grimly as he raised the antenna to his radio and pressed the transmit key. "HQ, this is Patrol Three. Come in, HQ. Over."

The shrubs by the ridge stirred and the pair turned to see Captain Todd emerge from the foliage. The SAS commander pointed his Sterling subgun at the driver. He ordered the patrolman to drop the radio. The thug with the French blaster released the binoculars and grabbed his FAMAS with both hands.

The gunman suddenly jerked and stood stiffly, eyes wide with surprise. He glanced down at the feathered shaft of a crossbow bolt lodged in his chest. Cyanide seeped into heart and lungs. The guy fell backward and toppled out of the Land Rover. His fingers still clutched the FAMAS rifle, but the man was already dead before he hit the ground.

"Jesus!" the driver exclaimed as he raised his hands in surrender. "I give up, damn it!"

"Get out of the vehicle," Todd ordered. "Put your hands on the bonnet and spread your legs."

The driver obeyed with great speed. David McCarter emerged from the bushes with the Barnett crossbow in his hands. Todd cast a hard gaze at the British ace. The officer relieved the enemy driver of a pistol and frisked the man for other weapons. He bound the guy's wrists behind his back with a set of plastic riot cuffs as McCarter approached the vehicle.

"It doesn't appear that your plan has worked out very well so far," Todd remarked dryly.

"Oh, it hasn't really gone all that badly, either," McCarter replied with a shrug. "Besides, we're not done yet."

21

Two Land Rovers headed for the range where Patrol Three had reported to headquarters just before radio transmission had ended. The Land Rovers encountered stampeding cattle as they approached the grazing area. The vehicles moved clear of the panicked cattle and reported the discovery to the security headquarters. Something was definitely wrong, and the others were warned to prepare for the worst.

The patrols noticed that no wranglers accompanied the steers, but they were surprised to see the small truck and trailer following the stampede some distance behind the cattle. That was particularly odd, since the trailer was used to store gear on the range and as a communications center for the wrangler teams to stay in contact with the ranch base.

The two Land Rovers approached the truck. One moved in from the right and the other from the left. The truck slowed down as the patrol vehicles drew closer. Both Land Rovers came to a halt. Passengers armed with assault rifles sprang from the patrol cars and pointed their weapons at the truck and trailer rig. The drivers of the Land Rovers also stepped from their vehicles and unsheathed pistols from hip holsters. The truck stopped fifty-odd feet from the improvised roadblock.

"Hold it right there!" a patrol gunman shouted at the trailer-toting rig.

"What the hell do you blokes think you're doing?" the man behind the wheel of the truck yelled from his window. "We've got an injured man on board! Got gored by a steer when they stampeded! We have to get him back to the ranch."

"Bullshit!" another patrolman snapped. "Get out of the truck with your hands up!"

Suddenly another vehicle appeared behind the truck and trailer. The patrol members were startled to see the Land Rover approach. It was the Patrol Three vehicle. The driver and his passenger wore bush hats. From a distance the pair seemed to be Hellson security personnel, but the camouflage military uniforms labeled them as imposters as the Land Rover drew closer.

The patrol blockade was distracted by the third Land Rover. They didn't notice the figure of David McCarter climb from the rear of the trailer onto the roof. The Briton sprawled on his belly, the Barnett crossbow in his fists. He put the skeletal stock to his shoulder and peered through the Bushnell scope. McCarter chose a target and triggered the crossbow.

An enemy rifleman dropped his assault rifle and raised both hands to the shaft of the crossbow bolt that jutted from the side of his neck. The man collapsed to the ground and thrashed around in a cyanide-induced fit. The convulsions were brief, and his body soon lay still in the total relaxation of death.

Calvin James and an SAS sharpshooter appeared from the rear of the trailer and fired assault rifles at the pair of patrolmen beside the second Land Rover while another soldier in the Patrol Three vehicle aimed his FAL at the survivor by the first blockade car. Silencers barked muted reports, and high-velocity rounds hammered the enemy positions. The door to the trailer sprang open and Rafael Encizo emerged with his M-16. The Cuban dropped to one knee and contributed to the firepower. Sergeant Winslow also climbed from the passenger side of the truck and swung an assault rifle at the besieged patrolmen.

Enemy gunmen jerked and twisted around from the impact of multiple projectiles. Windshields shattered, and bullets raked the doors and frames of both Land Rovers. The tidal wave of automatic fire chopped the remaining patrolmen into three lifeless clumps of bloodied meat. McCarter swung down from the roof of the trailer and landed next to Encizo.

"A bit messy," the Briton remarked, "but it worked."

"Yeah," Encizo agreed as he canted his M-16 across a shoulder. Smoke still curled from the silencer attached to the barrel. "It worked this time, but the enemy won't be as easy to take on when we reach the ranch house. They certainly know they've been invaded by now, and they're putting up defenses."

"Including the nuclear cannon?" Captain Todd inquired, his voice taut with tension.

"That's a risk we have to take," Encizo replied. "No turning back now, Captain."

"What if they use the cannon?" Todd asked, certain he wouldn't like the answer.

"Well, then we'll all be killed," McCarter said with a fatalistic shrug. "Getting vaporized by a nuclear explosion isn't my idea of a joyous end, but at least the other side will go up in the mushroom cloud along with us. Fewer people will die if the explosion goes off here than in a heavily populated area."

"We'll be among the 'fewer people' who'll buy the farm, man," James commented as he appeared from the rear of the trailer and joined the conversation. "Still, we've got to play the game with the hand dealt to us. The only thing that might save our butts now is if we can hit the bastards fast and hard. Maybe we can take 'em out before they have a chance to use the nuclear hardware.''

"We can move faster in the vehicles than on foot," McCarter added. "I wonder if those Land Rovers will still run now that we've shot the shit out of them."

"I guess we'll find out," James replied. "You know, this is really an insane way to make a living."

"True," Encizo agreed, "but I could never imagine myself going to work in a suit and tie. That sort of thing would probably give me high blood pressure, a bleeding ulcer and all the other ailments that come with a stressful office job."

"Might have had a heart attack or stroke by now if any of us had to go through that crap," McCarter added. "Reckon that puts us all on borrowed time, anyway, eh?"

"I just sort of wonder when that time will run out," James said with a sigh. "Aw, shit, let's boogie."

GUSTAV KUBLER MOPPED his brow with a sweat-stained handkerchief as he held the Heckler & Koch MP-5 submachine gun in his other pudgy hand. The Austrian munitions expert was more familiar with designing weapons than actually using them. The H&K felt awkward and alien in Kubler's hands. The obese, middle-aged Austrian had no illusions about his ability as a fighting man. He was a technician, not a warrior.

However, the four mercenary soldiers in Heller's office were young and fit. Their lean bodies were hard and muscular. The mercenaries carried weapons with confidence based on combat experience. There were two Australians, an American of Nordic descent and a German, all four of whom had light brown or blond hair and clear blue eyes. Adolf Hitler would have regarded them as superb examples of Aryan breeding for the master race.

Kubler snorted bitterly at the notion. Hitler had been a crackpot who had led Germany into a destructive world war. The Nazi master race had been pounded into the ground. Heller seemed to have some of the same racist notions as Hitler, Kubler thought. The American wouldn't hire any-one except whites, unless he needed someone with a unique skill to accomplish his ambitious goals. Professor Morarji had been the only exception to Heller's policy of "whites are right." Kubler felt sorry for the Indian scientist if Hellson Metallurgy was also under siege. Morarji was even less suited for battle than the Austrian.

"That metal casket contains a nuclear shell for the atomic cannon," Kubler instructed as he shoved a loaded maga-zine into the well of the MP-5. "Each of you grab a han-dle, pick it up and carry it to the barn."

"Mein Herr," the German merc said. *"Sie nicht—"*

"Speak English for the sake of your comrades," Kubler demanded. "We're all facing the same dangers. This is not the time to keep secrets or have others suspicious of the men on our side. Let everyone know exactly what you have to say."

"Yes, sir," the German soldier of fortune said in un-steady English. "Do you really intend to use the nuclear weapon? That is a very drastic decision. We'll all die if you do that."

"We knew the risk when we signed on, mate," an Aus-tralian mercenary commented. "We got paid high 'cause the risks are high."

"Yeah," the American merc remarked. "I realized that, too, but I didn't figure that meant I'd get my ass nuked, for Chrissake. I think we should choose the better part of valor and make a run for it. The attack seems to be coming from only one direction. Maybe some of us can get away if we all bolt in different directions."

"Be realistic, my friend," Kubler urged. "They may have sent a small assault team to penetrate the ranch property, but they have certainly established military and police blockades beyond the perimeters. We won't be able to escape that way."

"Maybe it's the Arabs and not the New Zealand government or the CIA or whoever," the American suggested. "They came here a few days ago to buy one of the atomic cannons and shells to go with it, right? Maybe they figured it would be cheaper to just come back and steal what they want instead."

"Possible," Kubler agreed, thankful for any reason to hope all wasn't lost. "Still, we have to prepare for the worst, just in case. Carry the casket and follow me."

The Austrian led the mercenaries from the ranch house. Kubler held the H&K tightly in his perspiration-slick hands, and the mercs carried the metal coffin like pallbearers on the way to a grave site. Symbolic perhaps, Kubler thought, since the weapon in the big steel box might mean the collective funeral for all of them. If Kubler had to use the atomic cannon, everyone would receive an instantaneous cremation, and their radioactive ashes would be scattered to the four winds.

The other mercenaries at the ranch were busy trying to set up defenses. Men carried light machine guns from the billets to sandbagged mounds. They selected tractors and silos for cover. Hired killers checked their weapons and magazines as the bellow of frightened cattle and thousands of hooves pounded the ground with artificial thunder in the distance. The clouds above the ranch gradually became darker, as if to set the stage for the grim life-and-death drama that was about to unfold.

Suddenly a large, dark shape appeared above the hill. The truck and trailer paused for a moment as a human figure slipped from behind the wheel and bailed out the open door. Then the truck rolled forward. It gained momentum as it headed down the incline. Machine-gun nests opened fire. Orange flame streaked from automatic weapons, and tracer rounds marked the progress of streams of bullets that pelted the rampaging vehicle.

"Keep moving!" Kubler told the mercs with the casket. *"Schnell! Schnell!"*

The pallbearers double-timed to the barn. They made better, faster progress than Kubler. The fat man was huffing and puffing by the time he reached the entrance of the barn. The roar of an explosion and the yellow glare of a sudden burst of light chased them as they ducked inside the shelter. Kubler glanced outside and saw that the truck had burst into a ball of rolling flame. Fire jumped from shattered windows and filled the seat behind the wheel with an inferno. The trailer wobbled behind the burning truck. Machine-gun rounds continued to blast the vehicle. Tires rolled despite the flames. Bullets punctured rubber, but the truck's path was already destined. It would roll on just the wheel rims if necessary.

The truck hadn't caught fire because the fuel tank had been hit, Kubler observed. Someone had purposely set something flammable in the front seat. A can of gasoline, perhaps, or even the butane stove from the mess equipment. The explosion had been deliberate. The enemy had wanted the truck transformed into a rampaging fireball. Kubler saw why. It was headed directly for the ranch house.

Too late, mercenary soldiers tried to stop the vehicle by lobbing grenades at it. The truck was too close. One grenade exploded beside the trailer and blasted it loose from the towing gear. Another grenade bounced off the hump-shaped roof of the trailer. The explosive egg ricocheted straight back at the sandbagged mound that it had come from.

Voices cried out in alarm and fear as men scrambled to get away or tried to grab the grenade in a vain effort to throw it away before it went off.

The flaming truck smashed into the side of the house. It caved in brick and plaster and charged into Heller's precious home. Fire broke out within the dwelling. The grenade on the sandbagged mound exploded, and fragments of dismembered mercenaries erupted from the shelter. Bodies and parts of bodies were flung several feet and landed near unnerved survivors.

Without warning the trailer section exploded in another burst of fearsome flame and flying shrapnel. The powerful C-4 explosion sent shards of metal rocketing among the mercenary forces like bullets from a Gatling gun. Men screamed and toppled to the ground. Flesh was punctured and bones splintered. Eyeballs were pierced and noses sheared from bloodied faces. Three mercs were killed by the wave of heat from the blast that scorched their lungs and burned tongues into swollen globs trapped in constricted throats.

"Gott in Himmel!" Kubler rasped in astonished horror as he witnessed the carnage from the open barn door. "It's as if devils from hell have been sent to destroy us!"

THE THREE PHOENIX FORCE commandos and their New Zealand SAS allies had witnessed the success of their "truck bomb" tactic. It had been a success on more than one level. The unmanned vehicle had delivered a devastating blow to the enemy camp and had also forced the mercenary soldiers to reveal several of their positions when they fired on the truck. The way the Heller goon army responded to the attack also told the Phoenix Force and SAS observers something about their opponents. The mercenaries were very well armed and appeared to have a vast supply of ammunition. They were obviously familiar with their weapons and accustomed to combat, but they showed little united effort or team coordination. The mercs had fought battles in the past, but they had never fought as a unit before. Judging from their performance thus far, Heller's private army had never really trained together and, until that day, they had probably thought it unlikely they would have to physically defend the ranch from invaders.

James, McCarter, Encizo and five SAS commandos observed the situation at an uncomfortably close position. They approached the enemy base while the mercenary forces concentrated on the obvious threat of the rampaging truck and trailer. The flames and explosions provided an excellent distraction as the strike team members crawled closer to the ranch center. Captain Todd and the remaining members of the SAS team remained near the summit of the hill. The best sharpshooters of Todd's men were with the officer. They had removed the silencers from their FAL rifles because the devices muffled sound and reduced muzzle-flash but also reduced accuracy and muzzle velocity of projectiles. The New Zealand military marksmen peered through sniper scopes and waited for the next round of combat with Heller's forces. Todd crouched by a Land Rover and anxiously waited for the signal that the next phase of the battle was about to begin.

James and McCarter crawled to a manure spreader in the fields about twenty yards from the enemy stronghold. The large metal bin and tractor-style tires were the best cover available to the pair. A young SAS corporal, a Maori with dark skin and proud Polynesian features, accompanied them and squatted behind a tire with his Sterling submachine gun cradled in his arms. James carefully peered over the top of the bin and estimated the distance from their position to a machine-gun nest.

The black badass from the Windy City eased the barrel of his M-16 over the bin, aimed as best he could and triggered the M-203 attachment. A 40 mm grenade burst from the launcher, sailed in a high arc and descended on the sand-bagged mound. It exploded and flung the mangled, twisted metal stalk that had formerly been a mounted machine gun high into the air. Ragged chunks of butchered mercenaries also showered down from the sky.

Only two or three mercs fired at the manure spreader. The others failed to see what direction the M-203 grenade had come from, let alone pinpoint the source. The others were more concerned about the shape that rolled over the top of the hill and headed for the ranch house.

The mercenaries fired at the Land Rover as it charged forward. They didn't blast the vehicle with fury equal to that exercised against the truck. Heller's goons assumed that the Land Rover was unoccupied and wasted little ammo in shots fired at the windshield or windows. They concentrated on firing at the tires and flank of the four-wheel-drive vehicle. The mercs wanted to slow it down or hit the gas tank and blow up the vehicle before it could get close enough to do serious damage among their ranks.

Some of the enemy lobbed grenades at the Land Rover when it came within range. They assumed it was another "car bomb" like the truck and trailer rig had been. Grenades exploded near the vehicle and blasted the Land Rover apart. The fuel tank exploded, and flaming gasoline erupted. However, the car hadn't been loaded with explosives, and the blast was less spectacular than the enemy had expected.

The Land Rover had served its purpose from the Phoenix Force/SAS point of view. The enemy was distracted by the Rover. Their attention was fixed in the wrong direction. Some of the mercs had even stood up when they'd thrown their grenades, presenting clear targets for the SAS marksmen on the hill. Todd's riflemen were ready and quickly zeroed in on the exposed opponents. Three careless mercenaries fell among their comrades, shot by one or more 7.62 mm NATO bullets in either the head or upper torso.

The distraction also allowed the three Phoenix commandos and the soldiers with them to close in on the enemy ranks. McCarter and the Maori trooper lobbed flash-bang grenades at the sandbags as they ran forward. James had reloaded his M-203 launcher but held his fire as he followed the pair.

The grenades exploded with blinding light and earsplitting force. Dazed mercenaries staggered around half-blind and disoriented. McCarter bounded over the sandbags and jammed his crossbow into the chest of a stunned opponent. The Briton triggered the weapon and fired a bolt. The projectile rocketed from the powerful bowstring and punched clean through the man's body. The mercenary staggered back three steps as blood seeped from the entrance and exit wounds in his chest and back.

Another Heller flunky screamed and doubled up. He had been standing behind the first merc when McCarter had fired the crossbow. The bolt had pierced his stomach after passing through the first opponent. The second man actually died first as the cyanide mixed with his blood and rapidly claimed the corrupt adventurer's life. The first merc had suffered a fatal wound but didn't even realize he was dying because the bolt had shot through him so fast that he'd barely felt it. McCarter switched the crossbow to his left hand and slashed the right in a karate chop at the stunned man's neck muscle. The merc collapsed in an unconscious heap, permanently.

Two other mercenary pieces of trash saw McCarter. They hesitated for a split second because they could hardly believe anyone would be bold enough to actually charge into their stronghold to take them on face-to-face at such close quarters. The startled thugs raised their weapons, but they had wasted too much time already. The SAS corporal rolled over the sandbags and fired his Sterling SMG at the pair. The British chattergun was still equipped with a silencer and rasped harshly as it spit out a lethal dose of half a dozen parabellum rounds. The hoodlum troopers toppled to the ground.

James leaped over the sandbagged wall and landed feet-first on the chest of a mercenary opponent. The powerful kick sent the man hurtling backward into another gunman. The black warrior gripped his rifle in both hands and jabbed the butt stock into the face of his first opponent. The hard plastic connected with the man's chin. He slumped, unconscious, and James slashed the rifle barrel at the second man's skull.

Although stunned and taken off guard, the merc managed to raise an arm to block the gun barrel. He hissed from the pain of hard steel against his forearm, but he still tried to grab James's weapon with his free hand. The Phoenix pro struck first and raised the butt stock in a fast uppercut to his opponent's jaw. The merc's head recoiled from the blow, and he collapsed beside his senseless comrade.

McCarter charged a pair of mercenaries behind a tractor. The Briton held the crossbow in one hand and the micro-Uzi in the other. The astonished thugs had barely realized they faced an enemy invader before McCarter's machine pistol sputtered a ruthless three-round burst into the face of the closest merc. The guy's head exploded and splattered the second man with gory debris. The mercenary was stunned and horrified by the ghastly shower. McCarter terminated the man's shock with a trio of 9 mm slugs through the heart and lungs.

James swung his M-16 at one of the enemy billets and fired his M-203 launcher. A 40 mm grenade jetted across the area and smashed through a windowpane. It exploded inside the merc barracks. Half the roof erupted into a shower of tar-draped kindling. The screams within the building revealed that it was still occupied when the grenade went off.

The Maori trooper dropped to one knee and fired his Sterling into a trio of enemy soldiers. One opponent went down instantly. Another doubled up and clutched his bullet-torn abdomen. The third pointed a Bren subgun at the SAS warrior, but Calvin James fired his M-16 from the hip and drilled a pair of 5.56 mm slugs through the gunman's face. A bullet split the bridge of the guy's nose and tunneled through his brain.

McCarter crouched by the tractor and yanked the pin from a concussion grenade. He lobbed it through a window of the ranch house. The grenade exploded and blasted two other windows from inside the building. Shards of glass spewed from the shattered panes and slashed into the faces and necks of two unfortunate mercenaries. The pair screamed in agony as they clawed at bloody cuts in their flesh. One man pulled a two-inch sliver of glass from a punctured eyeball.

The British warrior hosed the pair with his micro-Uzi. Their agony ended abruptly as 9 mm slugs chopped them into oblivion. Bullets sliced air inches from McCarter's head. He spun around and pointed his weapon at the guy who had nearly greased him. The Briton fired the machine pistol one-handed and hit his startled opponent with the last three rounds from the micro-mag. The enemy gunman fell, twitched and died with his Bren chopper still clutched in his fists.

McCarter jogged to the house, dived forward and shoulder-rolled to the side of the building. He crouched low and ejected the spent magazine. The Phoenix commando reloaded the micro-Uzi and charged through the doorway. A hard kick moved the door out of his path. It swung on broken hinges and fell to the marble floor in the hall.

Rafael Encizo and four other SAS soldiers had reached another row of sandbags. One of the more eager and reckless New Zealand soldiers charged the mound first and blasted a pair of mercenaries with his Sterling. One opponent slapped both hands to his bullet-shattered face and slumped lifelessly to the ground. The other bellowed in pain as a 9 mm slug burned through his left shoulder and smashed the joint. However, the merc raised his Beretta M-12 submachine gun and returned fire. The slugs ripped open the young SAS commando's chest and sent his corpse tumbling over the sandbags.

Encizo hit the bags sideways and slid on his back as he entered the enemy lines. The merc with the Italian blaster was taken off guard by this unorthodox entry. He tried to adjust the aim of his Beretta, but Encizo's M-16 fired first, canceling the thug's ticket.

A shape appeared near the Cuban's head. He shifted his shoulders and swung his rifle toward the mercenary, but his opponent butted the M-16 from his grasp. Encizo glimpsed a rifle butt about to slam down into his face. The Phoenix pro moved his head, and the walnut stock of the enemy's weapon stamped the ground near his right ear.

Encizo grabbed the gun stock with both hands and swung a boot up into his attacker's ribs. The merc grunted and fell sideways. The Cuban held on to the enemy's rifle with one hand and pressed the barrel down on his opponent as he rolled onto the man's back. His left hand grabbed the hilt of his Tanto knife and drew it from the belt scabbard. The six-inch blade jutted from the bottom of his fist in an "ice-pick grip." Encizo raised his arm and swung the Tanto hard.

The reinforced Cold Steel point pierced the mercenary's right kidney. He shrieked and arched his spine in a backward curl. Encizo executed another knife stroke and stabbed the Tanto into the base of his opponent's neck. The heavy blade severed the man's spinal cord. His opponent's body went limp as Encizo cut the blade through muscle and skin to yank it from the corpse.

The Cuban pushed the dead man and tried to pull his micro-Uzi from beneath the lifeless body. He glanced up and saw another merc towering over him. The man aimed a blueblack pistol at Encizo. A twisted smile crept across the hoodlum's face as he prepared to blast the Phoenix commando into eternity. Then the pistolman suddenly jerked backward as three exit wounds appeared across his chest. Blood spurted from the ragged bullet holes in his khaki shirt. He raised his arms and fired a harmless round into the sky before he wilted to the ground. An SAS commando stood behind the slain opponent, Sterling subgun in his fists.

"You all right, mate?" the New Zealander asked.

"I am now," Encizo replied with a sigh of relief. "Thanks to you."

He pried the dead man off his micro-Uzi and got to his feet. His SAS companions were busy hosing enemy troops with automatic fire. One man threw a grenade at the undamaged billets. Another SAS soldier followed his example, and the twin blasts tore the door from the entrance and blasted two windows apart. Encizo spotted a mercenary gunman at the mouth of the barn. He fired his machine pistol, and the man pitched backward as if yanked off his feet by invisible wires. The guy hit the ground in a lifeless clump as someone inside the barn shoved the heavy door shut.

A head appeared above a pile of sandbags. The gunman slid the barrel of a subgun over the top bag. Encizo spotted the guy and fired a burst of 9 mm rounds at the opponent. Slugs tore into the canvas sacks, and sand flew into the gunman's face. The man ducked back under his shelter. Encizo yanked a concussion grenade from his belt, pulled the pin and tossed it into the sandbagged cover. The grenade exploded, and three mercs were hurled from the mound.

"Better than I expected," the Cuban muttered as he scanned the area for more opponents.

David McCarter discovered that the interior of Heller's ranch had suffered considerable damage during the battle. Plaster dust leaked from cracks in the walls and ceiling. The dining room was ablaze, and columns of smoke billowed in the hall. The statues of Mars and Fortuna—Heller's favorite deities of war and fortune—had fallen to the marble floor and shattered beyond recognition.

The Briton left the Barnett crossbow and quiver of bolts in the hall and gripped the micro-Uzi in both hands. He moved to the corridor and carefully peered around the corner. There were no opponents waiting for him, but he saw two doors. Both were closed. McCarter took a concussion grenade from his webgear, pulled the pin and tossed the blaster down the corridor.

The Phoenix warrior stood clear of the corridor and waited for the grenade to go off. He didn't have to wait long—the explosion shook the house within seconds. Plaster and dust hurtled from the corridor. McCarter let it settle a bit, then moved around the corner. Both doors had been blasted open by the explosion. Micro-Uzi held ready, McCarter approached the first door and peered inside. It was a large closet filled with clothing, shoes, boots, hats and boxes. The Briton poked the jackets and shirts with the machine-pistol barrel to make certain no one was hiding behind them and even checked the shelf in case an opponent had climbed onto it.

Moving to the next doorway, he peered inside. The room was Heller's den. Several bottles and glasses had been knocked over by the blast. Broken glass littered the floor near the fancy leather-topped bar. Alcohol formed a puddle around the shattered pieces. Aside from a sprinkling of plaster dust, the expensive furniture hadn't been harmed, although a jagged crack marred the wide-screen television set.

However, McCarter's main concern was the burly mercenary in the center of the room. A muscular figure clad in khaki shirt and shorts, the guy had been bowled over by the blast that had smashed in the door. The merc was slightly dazed, but the door had protected him from the full fury of the explosion. A French FAMAS rifle lay on the floor beside him as he started to rise. The merc glanced up at the micro-Uzi in McCarter's fist.

"Reach for the gun and I'll cut you in half," the Briton warned. "Get up slowly and keep your hands where I can see them."

"You sound like a Brit," the merc muttered as he got to his feet. His accent suggested he was a native New Zealander, McCarter thought. Probably a hood from Auckland or Wellington.

"All you need to know is that I have a gun in my hand and you don't," the Phoenix fighter told him. "Speaking of which, kick that rifle across the floor. I don't want the temptation to make you do something stupid."

"Don't worry," the man assured him as he raised his hands and booted the FAMAS hard enough to send it sliding across the room. "I know when I'm beat. You're a cockney, right? I was in London once."

"I don't care if you used to work for bloody Scotland Yard," McCarter told him. "From the descriptions of this place, Heller keeps some of his nuclear shells in this room. Where are they?"

"Heller?" The mercenary raised his bushy brown eyebrows. "So you've already blown Hellson's precious cover. I always wondered why he picked a phony name that sounded so much like his real one. He's an arrogant bastard, of course. Fond of himself. Does all that weight lifting and such. Reckon he wanted a name as close to his real one as he could manage."

"If you don't answer my question, I'll shoot your kneecaps off and leave you here," McCarter warned. "Maybe the building will cave in on you, or you'll bleed to death before we get around to you again. Now talk or I'll find somebody else who will."

"All right, all right," the mercenary replied quickly. "Heller took some of the shells with him. Three or four. I don't know how many. He and House left with the Chink."

"What do you mean by 'the chink,'" McCarter demanded.

"Chinaman," the merc explained. "Maybe he ain't a Chink, but he's Oriental. Jap, Korean, whatever. Ugly fish-faced bloke with a steel hook for a hand."

"And Heller left with this Asian character and some of the nuclear shells?" McCarter asked. "Where did they go?"

"Australia, I reckon," the mercenary said with a shrug. "You've heard about the explosion, haven't you?"

"What explosion?" McCarter demanded, his stomach twisting as he thought of the innocent lives that could be destroyed by a single nuclear cannon shell.

"In the Aussie outback," the man replied. "It was on the news. Nuclear explosion out there in kangaroo land."

"Oh, God," McCarter rasped. "Where are the rest of the shells?"

"They make 'em at the metallurgy plant," the merc said. "I suppose most of them are there. Two of them are in those steel coffins over there."

He tilted his head toward a pair of long metal boxes near the window. "Kubler took the other one out to the barn," the mercenary continued. "He's got a goddamn cannon out there, you know. Might just blow us all up."

"Bloody hell!" the Briton muttered.

McCarter felt something hard jam into the small of his back. The cylinder-shaped object was no stranger to the Phoenix pro. Someone had stuck a gun barrel in his back.

"Freeze, you limey scumbag," a voice snarled less than a foot from McCarter's right ear. "Make a fast move and I'll bust your backbone with a .45 slug."

The Briton groaned. He had wondered why the merc had been so chatty when he had the guy at gunpoint. The bastard had been stalling for time to allow the fellow behind McCarter to get into position. The second gunman had probably been hiding behind the bar since McCarter had entered the den, the Phoenix fighter thought, disgusted with himself for not checking the room carefully before conducting a session of twenty questions with his prisoner.

"Took you bleedin' long enough, Karas," the merc complained as he lowered his hands.

"Sorry," the man with the gun at McCarter's spine replied. His accent sounded as if it hailed from the American Midwest. "There's a lot of broken glass on the floor, and I had to be careful not to step on any of it. Didn't want the sound to tip off this son of a bitch."

McCarter raised his arms to shoulder level. He held the micro-Uzi in his left hand by the frame, fingers away from the pistol grip and trigger. Karas, the guy with the pistol, still had his weapon pressed against the Briton's back.

"Tempted to kill you outright," Karas declared, "but I figure you might be more useful as hostage. Get his gun, Loomis."

The New Zealander reached for the machine pistol in McCarter's hand, but the Briton suddenly tossed it sideways, out of reach. Hoping both opponents were distracted, McCarter whirled to the right and slammed his forearm into Karas. The blow struck the guy's arm above the Colt .45 in his fist. The pistol was knocked away from McCarter as the Briton swung his left fist into Karas's broad face.

McCarter grabbed the guy's wrist and yanked the Colt toward Loomis. The New Zealand merc was about to help his comrade, but he froze when he saw the pistol pointed at his belly. McCarter whipped a knee into the American's abdomen and twisted the man's wrist. Karas dropped the Colt and kicked it across the floor, unwilling to let McCarter claim it.

The Phoenix pro cupped a palm behind Karas's head and pushed as he stepped behind the merc. He shoved with both hands and sent the American stumbling into Loomis McCarter took advantage of the confusion and attacked the pair. He snap-kicked Karas in the stomach and hammered his right fist between the American's shoulder blades. McCarter's left shot out in a fast jab to Loomis's face. Knuckles crashed into the New Zealander's nose, and Loomis staggered back two feet.

Karas slashed a clumsy karate chop at McCarter's chest. The Briton grunted and stepped back as the American merc swung a left hook at McCarter's face. The Phoenix commando dodged his opponent's fist and grabbed the guy's arm. He chopped his other hand across the merc's right forearm before the guy could throw another punch, then quickly snapped his head forward. The hard frontal bone of McCarter's skull crashed into the bridge of his opponent's nose. Karas moaned as blood seeped from his nostrils.

McCarter hooked his left elbow into the side of Karas's jaw and followed with a right uppercut that lifted the American merc off his feet and dumped the man on the floor. Powerful arms seized McCarter from behind as Loomis rejoined the battle. The Phoenix ace immediately stomped a boot heel into his opponent's instep and thrust his head backward to butt the back of his skull into the merc's face. He heard Loomis groan and felt the man's grip weaken. McCarter then swung a back kick and whipped the back of his heel between the New Zealander's legs.

Loomis wheezed in breathless agony as McCarter broke free of the man's hold and punched the point of an elbow into Loomis's solar plexus. The mercenary started to double up from the blow, but McCarter scooped an arm around the guy's neck. He clasped the back of Loomis's head with his palm and squeezed the side of the man's neck with his biceps. Then the British commando seized the forelock of Loomis's hair with his other hand and pulled hard. Mc-Carter dropped to one knee, and his opponent sailed over his back. Loomis tumbled head over heels and crashed to the floor beside his unconscious comrade. Just to make certain, McCarter kicked the fallen thug behind the ear for good measure.

"You two bastards have a nice nap," he growled as he retrieved his micro-Uzi. "I've got to see a man about a nuclear cannon."

22

Calvin James blasted the billets with another 40 mm grenade from his M-203. The roof caved in from the explosion, and walls collapsed. Two mercenaries bolted from the wreckage, and James picked them off with the last rounds from the magazine of his assault rifle. The black warrior discarded the M-16 and gripped his micro-Uzi with both hands as he glanced about to see how the battle was going.

Heller's forces were obviously losing. Khaki-clad corpses littered the battlefield. Shot, stabbed and blown to bits, the mercenaries had been destroyed by the bold and well-orchestrated attack of the Phoenix trio and their SAS allies. Both billets had been leveled by grenades, the machine-gun nests had been wiped out and Heller's ranch house was gradually burning to the ground. The barn had suffered severely from the effects of explosions. Holes had been hammered through the wooden walls, and the roof was ablaze, yet it had fared better than any of the other structures in the combat zone.

Encizo and the SAS troops with him had captured several mercenaries who had decided to surrender rather than die. James heard a karate shout and turned to see the young Maori trooper engaged in hand-to-hand combat with a much larger opponent. The mercenary swung an empty rifle as if it were a club, but the Maori ducked and snapped a kick at his opponent's wrist. The rifle flew out of the goon's hands, and the SAS corporal lunged with a Commando dagger in his fist. The double-edged blade sunk between the merc's ribs. The man screamed as the Maori soldier pulled him to the ground and finished him off with a knife stroke across the throat.

"Hold your fire!" a voice boomed from a megaphone inside the barn. "I'm warning you all. Cease fire immediately!"

"Now what?" Encizo wondered aloud as he approached James.

"I don't know," the badass from Chicago admitted, "but it doesn't sound too good."

The barn doors slowly swung open and the massive barrel of a howitzer-style cannon poked through the opening. The bore was as big as the gun on a Soviet tank, but the metal barrel was thicker, designed to handle powerful projectiles. The battlefield virtually fell silent. Flames crackled and wounded men moaned; otherwise the ranch was as quiet as a graveyard.

"This is a 115 mm atomic cannon!" Kubler's amplified voice bellowed through the megaphone. "I personally designed this weapon and supervised its construction. All of you know this is true. You know I'm not bluffing. If you don't follow the orders that I give you now, I'll fire the cannon and everyone will die!"

McCarter emerged from the house, crossbow once again in his hands. He waved to James and Encizo. The Briton worked the cocking lever on the Barnett and drew back the bowstring. Then he fitted a bolt in the weapon and cocked his head at the barn.

"You will now throw down your weapons!" Kubler's voice continued. "I want to see you line up in formation in front of the barn, unarmed and with your hands raised. Do it now! I've got nothing to lose by firing the cannon except my life, which would be of little value to me in a prison cell, anyway. Do as I say unless you're all prepared to die, as well!''

"Good God," Sergeant Winslow whispered as he approached James and Encizo. "What do we do now?"

"Keep your men away from the barn," Encizo told him as he placed his micro-Uzi on the ground. "If Todd or the guys with him approach, wave them away from the barn, as well."

"You thinking what I'm thinking?" James asked as he lowered his machine pistol to the ground.

"How do I know what you're thinking?" the Cuban said with a shrug. He drew his P-88 from shoulder leather and stuck the Walther pistol into his trousers at the small of his back.

"I'm pretty sure we've got the same idea," James remarked as he concealed his pistol in the same manner. "You know, this is an old trick."

"Sometimes old tricks work," Encizo said as he removed his shoulder holster rig and tossed it aside. "They'll probably be suspicious of us, but maybe we can stall long enough for our friend with the William Tell gear to get into position."

"You're going to confront the men with the cannon?" Winslow asked nervously.

"Yeah," James confirmed as he discarded his shoulder holster and made certain the Walther at the small of his back was out of sight but still as readily available as possible. "I just hope they don't ask us to turn around."

"This isn't a fashion show," Encizo said. "Just try to act as if you're not hiding anything behind your back."

"Gee," James snorted. "You ever think of going to Hollywood and starting a new career as an acting teacher?"

"All the time," Encizo replied with a straight face.

Encizo and James approached the barn, empty hands held high. Two mercenaries stood by the entrance, Bren submachine guns in their fists. They watched the Phoenix pair suspiciously. The commandos slowly walked to the front of the barn and peered inside. The great black metal cannon stood before them. Kubler was barely visible behind the massive piece of awesome weaponry. The Austrian munitions expert crouched low by the controls at the rear of the cannon.

"I said I wanted all of you people to throw down your weapons and come here," Kubler declared. His voice was high-pitched due to stress, and he was wheezing heavily as if he might have a heart attack before he could carry out his threat.

"We're the commanders of the unit," Encizo explained. "Let's talk before you vaporize us. Maybe we can make a deal."

"Screw you, fella," one of the mercenaries growled.

"Maybe we should listen," a third merc near Kubler suggested. "What harm can it do?"

"Shit," the American soldier of fortune snorted. "These suckers would say anything to try to get us to back down. They'll lie through their teeth and throw us to the wolves, if they don't just gun us down as soon as we drop our guard."

"How does immunity sound?" James asked. "You guys could turn state's evidence. That's bound to go in your favor, meaning you might get immunity if you help us enough."

"Immunity?" Kubler scoffed. "What am I supposed to tell you that you don't already know? You wouldn't even be here if you didn't already know everything about Hellson and his schemes. Most likely you've already caught Hellson in Australia. He probably turned state's evidence against *us* to save his own neck.''

"No, that's not true," Encizo said urgently. He hoped he sounded convincing. "We didn't even know Heller was in Australia until now."

"But you do know Hellson's real name!" Kubler snapped, convinced they were lying.

"Yeah, we know who he really is," James said. "But not because we caught up with him and beat the truth out of the son of a bitch. We found out about him after we interrogated his flunkies in Antarctica. Man, you must know who Naakon was. He was digging uranium out of the ground in Antarctica to get materials for these goddamn nuclear shells you guys made."

"That part's true," Kubler said thoughtfully. "Still, how do I know you men will keep your word?"

"What do you want from us?" Encizo asked with a shrug. "We didn't bring a stack of Bibles to swear on. We can't tell you for certain what kind of deal we can cut, anyway. We can tell you we have White House authority. That means you can get a pardon from the President of the United States and possibly get some political strings pulled to get a pardon from the New Zealand prime minister, as well. You guys are little fish. Heller's the one we want, especially if he still has any nuclear shells."

"Oh, he has the shells and a cannon," Kubler confirmed. "And it's probably too late to stop him and Ton, anyway. I've participated in an act of mass murder. They're not going to pardon me for that. God Almighty won't pardon me. So I guess I might as well take a few more lives personally!"

"No!" one of the mercs cried as he swung his Bren chopper toward Kubler.

He gasped in astonishment and horror as he saw a feathered fiberglass shaft suddenly appear in Kubler's right eye socket. The Austrian wobbled slightly as a ribbon of blood trickled from the punctured eyeball. The crossbow bolt had pierced his brain and would have caused instantaneous death even if it didn't contain a dose of cyanide. Kubler tumbled backward and fell heavily to the barn floor.

The mercenaries turned toward the sound. James and Encizo threw themselves to the ground and swiftly drew their Walther pistols. The mercs swung their attention back to the Phoenix pair, but they weren't prepared to deal with adversaries on the ground. Encizo fired his Walther into the stomach of one mercenary. The guy doubled up, and the Cuban warrior shot him again and split the guy's skull with a 9 mm parabellum.

James aimed his P-88 at another opponent and drilled a 124-grain Hydra-Shok slug through the center of the man's chest. Another pistol cracked as McCarter drew his Browning, snap-aimed and fired. A second 9 mm round slammed into the merc's chest and blew his heart into bloodied mush. The merc killer collapsed.

"Oh, Christ!" the man who had tried to convince Kubler to surrender cried out as he dropped his Bren and raised his hands. "Don't shoot! Don't shoot!"

"Just shut up and come here!" James ordered. "Face the barn and spread 'em."

"Sure, sure," the man agreed as he obeyed instructions.

McCarter approached his teammates and whistled softly when he got a better look at the cannon. "That's one hell of a piece of work."

"Yeah," Encizo said, nodding. "Nice shot with the crossbow. A bull's-eye if ever there was one."

"Thanks," the Briton replied, "but it's not over yet. Heller's in Australia."

"That guy told us as much before you drilled him with the crossbow bolt," Encizo said.

"Did he also tell you the bastard set off a nuclear explosion there?" McCarter asked.

"¡Madre de Dios!" Encizo exclaimed, frustrated and astonished by the news. "Maybe we're too late after all."

THE CARGO SHIP HAD DOCKED at the island harbor. It was a busy port, and no one paid special attention to the crates hauled from the hold by cranes and transferred to a forklift. Many in the port recognized Edward Hellson as a wealthy businessman from New Zealand. Some recalled Hellson when he was known as Mr. Smith or Mr. Jones. They remembered him as a narcotics smuggler, gunrunner and a man with dangerous associates. He was now regarded as a respectable and honest dealer in metal products, beef and leather goods.

Yet those who knew the truth about Hellson—part of the truth at least—realized he had never severed the dark ties of his past. They also knew it was wise to look the other way and not ask too many questions about the mysterious American. People died from being too curious about such men. The fact that Hellson was at the port and personally supervising the handling of the cargo from the ship suggested that whatever he was involved in was something very important, something no man who valued his health or the safety of his family would want to know about.

Heller watched the forklift haul the last crates to another crane next to a ship with *Celebes* painted across the freeboard of the stem. He frowned as the crew members of the vessel struggled with the crates and lowered the burdens into the cargo hold of the *Celebes*. They were dark-skinned with Asian features. Some wore turbans and necklaces made of shark's teeth. Most were barefoot and dressed in ragged clothing. Many, if not all, bore scars from knife fights, and a few had angry, puckered welts that appeared to be old bullet wounds.

"I can't say I fancy going to sea with this lot," Jason House commented as if reading Heller's thoughts.

"Ton seems to trust them," the American arms merchant replied.

"Who the hell trusts him?" the British merc snorted.

Heller grunted. He saw General Ton at the bow with a young hard-faced man dressed in black cotton trousers, a black leather vest and sandals. The man's body was lean but muscular, and he carried two hardwood sticks thrust into a sash around his narrow waist as well as a long-bladed knife in a wooden sheath at his hip. Ton noticed Heller and House. He gestured with his steel hook for the pair to come aboard. Reluctantly they walked up the gangplank to the deck.

"Gentlemen," Ton said, "this is Ramón Bontoc. This is his ship and these are his men."

"So you're the captain?" Heller inquired.

"I'm more than that," Bontoc replied. His narrow eyes seemed cold, as if glazed with ice. Bontoc's lips were curled in an arrogant sneer that never changed much with the rest of his expression. "I'm the cell commander. My comrades run this ship because I tell them to do so."

"You mean you blokes are revolutionaries?" House asked, managing to keep the sarcasm from his tone.

"The Philippine People's Liberation Army," Bontoc said with pride. "These are my soldiers. Don't let their appearance fool you. They're all dedicated to the revolution and to liberating our nation from the imperialist government that oppresses our people."

"Uh-huh," Heller said dryly. "Well, your revolution is your business. Getting our cargo to its destination and getting payment is mine."

"Yes," the Filipino said as he fixed a frigid stare on Heller's face. "You're an American. You care about nothing except money and gold. Americans think they can solve everything with money."

"Spare me the Marxist sermon," Heller said. He turned to Ton. "We've got a problem here. Your friend sounds as if he'd like to cut my capitalist throat. I find myself wondering if I might be making a serious mistake doing business with him."

"You're doing business with me, Hellson," Ton insisted.

"And you're dealing with him," Heller declared. "He's one of those righteous, dedicated revolutionaries you're always talking about, right?"

"Does that frighten you?" Bontoc asked with a snicker.

"I don't give a damn about your revolution one way or the other," Heller told him. "You can blow up every island in the Philippines and kill everybody there, including the U.S. servicemen stationed in your country if you want, I'm just concerned with getting paid and going home alive to enjoy my nasty capitalistic gains before all you international Communist Robin Hoods come along and take it from me so that you can redistribute the wealth to the unwashed masses."

"You mock our cause?" Bontoc snarled, a hand on the hilt of his knife.

"Only a fool would commit murder in broad daylight in front of so many witnesses," Heller said. "Save your threats. I'm not impressed. As for your cause, I don't have any great respect for anyone's cause except my own."

"You needn't worry, Hellson," Ton assured him. "We'll still want to do business with you in the future, even if you are a greedy capitalist pig. As you stated when we met at your ranch, you're the only source available to us if we want to purchase nuclear weapons. To kill you would be to chop off our supply. Kill the goose that lays the proverbial golden eggs because we don't like the annoying honking noises it makes? Come now, Hellson, we're not stupid."

"Then show us a gesture of good faith to reassure us this won't be a one-way trip," House suggested. "I'm just a soldier and a bodyguard. Politics and wheeling and dealing aren't my specialties. I'm concerned with the security of Mr. Hellson and the merchandise. Let's make a compromise."

"We're all reasonable men," Ton replied.

House glanced at the crew. They looked like a collection of the worst cutthroats from the Pacific islands. The merc directed his remarks to Bontoc. "Leave half your crew here and let Mr. Hellson's people handle the rest of the ship's duties for the journey," he said.

"Replace my comrades with his hired hoodlums?" The Filipino glared at House. "That's an insult. I'll lose face."

"You'll lose the bloody cannon and the nuclear shells if you don't go along with it," House insisted.

"It's a reasonable request," Ton agreed with a sigh, looking at Bontoc. "None of us feel much trust for one another. Mr. Hellson isn't on our side, but he isn't our enemy, Comrade."

"I'm with any side that's profitable for me," Heller said. "Is it a deal or not?"

"Very well," Bontoc agreed reluctantly. "But tell your people not to antagonize my men. It won't take much to provoke them."

"Just tell your people to do the same," Heller insisted.
"Very well," Bontoc said. "Let's get on with it."
"I can hardly wait," Heller said dryly.

23

Phoenix Force and the New Zealand SIS case officer Gavin Ford arrived without incident at the Canberra airport. Their plane was a New Zealand official's personal craft, well-known to the Australian air traffic controllers. A limousine bus was waiting for them at the runway. Ford recognized the man standing next to the bus. A tall man with broad shoulders, wavy silver hair and a discreet mustache, he could have easily been mistaken for a bank president or a senior executive with one of the major corporations in nearby Sydney. His powder-blue suit was expensive and well tailored, but his alligator skin boots seemed out of place. The Australian also wore steel points on the collar of his shirt, a fashion popular with Texans.

"Gentlemen," Ford said, "this is Luke Crenshaw. He may look like a lunatic, but bear in mind he's an Australian. Luke is also the third-highest-ranking chap in the Australian Security and Intelligence Organization."

"If I wasn't trying to make a good impression on these blokes, I'd tell you to sod off," Crenshaw remarked. "Lots of room in me bus, gents. Load up your gear and we'll be on our way. I was told you fellows carried a lot of hardware."

He looked at the aluminum cases and briefcases carried by Phoenix Force. Crenshaw assumed the long metal containers held assault rifles and spare magazines. He had dealt with American Intelligence agents over the years. The CIA and the NSA were more apt to haul crates of computers around than firearms. These five strangers were clearly a different breed. Whoever and whatever they were, the team had White House authority, and they were able to get the U.S. President to pull strings with the Australian prime minister, as well. Crenshaw had been impressed by the mystery team even before he'd met them.

Phoenix Force loaded their luggage into the bus and climbed inside. Ford and Crenshaw joined them. The Australian closed the doors and tapped the glass panel that separated passengers from the driver. The man behind the wheel nodded and started the engine.

"This vehicle is made of reinforced steel with lead lining, and the windows are bulletproof," Crenshaw announced as he opened a compartment to a service cart. He pressed a switch on the control panel. "I just activated an electronic scrambling device. Don't ask me how it works exactly, but it receives radio transmissions on several frequencies simultaneously. These are played on tiny speakers built into the window sections. If you place an ear to the glass, you might hear a slight garbled sound. Voices, music, whatever, all tumbled together like a radio receiver gone wild."

"Which means no one can listen to our conversations with a long-range microphone, rifle mike or laser microphone," Gary Manning commented. "All they'll hear is unintelligible gibberish."

"Sort of like the speeches politicians make when parliament's in session," Crenshaw said, grinning. "So we can talk about top-security matters. I understand you can tell us something about that nuclear explosion that scared the shit out of everybody in Australia. You'd best have some convincing information, because people here are seriously considering keeping the Americans as well as the Soviets the hell out of our country.''

"Then they'll be blaming the wrong source," Katz said. "I heard that the explosion occurred in the outback. How serious was it?"

"It happened in the Gibson Desert, to be exact," Crenshaw explained. "I suppose if you have to have a nuclear explosion, the Gibson is a better place than most for it to happen. We don't know for certain if anyone was killed, but aborigines sometimes wander around the desert. If so, there's literally nothing left of them. I'm told it was a small explosion by today's standards in nuclear weapons."

"It was a 115 mm nuclear shell fired from an atomic cannon," Rafael Encizo explained. "We confiscated a weapon just like it with three rounds of nuclear warhead ammo at Erik Heller's ranch less than five hours ago."

"Well, I'll be damned," Crenshaw said, stunned by the news. "You blokes really do know some details the rest of us don't. Maybe you'll be good enough to tell me what the hell's going on here."

Phoenix Force explained how their mission had started in Antarctica and led to direct action against Heller's property in New Zealand. The Australian listened in amazement as they told him how Erik Heller had started a private nuclear arms trade and had apparently used the Gibson Desert to test his cannon and shells.

"From interrogating prisoners we learned that Heller has apparently closed a deal with a client named Ton," Katz said. "We now know that he's a senior officer in the Vietnamese army."

"When I was in Nam, I was involved with some SOG operations behind enemy lines," Manning explained. "There was a Major Ton who was noted for being a particularly ruthless commander in the NVA. 'Ton of Fun' some called him. That was a real gallows-humor nickname, since Ton slaughtered entire villages as an example of what would happen if they resisted the Communists and sided with the South."

"And you think this is the same man?" Crenshaw asked with a frown. "That was quite a few years ago."

"We checked with our control officer in Washington," Katz explained. "He had a computer run done and discovered that Ton Chi Dai is currently a general in the Vietnamese army. He received promotions due to his status as a war hero and his work in Cambodia. He's a wounded war hero at that. Lost his right hand in combat during the war." Katz raised his prosthesis and displayed the three metal hooks at the end of the artificial limb. "Ton now has a steel hook at the end of his arm," the Israeli said, smiling. "Sinister, isn't it?"

"This whole business is bloody sinister to me," Ford commented. "I can vouch for most of what these men have told you, Luke. I've seen the nuclear shells myself, and I was present when they questioned the prisoners under the influence of scopolamine. A number of brave young SAS soldiers were killed during the raids on Hollnon Metallurgy and the ranch."

"I'm convinced this is real," Crenshaw assured him. "I certainly agree we have to find Hellson or Heller or whatever his real name is."

"As I understand it, Hellson-Heller is no stranger to Australia," James said. "He has business deals going on here as well as in New Zealand. He's even supposed to be part-owner of some outfits in this country. That's not the kind of guy who's going to be totally invisible. Besides, he's accompanied by an Asian dude with a hook for a hand, and they're packing a cannon that weighs more than a ton. It's not going to be easy for them to get around without attracting some attention in Australia.''

"I hope you're right," Crenshaw said with a sigh. "Australia's a large country, you know. There's a lot of uninhabited territory here. A lot of space where you could run a herd of elephants in just about any direction for hundreds of miles without anyone knowing.''

"Heller may not even suspect anyone's hunting him," McCarter said with a shrug. "As far as we know, none of his people were able to contact him before we busted their chops. I don't imagine they had much time to radio the boss.''

"We're keeping as many facts from the media as possible," Ford declared. "But New Zealand isn't a bloody dictatorship, you know. My government can't really censor television and newspapers. So far the police are telling the press they can't give them full details about what happened at Hellson Metallurgy. Right now they're putting out the story that it was a fire caused by a band of armed arsonists. They won't be able to sit on the truth for long, but they should be able to prevent the story from becoming an international news item for the time being.''

"There's no way we can know how many people worked for Heller on the outside," Katz reminded the others. "We took out his operations at the plant and his ranch, but he could have dozens of informers and contract goons who work part-time for him and who escaped detection. They may have contacted him by now. Still, there's a chance he's still in Australia and doesn't realize his empire's crumbling.''

"I'm not so sure he'll stay in Australia," James remarked. "Heller's selling the cannon and shells to General Ton, right? Why the hell would Ton want to use it here? I've never heard of the Vietnamese conducting terrorist activities in Australia.''

''We've had a number of crackpot political groups call the newspapers, the police and the prime minister's office to take credit for the Gibson Desert explosion,'' Crenshaw said. ''Left wing, right wing, religious, environmental and just plain bonkers. They've all claimed they set off the bomb for one reason or another. Only one or two are even being taken half seriously, and apparently those were liars, too. None of them are alleged to be connected with the Vietnamese.''

''Maybe Ton plans to take the cannon back to Nam,'' Manning mused. ''The Soviets aren't too generous when it comes to giving their allies nuclear weapons of any sort, not without Russian advisers and troops to maintain control of the weapons. Could be Vietnam has decided to get their own weapons without having to kiss Moscow's ass.''

''Well, if Ton is taking the cannon back to Vietnam,'' Encizo said with a frown, ''he's probably doing it on his own. Our Intel tells us he's a rogue, like Heller. If Heller's god is money, Ton's is some cracked idea about one-world communism.''

''We can kick around theories all day,'' McCarter said, grunting sourly as he reached for his Player's. He decided he shouldn't smoke in the bus and left the cigarettes in his pocket. ''Fact is, we're still stumbling around in the dark. What we have to do, and fast, is find that bastard Heller.''

''We'll find him,'' Crenshaw vowed. ''If the ASIO doesn't have a file on Heller, I'll contact Interpol, the Business Commission and whoever else I have to talk to in order to get a lead.''

''Heller had a number of Australians on his payroll,'' Katz said. ''Most had criminal records, according to the CID in Wellington. I suspect the police here will have a record of Heller's activities in Australia and a list of his associates."

"Sounds like a good place to start," the ASIO man agreed. "When we arrive at headquarters, we'll get to work right away. Anything you blokes need?"

"We're getting low on ammunition," Manning replied. "If you can get us about two or three thousand rounds of 9 mm parabellum and one or two thousand 5.56, we'd certainly appreciate it."

"You want thousands of rounds of ammunition?" Crenshaw asked with surprise. "You lads must be trigger-happy."

"Not really," McCarter replied with a shrug. "We just had to shoot a lot of people recently."

"I'll see what I can do," Crenshaw assured them. "I'm almost afraid to ask if you want anything else."

"Some food," Encizo said. "I don't know about the rest of you, but I'm getting hungry enough to eat the leather straps on my shoulder holster."

"I know a couple of restaurants in Canberra that serve food that tastes rather like that," Crenshaw told him. "You're in luck, mate. One of them delivers."

The limousine bus passed rows of museums and embassies. The traffic was light and easily negotiated. Australian drivers tended to be as courteous and good-natured as those of New Zealand. The bus whipped by the Australian parliament buildings, then skirted the War Memorial, a large structure that housed entire tanks and planes, mementos of wars Australia had taken part in. Finally the bus rolled into an underground garage belonging to a small, nondescript office building. The driver stopped inside, and Crenshaw told his passengers they had arrived as he opened the nearest door.

The ASIO case officer escorted the Phoenix commandos and Ford to an elevator. They rode the car up to the third floor and exited into a hall of tile and mercury tube lights. Crenshaw led them through the corridor to his office, which was too small for seven men to squeeze into with reasonable comfort.

"Why don't you blokes go to the conference room and relax a bit while I talk to my people and contact Interpol?" Crenshaw suggested. "I'll also get some food for you gents and see about that ammunition. Fair enough?"

"Sounds fine," Katz agreed with a nod.

"I'll let you know what we come up with as soon as I know anything myself."

"We can't ask for more than that, Mr. Crenshaw," Manning replied.

"Just call me Luke," Crenshaw told him. "This is Australia, mate. We don't go in for much formal snobbery here. Not in this office, anyway. Sometimes we come up against that 'coppers mentality' among the Interpol blokes. They reckon everybody's a member of the public unless he carries a badge. It's pretty obvious they feel those 'members of the public' are just there to pay the police salaries and serve as witnesses when the cops need them."

The five members of Phoenix Force weren't surprised to hear Crenshaw's criticism of Interpol. Law-enforcement and Intelligence organizations tended to regard one another as rivals. Local police didn't like dealing with the federal cops. The FBI and the CIA in the U.S. didn't have much good to say about each other, either. Even the Soviet KGB state security and the GRU military Intelligence didn't get along very well. Obviously the ASIO and Interpol weren't bosom buddies, either.

"Just remember we need their cooperation," Katz urged.

"Don't worry," Crenshaw assured him. "I'll be tactful, but a kick in the arse gets better results from Interpol than trying to kiss their backside. More agreeable, too."

"Not if it prevents us from finding Heller," Encizo said. "There aren't many things more disagreeable than nuclear weapons in the hands of someone who doesn't mind using them on innocent people."

THE FOOD DELIVERED to Phoenix Force tasted better than leather shoulder holster straps, but it was hardly a flattering example of Australian cuisine. The beef was tough, the bread slightly stale and the kangaroo tail soup was so oily that it tasted as if it had originally been intended for a car engine. Dessert was better—chocolate cake with French vanilla ice cream. Katz was pleased with the tea, but it was too strong for James's taste. The Windy City commando was accustomed to American teabags. McCarter was lucky enough to get a chilled bottle of Coca-Cola, and Encizo and Manning enjoyed some Australian lager.

"Not the best meal I've ever had," the Canadian said with a shrug, "but God knows I've had worse."

"You think the kangaroo tail soup is a put-on?" James wondered aloud. "It sounds like it might be a joke."

"No," McCarter assured him. "I've had it before. The soup is usually better than this stuff was. I reckon this kangaroo had his tail raised just before they chopped it off."

"That's disgusting," Encizo muttered, shaking his head.

The door to the conference room opened. Crenshaw and Ford entered. The Australian carried a coffeepot and some disposable cups. He grinned as he placed them on the table. "I know Americans like coffee, so I managed to get some for you gents," Crenshaw said as he poured some dark, steaming liquid into a cup. "How would you like it? Black or white?"

"Black!" the Phoenix Force commandos chorused.

"Glad to see you all survived the meal," Crenshaw said. "You blokes must be tough."

"We try," Katz replied. "Any luck with Interpol?"

"At first my conversation with them wasn't going along very well," Crenshaw answered. "However, after a while, Interpol got a bit more cooperative. Turns out they've been keeping tabs on Hellson-Heller, just as you suspected."

"Do they know where he is?" Manning asked eagerly, sipping some coffee. It was weak and not as hot as the Canadian liked it, but he didn't complain.

"Not exactly," Crenshaw answered. "Oh, they knew he was in Western Australia with a bloke named Jason House, a British soldier of fortune who's been associated with Heller for quite a while. House is a sort of personal bodyguard and chief enforcer for Heller. An Asian with a steel hook for a hand was also with Heller. The bloke's supposed to be a Taiwanese businessman named Han, but I'd say there's no doubt who he really is. Interpol doesn't have any evidence that Heller and his friends were in the Gibson Desert when the nuclear explosion occurred, but I don't think there's any doubt about that, either."

"Well, hot diddly damn," McCarter snorted as he rolled his eyes toward the ceiling. "You really haven't told us anything we don't already know."

"Let the man finish," Katz told the impatient Briton.

"Thank you," Crenshaw said with a nod. "The Intel from the Interpol gents also included a rundown on Heller's businesses here in Australia. The important one is part ownership of a shipping outfit in Darwin. Import and export. Now here's the most important part. Heller and his mates set sail in a cargo ship headed for New Guinea. Papua New Guinea, actually."

"New Guinea," Encizo repeated thoughtfully as he rose from his chair and moved to a wall map. "That's just north of Australia."

"They have quite a head start," Manning remarked. "Do you figure they'll already be in New Guinea?"

"Probably," Encizo replied. "How fast a vessel travels depends on size, weight, condition of equipment and other factors. We'd better assume they've reached their destination or soon will."

"So let's get a plane and fly out to New Guinea," McCarter said eagerly. He spread his arms wide in a massive gesture. "I'll fly the bloody thing. If they're trying to transfer the cannon to Vietnam, they won't hang around New Guinea very long before they head for Southeast Asia."

"A plane?" Ford inquired with a slight grin. "You might recall that we arrived in one from New Zealand. In fact, you were the pilot."

"Fine," the Briton agreed. "We'll fuel up and be on our way."

"That's sort of rushing it, isn't it?" Crenshaw remarked, surprised by the sudden decision. "Papua New Guinea's a sovereign nation. Australia had control of it once. We beat the Germans in New Guinea during World War I and retained control until 1975—"

"I'm certain the history involved is fascinating, but we really don't have much time," Katz told him. "We need to contact the New Guinea government. What have they got? It's a parliamentary democracy, isn't it?"

"Yes," Crenshaw confirmed. "It has a governor-general and a prime minister. New Guinea's a Commonwealth nation and still has close ties to Australia. We can certainly get the authorization you'll need to continue your mission there."

"Then let's see about arranging their cooperation so we can cut through any red tape that might slow down our progress," the Phoenix commander replied. "And let's do it quickly. Time's something we can't afford to waste."

24

Ramón Bontoc stood on the deck of the *Celebes* at the port quarter. Several fellow members of the Philippine People's Liberation Army sat on crates and ropes. Some ate boiled rice and *rellenong manok*, boneless chicken stuffed with sausage and eggs. Others cleaned and oiled disassembled firearms. The night air was pleasant and carried the scent of saltwater. The atmosphere encouraged the men to relax, but Bontoc didn't intend to let his men get careless. The PPLA commander didn't trust Heller and his followers, and the cargo was even greater reason for concern.

"Comrade Bontoc," General Ton said in a low voice as he appeared from the port side. He continued to converse in English because he didn't speak Maguindanao, Bontoc's native language, and the Filipino didn't understand Vietnamese or French. "We need to take care of the problem we discussed earlier."

"I'm ready," Bontoc replied, and drew the hardwood batons from his sash.

Abe Samels, Bart Tibbs and Rob Ethan emerged from the cargo hold on the starboard side of the ship. The Australians had seldom been apart since they'd boarded the first ship at Darwin. Tibbs and Ethan weren't accustomed to ocean travel, and they didn't know any of the men aboard except Samels. The pair were extremely uncomfortable around General Ton and the Filipinos. They tried to avoid the Asians as much as possible, but that was difficult aboard the *Celebes*.

"Come here, gentlemen!" Ton called to the trio. He waved them forward with his steel hook. "You ought to see this."

"What's that rice slurper want?" Ethan whispered to his companions.

"Watch your mouth," Samels warned. "Hellson told us not to cause any trouble and to try to get along with these blokes. Just be polite."

"I just hope this doesn't take long," Tibbs muttered as they approached the Vietnamese officer.

The three Australians hesitated as Bontoc raised the sticks, one in each fist. The Filipino suddenly crossed his arms on his chest, uttered a shout similar to a karate *ki-ya* and slashed the clubs through the air. Bontoc delivered a series of jabs and swings with the batons in a set of *kata*-style exercises. He occasionally threw a kick at the invisible "opponent" during the "practice."

"Are you gentlemen familiar with Filipino martial arts?" Ton inquired. "Comrade Bontoc is quite accomplished in at least three styles. *Escrima* is a form of knife fighting and fencing, *kun-tao* is a bare-handed fighting art like karate or kung fu, and the type of martial art he demonstrates for us now is the stick fighting art known as *estocada*. Have any of you seen it before?"

"Not that I recall," Tibbs admitted, "but it looks like it works mighty well as long as you don't go up against a bloke with a gun."

"Really?" Bontoc said as he glanced at the revolver jammed in the waistband of Tibbs's trousers. "The man with the gun would have to get it first."

He suddenly thrust one stick and jabbed the end into Tibbs's slender abdomen. The Australian doubled up with a surprised gasp of pain. Bontoc's other baton slashed a blow to Tibbs's collarbone. The Filipino snap-kicked Tibbs in the chest and slammed the ball of his bare foot into the man's breastbone. The kick straightened Tibbs's spine and raised his head as Bontoc swung a cross-body stroke and smashed a baton across the side of the Australian's head.

Bontoc slashed rapidly with his arms and hammered Tibbs's head and neck with three more blows. The scrawny Australian dropped to his knees, blood oozing from his nostrils, mouth and a cut over his right eyebrow. The Filipino crashed a stick across the back of his opponent's skull, and Tibbs slumped at his feet, unconscious.

Ethan had tried to assist his friend, but General Ton had seized the big Australian from behind. The Asian rammed a knee into Ethan's kidney and grabbed the man's hair with his left hand, yanking Ethan's head back. Ton swung his hook around his opponent's shoulder and plunged the steel point into the hollow of Ethan's exposed throat. The general pulled hard and ripped open flesh as the hook tore through the Australian's windpipe and served the carotid artery. Ethan's body collapsed onto the deck and twitched violently as more blood spilled from his ravaged throat.

"Jesus Christ!" Samels exclaimed as he jumped back from the carnage and desperately reached for a pistol in his belt.

"Don't try it!" Ton snapped as he pointed his bloody hook at the surviving Australian. "We planned to spare you. Don't force us to change that plan by doing something stupid."

Samels moved his hand away from his pistol. His fingers trembled as he slowly raised his arm and watched with hatred as Bontoc gestured for two of his terrorist followers to come forward. The Filipino ringleader barked some orders in rapid Maguindanao. His men nodded and picked up Tibbs's senseless form. They carried him to the handrail and tossed the bleeding, unconscious Australian overboard.

"What the hell do you think you're doing!" Erik Heller shouted as he rushed from the bow to witness the improvised funeral at sea.

"They murdered Tibbs and Ethan!" Samels answered, still shaking with anger and fear. "Killed them right before my eyes!"

Jason House appeared behind Heller. The British merc held his .38 revolver in his fist but didn't point it at Ton, Bontoc or any of the Filipino terrorists. Two PPLA flunkies scooped up the limp body of Rob Ethan, hauled it to the rail and hurled it overboard. The men aboard the *Celebes* heard the splash as the body plunged into the ocean.

"Those two had to be removed, Hellson," Ton declared as he calmly wiped the blood from his hook with a rag. "You know that as well as I do."

"We discussed what had to be done about them earlier," House whispered to Heller. "We would have had to terminate them sooner or later."

"This stunt was out of line, Ton!" Heller declared. He ignored House's comment, none too happy that his bodyguard seemed to sympathize with Ton's actions. "You had no right to do this."

"We have a perfect opportunity to dispose of troublesome individuals out here," Ton explained. "No witnesses and a vast ocean to swallow up the bodies. Comrade Bontoc tells me there are many schools of sharks in these waters. When the killer fish smell blood in the water, they'll take care of the remains and nothing will wash up onshore."

"So you and Bontoc just decided to be judge, jury and executioner for a couple of men you didn't approve of,"

Heller snorted. "The rest of my men are going to be thrilled with that. If you trigger a mutiny on this ship, I'll personally kill both of you."

"Come and try, Yankee," Bontoc invited, the *estocada* sticks still in his fists.

"Don't tempt me," Heller growled. "This is putting a strain on our partnership, Ton."

"It had to be done, and I had my doubts you would do it," the general replied with a shrug. "Two less men who need to be paid. I'd think that would please you, Hellson. It saves money for you."

"We won't tolerate any more surprises like this, Ton," Heller warned. "If we weren't within a few hours of our destination, I probably wouldn't put up with it now."

"You're going to let them get away with this?" Samels asked, stunned by Heller's behavior.

"For now," Heller replied. "Come with me, Samels. We need to talk."

The Australian followed Heller and House to the bow. The renegade American didn't care if Samels was upset. Samels was expendable. The two Australian thugs who had been tossed into the sea for the sharks had been even more expendable. House had been correct when he'd said the pair had to be terminated. Heller had intended to have them killed—and probably Samels, as well—after they had delivered the cannon and received final payment from Ton.

What worried Heller was Ton's willingness to conspire with Bontoc to kill two of his men before they reached the Philippines. Such an action reduced the number of Heller's employees—the men who would fight on Heller's side if Bontoc tried to turn on them in order to kill the arms dealer and claim the cannon without paying for it. Ton had assured him they wouldn't kill the goose that layed the radioactive eggs, but Heller was less than convinced, especially since the general and Bontoc had murdered the two Australians.

"Let's not overreact now," House urged in a soft voice.

"Shut up, Jason," Heller snapped. "I don't need to hear that from you right now. It's bad enough that I have to worry about Ton and those fish-faced bastards. I don't want to have any doubts about where you stand, as well."

"I've always been there for you, all the way back to the days when we smuggled dope for the bloody triads," House assured him. "It's just understandable why he offed those two."

"Well, I don't understand it," Samels declared. "What the hell is this, Mr. Hellson? Why are you letting them do this?"

"Because we've come this far to get our hands on a fortune in gold and precious stones in exchange for the cannon," Heller replied. "We're not going to lose that chance now because two scummy low-life hoodlums were killed. That's all Tibbs and Ethan were, so don't expect me to shed any tears over them. Their deaths don't matter, but the success of this operation does."

"Are you greedy enough to get us all killed for a profit?" Samels demanded, eyes wide in astonishment and outrage.

"Greed's the reason you're here, too," Heller reminded him. "We have two choices, gentlemen. We can arm ourselves, get the others from the cabin section and try to take on Ton and the Filipinos, or we can go on to make the deal, get our payment and go home extremely wealthy."

"I think we can take the group on board now," House said. "There'll be more of them when we reach the site for the exchange in the Philippines. The odds will be less than fifty-fifty for us then."

"The risks are high," Heller said with a smile. "That's how it works. We all know that from past operations. Some of those have been nearly as dangerous, but the possible rewards for those risks were never as high as they are now."

"Money isn't much good to dead men," Samels grumbled.

"Then I suggest we try to stay alive," Heller replied.

MAJOR TUKARNO WASN'T in a good mood. He had been rousted from his bed and ordered to meet some mysterious team of experts from the United States at an obscure airfield near Amboina. Tukarno let his wife sleep and left a note for her to explain his absence. He dressed in the bathroom and donned the standard fatigue uniform of the Police Mobile Brigade. Tukarno glanced at the mirror and saw a slender, dark man in his early forties peering back at him.

He examined the uniform due to his habit of neatness and the belief that a good officer must always serve as an admirable example for his men. An eagle head and a lightning bolt symbol adorned the shoulder patch, and the gold wings and parachute badge of a police parachutist was above his breast pocket. Tukarno slipped the blue beret onto his head and nodded with satisfaction at his image.

Tukarno moved to the front room where his aide waited. He paused for a moment at a book stand and opened a large leather-bound copy of the Koran. Tukarno read a passage, kissed the Islamic holy book and bowed to Mecca as he prayed for Allah to grant him courage, wisdom and patience, and to protect his wife and children. Then he offered his aide the Koran and some time to pray. The soldier faced Mecca, kissed the book and gently returned it to the stand. Then both men left Tukarno's quarters.

"I have some coffee in a thermos, Major," Jatta, his aide, declared as he slipped behind the wheel of the jeep.

"Thank you, Sergeant," Tukarno said with genuine gratitude. He sat beside his aide as Jatta started the engine. "You know where the airfield is?"

"We've used it for training operations," Jatta replied. "I don't know what the Americans want with us. Probably another complaint about alleged violations of human rights in East Timor."

"That would be a complaint for the politicians in Jakarta," the major stated. "They wouldn't call on the Police Mobile Brigade stationed in the Moluccas because of human rights in East Timor. More likely it's some sort of terrorist activity here that threatens American interests somehow."

The headlights knifed through the darkness as the jeep rolled over the badly paved road. There was no traffic. Not even a bicycle or a goat shared the road, which allowed Jatta to step on the gas. Tukarno considered the reasons for the arrival of the Americans. The Molucca Islands were part of Indonesia, a fairly small and somewhat distant part. The Americans wouldn't be coming to Amboina unless the problem concerned something in the Moluccas themselves. Tukarno may have been selected to contact them because he spoke English, but many Indonesians spoke English. They could have found someone else to be a translator. Tukarno had clearly been selected because he was an officer in the PMB.

The Police Mobile Brigade was, among other things, Indonesia's antiterrorist unit. That was probably the reason Tukarno had had to leave his bed and his beloved wife at four in the morning. He wondered what kind of lunatic band was causing trouble now. Communists, he figured. The United States seldom had much interest in Indonesia unless they were worried about a Communist takeover or unless they wanted to criticize the government for violating human rights. Now that the Americans were trying to improve relations with the Soviet Union, they seemed more concerned about Islamic terrorist outfits these days.

Tukarno was a devout Muslim, and he didn't like the idea of hunting down people of his own faith. Still, he had to admit there were violent fanatics among the followers of Islam. If he had to take on Muslim zealots for the sake of his country, Tukarno would do it.

They reached the airfield and discovered that the plane had already landed. Phoenix Force was waiting for Major Tukarno next to a green minibus. The Indonesian officer climbed out of the jeep and approached the five strangers. "Welcome to the Moluccas," he said with a polite nod. "I understand that you just flew in from Port Moresby in New Guinea."

"Yeah," Calvin James muttered. "It turned out to be a bum steer. The guys we were after never arrived there."

"We wasted a lot of bloody time flying from Australia to New Guinea only to find out that Heller had claimed his ship was off course and that he'd have to head up to these islands for repairs."

"I hate to admit this," Tukarno began, "but I have no idea what you're talking about."

"It's a long story," Yakov Katzenelenbogen admitted. "We're short on time, so we'll have to give you the edited version."

A thin man dressed in baggy white cotton shirt and trousers emerged from the bus as Phoenix Force told Tukarno about their mission. He was Carlos Leyte, a CIA case officer. A native-born Filipino, Leyte had served in Vietnam with the SOG and had later become an operative for the Company in the Philippines, Indonesia and Malaysia. Currently stationed at a listening post in Borneo, Leyte had been contacted by Phoenix Force from New Guinea and had been told to meet them at Amboina in the Moluccas.

"So you went to New Guinea after these men, but they weren't there," Tukarno said after hearing the commandos' story. "Now you're convinced they're here."

"I know this isn't good news, Major," Katz said with a sigh. He fired up a Camel cigarette as he spoke. "The authorities in Papua, as well as the CIA and the NSA stationed there, radioed personnel in surrounding islands. They contacted ports, military bases and coastal patrols. Heller's cargo ship arrived here in Amboina."

"You're certain of this?" Tukarno asked, surprised.

"The foreman of a stevedore crew recognized Hellson-Heller and the one-handed man who was claiming to be a businessman named Han from Taiwan," Rafael Encizo explained. "That's good enough for us to come here looking for the bastards."

"And they're armed with a nuclear cannon?" Tukarno asked, still finding the story hard to believe.

"That's what they say," Leyte remarked. "These fellows have White House authority, and they're also backed up by the prime ministers of both Australia and New Zealand, as well as the president of Indonesia. I'd say that's a lot of clout, Major."

"I agree," Tukarno said. "I can call in twenty more PMR troops on short notice. In four hours we could have a small army on this island."

"We don't have that much time to spare," Katz explained. "Mr. Leyte brought a vehicle large enough for us to use, and you have local military and law-enforcement authority here. That's all we need right now. If Heller and his people are still on the ship, that'll mean the cannon's still disassembled and harmless. If they put up a fight, we can simply blast the ship's hull and sink it to prevent them from using the cannon.''

"My driver knows Amboina perfectly," Tukarno declared. "He'll take me to the harbor. You gentlemen follow and try to keep up with us."

"Let's do it," McCarter said eagerly.

25

Yakov Katzenelenbogen and Gary Manning approached the gangplank of the cargo ship. The Israeli carried his micro-Uzi braced across his prosthesis, a nine-inch silencer attached to the stubby barrel. The Canadian warrior held his machine pistol in one fist and a tear gas grenade in the other. Both men wore gas masks in addition to their other combat gear. They had also donned black camouflage uniforms and matching skintight gloves.

The docks were fairly quiet at that predawn hour. A Malaysian vessel had been unloading a shipment of electrical equipment, but Major Tukarno had ordered the crew to stay on the ship and take cover. Dockworkers, too, stayed clear of the pier as the two Phoenix commandos boarded the port side of the cargo ship from Darwin, Australia.

A figure appeared on the bridge and peered down at the two black-clad armed invaders with inhuman heads of black rubber, plastic filters and buglike lenses. The man raised an AK-47 and opened his mouth to shout an alert, but he heard an odd hiss and glimpsed the blur of a projectile a split instant before a sharp pain exploded in his chest. The man glanced down at the fiberglass crossbow bolt that jutted from his punctured heart. His Kalashnikov rifle slipped from his fingers and clattered on the bridge deck. The cyanide took effect before the man could cry out, and his corpse wilted beside the fallen AK-47.

David McCarter lowered his Barnett Commando crossbow and worked the cocking lever to reload the weapon. The British ace was concealed behind a stack of crates on the dock. In addition to the crossbow and other standard weapons, McCarter also had Calvin James's M-16 with its M-203 launcher attachment. James hadn't taken the rifle because he and Encizo were approaching the ship from a different direction.

The ex-SEAL and the Cuban swam below the surface of the bay waters from under the pier to the starboard side of the vessel. Their black wet suits and flippers protected them from the chilly water as they breaststroked to the hull. Neither man needed air tanks for such a brief swim, but they wore diving masks to protect their faces and eyes from the cold saltwater.

They swam along the draft, heads above water to inhale deeply after holding their breath during the swim. Both men carried thick waterproof bags on their backs. They climbed up from the water and hauled themselves onto the handrail. Encizo and James scanned the deck fore and aft. They saw no one and climbed on board. The pair removed their masks and fins and unbuckled the straps on the bags. Inside the rubber containers were micro-Uzis, a pair of tear gas grenades and a mask for each man.

Encizo and James were preparing to open the bags just as a man appeared at the port quarter. A dark-skinned figure, clad only in cutoff trousers and a straw hat, the sentry carried a French MAT-49 submachine gun. He saw the pair and started to swing his weapon at the Phoenix commandos. Neither the black tough guy from Chicago nor the Cuban crusader could hope to open a bag and draw a micro-Uzi fast enough to beat the enemy to the trigger.

James's hand swooped to his ankle and snatched the Blackmoor Dirk from a sheath. He swung his arm high in a desperate underhand throw, and the knife rocketed from his fingers and struck the sentry in the stomach. The sharp steel punched skin and muscle. Blood oozed from the wound as the sentry doubled up and screamed. He triggered his subgun, but the barrel was pointed downward. Nine-millimeter slugs splintered wood from the deck near the sentry's feet.

Rafael Encizo drew a *shaken* throwing star from his diving belt and whipped his arm forward. The steel star hit the gunman in the head. The sharp tines pierced his skull at the hairline above and between the eyes. The guy's head snapped back, eyes wide with astonishment. Then he collapsed onto the deck as more voices shouted from the cabins and hold of the ship.

Katz and Manning lobbed tear gas grenades through the cabin windows. A slight figure emerged from the cabin section, an AK-47 in his fists. His eyes were closed, trying to hold back the tears. Almost blind, he nearly ran into Gary Manning.

The big Canadian grabbed the barrel of the man's assault rifle and pulled hard. The guy staggered forward, and Manning shoved a boot into his hip. The kick sent the opponent hurtling into a handrail. He cried out in surprise and terror as he toppled over the rail and plunged into the ocean.

Katz sprayed the cabin windows with micro-Uzi rounds. Glass shattered and bullets raked the walls inside. Voices yelped in terror. One man shouted something in a language neither Katz nor Manning understood.

"We give up!" another voice declared in broken English. "No shoot! We give up!"

Two men stumbled from the gas-filled cabin and emerged with their hands raised. Manning and Katz shoved the pair to the gangplank and told them to get off the ship. McCarter waited for the pair at the dock, a micro-Uzi held ready in case either man decided to change his mind about surrendering. The Briton frowned as the men staggered down the plank. They were both brown-skinned with Asian features and straight black hair.

"I thought Heller didn't hire nonwhites?" Manning remarked. He had also noticed that the men aboard the cargo vessel didn't fit the usual description of Heller flunkies.

"Except the Indian scientist you found at the plant back in New Zealand," Katz reminded him. "Maybe these men work for Ton."

"Maybe," the Canadian muttered under his gas mask. "I'd hate to think we may have hit the wrong boat."

"More coughs and angry shouts erupted from the ship's hold as James and Encizo lobbed more tear gas. An enemy inside the hold blasted automatic fire through the opening. The Phoenix commandos stood clear of the hold as the orange muzzle-flash tore through the cloud of gas fumes.

"Dumb move!" James shouted, returning fire with his micro-Uzi. He fired another short burst into the hold and was rewarded with a scream for his effort. An M-16 assault rifle was hurled up from the hold. The enemy also tossed out a Colt .45 and a sawed-off shotgun.

"We come out!" a voice shouted from the hold. "You have our guns now! Don't shoot us!"

Two more figures emerged from the hold. One held his hands high in surrender while the other clutched a bullet-shattered forearm as he staggered onto the deck. Encizo escorted the pair toward the bow while James descended into the hold, machine pistol ready in case there were more opponents waiting below.

"Found a couple of more ship rats, eh?" Manning remarked as he met Encizo at the bow. "I'll get them off the ship for you. Where's Jackson?"

"Checking the hold," Encizo replied, eager to hand over the prisoners to the Canadian. "I'll get back there and see if he needs any help."

Manning pointed his micro-Uzi at the captives. They resembled the other enemies aboard the vessel. All were young, dark and seemed to be Asian or Eurasian. Encizo turned and headed back to the hold, only to find that James had already completed his investigation below.

"The goddamn cannon isn't down there," James announced, angry and frustrated. "I bet nobody's found Heller or Ton, either. That son of a bitch has slipped past us again."

MAJOR TUKARNO AND CARLOS LEYTE helped Phoenix Force with the prisoners. The CIA case officer instantly recognized the accent of the captives' broken English and snapped questions in a language totally alien to the five commandos.

"What are these guys speaking?" James asked.

"Maguindanao," Leyte replied with a nod. "These guys are all Filipinos. They're not answering questions worth a damn. Lots of colorful profanity, but not much else."

"Did you ask them what they were doing on an Australian cargo ship?" Katz inquired as he began to pace in front of the prisoners. The Israeli clicked the steel hooks at the end of his arm to make certain the Filipinos noticed the prosthesis.

They had taken their captives to a dock warehouse in order to interrogate them. The Filipinos sat on the wooden floor and stared up at Katz's artificial limb. Calvin James examined the man with the wounded arm and insisted that he be excused from interrogation.

"I've got to take care of this dude," the black commando declared. "Bullet went clean through his arm, but it broke the radius bone and tore the flexor carpi muscle pretty badly. If I don't disinfect the wound and set the bone, he could be crippled for life."

"Do what you have to," Katz agreed. "Four uncooperative prisoners will be as much use to us as all five have been so far."

"Ordinarily I would never suggest this," Major Tukarno said grimly, "but this situation is so serious that I must say it, anyway. If we cause these vermin enough pain, they'll answer our questions. As Allah is my judge, I find such methods repulsive, but so many lives are at stake—"

"We don't use torture, Major," Katz told him. "It's unreliable as well as immoral. Besides, I can already tell that these men have encountered Ton recently. They looked at my prosthesis with more than passing curiosity. I've had this steel hook for a hand—and ones like it—for more than twenty years. I'm used to people staring at it. After a while one learns to read people's expressions when they see it. These men's faces tell me they've seen something like it recently. There's a glimmer of recognition in their eyes."

"Well, they won't tell me why they were on the ship," Leyte said with an exasperated sigh. "One thing's certain, they weren't just a bunch of innocent wharf rats who decided to take a nap aboard the vessel. Not when they were all armed with automatic weapons."

"Yeah," Gary Manning said. "Soviet-made assault rifles, French submachine guns, American M-16s and Colt .45s. Does that sound familiar, Carlos?"

"Vietnam," Leyte said with a nod. "The Communists in the North got all sorts of weapons from both the Russians and the Chinese. They also had a lot of French guns left over from when they were fighting the Europeans and, of course, they got their hands on a lot of American arms when the U.S. was there."

The CIA man stared at the captives. "Those types of weapons also fit the sort of arsenal used by certain terrorist outfits in the Philippines. Since these jokers are speaking Maguindanao, it's likely they came from Mindanao, the southern island of the Philippines. The pro-Marcos extremist groups aren't getting weapons from the Communists, but they could have purchased AK-47s from black market arms dealers who don't care about politics."

"Where's the manager of the docks?" Katz asked. "I think we should have him check to see if there was a ship from the Philippines here when Heller arrived. I also want to talk to the stevedore foreman who recognized Heller when he saw him supervising other workers on the pier."

"They're both at the office," David McCarter said. The Briton stood guard over the prisoners, his micro-Uzi pointed at the Filipino fanatics. "Go talk to them. I'll keep an eye on these blokes."

Katz, Leyte and Tukarno met with the manager and foreman. After discussing the matter and checking the dock records, they learned that a Filipino ship called the *Celebes* had been in port when the Australian cargo vessel had arrived. The foreman also recalled the man who seemed to be in charge on the *Celebes*, because he carried two wooden batons in a sash as well as a long-bladed knife.

"Bontoc!" Leyte exclaimed when he heard the description. "Ramón Bontoc is the cell leader of the most ruthless gang of terrorists in the Philippines. It's a branch of the Philippine People's Liberation Army, a real demented leftist group. Bontoc and his gang are the worst of the lot. The Company has a file on those scum thick enough to choke an elephant. Bontoc is wanted for murder, kidnapping, sabotage and God knows what else."

"Have these terrorists been getting support from Communist countries?" Katz inquired.

"They were getting arms and supplies from the Soviets through sources in Southeast Asia," Leyte confirmed. His eyes widened. "Of course, Bontoc could have connections with Ton. Since this *glasnost* business, the Soviets haven't been giving the Filipino terrorists the kind of assistance they're used to, but maybe the Vietnamese have decided to pick up where the Russians left off.''

"Or Ton himself is taking things a bit farther," Katz said grimly. "The *Celebes* left here and headed back for the Philippines, right?"

"I'm afraid so," Tukarno answered. "They've got quite a head start. Still, a plane is much faster than a ship."

"Well, here we go again," Katz said with a sigh. "Carlos, you're familiar with the Philippines and CIA operations there. Can you contact the Company and the local authorities to find out what port the *Celebes* is supposed to arrive at?"

"I can do more than that," Leyte replied. "I'm going with you to the Philippines. I was born near the rain forest where the PPLA has been hiding out. I can help you hunt those bastards down, Mr. Ginsberg. I know the jungle, and I've had combat experience in Nam."

"We'd appreciate your help," Katz assured him. The Israeli turned to Tukarno. "You'll take care of the men we hauled off the ship?"

"Of course," the Indonesian officer confirmed. "Although we still don't know how crew members of the *Celebes* wound up on that vessel. Why didn't they go with the others back to the Philippines?"

"We can only guess," Katz said. "From what we know about Heller, I'd say he probably insisted on taking his own crew to the Philippines. The man appears to be a racist, and he wouldn't feel very comfortable sailing off to sea with a ship full of Filipinos. However, since he's a mercenary opportunist just interested in making a profit, and the terrorists are Marxist fanatics, Heller might have a more valid reason to feel uncomfortable with his new clients. At any rate, the Filipinos left behind clearly had nowhere else to go, so they boarded the Australian ship because they knew the crew was gone."

"This could all be wishful thinking," Leyte warned. "The foreman said he saw Heller and Ton with Bontoc aboard the *Celebes*, but he's not certain they were on the ship when it departed. Heller could still be here in the Moluccas."

"I think the evidence strongly suggests the Philippines," Katz insisted. "Too many things point to it. It looks as if Ton's either nudging his country toward membership in the nuclear club or he's making his own play for one-world communism. Indonesia has a certain degree of political unrest, but not nearly as much as the Philippines. Corazon Aquino's regime might be popular, but it has also gotten a lot of criticism for handling the economy and other government matters badly. Communist insurgency has continued, and pro-Marcos groups and Moro separatists have added to the strife and tension."

"I see what you mean," Leyte said. "If Bontoc and his boys fire a nuclear shell at Manila, the Philippines will explode in violence and chaos, a perfect atmosphere for another revolution. I doubt if Bontoc could seize control of the country that way, but he's nuts enough to think he could pull it off. He's also violently anti-American, you know."

"That doesn't surprise me," Katz replied. "Aren't all Marxist extremists anti-American?"

"All that I know of," Leyte agreed. "My point is that there are thousands of U.S. naval personnel stationed in the Philippines. One of those bases might very well be Bontoc's intended target instead of Manila."

"They have more than one shell for the atomic cannon," Katz said grimly. "Maybe Bontoc plans to take out both targets, which is all the more reason for us to get to work. We have a lot to do and very little time left to do it in."

26

David McCarter expertly landed Gavin Ford's plane on yet another narrow runway at a little-known airfield. This time the landing gear touched down outside of Maganoy, the capital of the Philippine province of Maguindanao.

A group of men dressed in camouflage military uniforms waited by the runway beside the U.S. Army deuce-and-a half and a jeep. They waited for the plane to taxi to a stop before two soldiers approached the craft.

"Good morning," Carlos Leyte greeted as he climbed out of the plane. The CIA case officer wore a U.S. Marine Corps tiger-striped uniform and a boonie hat. His webgear included a Beretta 92-F in a hip holster, with magazine pouches for an M-16 as well as the 9 mm pistol.

"Good morning to you, too," one of the Filipino soldiers replied. "Allow me to introduce myself. I'm Captain Juan Galdo, Philippine Special Forces."

Phoenix Force emerged from the plane as the officer identified himself. Galdo was a short, stocky man, thickly muscled rather than fat. His name was written in black on a white name tag over the left breast pocket of his uniform shirt. A Philippine army badge was pinned to his left collar and a trio of silver triangles on the right labeled his rank as captain. The soldier beside Galdo wore dark blue chevrons on his sleeve, three pyramid-shaped stripes with three bars under it to mark his rank as a master sergeant. All the Filipino troops wore regulation bush hats with gold cords and blue-and-white parachute badges on the turned-up brims.

"I'm afraid we have little time for social niceties, Captain," Yakov Katzenelenbogen declared. "Have you received word about the *Celebes*?"

"Yes," Galdo confirmed. "The ship docked at a harbor on Sarangani Bay approximately two hours ago. Another detachment of Special Forces troops raided the vessel. I received word of this by radio not fifteen minutes ago. There were only two men on board, both Filipinos. There was no sign of the men you seek or the cannon. May I ask why this weapon is so important that a team of special agents from the United States has come to retrieve it?"

Galdo hadn't been told that the cannon fired nuclear shells. Katz promised to explain later and asked if they had any idea where Heller and the others had gone.

"Fortunately," the captain said, "dockworkers noticed the Taiwanese man with a steel hook for a hand." The officer stared at Katz's prosthesis with surprise.

"Yes," the Israeli said. "I know I have one, too."

"Sorry," Galdo said, slightly embarrassed. "Seeing the man with the hook was...unusual, so the dockworkers paid more attention than they ordinarily would as this Taiwanese and a group of white and Filipino men loaded some crates into a pair of military-style trucks. They also commented that two of the crates resembled metal coffins. Then they drove north with the cargo and men in the vehicles."

"Isn't anybody inspecting cargo that comes off ships these days?" Rafael Encizo asked, frustrated by Heller's ability to shuffle his nuclear weapons from port to port at will.

"The dock at Sarangani where the *Celebes* arrived is a small harbor that doesn't seem too concerned about following regulations very closely," Galdo said with a shrug. "I suspect they have ships dock there often that are involved in illegal activities, but the officials tend to turn a blind eye to such matters and probably accept bribes to remain disinterested in cargo.''

"That's probably what's happened from the beginning," Calvin James remarked. "Heller's been coasting right through inspections because people have either been bribed or they were afraid of him or they didn't want to offend a rich and 'respectable' businessman. In other words, the son of a bitch has operated the same way big-time drug smugglers do. Hell, he used to be a dope smuggler, according to some of the stooges we've interrogated. I haven't met the guy yet, but I sure as hell am looking forward to it.''

"Well, we've been lucky enough to track Heller this far," McCarter commented, taking out a pack of Player's. "Now we're finally in the same neighborhood those dirty sods are in. There's got to be a way to nail them now.''

"The Philippine People's Liberation Army is most active in this area," Galdo stated. "It's well-known that one of the most ruthless cells is hiding in the jungle here. Heller and the others are headed in that direction.''

"Jungle," Encizo began as he glanced at the banyan forest that extended beyond the airstrip. Parrots cawed in the trees. "That must cover a lot of territory here.''

"A great deal," Leyte confirmed. "But that's an advantage. Since they have to transport the cannon by truck, there are only a few roads into the jungle. None are very good. Better suited for water buffalo than motor vehicles.''

"We've considered that," Galdo declared. "The terrorists would certainly choose the least-traveled path. They'd avoid the larger villages. One of my men was born in a village in this area. He can certainly help us. If we move now, there's a chance we can catch them. The terrorists were seen moving northeast of the bay. That means they're actually southwest of our position.''

Manning smiled. "They can't travel through a jungle very fast, and they won't want to risk an accident carrying their cargo or attract attention by trying to break speed records. Maybe we can head 'em off at the pass, so to speak."

"Not if we stand around jawing about it," Katz declared.

Phoenix Force, Leyte and the Filipino Special Forces left the airfield in the army vehicles. They passed small towns that seemed to be built of plywood and thatched roofing. Chickens wandered in the streets, and children chased an old tire as it rolled past a row of outhouses. Elderly men and women sat on stone stoops. They smoked hand-rolled cigarettes as they calmly watched the jeep and truck drive by.

The morning grew steadily warmer. Encizo had finally found the tropical sun he had longed for in Antarctica. The other members of Phoenix Force found the ninety-degree heat and extreme humidity less welcome. The vehicles bounced over dirt roads and jarred the passengers, which did nothing to increase the comfort of the men enclosed in the hot, crowded transport truck. The Filipinos were accustomed to the weather and bad roads. They passed the time by inspecting their M-16s.

They saw fewer people as they reached the rain forest. High, coarse grass, unfit for cattle, lined the dirt path. Bamboo and rubber trees formed walls of thick foliage. Insects became more troublesome as flies and gnats bombarded the vehicles. The cries of jungle birds filled the forest. Their progress was occasionally impeded when they encountered tangles of vines on the road.

The jeep came to a halt and the truck followed suit. A Special Forces sergeant approached the road ahead of the vehicles and examined the ground. Manning was an accomplished tracker, so he joined the Filipino soldier in the investigation. The man spoke a smattering of English, and

Manning conversed with him briefly. They both nodded in agreement and returned to the vehicles.

"What was all that about?" McCarter asked as he took a canteen from his belt.

"We've reached the area that the local guy figures Heller's gang would use to go into the jungle," Manning explained. "Looks like he was right on the money. There are tire tracks on the road. The size fits a deuce-and-a-half. Two army trucks to be exact. The prints are deep and suggest that the rigs carried heavy loads, one heavier than the other. The tread marks are worn and were probably made by old army surplus vehicles with tires that have seen a lot of miles."

"Any idea how long ago the vehicles went through here?" Katz inquired. The Israeli's hooks clicked anxiously.

"The sergeant knows the territory, and he's familiar with how long grass takes to spring back up this time of year after being trampled by a heavy weight," the Canadian told him. "He figures they drove through this area less than ten minutes ago."

"Jesus," James said, clenching his fists in frustration. "Let's move it!"

"If they realize we're chasing them, they could set up an ambush and blow us off the road before we even see them," Encizo warned. He gazed at the thick foliage of high grass, ferns and close-set bamboo stalks. "There's lots of concealment available for the enemy to use along the road."

"You're right," Leyte said grimly. "This is like Vietnam all over again."

"I don't remember too many roads when I was in Nam," Manning replied. "We'll just have to do what we did then. Have a couple men go forward ahead of the vehicles as pointmen. On foot they'll have a better chance of spotting an ambush."

"A better chance of getting killed first, too," James added.

"Right," McCarter said with a shrug as he put away his canteen and gathered up his Barnett crossbow. "So who's going to walk point with me?"

"Ask the Filipinos," Manning replied. "We know you too well."

27

Jason House felt the hairs on his neck rise. He placed a hand on his holstered Smith & Wesson and glanced over his shoulder at the road and surrounding jungle. The British merc had survived in a dangerous business for a lot of years, and he credited a large part of his success to his instincts. Right now that sixth sense was signaling danger.

The mercenary didn't need ESP to appreciate the fact that there was good reason for concern. Bontoc's PPLA goons had driven the deuce-and-a-half trucks into the jungle with House, Heller, Ton, the surviving members of Heller's crew from Australia, the nuclear cannon and the shells. The two-vehicle caravan had traveled deep into the rain forest until reaching the blockade in front of them now. Half a dozen figures stood in the road by a pair of battered, old motorcycles. They were a scruffy-looking group—clothing torn and dirty, hair and beards unwashed and matted.

They were also armed with AK-47 assault rifles and submachine guns of Soviet, Chinese and French manufacture. Some also carried handguns and ammunition belts slung across shoulders and chests. Two men held machetes. House didn't need Bontoc to tell him that these blokes were more members of the Philippine People's Liberation Army.

The trucks came to a halt, and Bontoc snapped orders in Maguindanao. His terrorist flunkies hurried to the rear of the trucks as the passengers climbed out. Heller and his men stepped back to give the Filipinos ample room to get inside the vehicles. General Ton separated from the others and watched as if he were a disinterested third party. The Vietnamese officer had donned a gun belt with a Makarov pistol on his left hip. He had claimed he'd done so because he wanted to be ready in case the Philippine authorities or the CIA tried to stop them. House was suspicious of Ton's motives for deciding to carry a gun. If violence erupted between Heller's forces and Bontoc's people, there was little doubt which side Ton would support.

House didn't have much doubt how such a conflict would turn out, either. The Briton was armed with his .38 revolver and the hidden derringer under his left sleeve. Heller didn't carry a gun, but the Australians all packed pistols. However, the Filipinos were armed with automatic weapons, and they outnumbered Heller's group more than two to one now that reinforcements had joined up with them. Worse, House thought, there were probably more PPLA fanatics concealed among the trees and tall grass.

Yet what puzzled House most was the sense of danger from the road in the direction they had come from. It was as if an even greater threat were coming their way. The Briton tried to shrug off the sensation, putting it down to nerves caused by the obvious tension. Nonetheless, the creeping fear remained.

The PPLA flunkies hauled the steel caskets from the truck. Bontoc ordered them to carry the crates into the trees. Other men dragged out the crates that contained the disassembled cannon. House examined Heller's face. The renegade American's expression seemed assured, almost arrogant. The merc glanced at Samels and the other Australians. None of them shared their leader's apparent self-confidence. Maybe Heller figured his bodybuilder muscles would protect him from bullets, House thought sourly. If shooting broke out, Heller would certainly learn otherwise.

"General Ton," Heller declared. "Your merchandise has been delivered as we agreed. I trust you haven't forgotten the rest of our deal."

"Of course not," the Vietnamese assured him. Ton turned toward Bontoc. "My associate wants his thirty pieces of silver, so to speak."

"It's a bit more than that, General," Heller reminded him. "I'm a very expensive Judas, but I'm worth it."

"Follow us into the jungle," Bontoc told him, and promptly pursued his men with the crates.

Heller leaned toward House. "Stay on your toes, Jason," he whispered. "This is it, one way or the other."

Reluctantly Heller and his men followed Bontoc. Ton and most of the PPLA stooges also marched through the yard-high grass and pushed their way through the bamboo to stay close to their terrorist commander. The shade from the hardwood trees and oil palms shielded them somewhat from the fireball in the sky, but none of them noticed the noonday sun as they struggled through the bush to a clearing. Bontoc ordered his men to put down their burdens. Heller opened one of the caskets to allow the Filipinos to examine the torpedo-shaped shell inside.

"That's it," Heller announced. "A 115 mm cannon shell with a uranium warhead. The general has certainly told you that it works. Of course, you don't have to take his word for it. The test firing in Australia has been reported by news agencies around the world."

"The first of many nuclear strikes without the approval of the United States or the Soviet Union," Ton declared with a smile. "The revolution should have these weapons. Only revolutionaries are willing to continue the fight, not fat and fearful members of the politburos who no longer have the stomach for war."

"We'll certainly make our collective voice heard!" Bontoc announced with fanatic fire. "It's just a question of which target to strike first. The American naval bases or the puppet government in Manila.''

''Do what you want with these weapons,'' Heller invited, ''but pay me first.''

Bontoc snapped some orders at his men. Three PPLA zealots scrambled to a cluster of pepper plants surrounded by fallen leaves and logs. They moved the latter and tore several iron spikes from the earth. The trio brushed aside some leaves and seized the corners of a canvas tarp, peeling it back. The pepper plants were attached to the center, and loose dirt slipped from the tarp as they removed it from a trench. Heller stepped forward and peered into the pit. Several metal boxes covered the bottom of the six-foot ditch.

''There it is, my American Judas,'' Ton said. ''Gold, jewels, precious jade.''

''You don't mind if I take a look?'' Heller asked.

''Be my guest,'' the Vietnamese invited, gesturing with the steel hook.

Just then a burst of automatic fire erupted from the road. Screams accompanied the gunshots. Ton raised his head and stared at the road, but the foliage blocked his view. Both Filipinos and Australians immediately responded to the shooting by firing at one another.

A PPLA thug raised his AK-47 to point it at Heller. House thrust his left arm forward, and the derringer appeared in his fist. He triggered the diminutive pistol, firing a .38 slug into the face of the Filipino gunman. The terrorist collapsed against Bontoc. House drew his revolver and fired two shots into the torso of another PPLA zealot as he jumped for cover behind the closest tree trunk.

Heller charged a Filipino who was about to fire a Chinese assault rifle. He slammed his powerful forearm into the Chinese rifle, knocking the weapon from his opponent's hands. Heller then hammered the man in the side of the neck and dropped him to the ground. The renegade American scooped up the rifle and shoulder-rolled as another terrorist fired a MAT-49. The French SMG blasted a trio of bullets into the ground near Heller's hurtling form, but the American rolled to cover behind an oil palm.

Samels drew his pistol. A PPLA gunman shot the Australian in the center of the chest with an AK-47 and sent the man tumbling backward into the open pit. Samels's corpse fell across the metal boxes as both sides continued to fire at each other. Two more Australians collapsed, and Heller triggered the Chinese assault rifle from his cover, drilling the Filipino who had taken out Samels.

"HOLY SHIT!" Calvin James rasped as he peered through the bamboo stalks at the battle within the jungle. "These crazy bastards are killing each other, man!"

"Nice of them to make our job easier," Rafael Encizo replied.

Phoenix Force and their Filipino allies had continued on the road with McCarter and a Special Forces NCO on point. They had finally discovered the enemy vehicles, and the PPLA terrorists guarding them had started shooting. McCarter had taken out one with a poisoned crossbow bolt, and his teammates had rushed to the battle scene when they'd heard the shots. The terrorists on the road had been chopped down by a wave of automatic fire. A couple had managed to flee into the jungle, only to discover that their gunshots had also triggered a battle between Heller's group and the PPLA.

"Let's take advantage of this," Katz instructed. "Captain, take a detachment to the east and we'll get them in a cross fire. Block their escape routes and don't let them get away with those steel coffins. The nuclear shells are inside."

"Right," Galdo replied.

"I just love it when my enemies turn out to be this stupid," McCarter commented as he put down his crossbow and gripped his micro-Uzi with both hands.

"Don't get cocky," Katz warned. "There are still enough of them left to kill you."

"Only takes one," Gary Manning added.

The enemy was located in a confined area, which meant using close-quarters weapons. Phoenix Force held their micro-Uzis ready and carefully approached the battleground. Filipino terrorists and Australian hoodlums still exchanged fire with one another. Several slain opponents littered the ground. The combatants concentrated on one another and failed to notice Phoenix Force and their allies closing in.

An Australian gunman crouched behind the trunk of a tree as he reloaded a Heckler & Koch pistol. He snapped the slide forward to chamber a round and prepared to fire at the PPLA positions. The guy didn't hear Manning slip from the bushes behind him. The Canadian crept closer and swung his machine pistol against the back of the Australian's skull. The steel frame smacked the man's face into the tree.

The gunman collapsed at the base of the tree. Manning relieved him of the H&K autoloader and stuck it in his belt. A second Australian lowlife leaned around the trunk of another tree to try to see if his comrade had been shot by the Filipino terrorists. Instead he discovered Manning standing over the senseless form of his pal. The Australian cursed and swung his .357 Magnum toward Manning. The Canadian's micro-Uzi spit a three-round burst, and the enemy gunman cried out as his sternum exploded and a bullet tunneled through his solar plexus on the way to his heart. The second opponent went down forever.

Manning heard something hit the tree trunk near him. The snarl of automatic fire and a stray round that had nearly taken off his ear warned the Canadian that the PPLA gunmen were using his position for target practice. The Phoenix fighter braced his back against the trunk and tucked in his arms and legs to avoid catching a bullet. He took comfort in the knowledge that the Filipino opponents were also being stalked by his teammates and the Special Forces troops.

Captain Galdo and several of his men approached the PPLA enemy lines from behind. One terrorist had been shot in the left thigh and was trying to tie a tourniquet while three of his comrades continued to fire at Heller's forces. The wounded man spotted the soldiers in the high grass and shouted a warning to the others.

M-16 rifles spit flame as Galdo's men concentrated on their opponents. The wounded terrorist saw the PPLA fanatic closest to his position jerk wildly and fall against a tree trunk to slide to the ground, lifeless. Blood stained the slain fanatic's shirtfront.

Another terrorist triggered his MAT-49 and sprayed the grass with parabellum slugs. A Special Forces trooper dropped his rifle and clasped both hands to his bullet-shattered face. Blood trickled between his fingers as the soldier rolled onto his back and died. Galdo and the other troops returned fire. Blasts of 5.56 mm slugs ripped into the body of the terrorist who had killed the soldier. Blood spurted from the PPLA gunman's stomach and chest. His biceps was sliced by bullets, and the French subgun fell from the man's quivering fingers.

The terrorist with the injured leg stared at the crimson pulp that his comrade had become. The terrified revolutionary raised his hands and held them over his head. The remaining PPLA killer blasted Galdo's position, missing the captain by scant inches. The soldiers returned fire as the terrorist dived for cover behind another tree trunk.

Suddenly the terrorist's weapon dropped from his hands as the extremist began to flap his arms as if attempting to fly.

Bullet holes burst in his chest. The man had run directly into Erik Heller's line of fire, and the renegade had shot him between the shoulder blades with his captured Chinese assault rifle.

RAMON BONTOC TRIGGERED the last rounds from the magazine of his AK-47. The terrorist leader didn't carry spare magazines or ammo, so he dropped the Kalashnikov in disgust and glanced around, hoping to find a PPLA comrade close enough to toss him another firearm. But Bontoc groaned with anger and frustration when he discovered that his nearest comrade was dead.

The Filipino terrorist saw another AK-47 on the ground beside the corpse. He judged the distance to the rifle to be roughly ten meters. Not far, but the shooting between combatants had escalated. Damn Heller, he thought with bloodthirsty anger. The capitalist bastard must have had a unit of reinforcements follow them into the jungle—reinforcements armed with automatic weapons.

The terrorist leader didn't like firearms, and he wasn't very good with a gun. Bontoc thought guns were almost cowardly because they allowed men to kill each other at a distance. Men ought to fight face-to-face, he believed, eye-to-eye as they tested their skill with blade, club or bare hands. Anyone could pick up a gun, point it and pull the trigger, Bontoc thought with contempt. That attitude was the reason the PPLA leader was inept with firearms, but he always blamed his lack of accuracy and control of the weapon on the mechanics of the gun instead of his own limited ability.

Regardless of his personal prejudices, Bontoc realized he needed a gun. The terrorist leader prepared to dash for the AK-47, but a sharp whistle startled him, and he froze in place as his head slowly turned toward the sound. Rafael

Encizo had emerged from behind a giant fern, his micro-Uzi aimed at Bontoc.

"Going somewhere, *cabrón*?" the Cuban asked. "You can go to a prison cell or a graveyard. Take your pick. It's okay with me either way."

Bontoc raised his hands to shoulder level and slowly turned to face Encizo. The Phoenix crusader was surprised to see the fighting sticks in the man's sash and the large knife in a wooden scabbard on his hip. He recalled the description of the cell leader of the Philippine People's Liberation Army and realized he had captured Bontoc himself.

"All right," Encizo said as he drew closer in order to use the cover of the trees if necessary, "I know you're an expert at *estocada*."

The Filipino terrorist smiled contemptuously.

"Try any fancy tricks with those sticks or the knife and I'll blow your head off. Is that clear enough?"

"I understand," Bontoc assured him.

"Good," the Cuban said. "Now use one hand, only the thumb and forefinger, and pull the sticks out one at a time. Then drop them on the ground. Keep the other hand raised. Screw up my instructions and you'll get to know this machine pistol better than you'd like."

A figure appeared next to an oil palm, a Chinese subgun in his fists. Encizo saw the motion out of the corner of his eye. He whirled, snap-aimed and fired at the ambusher. The PPLA killer stopped four 9 mm parabellum slugs with his chest and face, fell backward and triggered his submachine gun, blasting a useless volley of 7.62 mm rounds into the triple canopy above.

Encizo swung the micro-Uzi back toward Bontoc, but the PPLA ringleader had already drawn his *estocada* sticks and was charging the Phoenix pro. One club slammed into the micro-Uzi in a cross-body stroke, and the other chopped Encizo across his collarbone. The machine pistol was torn from the Cuban's grasp, and his head and shoulders were forced into a painful bow by the blow on the collarbone.

Bontoc thrust a stick in a hard jab and stabbed the wooden end into Encizo's belly. The Cuban doubled up from the blow, the breath driven from his lungs and his chest constricted with numbing pain. The Filipino terrorist raised a club to bash Encizo across the skull, but the Phoenix warrior suddenly lunged and rammed a shoulder into Bontoc's abdomen.

The unexpected tactic drove Bontoc backward several steps, but he managed to maintain his balance. Encizo raised a knee and tried to drive it into his opponent's groin. He hit the Filipino in the thigh muscle. Bontoc hammered the butt of an *estocada* stick into Encizo's shoulder blade. The blow doubled up Encizo again, and Bontoc slammed a knee into the Cuban's face.

Encizo fell backward. His head filled with pain, and his vision blurred as he felt himself descend. The Phoenix commando's back struck the ground, and lights burst in front of his eyes. He moved a hand to the Walther in shoulder leather, but his arm seemed to be made of lead, and his fingers groped without finding the pistol.

Bontoc charged forward and swung both clubs at Encizo's head. The Cuban saw the blur of motion through a gray veil. He rolled away from the attacker and moved his head. Bontoc's sticks hammered the ground near Encizo's ear. The Phoenix fighter swung a boot and kicked Bontoc under the ribs. The terrorist grunted and staggered sideways from the blow. Encizo got to his feet as his vision cleared. He drew the Cold Steel Tanto from its belt sheath with one hand and yanked the Gerber fighting dagger from the boot sheath with the other. Now he had a knife in each fist. Bontoc looked at him with surprise. He had thought the Cuban was beaten, but the determination in the commando's eyes made it obvious the man wasn't about to roll over and die.

"What are you waiting for?" Encizo demanded. He spit blood and added, "Come on. Let's finish it."

Bontoc nodded and suddenly hurled a club at Encizo's head. The Cuban ducked, and the *estocada* stick whirled above his skull. The terrorist drew his long-bladed *kali* knife from the scabbard on his hip and attacked. Bontoc slashed the air with the stick in one fist and thrust with the *kali* in the other. Encizo dodged the stick stroke and crossed the blades of his Tanto and Gerber to block the Filipino's blade.

Steel clashed on steel. Bontoc snarled and lashed out with the stick again. Encizo turned toward the attack and aimed his Tanto high. The ultrasharp edge sliced Bontoc's wrist behind the club. Blood squirted from the severed artery, and the terrorist's fist popped open. Bontoc screamed as the stick fell to the ground. He swung the *kali* in a vicious swipe aimed at Encizo's neck in an effort to decapitate the Cuban warrior.

Encizo suddenly dropped to one knee, and the long Filipino knife slashed air above his head. The Cuban thrust an arm forward and punched the double-edged blade of the Gerber into Bontoc's belly. Steel pierced the terrorist's stomach. Bontoc bellowed in agony, and Encizo jumped up and shoved a forearm under the Filipino's elbow, knocking Bontoc's knife hand overhead. With his other hand Encizo slashed the Tanto across his opponent's throat.

A wound opened, and blood poured from the cut, splashing Encizo's shirt. Bontoc staggered backward. The blade of the Gerber was still buried in his belly, and crimson continued to flow from his slit throat. The PPLA leader dropped to his knees and swung the *kali* in a mindless stroke, chopping the ground vainly. Then the terrorist dropped to the ground and twitched feebly as a pool of his own blood formed around his body.

Encizo felt a dozen bruises from the battle as he walked unsteadily to his discarded micro-Uzi. The Cuban stooped to pick up the weapon. But his head spun, and he knelt next to the machine pistol, shaking his head to clear it. Bontoc had gotten in some good licks, but Encizo had survived worse. He had no broken bones or serious wounds. The Cuban grinned.

A SPECIAL FORCES SERGEANT crept toward the clearing from the east. He spotted the crates and remembered the description of the metal boxes that contained the nuclear shells. The casket-shaped crates were among the cargo in the clearing. The soldier sighed with relief. Even if some of the terrorists managed to escape, they wouldn't have the cannon or the nuclear projectiles.

He didn't notice General Ton concealed behind some bamboo stalks. The Vietnamese officer recognized the uniform and bush hat that the NCO wore. Philippines Special Forces, Ton thought grimly. That meant the CIA was probably after them, as well. The general didn't intend to give up his dream of renewing the fires of revolution. He had devoted too many years and too much effort to this mission. They would have to kill him before he would stop now.

Ton thrust his left arm from the bamboo, a Makarov pistol in his fist. The general aimed carefully and squeezed the trigger. The sergeant's spine arched as a bullet hit him between the shoulder blades. Ton shot the soldier again and drilled the second bullet under the NCO's left shoulder blade. The round punched through the Filipino's heart and exited at his chest. Ton watched his victim fall facedown on the ground.

The general emerged from his hiding place and approached the dead trooper. Ton needed more firepower than the Makarov. He returned the pistol to the hip holster and reached down to seize the slain soldier's M-16. The Vietnamese grunted with recognition. The M-16 had been the assault rifle used by the Americans in the war. Ton had fired such weapons in the past, but not since the loss of his right hand. It would be a bit awkward, and he realized he wouldn't be very accurate with the unfamiliar rifle, but he would have to make do with what he could get.

Ton picked up the rifle by the barrel as another figure appeared from the bush. Katz had heard the pistol shots and had headed toward the sound. He found Ton bent over the dead Special Forces sergeant, the man's M-16 in his left fist. The Phoenix Force commander and Ton made eye contact. Ton froze and stared at Katz's machine pistol. The Vietnamese officer realized he couldn't hope to adjust his grip on the M-16 to grab the pistol grip and trigger the rifle before Katz cut him in two.

"Try it," Katz invited as he stepped closer. "Please."

Ton sighed and started to straighten his back, hand still wrapped around the rifle barrel. Then, suddenly, he swung his arm and hurled the M-16 at Katz. The rifle slammed into the Israeli's machine pistol just as he fired. The blow threw his aim off target, and the three-round burst missed General Ton by almost a foot. Ton followed his desperate move with a charge forward and a roundhouse kick at the micro-Uzi. He booted the weapon from Katz's fist and slashed his big steel hook at the Israeli's throat. Katz dodged the attack, but Ton's hook ripped his shirtfront and clawed a shallow cut across the Phoenix pro's chest.

The Vietnamese officer yanked his Makarov from his hip holster, but Katz's prosthesis struck out like the head of a cobra. Steel hooks slammed down on the frame of Ton's pistol and knocked the weapon out of the startled general's hand. Katz swung his left fist at the side of Ton's jaw. The general was staggered by the blow, and he raised his arms. Katz adopted a fighting stance with his left fist and prosthesis claw at chest level. Ton's eyes widened with surprise at the sight of the Israeli's artificial arm.

"Small world, isn't it?" Katz cracked.

Ton feinted an attack with his hook and threw a kick at Katz's groin. The Phoenix fighter stamped a boot on his opponent's shin to stop the kick and slashed his hooks at Ton's left arm. Ton grabbed the prosthesis above the steel claws and swung his own hook at Katz's head. The Israeli's left forearm rose to block the attack. Forearm struck forearm, and the point of Ton's hook danced inches from the Phoenix commando's left eye.

Katz stamped a heel on Ton's shin a second time, then stomped the man's other instep. Ton hissed in pain, and Katz turned suddenly to yank his prosthesis from the general's grip. He punched the hooks into the Vietnamese man's solar plexus. The curved steel of the hooks hit hard, and Ton gasped. The Vietnamese slashed his own hook at Katz's face, but the Israeli dodged the attack.

Ton altered the stroke to a backhand sweep and hammered the curved portion of his hook into Katz's chest. The Phoenix commander staggered back. He felt blood ooze from the cut in his chest, and the wound stung. Ton thrust out his left hand in an effort to seize Katz and yank him forward so that he could employ the hook again. But Katz swung his prosthesis in a sideways stroke, raking the hook across the inside of Ton's forearm. Cloth at the sleeve tore, and blood dripped from a cut in Ton's flesh.

The Vietnamese snarled with pain and rage as he swung his hook in a diagonal stroke. Katz jumped back to avoid the steel claw and slammed the side of his left hand against his opponent's arm. If he could deflect Ton's arm and drop the man's guard, Katz could launch an effective attack at one of Ton's vital points. However, Ton swung his hook in a fast figure eight stroke to avoid Katz's hand. Then he swooped in for another attack on the right side of the Israeli's face.

Katz raised his prosthesis. Steel hooks clashed. Katz's trident claw snapped shut around Ton's larger, single hook. The general gasped with surprise when he found that Katz had trapped his hook. The Israeli stepped to the left and grabbed Ton's right arm with his left hand. The Phoenix commando raised the captured limb, ducked under Ton's arm and pulled hard. His left hand pushed Ton's elbow while the hooks held on to Ton's steel extremity. The general's arm locked, and his body was tossed forward with the force of Katz's push. Ton plunged head over heels, and Katz moved with his opponent to hold on to the man's hook. The Vietnamese crash-landed on his back.

Katz quickly stomped the edge of his boot on Ton's throat. The general's hook jerked in an effort to get free of Katz's prosthesis grip, but the Phoenix commander held on. Blood bubbled from Ton's lips as his windpipe was crushed by the boot. His body twitched briefly and lay still. Katz stared down at the general's open, lifeless eyes, then released the man's hook and let it fall limply beside his body.

28

The battle was virtually over. Erik Heller had realized that another force had joined the fight and had taken on both his men and the PPLA. Whoever they were, they had crushed the terrorists and picked off most of the remaining members of Heller's crew. Only Heller, House and one Australian thug remained.

"We have to get out of here!" House declared. "Our only chance is to get to the road and make a run for it!"

Heller glanced at the crates that contained the atomic cannon and the nuclear shells. He saw the pit where his treasure in ill-gotten Cambodian gold and precious gems lay. Everything he had worked and schemed for years to accomplish stood in the clearing. Now he had to turn from it and run for his life.

"Let's do it!" Heller agreed reluctantly as he swung his Chinese assault rifle around the trunk of a tree and triggered a short burst at his mysterious opponents.

The renegade broke cover and bolted for the road. House followed him, and the last Australian flunky shoved a full magazine into the butt well of a Glock 17 and triggered three shots at Gary Manning's position to keep the Canadian pinned down while the others made their break for freedom. Heller fired his Chinese assault rifle at the trees and foliage that had formerly been cover for the PPLA and now supplied shelter for Katz, Encizo and several Filipino Special Forces soldiers.

The Phoenix commandos and their allies returned fire. A 5.56 mm slug tore cloth on House's bush shirt, the bullet grazing his ribs. The British mercenary hardly noticed as he concentrated on running for the road. A Special Forces trooper emerged from a tree trunk and dropped to a kneeling position with his M-16. House snap-aimed his Smith & Wesson and fired as he ran. The .38 Special round smashed into the soldier's left cheekbone. The trooper toppled backward and clutched his face as other soldiers continued to fire at the three remaining enemies.

The Australian broke cover and fired blindly as he ran. Manning triggered a stream of 9 mm rounds into the path of the hoodlum, and the guy ran right into it. His chest sprouted crimson bullet holes as he went down. The Australian lowlife blasted a Glock bullet into a tree branch on his way down.

James and McCarter spotted the two last opponents and triggered their micro-Uzis as the pair darted from tree trunk to tree trunk while attempting to flee. Bullets chipped bark and snipped off twigs, but Heller and House kept moving. McCarter lowered his aim and sprayed a salvo of 9 mm rounds as the pair bolted for the edge of the forest. House spun around on one foot and nearly went down as two parabellums crashed into his left thigh. The mercenary returned fire with his revolver and hobbled after Heller. The American traitor remained untouched by flying lead and conserved his ammo, aware he only had a few rounds left in the assault rifle.

"They're headed for the road," James yelled as he ran for the trucks.

McCarter followed the black commando. They bull-dogged their way through a wall of bamboo plants and peered through the foliage to see Carlos Leyte and a Filipino Special Forces solder jog up the road to try to cut off Heller and House. The Chinese assault rifle snarled and the British merc's Smith & Wesson boomed twice. Leyte staggered backward and fell to one knee. The CIA agent jammed the butt of his M-16 into the ground in an effort to haul himself erect. The Filipino soldier was sprawled beside him, blood and brains oozing from his bullet-shattered skull.

James and McCarter frantically pushed through the foliage to try to reach the road. Leyte wobbled unsteadily and started to aim his M-16 at the opponents, who were still out of view of the Phoenix pair. A three-round burst of automatic fire nailed Leyte in the center of the chest. The CIA man toppled to the ground, the M-16 still clutched in a frozen death grip.

The Phoenix commandos reached the edge of the forest. They saw Heller behind a deuce-and-a-half, with House limping after him. The British merc glanced over his shoulder and saw James and McCarter. He pointed his .38 at the pair, but McCarter fired first. Parabellums slammed into House's right arm and shoulder. The revolver flew from his fingers as the mercenary dropped to his knees, his right arm dangling uselessly.

The truck bolted forward with Heller at the wheel. James triggered a 9 mm salvo at the vehicle. Bullet holes appeared in the cab door and canvas tarp, but the truck kept going. McCarter stepped onto the road and drew his Browning Hi-Power. The British commando had exhausted his micro-Uzi ammo, so he pointed the Browning at House while James sprinted across the road to the trio of motorcycles.

"I'm not letting that son of a bitch get away again," James vowed as he mounted the nearest motorcycle and started the engine.

The motorcycle roared to life. The black commando gripped the handlebars and hung on as the bike shot forward in pursuit of the speeding truck. McCarter kept his Browning pointed at House as he watched the motorcycle rocket down the road.

Jason House shook his head. Beads of sweat flew from his hair and brow. He had lost a lot of blood, and the pain in his bullet-smashed limbs had sapped him of his strength. The mercenary felt faint and feared he might pass out. He glanced up at McCarter and considered his options. "I'm as good as dead," he croaked hoarsely, slowly raising his left arm.

"You're about halfway there already," McCarter agreed, pointing the Browning at the mercenary's face.

House worked the levers in the sling concealed in his left sleeve. The derringer popped into his palm. He had one bullet left in the diminutive gun, and he intended to use it to take McCarter out.

But it was too late. A 9 mm slug crashed through the frontal bone in House's skull. It burned a violent tunnel through his brain and blasted a gory exit at the back of his head. Jason House was dead before he could hear the report of the Browning autoloader. David McCarter had shot him between the eyes the instant he'd seen the derringer appear in the mercenary's hand.

"Congratulations," McCarter commented as he lowered his Browning. "Hope you like your new home in hell."

THE MOTORCYCLE WAS faster and better suited for the dirt path than the deuce-and-a-half. James soon closed in on the truck. Flying dirt and dust assaulted the commando's face and eyes. He squinted as he peered through the grimy curtain and saw the open back of the truck yawn ten feet away. Holding the handlebars with one hand, James grabbed his micro-Uzi with the other and fired at the rear tires. The truck and the motorcycle bounced around on the rugged path. It was impossible to aim, and firing one-handed didn't help James's accuracy.

Bullets sparked off metal and tore into the road. One or more slugs may have struck a tire, but the thick rubber and tough axle didn't seem impressed by the effort. Heller glanced at the rearview mirror and saw the rider pursuing on a motorcycle. He stepped on the gas, although he realized he couldn't hope to outrun the motorcycle.

James exhausted the micro-Uzi magazine, but he still had his Walther in shoulder leather. James considered riding up alongside the truck to get a shot at the window of the cab on the driver's side. Unfortunately there was hardly enough room on the narrow road for the truck, let alone trying to ride next to it. Besides, James realized Heller would see him in the mirror, and it would be easy enough to force him off the road with the big truck.

Got to try something else, James thought as he reached for a concussion grenade on his webgear. The black commando hooked the pin ring over his left thumb as his fingers held on to the bike's handlebars. He tugged and pulled the pin loose. Then he aimed carefully and tossed the grenade underhanded.

It sailed into the open rear of the truck. James turned the bike to steer it away from the deuce-and-a-half, and reduced speed. The truck rolled twenty yards before the grenade exploded. The deuce-and-a-half rose awkwardly and crashed onto its side as it skidded into the jungle. The blast reached James and knocked the bike out of control. He bailed out, hit the ground hard, rolled with the impact and collided with the base of a rubber tree.

"Oh, shit," he moaned as he slowly crawled away from the tree and started to rise.

His right shoulder and upper arm ached. His head felt as if he had come in second place in a butting contest with an angry ram, and his left hip was badly bruised by the abrupt encounter with the tree. James got onto his knees and reached under his left arm to draw the Walther P-88. The micro-Uzi had been lost in the fall. He took a deep breath and slowly stood up.

James walked unsteadily toward the truck. The motorcycle lay on the side of the road, its tires still spinning. The truck was in worse condition. Its belly was jammed against two tree trunks, its windshield scattered all over its dented hood. The truck resembled a dying dinosaur as it lay sideways, engine sputtering, tires rolling slowly in the air.

The Phoenix commando approached, pistol held ready. The door on the driver's side was shut and battered, probably jammed. The passenger side was on the ground. Heller was probably still in the cab, hopefully trapped. James wasn't sure if the guy had any ammunition left in his assault rifle, or if the renegade had a spare magazine. He had glimpsed Heller and seen enough to appreciate the fact that the man was big and powerful. But the arms dealer still might have been killed or knocked unconscious when the truck had crashed. Nonetheless, James approached the deuce-and-a-half with care, assuming Heller would still be capable of putting up a fight.

He shuffled to the cab, gripping the Walther in both hands. James pointed the pistol at the shattered windshield and peered into the cab. He saw the steering wheel and backrest. James shifted position and examined the rest of the cab. Erik Heller wasn't inside.

A bellow of rage startled James. He saw a flash of movement at the nose of the cab and turned to face Heller. The big man held the Chinese assault rifle by the barrel and swung it like a club. The wooden stock crashed down on the Walther, knocking it out of James's hands. The black warrior immediately swung a karate kick at Heller's forearm. The Chinese rifle clattered to the ground.

James snap-kicked his opponent in the abdomen. Heller's stomach muscles seemed to be as tough as a flak vest. The renegade's face was contorted with rage, and his eyes burned with hatred. James hit him with a solid right cross. His knuckles stung from the blow, but Heller's head hardly moved. The renegade responded with a short left hook that lifted James off his feet and pitched him four feet.

The Phoenix commando hit the ground. His jaw ached as if he had been kicked by a mule. James started to get up, but Heller charged forward and kicked him in the ribs. The blow sent the black commando tumbling across the road. Heller followed and raised a big boot to stomp the life out of his opponent.

James shifted his weight on the small of his back and slid clear of the attack. Heller's boot heel stamped the ground near James's head. The black commando lashed out with his right boot, hitting Heller between the legs. The steel toe crashed into Heller's genitals. The big man doubled up in agony, and James swung his left boot against the side of his opponent's face. Heller stumbled backward. James scrambled away from him and got to his feet. An ordinary man would have been flat on his back from the punishment Heller had endured, but the powerful bodybuilder stood firmly on both feet, eyes fixed on James as he hissed through clenched teeth. "You fucking nigger, I'll tear you apart like an insect for that!"

"Just don't talk me to death. This is judgement day, asshole. You've got a lot to answer for, and I'm in charge of payback."

Heller charged. He thrust a left jab at James's chin. The black warrior danced clear of the fist and snapped another kick at Heller's muscular belly. Heller jabbed again and hit James in the chest. The blow staggered the Phoenix fighter, and Heller swung a right cross at his head. James ducked and hooked a left at Heller's kidney, followed by a right uppercut at the ribs. Heller didn't seem to even feel the punches as he whipped a fist at the commando's head.

James fell back against the roof of the truck. Heller galloped forward and launched a vicious kick. James dodged the boot and drew his Blackmoor Dirk from the sheath under his right arm. He slashed the double-edged blade across Heller's calf muscle. Heller yelped and hopped back on his other foot as blood trickled from his cut leg. James lunged with the knife. Heller moaned when the point raked his ribs, but he grabbed James's wrist with both hands and twisted hard. The knife slipped out of the Phoenix pro's fingers.

The black warrior's other hand rose to Heller's face and jabbed a thumb in the renegade's eye. The big man howled and jerked his head back. He released James's wrist and drove both fists into the commando's chest. The blow drove James back into the cab roof once more. Heller lashed a cross-body karate chop aimed at James's throat. The Phoenix commando slid along the metal roof to avoid the blow.

Heller's hand smashed against the roof. James stepped behind his opponent and slashed a karate stroke at Heller's kidney with one hand and hammered his other fist between the brute's shoulder blades. Heller fell face first against the cab roof. The Phoenix crusader stomped a boot on the back of Heller's knee, choosing the leg that had already been slashed during the fight. The renegade's leg buckled, and he fell to one knee.

James raised his arm over his head and bent his elbow. He put all his strength behind the stroke and slammed his elbow down on the nape of Heller's neck. Vertebrae cracked, and Heller's body collapsed at James's feet. The Phoenix warrior stepped back and watched the American death merchant's corpse twitch slightly. Then he kicked the body under the armpit to be certain the guy was dead.

"Payback," James said breathlessly as he walked away from the corpse.

His knees felt like rubber, and he gasped for air raggedly. A truck rolled along the road toward James. Unarmed and exhausted, he could only hope the vehicle didn't contain enemy forces. It came to a halt, and Katz emerged from the passenger side of the car. McCarter opened the other door and climbed out from behind the steering wheel.

"Are you okay?" Katz asked as he approached James.

"Nothing a hot bath and a couple of ice packs can't cure," the black commando replied with a weary nod. "I got Heller."

"So I see," Katz said as he glanced at the dead man next to the crippled truck. "That wraps it up, Cal. The rest of the bad guys are either dead or held prisoner by Captain Galdo and what's left of his Special Forces troops."

"He lost a number of men, and Leyte's dead, too," McCarter added. "But we got the cannon and the nuclear shells. Heller and the others are history. All we have to do now is head for home and report the good news to Brognola."

"Sure," James said. He felt too bruised and battered at the moment, but he knew he would be one happy dude later. "I just hope it'll be a while before we have another mission like this one."

"Yeah," Katz said, wincing. "This one was close. Too close." The Israeli shuddered as he thought about Heller's nuclear stash. "Let's go home, guys. I think we've all earned a rest."

**A treacherous tale of time travel
in a desperate new world.**

JAMES AXLER

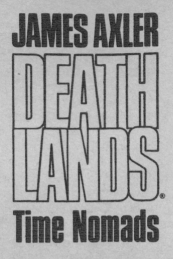

DEATHLANDS®

Time Nomads

Trekking through the blasted heart of the new America, Ryan Cawdor and his band search the redoubts for hidden caches of food, weapons and technology — the legacy of a preholocaust society.

Near death after ingesting bacteria-ridden food, Ryan Cawdor lies motionless, his body paralyzed by the poison coursing through his system. Yet his mind races back to the early days in the Deathlands...where the past is a dream and the future is a nightmare.

GOLD
EAGLE

DL 11-1

More than action adventure...
books written by the men who were there

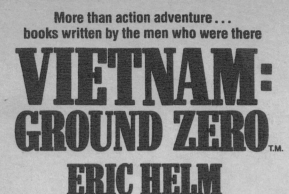

VIETNAM: GROUND ZERO T.M.

ERIC HELM

Told through the eyes of an American Special Forces squad, an elite jungle fighting group of strike-and-hide specialists fight a dirty war half a world away from home.

These books cut close to the bone, telling it the way it really was.

"Vietnam at Ground Zero is where this book is written. The author has been there, and he knows. I salute him and I recommend this book to my friends."

—Don Pendleton
creator of *The Executioner*

"Helm writes in an evocative style that gives us Nam as it most likely was, without prettying up or undue bitterness."

—*Cedar Rapids Gazette*

"Eric Helm's Vietnam series embodies a literary standard of excellence. These books linger in the mind long after their reading."

—*Midwest Book Review*

Available wherever paperbacks are sold.

VIE-1